D1414337

Also by Larry Baker

The Flamingo Rising

This pitch perfect first novel is reminiscent of the best of John Irving. Like the giant July 4th fireworks display toward which the story builds, this engaging, moving novel sends up one sparkler after another on its way to a crash-bang, heart-stopping ending. —*Publishers Weekly*

Athens, America

Larry Baker's immense knowledge of local politics comes from his own experience, and that knowledge is put to dramatic effect in this story. But this is more than a political novel. It is also a highly moral and humane story, with a narrator who is both astute and forgiving of human foibles. And, ultimately, while being a story about a certain kind of American, it's also a very tender love story.—Haven Kimmel, author of *The Solace of Leaving Early*.

A Good Man

In Harry Ducharme, Larry Baker has created a main character as memorable and complex as John Updike's Rabbit Angstrom or Richard Ford's Frank Bascombe. Not since Robert Stone's *A Hall of Mirrors* have we been this privy to the troubled soul of a disc jockey. Fans of Baker's previous novels won't be disappointed while readers new to his work will be bowled over. —John McNally, author of *Ghosts of Chicago* and *The Book of Ralph*

Love and Other Delusions

Some art just points us at the direction it wants to take us. Other art takes us gently by the hand to lead us towards its goal. Larry Baker's art in *Love and Other Delusions* does a bit of both, but most of the time it engages us more fully, in an deeply intellectual wrestling match with matters of the heart, if not the soul. And at its best, and for what I suspect will be the case for many readers, the heart involved is our own. —Robert Leonard, KNIA Radio

The
EDUCATION
of
NANCY ADAMS

LARRY BAKER

Ice Tea Books
North Liberty, Iowa

The Education of Nancy Adams
Copyright @2014 Larry Baker

ISBN 9781888160789 paperback
ISBN 9781888160802 hardback

Library of Congress Control Number 2013957645

Ice Tea Books, fiction imprint of
Ice Cube Press, LLC (est.1993)
205 North Front Street
North Liberty, Iowa 52317-9302
Larry Baker contact: flamingo@avalon.net
Publicist contact: nancyadams@netexpress.net
Publisher contact: steve@icecubepress.com

Limited first edition hardcover printing of 200 copies, available only
from publisher directly or at bookstores. Paperback printing to follow,
but also available only from publisher directly or at bookstores. E-book
version available on-line.

Manufactured in the USA

Pictures of Henry and Clover Adams are public domain.
River dock photo: Lorraine Portman
Vietnam photos: Fred Tymeson
Cover, City, and West High schools in Iowa City: Howard Horan
Additional West High School photos: Ginny Ordman and Leah Best
Grade book and swimming pool photos: Jennifer Lord
Author Photo: Jennifer Lord

Acknowledgements:

As usual, first thanks go to Steve Semken for his generous, often stoic, support of my writing.

Jody Hansen was an early and encouraging reader who also caught a few hundred typos, phrasing problems, and other mechanical errors. Any remaining errors are all mine.

Thanks to Jerry Arganbright at West High School and John Bacon at City High School for permission to photograph inside their schools. Thanks also to Mike Moran for permission to photograph inside the Mercer Park Recreation Center.

Amy Kanellis is not a character in this book, but I could not have created one of them without knowing her first.

Fred Tymeson is not in this book (unlike two others), but knowing him helped me understand the Vietnam experience of one of my fictional characters.

Finally, in a list that is not meant to be exhaustive, the following people are all part of my understanding of the high school experience: Charles Yates, Scott Bennett, Nita Rios, Terry Abbott, Robert Anderson, Carol Austin, Cecil Perdue, Rose Lynn Scott, Julie Martin, Helen and Lanny Bassham, Carlye Calder, Garey and Patsy Kirk, Mary Brumbach, Alicia Golsan, Sue Ray and Harlan Hammond, Nancy Hubbard, Michael Carmean, Billy Roberson, Dianne Smith, Mary Haltom, Nancy Patterson, Gary Wimmer, Clinton Gorney, Lois Jenkins, Linda Combs, Ronnie Day, Ronnie Rockwood, Charles Anderson, Donna Frank, Chari Kensinger, Elaine Fink, Linda Laine, Sandra Cunningham, Joe Holub, Mary Brown, Michael Owens, Diana Ford, Barney Capshaw, Gene Merrell, Cheryl Zelt, Chickie Williams, Dell Ray Dearing, Joe Skipper, Jamie Smith, Larry Morphew, Martha Harding, Pam Morgan, David Pillow, Bruce Hartin, Michael Stewart, John Stevens, Debbie Whitaker, Danny Currie, Glenda Gosdin, Paul Slaughter, Jaynie Baker, Janet Nichols, and June Davis.

The Education *of* NANCY ADAMS

Nothing in education is so astonishing as the amount of
ignorance it accumulates in the form of inert facts.

—Henry Adams—

Thirty Years Ago

Education, n.: That which discloses to the wise and disguises from
the foolish their lack of understanding.—Ambrose Bierce

I have perfect vision and low blood pressure, assets that make me
a great shot. I can sit on the dock that slopes away from my house
and finish a box of shells in an afternoon. I like to shoot things.
That scares some men. A woman with a gun. Too bad it never
scared the men it should have. My theory is that being educated
and being armed ought to reinforce each other. Wrong.

I used to watch my father shoot from the same dock thirty
years earlier. He was a lousy shot, and my mother had always in-

sisted that he keep his gun pointed toward the water of the St. Johns. Odd, I always thought to myself, because daddy was much safer to be around than my mother. Frances Adams had a short fuse, and dishes were always breaking if she lost her temper. Dishes and cats and pictures on the wall, nothing was safe. I had seen her launch an empty coffee mug at my father, poor hapless Charles, and then they laughed at each other. My parents were strange. PhDs or not, teachers or not, mother hot and father cool, but cool in a good way, two parents who adored their perfect only child, me, I could never make them as normal as my friends' parents.

Like my father, I'm not a hunter, and I don't shoot in front of other people. I've got no illusions about protecting myself with either the twenty-two rifle or my small gauge shotgun. They're always unloaded and locked away most of the time. If I can't talk a murdering raping flesh-eating burglar into leaving, I'm in big trouble. No, I just like the feel of the stock on my shoulder, the imaginary line down the top of the barrel as I aim, the jolt as I fire, the sight of the target exploding. I seldom miss. I wear ear plugs, but not so thick that the explosion is simply muffled into a mere whisper. And the smell, I really like the smell.

Daddy taught me to shoot, but he told me to never kill anything. Even ant hills were off limits. He was an ideal role model for gun safety, a liberal through and through, except for the time an alligator wandered into our yard. Me, I thought he was the bravest man in Florida that evening.

It was hot and humid, and the sunset brought no relief. He and I had been shooting off the dock, and we hadn't seen the gator crawl out of the water behind us. When we turned around, the gator was between us and the house. Daddy fired a few shots into the ground around the gator, intent on scaring it back into the St. Johns, but the gator had an agenda and was headed for the house.

I looked up at my father and wondered what he would do next. He looked down and smiled, "You got any more bullets?" It was a moment I always use to explain him to others. I shook my head, terrified at the implication. He smiled again, "Well, I better make my last one good, right?" He quietly explained his plan, as if he had prepared all his life for that moment: Get the gator's attention, turn it to face us, make it come toward us, and shoot it in the eye. A twenty-two shell would probably bounce off the gator's hide, and even a shot in the jelly eye wouldn't kill it, but it might scare him off. Daddy seemed confident. I was about to pee in my pants.

He assigned me the key role, as if I had proven myself in a crisis a hundred times before. Run toward the house making as much noise as possible, and when the gator turned toward the noise I was to run back toward my father, remembering to stay out of the line of fire. That was my favorite part of the story to re-tell, because I always remembered my first thought: *You want me to do what?* But I did as I was told, and as I started running toward the house I wondered how mad my mother was going to be when she found out that daddy had put me in harm's way, and then an absurd thought made me laugh...me and daddy were doing the gator a favor by keeping it away from her.

The gator snorted as it turned its head toward me. I screamed as I headed back toward my father, not seeing if the gator was after me or the house or him. All I heard was the single shot. When I opened my eyes again, clutching his legs as he was leaning down to kiss the top of my head, I looked out toward the orange ripply line that marked the setting sun's reflection off the water. Daddy picked me up and carried me to the house, whispering in my ear,

"He won't ever come back here, that's my guess." Ever since then, I've never been too sure.

Thousands of bullets and thirty years later, I'm still shooting Coca-Cola bottles. I like the 8 ounce bottles with a cork in the top. I can throw them far away into the St. Johns. They're small and they bob with the current, not an easy target. But when they're hit they make a satisfying shattering sound, and then the pieces disappear under the water. If I had enough money, I'd shoot bottles every day, but I was going broke last year. Facing the necessity of finally going to work full-time for the first time in my life, I had to decide if I was going to let Russell Parsons come to my rescue.

Guns and Books and Ghosts

Very likely education does not make very much difference.—Gertrude Stein

I have a habit that my dead husband Jack used to make fun of all the time. I pick a point in my life and sum it up. Or just a day. Sometimes just the things that happened that day. Jack said I was a control freak. I never understood that. His own office at home had always been a mess and he absolutely forbade me to touch anything. His office at the clinic was the same way. But his nurses loved him anyway, and they would joke with each other about having to sort out his files if anything ever happened to him. Then he died in a plane crash. I didn't touch his home office for a year. It was how I mourned. When I finally made the effort to reclaim the space, to box it all up and store it away, it was then that I found his journal. He had been uncharacteristically meticulous. He listed names and dates. Jesus, thinking about it now, I'm surprised he didn't have pictures too. It was the same day his partner called to ask me out to dinner, again, and I finally accepted the invitation. Put a gun to my head today, I couldn't tell you that guy's name.

The latest list for me? I'm a childless widow. My mama and daddy are dead. No brothers or sisters. I'm five feet seven inches tall and weigh less than I did when I was in high school. I have almost no money in the bank and now live in the house I grew up in, home again, escaping the distant suburbs of Atlanta. I had no real job there. I had been a substitute teacher in Atlanta when I felt like it, which was not all that often, but I hadn't stepped into a classroom since coming back home to Fort Jackson. If I had any identity in Atlanta, it was as a book reviewer. Mostly histories and biographies, never fiction. In a good month, I'd have two reviews in the *Atlanta Journal-Constitution*. In Fort Jackson, I had no identity. Oh sure, I was Frances and Charles's daughter, back in the old house. *Her.*

I was a virgin—seriously, this is the truth—when I married John "Jack" Vandergriff. I thought I was typical, the virgin thing. Jack had been five years older than me. After he died, I slept with a lot of men, most of whose names I don't remember. Too many times, a man, a man not named Jack, had asked me why I called him *Jack*. I told him it was my father's name, and that man seldom called back. For a long time all men were named Jack to me, and I saw him in them. I did it intentionally, call them Jack, tell them it was my father's name, and it creeped them out.

Then it was time to go home. I was almost out of cash, so I sold my double-mortgaged house in Atlanta in 1995 and headed south on I-75, back to live in the house in which I had spent the greater part of my first eighteen years. Almost five hundred miles later and seven hours of singing out loud to myself without music, songs my father had taught me when I was a little girl. *Fly Me to the Moon* and *Moon River*, some Janis Ian and the complete Carly Simon catalog, songs that I had lip-synced in high school, all the Anne Murray and Neil Diamond hits, and all the Harry Chapin ballads I could half way remember, songs that Russell Parsons had introduced me to after I moved to Atlanta, singing to myself in a voice that couldn't carry a tune, I pulled into my old driveway. I could smell the pines, and I had lost my voice. The first thing I did was walk down to my parent's boat dock on the St. Johns and stick my feet in the water. I wondered how long alligators lived, then I pulled my feet out of the water, wishing I had my father's rifle. Within a week, I bought myself two new guns.

An Older Woman

Give a girl an education and introduce her properly into the world, and ten to one but she has the means of settling well, without further expense to anybody.—Jane Austen

He wanted an answer to his question, but I wanted to talk about my name.

"I hate my name."

Russell was silent, trying to be his usual patient and considerate adult self. After all, I was dealing with the possibility that I would have to actually work for a living.

"So all I did with this phone call was trigger a name crisis with you?" he finally said, starting to laugh.

"I just always wanted to know why my parents named me Nancy. It's not a family name. None of their friends was named Nancy. And, please, that godawful middle name. Golden, seriously? Nancy Golden Adams? Why Nancy? I hate my name. I've always hated it. I'm not a Nancy."

"Nancy..." he hesitated..."this is all very interesting, of course, your approaching-40 crisis, but I still need an answer about that job."

He was right. I knew that, even at that moment I knew he was right, but I couldn't stop myself. "How many Nancys are there that anybody remembers or knows about? Who else is a Nancy?"

"The world is full of Nancys, *Nancy*. There's Nancy Drew..."

"Not real," I protested.

"Nancy Reagan...."

"Oh, please, Russell. Not her."

"She's a great woman, Nance."

"Russell, stop being a Republican for once in your life. Nancy Reagan is not a...." And it hit me then, could he *really* be a Republican? How did that possibility not sink in all these years? Did we never discuss politics?"

"Nancy Kerrigan."

"Keep going, please please please, before I start seeing those teeth. Keep going."

"If you really want to know, I *do* know why your parents named you Nancy. Your mama told me with her last dying breath. You were named after that girl in the Nancy cartoon strip, the one with Sluggo as a boyfriend. That's you. Nancy and Sluggo. Now, can I get an answer, please?"

"Does that make you Sluggo?"

"No, Nancy Adams, former star student of mine, all your teachers' Golden Girl, that makes me..."

That's all I was?"

Silence. I had the phone tight against my ear, listening for his breath.

"No, Nancy, you were always more than that," he said. "You know that, after all this time, you know that."

"I hate you, Russell Parsons," I finally blurted out.

He didn't skip a beat, "No, you don't. You love me, and we've worked around that for twenty years."

"You've worked around it for twenty years. Your marriage...my marriage...you've worked around everything."

"Nancy, you're not being fair, and you know it," he said quietly. "Maybe I was wrong about my offer, but I thought you needed..."

"I accept," I cut him off. "I'll take the job. But you still have to explain to me what happened last night."

I'm cursed by my education. I know just enough undergraduate psychology to categorize myself as having a father fixation, so I'm some sort of Sunshine Electra. The father I adored, he died while I was young. I married an older man. Textbook clue. Too obvious. The first great love of my life had been my high school history teacher, Russell Parsons. That great teenage love had just offered me a job. My former teacher, my future boss. I wasn't making progress. And I never had a good response whenever my best girlfriend Kris would ask me, *If you're so damn smart, why aren't you happy?* Touche, Kris, tu-fucking-shay.

Russell had asked me to meet him at the high school the night before. He was the principal; he had the keys. *It's almost romantic,* I told myself. I hadn't been inside Kennedy High since my ten year class reunion, but there I was the previous night, standing on the front steps of the main entrance, the Class of 1977 valedictorian, my mother's pride and my father's legacy, telling myself over and over, *I am not Emily Grierson, I am not Emily Grierson.* It was my greatest secret fear, becoming the town's crazy woman. Thank God, I reminded myself, thank God for Russell's wife. As long as Stella Parsons was around, I was a safe second in the crazy department.

He was wearing faded jeans and a knit sport-shirt, casual clothes that he seldom wore, clothes that didn't fit my image of him. Hell, nobody's image of him. Russell was a paragon of maturity. His public wardrobe was *old* even when he was young.

"Are we the only people here?" I asked.

"I assume so," he said, holding the door open for me.

I stepped into the hallway and instinctively reached for something to hold on to in the darkness. Outside, the security lights had turned the whole campus into a fuzzy orange dreamscape. Inside, the only light was at the end of the hall, a hundred feet away, and that distant white light created a harsh glare that bounced off the freshly polished floors. I could smell the wax. *Déjà vu* all over again.

He took my hand and held it for a second.

"Stand still until your eyes adjust. I don't want you walking into the lockers. Insurance is already too high. You hurt yourself and we'll have to cancel the music programs to pay off your lawyer."

"Is insurance the reason you can't afford to turn on the lights?" I asked, wondering how long he was going to hold my hand.

"No need for lights. You'll be okay."

My eyes adjusted, and he let go of my hand. Soon enough, I could see in the dark.

"You want a tour?" he asked, beginning to walk away.

"Has it changed all that much?"

"No, not really. Not the building. Just more stuff in it. A lot more memories. You were here for three years a long time ago. I've been here twenty-two years, almost half my life, certainly most of my adult life. Nope, you've probably changed more than this building, or me."

"Russell, you're beginning to wax sentimental, and something worse...profound. So, how come you asked me here?"

He turned around and laughed. "Absolutely right." Then, abruptly, "Race you to the end of the hall. One, two..." And then he was running down the hall toward the light at the end.

I was too stunned to do anything other than start running after him, yelling at the same time, losing my breath, unable to ignore how totally out of shape I was. "Russell! Why are we here? And why, for chrissake, am I running at my age!"

He stopped fifty feet away from me, then turned and started jogging backwards away from me as he answered, "Because I have a favor to ask of you. And you, Nancy Adams, had better get in shape."

"Russell! Russell!"

"Later, Nancy. Right now, as soon as... *if...* you catch me, I'll give you the grand tour of your former domain."

Reunited at the end of the hall, we walked through Kennedy High School. The more we walked, the less I cared if any of this made sense. I looked at him in the dim light. "You know what I feel like, right now?"

Russell turned toward me and shook his head.

"Like I'm just recovering from amnesia. Like I've been awake for a long time but not conscious. Not just since Jack's death, for a long time even before that. Does that make sense?"

"You said the same thing after your mother died. Remember?"

"So, you're telling me that this isn't the first time I've lost my mind." We were outside the classroom where he had first touched me a lifetime ago. Only the hall posters had changed: IF YOU BELIEVE IN YOURSELF, ALL THINGS ARE POSSIBLE—YOU CANNOT DISCOVER NEW OCEANS UNLESS YOU HAVE THE COURAGE TO LOSE SIGHT OF THE SHORE—A DAY WITHOUT WEIRDNESS IS LIKE A DAY WITHOUT SUNSHINE—MY BASIC PHILOSOPHY AS A PUBLIC SCHOOL TEACHER IS TO FIND A WAY TO CONNECT WITH WHOEVER SHOWS UP ON MONDAY—FRESHMEN NEED LOVE, TOO.

"Remember this room?"

Well, duh, I wanted to say, refusing to act my age. I was seventeen again, outside the room in which Kris and I had fantasized about our favorite history teacher. Standing across from him twenty years later, I had a thought that I didn't want to share with him, a thought that contradicted anything I felt only a few minutes earlier. I wanted to be alone at that exact moment, there in his old classroom. Somehow, as much as I had looked forward to being alone with him this night, for some reason I now wanted to be alone with myself. Somehow, he wasn't part of anything I wanted to think about at that moment. I wanted to walk around Kennedy by myself, to find my old locker, then Kris's locker, where we would always meet to go to lunch in the cafeteria where everyone sat according to their status in the high school pecking order. More than anything else, I wanted to go to the pool building.

"Let's get out of here. You got keys to the pool?" I said.

He had been staring at me. "You okay?" he asked.

"I'm fine. So, you got those keys?"

He stood up and pulled a ring of keys out of his jeans pocket. "Nancy, I am the principal of Kennedy High School. I have the master key to every locker in this building. Nobody has any secrets from me. Getting *into* the poolroom is merely a matter of us getting *to* the poolroom. You remember the way?"

Five minutes later we were sitting on opposite ends of a bench in a room as big as a typical high school gymnasium, looking up at a cloudless summer sky through an open roof. Of all the changes to the school as I remembered it, the biggest surprise was that the solid roof over the pool had been replaced by a steel and plexi-glass retractable roof. It was, as Russell admitted, an absolutely unnecessary improvement. But, like many things at Kennedy, it had been paid for by private donations, not by local taxes. I was sure that my mother had been one of the donors.

We opened the sliding glass doors along the side, and the wind created small ripples in the water. I could hear them gently lap against the side of the pool. The only light was from the outside orange security lights reflecting off the pool water. I wanted to go for a swim. I really wanted to get wet.

"If you know everything," I asked him, "do you know all the stories about this pool?"

"About the parties, the initiations, you mean all that?"

"I guess you do," I said, letting that subject drop. "Do you remember the first time we ever met?"

"At your mother's house. She was very proud of you."

"Oh, you were the one who made the big impression on everyone." I resisted the temptation to remind him that it was my house now, not my mother's. Instead, I walked to the edge of the pool. Then I asked, "You ever swim here by yourself? You know, you've got the keys. You are *the* man with the keys."

"Never," he said, standing up to walk toward me.

"You said you had a favor to ask of me." He stood next to me, both of us looking down into the water. Before he could answer, I took off my sandals and sat down on the edge of the pool, letting my feet dangle in the water. He looked down at me, looked at his own feet, and then he took off his shoes and socks to sit beside me with his feet in the water. I wondered if he remembered that I had asked him to do this with me, sit by the pool with our feet in the water, back when he was my teacher, and we were our own secret. Back then, he had said it was *not a good idea*. Always boundaries for us, all of them set by him.

"Yes, a favor," he said. "I want you to accept that job I've been offering you for years. I need you to do it this year."

I almost got hysterical, "For Christ's sake, Russell, I'm looking for a *life*! Not a *job*!"

"Nancy, I can't get you a life, but if you want a job I have an opening for this fall at school. Five classes, one an honors course. And I know you're qualified."

Of course I was qualified. I spent my entire life getting qualified. A major in history and a minor in English, and an MA in history. I went to Notre Dame to be a teacher, to be just like my parents. My father taught history at Gainesville. My mother taught English at Kennedy High. I set out to make both of them proud. I did my student teaching in a South Bend high school, but in the back of my mind was a plan to get a PhD so I could teach in college, not high school. I was my father's daughter, not my mother's, I was sure of that. I became certified, but I never became employed. After I moved to Atlanta with my new doctor husband, I had been on call for subbing jobs. Fifty dollars a day, no benefits, but no homework to grade either. I never needed a salary because I never had to support myself. After Jack died, I lived off his insurance, his stocks, our small savings. The few dollars I made from reviewing went to meals I never finished. God, to be *that* thin again.

"Russ, how can you..." I started to ask.

"Because, since I'm the principal of Kennedy High School, I can fill any sudden opening on a temporary basis if I want to. Those are the rules. So, if you accept, I'm your future boss. Can you live with that?"

Then it hit me, the absurdity of it all, of everything about thirty-eight years of going in a circle. He was offering me a job at the school I had left twenty years ago. As if my first paycheck was inside the diploma I had been given by the principal at Kennedy when I graduated.

"I don't have a Florida teaching certificate..." I started to protest.

"No problem," he said. "You can get a temporary license. You've got two years to get certified. Until then, your Georgia license is all you need."

"I don't have any full-time high school experience."

"No problem. That'll come soon enough," he countered.

"I hate teenagers."

"No problem. I do too."

He was joking with me, like the best of our old days, and we both began to laugh, to laugh so loud that I forgot how miserable I felt. "Russ, do me a favor," I said to him as we sat next to each other. "One of these days, would you explain to me how I got here at this moment."

"This exact moment? Nancy, I've got my own questions. My own problems. And until I figure out how *I* got here," he said, standing up and offering me his hand, "you're on your own. You've come back home. Jack is dead. You're alive. That's all that matters."

I just looked at him, wondering if he realized that the most attractive part of his offer was...*him*. He stared back, but the light was behind me so he could not see my face in the dark. "Oh, yes, my dear dead Jack," I sighed, at the same time reaching into the pool and pulling up a handful of water to throw at him.

"You do that again, Nancy, and I'm calling for Darrell," he said in a mock angry tone.

I laughed so hard that I began choking. Darrell was Kennedy's career janitor, rumored to actually live in his supply closet. He had been at Kennedy High longer than the original paint, and he always had a pocket full of Tootsie Rolls to offer the girls. As soon as I stopped laughing, I looked around. Nobody could *ever* be sure where Darrell was. He was Kennedy's Freddie Krueger, that was what Kris called him.

"Actually, Nancy, you need a job. I know your money situation. I know your emotional situation. You keep yourself buried in that house much longer, you're going to turn into..."

"Russ, if you mention me and any character from a Faulkner story in the same breath I am going to scream at the top of my lungs until Darrell thinks I'm being murdered and calls the police. Do you understand that!"

"Nancy...

"DARRELL!!!!!"

The great love of my adolescence scooped up his own handful of pool water and threw it in my face. I returned the assault. He kicked water up with his foot. We then called a truce. Domestic tranquility restored, he continued, "You taking this job is not a favor for me. You'll be a good teacher, if you give yourself a chance. But I can hire other people to do the same thing. The favor I need from you is more personal."

At last, at last, I told myself, *what I want to hear from him.*

"I want to tell you about someone else who needs your help too. Her name is Dana O'Connor. I want you to do her a favor. She had some problems last year, and I made arrangements for her to take some courses over this year, to do a second grade option to bring her GPA back up. She needed a break, and it worked like I thought it would."

"You let her take courses over?" I asked.

"Principal's prerogative: *A student may be allowed to repeat a course if the principal determines that extenuating circumstances prevented that student from performing at a level reflective of that student's abilities.* Something like that in the district guidelines. I love bureaucratic language."

"Circumstances?"

"Dana had a baby last year. She didn't drop out of school, but her work suffered because of all the problems. She was really distracted."

As he talked, I kept listening for a reason that would explain why he was telling me all this at that particular moment, alone at night in an empty building, after offering me a job.

"Why are we here?" I interrupted him.

"You wanted to see the pool," he said.

He just sat there swinging his feet back and forth in the water. I sat there like a stone, or a shrink waiting for the patient to finish talking. I wanted him to tell me that Dana whoever was just an excuse for the two of us to see each other without being seen by others. I wanted him to tell me what he thought of me...Nancy Adams. It was time to get the truth, any sort of truth. A few minutes earlier, I had wanted to be by myself. Now, I wanted him to tell me why he wanted to be alone with me.

"When you meet her, you'll understand. She's the most extraordinary young person I've met in years. A lot like you a long time ago. Full of questions. But not optimistic like you. She doesn't assume, like you did, that things will work out."

I was optimistic? I wanted to hear more about myself back then. I wanted him to describe the seventeen year old Nancy Adams. I was back to being a teenager, and the world revolved around me. It had to.

"The difference between day and night, you and Dana. Still, you had a lot of people who were looking out for you. Your mother, your teachers, and friends. Dana's got that in common with you, except for the mother and friends."

"Funny, I don't remember it that way," I said. "I remember feeling terribly misunderstood."

"You were almost eighteen. Being misunderstood goes with the territory."

"This Dana girl is seventeen, isn't she?"

"Dana is eighteen going on fifty, Nancy. She's got a baby with no father, two younger brothers that she has to raise in addition to her own baby because her mother is a total waste of human flesh. Christy O'Connor was in your class but dropped out. The father is dead and not missed."

"Christy O'Connor doesn't ring a bell." How small was the circle lived in, I wondered.

"Her and Dana's brothers live with their mother in a trailer half the size of your future classroom. Dana works. Worked two jobs and went to school and got straight A's and raised her brothers while her mother bitched at her for being...for not being a failure. I even think that her mother was glad that she got pregnant."

"Russell, you never answered my question."

I was looking across the pool to the other side of the room. Banners hung down from the ceiling, more proof of some championship team. I remembered the time when I had waited outside the door to the girls' shower room as Kris and the football captain had sex inside. Then the time Kris and I stayed in the building until nine o'clock, telling my mother that we were working late on the yearbook. We sneaked into the pool to swim naked, scrambling out when we heard Darrell making his rounds. I remembered swimming alone other times, slow laps back and forth across the pool, floating in the dark, wishing that Russell would find me.

"You want to know why we're here, right? You and me," he said.

"Right."

"To be as honest as I can be, this girl needs more help than I can give her. She needs an older woman as a friend. She needs..."

I was almost hysterical again, but I didn't know whether to laugh or cry. Of all the things I thought he might tell me, hearing myself described as an *older woman* wasn't on my list. I stood up, shoes in hand, and began walking away. He was on his bare feet following me in a split second.

"Nancy, I'm sorry. Believe me, you're the only person I could ask this of."

I stopped cold and spun around to face him. "Are you listening to me? Are you hearing me? Are you hearing *yourself*? For someone who always seemed to say the right thing, how can you *not* hear what you're telling me? The first really personal conversation we've had in years, and we don't even talk about *us*?"

We looked at each other in the faint glow of the orange lights from outside. His outline was more visible than his face.

"No, Russ." I said, straining to see his face, "I'm the one who's sorry. This is my fault. I guess I was the one who wasn't listening."

"Look, if you don't want...," he tried to say.

"I don't want to talk about this anymore. That's what I want. I want to go home."

An hour later, I was sitting at the end of my dock. I had stopped at the Curb Mart on the way home and bought ten six-packs of eight ounce bottled Cokes. I sat on the dock and stacked them beside me, opened each one and emptied it into the St. Johns and then corked each empty. I kept a bucket of corks in my kitchen just for these moments. Let's face it. I *was* Emily Grierson. I was a single white female pushing forty who was still sorting out a few minor issues from her past. Would rat poison complete the circle? Would the town gentlemen protect me from my own madness? Thank God, I told myself, I wasn't an English major. I would be even more insufferable in yanking analogies out of thin air. Nope, I was stuck in history, just like daddy, just like that goddam Henry Adams I studied at Notre Dame. Russell wanted an older woman for his new star student, and I was the designated oldie. I was the fossil. *Nancy Adams, welcome home.*

Sixty targets, a full box of ammunition, I tossed the bottles in the water one at a time, shooting at them by the light of the full moon. I could fool a lot of people, but not myself. "You are a complete and utter idiot," I said out loud. My reflection did not disagree. "You're still mad at your dead father, at your dead husband, and you're probably about to accept a job from a man who broke your heart twenty years ago. You know, Nancy, for an educated woman, you're not making a lot of smart decisions. And you talk to yourself out loud. What is that all about?" My reflection seemed amused. "And you're going to stand up in front of a bunch of kids and be an adult?" My reflection withheld judgment. "Jesus, those poor kids." My reflection nodded.

The Long and Winding Road

The whole purpose of education is to turn mirrors
into windows.—Sydney J. Harris

Jack Vandergriff had disintegrated in a plane crash, and there
hadn't been a single identifiable piece of him to bury, not even his
dick. Russell had offered to come to Atlanta to drive me home,
but I told him that I would see him at the funeral. I had known
he would call, knew he would offer. He was the most considerate
man I had ever known. Russell Parsons: My first serious schoolgirl
crush, my first love, my high school history teacher, my first older
man, the first major cliché of my life, my future boss. We were

still friends after all those years. Cards and letters when I went to college, not too personal because we had reached an *agreement*. He got married. I got married. My husband died. His wife went crazy.

Back in high school, he had been ten years older than me. But not now. Ten years between adults was not the same as ten years between an adult and child. His hair, wavy black and thick then, was now wavy gray and thick. He always looked like he needed a haircut. I liked that.

At my eighteenth birthday party, I had been the center of attention. I had been accepted into Notre Dame on a full scholarship. My mother was very proud of me, and she kept telling me how proud my father would have been if he were still alive. Russell had told me then, back in 1977, when we were alone on the porch, that I was the "star" of the class. I was the Kennedy High valedictorian. President of the senior class and the Literary Club and the Future Teachers. *Yeah, I am miserably popular*, I wanted to tell him. I had never dated any boy longer than a month, and it was his fault. I was a pathetic lovesick puppy, and he was oblivious.

In those days, my best friend Kris Fuller would always sneak up behind me and whisper, *You are a bitch and don't you ever forget it*. Then she would pinch me and run off laughing. We would chase each other through the Kennedy halls, screaming the loudest when we passed Mr. Parsons's room, and he would always step out and give us that fake frown that broke our hearts.

After Jack died, Russell listened for years to all the Jack stories I hadn't told anybody else. Jack's affairs, with men and women. I had been ashamed and angry. I had even asked him if he was interested in going to bed with me. "Surely," I had said to him, you have to have thought about it. It was a silly proposition, and he saw right through me. "That would be a mistake," he had told me, "after all these years." I had asked again, "Haven't you ever been curious?" He had smiled that considerate smile of his. "That's killed a lot of cats throughout history."

Me and Kris both agreed back in high school. We loved Russell Parsons, but we hated Stella Malone, the sophomore English teacher. Too pretty, too snobby, too cold, too tall, and too much the obvious object of Russell's desire. *Stella, Stella, she can go to Hella* or *Stella Malona, full of bolona* we would write in notes back and forth to each other. Who, we asked with serious intent, would ever name their daughter *Stella*. If you were named Stella, we reasoned, wouldn't you have to turn out like Stella Malone, the ice princess from Orlando.

The other girls back then had always agreed with Kris about why Stella really bothered me. She was just an older version of... *me*. Smart but cold, pretty but cold, friendly enough but cold. Sometimes funny, but always cold. Kris once called me *Stella's little sister* and I didn't speak to her for a week. Thanks to Kris, everyone seemed to know that I had a crush on Russell, and some of them even seemed to understand how I felt. It was so simple: If Russell could love someone like Stella, why not me? I was just as cool as her. Both of us, so very cool. Cold was cool, right? And the real irony? I had always thought of myself as being like my mother, hot-headed and loud, not anything like *cool*.

I would study Russell like he was the subject of my class, not the teacher. Especially after we started sneaking out of town to see each other privately, I would then go home and write to him in my journal, as if he might eventually read it and know how perceptive I was about him. I look at those journals now and wonder what happened to the girl who wrote them.

Like a slow motion car wreck, Stella and Russell headed for the altar. When I got the formal announcement in the mail, I called Kris and we both cried, then we started laughing, making up stories about our former teachers' honeymoon.

Even more years later, at a welcome home party given for me by Kris, after I had come back from Atlanta in my widow wardrobe, I had fortified myself with two glasses of wine and maneuvered Russell to the kitchen where we could be alone, and I asked him about Stella. He flinched. "She's fine, just not feeling well today."

"Tell her I said hello, and that I was sorry I missed her," I had lied.

He had nodded without looking at me, and there was a moment when neither of us knew what to say. Then I saw his face brighten, and the lines around his mouth softened. I kept thinking, the more I looked at him, that time had been very good to Russell. I thought to myself that I might be ten years younger than him, but I didn't look as good.

He had reached into his back pocket, not saying a word, pulled out his wallet, and opened it to show me the latest picture of his daughters. I looked at it and then looked up at him. He was looking at it, not me, and his face gave him away. He worshipped his daughters. That wasn't a surprise. I had known it for years. At that moment, he had that look my own father had when I would sometimes catch him looking at me when he thought I wasn't looking: Wonder, awe, love, pride, and fear.

I always remembered how I had felt when I looked at that picture. Sally and Theresa were identical twins. I had seen them before, but that picture made me disgusted with myself. *They were not pretty.* That was my first thought. Two very beautiful parents had produced two very plain children. Not unattractive, certainly not close to ugly, just unexceptional. Sally had longer hair, and a prettier smile. Theresa had a face that reflected Russell more than Stella, a sterner face. Twins or not, I saw the difference. I had sometimes imagined me and Russell as parents. Sally and Theresa were nowhere near how beautiful I had imagined my own union with their father.

How many stupid petty mistaken moments did I want back? That was one of them, on my top five list. I was far past thirty, but I didn't want a new life. I just wanted to go back and start over, grow up, be nicer, be happier. I didn't want to be someone else. I wanted to be myself, only better. In Kris's kitchen that afternoon, with Russell smiling as he looked at his daughters, I had wanted to kick myself. I had failed my father and mother by being so petty and selfish when I looked at that picture. Charles Adams had always told me that the purpose of life was to do good. Frances Adams told me that the purpose of life was to be happy. I had achieved neither goal. Instead, I had come home and proceeded to sleep for almost another year.

Home is Fort Jackson, Florida, and it is two places, depending on your color. If you are black you live in the town of Fort Jackson. If you are white you now probably live in Fort Jackson County.

Before I was born, there was only one place, the town. Seventy percent white, thirty percent black. Twenty thousand people whose color determined where they lived and how they worked. If you were black you lived on the north side. Whites lived on the south side, the side closest to the St. Johns River. Black men worked in the potato fields or tenant farmed the land owned by whites. Black women worked in the homes of white women. If you were white you worked in the lumber mill, the sugar processing plant, or you commuted to Jacksonville. I could have been the town historian, as much as I learned from my father. He always said, "Civil rights ruined this town." It was his acid test of irony. After the downtown schools were integrated, whites left Fort Jackson and built new homes and schools out in the county. Money for schools, but not for buses. My liberal parents had done the same. My earliest memories of our new home were that we were alone in the woods until I was six, and we spent most evenings on our boat going up and down the St. Johns. When I was fifteen my father died, and my parents' home became simply my mother's house.

The St. Johns had held us together. My happiest memories were the three of us in our boat on that river, going downstream to Fort Jackson, and then back upstream to get home. The St. Johns was a freak river, one of the few that flowed upstream. My mother always steered, with me in the middle, and my father sat at the bow. He always had a cigarette in his hand, and I loved the smell of his tobacco. When we floated back home after sunset, the red glow at the tip of his cigarette always led the way, making arcs in the dark sky as his hand pointed toward the stars or motioned toward the shore. My mother and I were his captive audience as he told stories about his teaching job in Gainesville or his work in the civil rights movement in Florida. I would listen to him and imagine the scenes: his meeting Martin Luther King, Jr., the bloody confrontations in St. Augustine, the marches in Jacksonville and Miami. For as long as I knew him, he had always seemed to move in slow motion, he was so easygoing. Floating on the St. Johns, however, listening to him talk about his other life, it always seemed to me that he was describing a different man than the one I knew.

Gossip and a Mother's Love

Every educated person is a future enemy.—Martin Bormann

You can never be overdressed or overeducated.—Oscar Wilde

My first official visitor from Kennedy High was Agnes Rose, an English teacher. Agnes wore solid white in stark contrast to her black skin. Her age was not revealed by her face. If someone had told me that Agnes was thirty, and someone else had said she was sixty, I would have agreed with both.

As long as anybody could remember, Agnes always wore clothes of one color. As I got to know her better during the year, I would see how the color for any particular day might have subtle shades different between a skirt and blouse or dress and scarf. The colors were never stark or glaring. Only her fingernails called attention to themselves. They were a half inch longer than her fingers, bright red, and polished hard with almost luminous intensity.

"Mr. Parsons asked me to come by, said you'd need some help getting organized." We were drinking sweet tea on the porch, late afternoon on a muggy day. I was in shorts, braless under a t-shirt, and I was dripping sweat. Agnes was covered from neck to ankle but still dry.

"You call him Mr. Parsons?" I asked.

"He's the boss now," Agnes replied, wiping the condensation off her tea glass with a napkin. "I tell my students that respect for authority is important. I even called Billy Smith *Mister* when he was principal, and he had about as much weight as this tissue here."

"Do all the teachers call him mister?"

"Lord, no," Agnes laughed, "just me in public or with new people. Of course, the students do. He'd like all of them to stop using the first names of the teachers, like everybody was in some big commune. Russell ...," she said, winking and looking around as if checking to see if she was being overheard, "...Russell wants the faculty to act like adults and be treated that way by the kids. I tell him he should have been teaching in the 1950s, not now. Lots of ways, he's out of step."

"Is he a good principal?"

"Honey, you know he only got the job a few years ago, and then he was lucky because the school board still had some long-timers who knew him. That new Chair... the Ms. Elizabeth 'Abeth' Elizondo... she wasn't happy." Agnes's mouth, voicing Elizondo's name, almost puckered up in disgust. "But she didn't have the votes then for her choice. That changed this year after the elections, but he already had the job." She sat back and rocked in her chair. "So, is he good? Me, I love the man. Most of the students do, too, though he drives them crazy with his rules. I'll let you figure out how the rest of the teachers feel about him on your own. The first faculty meeting is in August. Best show in town and you've got a good seat."

"Some of the teachers don't like him?"

Agnes grinned. "You think being a teacher keeps you from being petty and vindictive?" She paused, tapping her nails against each other. "Honey, being a teacher doesn't even guarantee you being smart."

"How long have you been teaching?"

Agnes was becoming a lot more interesting, and I started to wonder how the other teachers felt about her as well as Russell.

"Almost forty years. Since before the new schools were built, before *we* even had real schools." She emphasized *we* without being self-righteous or accusatory. It was merely a way to indicate how long it had been from then to 1996. "I was at the old downtown high school when somebody, in a weak moment, decided that Kennedy needed some more color on the faculty. So, me and my son were hired at the same time about fifteen years ago. Me and your mama became close, and I knew your father in the rights movement even before I met your mama."

"Your son?" I asked, imagining my own mother and me teaching at the same school at the same time. How tense would that be? It was bad enough that I was a student there when she was a teacher. But, colleagues?

"My boy, my oldest, Franklin Rose, the basketball coach."

Something about the name stopped me, and then it hit me. "Dell Rose! Your son is Dell Rose? He's the coach at Kennedy?"

How old was I, back then? I must have been a senior in 1977, when the amazing Franklin Delano Rose scored 54 points against us. Old downtown Jackson High creamed the new county Kennedy High 110-59. And then he went to Kentucky on a football/basketball scholarship. He left town trailing high school All-American credentials behind him and walking into college All-American expectations ahead of him. I had watched him spin the Kennedy players into humiliation, but all I really saw was the most graceful and dazzling human body I had ever seen. I saw physical perfection on the court that night, and it had nothing to do with sex. If told to create a new Adam and Eve, Kris and I both agreed, we would have chosen Dell Rose as Adam, to be the first man from which all other men sprang. I wrote *that* purple prose for the Kennedy newspaper, but it never got published. My mother was the newspaper sponsor. She nixed it. Said she was protecting me from myself.

"Oh, yes, that Dell is mine, and a bigger trial no mother ever had. Nancy, just don't make up your mind about him right away, and don't pay attention to those stories. My son is not like you'll hear. I didn't raise him that way, and he knows it."

It took me a year, but I eventually heard the real story about Dell Rose. Agnes had named all of her sons after American presidents. Franklin Delano was her first child, Dwight David was her last, and John Quincy was the middle son. Her daughters were named Eleanor and Jackie. Agnes had always been partial to Franklin

Roosevelt as the greatest of American Presidents. Her students, years after they had been in her class, at every reunion, would laugh when the shared experience of Agnes Rose was discussed. Jesus and FDR, the Great Depression, and World War II... how often could Mrs. Rose work those topics into every subject, even though she never taught history.

Agnes had five children alive, two dead husbands, and one child who died at birth. All of her children finished high school, all went to college, and all of them except Dell moved away from Fort Jackson. When her children had their own reunions, they would laugh when *their* shared experience of their mother was discussed. That laughter was usually tinged with the knowledge that big brother Dell was their mother's favorite child, but they long ago forgave their mother for her partiality. Dell came back home; they did not. Dell was the only child of her first marriage, to a man who had made love to her almost everyday and who had washed her hair every Sunday night. They were the children of a man who beat them and their mother and who drank himself into a car wreck that killed him and three other people. As a skinny child, Dell had thrown himself between their father and them, cursing him to his face, promising that when he got bigger he would kill him with his bare hands. It was how Agnes told this part of the story that made me realize how much she treasured him above all her other children.

At her second husband's funeral, Agnes had apologized individually to each of her children. She had no explanation for why she had chosen that man or why she allowed herself and her children to be abused. She told them that living with him was a valley that God was leading them through to a better life. For her children, Agnes Rose's faith destroyed their own. None of them, not even Dell, would go to church ever again after they got away from their mother's house.

I poured Agnes another glass of tea and changed the subject, "What can you tell me about Dana O'Connor?"

"How come you're asking?" Agnes replied, her tone noticeably cautious.

"Russell talked to me about helping her make up some courses she did poorly in last year, when she was having her baby. She seems to be very important to him."

"He's going to let her do those courses over?"

"As long as she keeps up her other work as well, which, he says, she should be able to do."

Agnes burst out laughing. "Oh, Lord Jesus, Dana can certainly do that. Making good grades is nothing to that young woman. Nothing at all. I was just thinking of April Bourne. I wouldn't want to be the one to tell her that Dana is going to be able to make up those grades."

"April Bourne?"

Agnes was laughing even louder. "April is counting on that valedictorian's scholarship. And the money's not even the issue. Up until she got pregnant, Dana was the mountain that April couldn't move. The only thing between her and being the best. Nancy, if I were you, I'd get a safe distance away from April when she finds out. A country mile away."

"Odd, Russell didn't mention April being in this equation," I said.

Agnes nodded, and, with her head down as if she was almost talking to herself, she said, "Nope, he wouldn't. Comes to Dana, April doesn't matter. Comes to Dana, not many people matter."

Introductions and History

Do you know the difference between education and experience?
Education is when you read the fine print; experience
is what you get when you don't.—Pete Seeger

The annual National Honor Society picnic was held at Agnes Rose's house in Fort Jackson, the same evening that the opening ceremonies for the 1996 Olympics were being held in Atlanta. For as long as my mother had been the sponsor of the NHS, the picnic was also the traditional new faculty introduction. New teachers meeting old teachers as well as the brightest of Kennedy students. But Agnes's house was much smaller than the house that was now mine, and her backyard was barely big enough for a garage. A rusty swing set, the remnant of raising five children, further cramped the green space, so she rented a wedding tent and had it erected in her front yard.

The old faculty wasn't invited to the picnic. Agnes apologized to her guests for the break in tradition, but I understood. The other new teachers and I, plus twenty senior NHS students, were enough of a strain on Agnes's hospitality. But I was disappointed that Russell wasn't there, even though he had been invited. In fact, I was beginning to think that he was avoiding me. He had called several times to see how I was doing, but he had ignored my suggestions for lunch or dinner. His only excuse was that his daughters took up most of his time during the summer.

I looked at the other new teachers and wondered if they were as nervous as I was. Two, in particular, stood out. Ashley Prose was a Language Arts teacher, fresh out of college with a bachelor's degree in Secondary Education. Like me, it was her first job. You ever meet somebody and dislike her in the first five minutes? It was not fair, it was often wrong, and I usually reserved judgment on people until I knew them better. Like an adult should. But Ashley Prose pissed me off from her first word. *Prose was a poser,* that was what I told Russell later. I also told him I should have gotten a Pulitzer for that line. He was not impressed.

Jerry Sinclair, on the other hand, was as real as rain. I knew that immediately. My first adjective for him, for lack of a better word, was *sweet.* There he was, cup of punch in one hand and cake plate in the other, kid in a candy shop look on his face. He had been teaching math and coaching basketball in Tampa, but he had wanted to get away from that big school. He had graduated from high school in 1980 in a senior class of eighteen students. His school in Tampa had just graduated six hundred and ninety.

Jerry was happy to be in Fort Jackson. Ashley was disappointed. She had let me know that as soon as we were alone after being introduced. "I wasn't going to get a job this year," she said. "I was going to finish my master's in Educational Leadership, so I didn't try for any of the major markets. But Bob Skinner, on the faculty here, called me and told me about this position, said it would be a good stepping stone up, that Kennedy was going to be doing some really innovative things in the future. So I assume you and I will be shaking up some of the old fossils here."

Did she just say fossil? Did she know who she was talking to? Thank God the picnic was alcohol-free. If I had been drinking, I might have asked Ashley who all the old fossils were at Kennedy. Was Agnes one of them? Russell? And since I was pushing forty and recently crowned *an older woman*, how close was I to being petrified?

"So this is your first teaching job?" I asked, orange juice in hand, looking over Ashley's shoulder to see Agnes leading two students to us.

"The first, but I'm ready," Ashley said, turning to see what I was looking at, and then morphing her face from serious to all smiles. "Agnes, you have a great house," she said. "And it was really kind of you to get us all together."

"Do it every year, Ashley," Agnes said. "Next year we'll be back in the woods at Nancy's place. Right, girl?"

"Yes, ma'am," I laughed. "Badminton and horseshoes, sack races, snipe hunts, and real drinks for the adults."

I could see Ashley debate with herself whether to laugh. I could also see that Agnes *was* one of the fossils that Ashley was aiming to bury. Before anyone had a chance to say anything else, and before I could slip in a joke about troglodytes, the female student with Agnes spoke up.

"Let me introduce myself. I'm April Bourne, president of the club, official greeter of new teachers." April shook hands with Ashley and me. "My job is to make sure you meet everyone here, and to make sure Freddy doesn't bother you for a campaign contribution."

The young man next to her stepped forward, extending his hand to me first. "Fred Stein, vice-president of the club, but president of the government and speech clubs. And all the stories about me are true, especially the ones about me having my pick of any girl at Kennedy."

I instantly liked Fred Stein. He was adorable. Obviously the bright nerd of Kennedy High, he was dressed in black denims, a black t-shirt, with black plastic glasses that looked like they were taken off Buddy Holly's dead body. With his black hair combed straight back and spritzed too much, he reminded me of a comedian I had seen on television. A manic talker, self-deprecating, ironic, Fred Stein's black power wardrobe faltered when anyone looked down and saw his white socks.

April was starched, long-legged, dressed in an outfit that was fashionably correct and actually looked good on her. Her long hair was brushed back and knotted in a ponytail. Her complexion was flawless and her face might have been on the cover of *Seventeen* magazine. I wanted to like April because when I looked at her I thought I saw myself twenty years earlier. But I also remembered that April was somehow in the Dana O'Connor equation.

"Freddy and April are two of our best," Agnes beamed, her arms across their shoulders. An orange outfit was her picnic fashion statement. "Up for top honors, the colleges should come knocking soon. We expect them to be our senior leaders."

"If I was just coordinated, I'd even get more offers than April here," Fred said. "Nothing like a smart Jewish jock to fill some quota at Harvard."

April grimaced. "Freddy, do you ever...."

"DA JEW! See what I mean," Fred almost shouted. "DA JEW is what I am to April. That's why I'll never be valedictorian. That's why..."

Ashley and I froze, but then I looked at Agnes and April, and realized that Fred was using a line he had used a hundred times before. Ashley and I were just a fresh audience. "Fred, how come your eyes are brown?" I asked him with a straight face.

"Uh?" he said, not following the transition from his comments to my question. "Say what?" But then he understood. "Because I'm full of crap?"

"Exactly," I said.

Fred reached out and grabbed my hand. "Miss Adams, I want you to know that you are my favorite teacher of all time and I think I love you. If you ever want to have an affair with one of your students, please keep me in mind."

I could tell that Ashley wasn't comfortable with the conversation, and I had to resist the temptation to make her even more uncomfortable.

"Freddy!!" Agnes and April both said at the same time. But neither was really upset.

"Fred, you'll be the first man I call when I'm in the mood," I said, squeezing his hand. Calling him Fred instead of Freddy, and squeezing his hand, I had made him the first of the Kennedy males who, I joked to myself, would fantasize about me while they sat in my classroom.

Agnes guided Fred and April through the other teenagers to meet Jerry Sinclair, who was standing by himself at the edge of the tent. Fred looked back over his shoulder as he walked away. I did a mock glare, one eye closed, and shook my head. He laughed, as I knew he would.

"Impressive kids," Ashley said. "Smart and articulate. Too bad there are never enough of them. And I admire your rapport with them. That's the best approach to teaching. Treat them like adults, they'll be adults."

I wondered if Ashley was as insincere as she seemed, or if she was just too serious for her own damn good. "Ashley, I didn't know I had an approach at all. I just liked him. I think I used to date someone like him when I was in school." I then wondered if Ashley dyed her hair.

She began talking about some theories of adolescent psychology that she wanted to put into practice in her classes, and I realized that although I must have had the same sort of classes sometime in the past I had no memory of them. My college training was a blur, and I found myself merely nodding as she talked, all the while trying to retrieve a theory from my own past. I was catching bits and pieces of Feminine Gender Esteem Acceleration mixed in with Reader Response Variables. And then the bits disappeared. I was clueless. Then for some reason, I remembered Henry Adams. And I told myself to tell Russell about the joke I made to myself about Ashley, stealing words but not weight from Henry Adams. *Ashley was a Dynamo. I was a Virgin. Pretty good, eh? Right, Russell?* But then I corrected myself. Ashley might be a dynamo, but my virgin days were history, and, unlike the Virgin Mary, I was hardly inspiration material.

Then I was alone. The same thing had happened a lot to me right after Jack was killed. I'd be having a conversation with someone, but I wasn't listening to that person. Then that person would be gone and I couldn't remember how the conversation had ended. Only that I was alone, as if waking up in a strange bed, wondering whom I had been with.

I wondered how I got there under the tent, from Atlanta to Agnes's yard. I started to tell myself that I had been wrong to accept Russell's job offer, especially because I had done it for the wrong reason. April Bourne, I told myself, was better prepared to be a teacher than I was.

I suppose a better question would have been how did I get from my mother's house to Atlanta. From my mother's house, the NHS picnic at the end of my junior year, when I met Russell. Then to now. He had been a hot topic even before his appearance. Kris had seen him before I did, and she dripped lust straight through the phone as she described him. But I was more interested in knowing that he had been in Vietnam, killed men was one rumor, and thus he must represent the dark force my father had warned me about, all that was wrong with America.

My father was anti-war before anyone else in Fort Jackson. Knowing what I know now, I wish my father had been more thoughtful. But his rage against Johnson and Nixon spilled over into a loathing for the poor boys who did the dirty work, and soldiers were no more than killers in his liberal mind. If he had been alive when my mother held the NHS picnic that year, he would have either confronted Russell or sulked in his study, refusing to come out. My father was angry, but he died before Russell came to our house. He died while Russell was in Vietnam. Probably some sort of wasted irony, I suppose. Still, I wish he had met Russell. It would have been good for both of them.

I was at the end of the dock back then, watching some of the other kids swimming in the St. Johns, and Russell came out of my house with my mother. He was wearing shorts, sandals, and a baggy shirt, sunglasses hiding his eyes, his skin too pale for Florida.

Cosmic coincidences? Russell met Betsy Elizondo before he met me, luckily for her. Betsy had gone into the St. Johns with her coven of friends, the other outcast smart girls who worshipped her. I had told them to stay close to the dock. Out in the middle of the St. Johns the current was deceptive, much stronger than was apparent on the surface, and sometimes it swirled downward like an inverted water spout. I told Betsy all of that, but she asked if I was merely trying to scare her. Betsy was my first feminist, even if neither of us had any idea what that meant back then. I was going to be valedictorian the coming year. She was my only competition. I told her about the dangerous currents, but she dived in anyway.

As I watched Betsy swim toward the center of the St. Johns, I heard my mother behind me, "Nancy, I want you to meet Mr. Parsons." I turned and he was there, extending his hand but looking past me toward the river. And then the screaming began.

Betsy was bobbing up and down in the water, and her little fishy mates were yelling for help as their entire coven school seemed to be floating toward Fort Jackson. The other fishies were screaming, but Betsy was absolutely silent. If she had been alone, nobody would have known she was about to drown.

Before my mother could finish my introduction to Russell, he had his shirt off and was in the water. The little fishies had not swum too far out, so they were soon safely back at the dock, but Betsy had disappeared, along with Russell. Everyone else was soon at the end of the dock, and then a head popped up out of the center of the St. Johns, then another. Of all the spectators, only my mother and I knew how strong that current was. Everyone else assumed the drama was over, but it was another fifteen minutes before Russell could reach the dock, his arm around Betsy's chest, and he held her until we could grab her arms and lift her up.

Everyone focused on the gasping but still silent Betsy, while I looked for him. I stood at the edge of the dock and he re-surfaced almost directly under me. His two hands on the wooden dock first, then his head rose over the edge followed by his shoulders and chest, and then he took another deep breath before he could lift himself completely out of the water. It was that moment, as the upper half of his body was suspended between water and wood, that was the moment I fell in love, or lust, or whatever. Like a pathetic silly sappy vapid shallow… girl. He was gorgeous, dripping wet and lined with muscles, and a damn hero. I could even ignore the fact that it was Betsy that he saved. If I could love him, how could my father not have at least respected him? And the scars on his rippled stomach? Two ugly red lines, how could they not mean that he was privy to some knowledge denied most men, of death and mortality. I wrote that in my journal, about the scars and death and mortality, as I began the process of mythologizing him. But I didn't write, didn't admit in print then, how absolutely turned on I was at that moment. Desire that was more than an abstraction, desire that was real and that I felt all over my body as he spoke to me for the first time.

"Is she okay?"

Even then, I was in second place.

I handed him his shirt, and we walked back to the house together, as lesser apostles shook his hand or patted him on the back, as even the fishies parted to let us through between them, their envy of me almost too wonderful. Only later would I remember that, of all the people who praised Russell, Betsy never thanked him.

I walked beside him, his escort, and I wanted him to be my trophy. Waiting at the door for us, my mother handed him a towel, and I could tell by the look on her face that she could read my mind, like she always seemed to do, and she almost seemed sad.

I went to my bedroom and called Kris. The National Honor Society picnic of 1976 was about to become an urban myth.

Ashley was at the other end of the yard, being introduced to some students by April while Fred was introducing Jerry Sinclair to another group of students. All the students were seniors, but some, like Fred and April, looked physically older than the others. I overheard bits and pieces of conversation around me. Something about going inside to watch the lighting of the Olympic flame in Atlanta. A sneer about the Kennedy football team. A mock-moan connected to some boy's name. Talk of scholarships. Laughter about Bob Dole. A snicker about Bill Clinton.

"You look like you need something to put in that juice," said a warm baritone voice behind me. I spun around to find myself staring into the chest of Franklin Delano Rose. I had to turn my face up to see his face. I blinked. "Vodka or gin?" he asked, flashing a smile of perfect white teeth.

I kept staring.

"I'm Dell Rose," he said, stepping back away from me and looking up and down my entire body in a split second. "Mama said to come over here and introduce myself. Said you were Frances Adams's daughter."

Of course you're Dell Rose, and just as, just as…yes, you certainly are, I told myself, so proud of my composure. "Nancy, call me Nancy" was the only thing I could say as I extended my hand.

"Mama told me that too. Pretty name, like a name in a song. Told me that you were hired by Mr. Russ himself. Mama gave me the whole story. I know all about you."

I just looked at him. The only other time I had ever seen him in person was when he played basketball for Jackson High, and he had been a hundred feet away from me as I sat in the bleachers. After that, I had seen him play on television once, but then he had disappeared from national attention. The sad classic story of a gifted athlete whose career ended too soon because of an injury. All I could think of there under the NHS tent was how big he was.

Dell Rose was six feet four inches tall. He had dark brown skin, full lips, broad shoulders, and a nose that did not look like the nose he had in high school because it had been broken, repaired, broken again, and then completely reshaped through plastic surgery. He had the best nose money could buy.

Seeing that I was not talking, he took me by the arm and walked me through the crowd to the refreshment table. Moving through those students, I could see some of them prodding others to look while whispering to each other. It was the oldest social glue in history… gossip. Fred Stein saw Dell and me together, and he looked disappointed. Agnes looked happy. April looked like she had just seen her parents naked.

Standing at the long table covered with chips and sandwiches, I watched Dell talk to the female students who came up to see him. I was only a few feet away from him, but he stood there, with his hands in his pockets, and ignored me. *Say what?* I was confused. Why bother bringing me with him if he was going to ignore me? Just as I was about to walk away, he spoke without looking at me. "Something I need to tell you when we get some time to ourselves."

I told myself to walk away. He was being rude, and arrogant. "You sure you can tear yourself away from your groupies?" I said with a phony sigh.

"Woman," he said first with a grin, and then with a real sigh. "I eat these biscuits for breakfast every morning. Butter, jelly, and jam on the side. You and me, *we* got serious business."

I walked away from him and went into his mother's house. Four students were in the living room, watching the Olympics. A few more were in the kitchen, but they stopped talking when I came through the door. I could hear someone in the living room shout to those outside, "They're bringing in the torch now!" After some quick perfunctory hellos, the kids in the kitchen left to watch television. I was then alone in Agnes's kitchen, a kitchen dominated by a poster-size framed picture of Jesus.

The living room was crowded and some of the teenagers were wondering out loud who the final torchbearer would be, the one to actually light the stadium flame.

Standing under Jesus, hearing footsteps, I slowly turned around to face Dell. "You know, I really like your mother." It was not what he expected.

"Don't let her fool you. She puts on like she's some sort of Aunt Jemima, talking country, but she's the best writing teacher this school's got. People shake their heads at the way she talks, but she tells them she ain't teaching speech. Her students learn the king's English when it comes to writing."

"You're very proud of her," I said, watching him beam.

"My mama's the best teacher at that school, and if you treat her right she'll be the best friend you ever have. But I'm not here to talk about her. You and me..."

"Got serious business, right?" I interrupted, liking him again.

"Nancy, I'm sorry about those comments out there. Sometimes I don't gauge my audience right. That's how I usually stay out of trouble. Knowing what to say to whom. Russell told me you were different. I should have remembered."

"Dell! Come quick, you've got to see this," a young voice yelled from the living room.

"Be right there...just a second," he replied. He then looked back at me. "I just want you to know that you can depend on me when you need me. You're getting into a nest of snakes, and that damned Betsy Elizondo is queen of the snakes. Russell hired you without their permission. All legal. He knows the smallest of small print. But they're rewriting the book all the time."

Before I could say a word, more students were calling for him. He held up one finger, pointed it at me, and then he touched my arm. "Dinner, drinks, conversation. You pick the place. I drive. Dutch treat," he said. Then he turned to go into the living room.

I followed him and stood on the opposite side of the crowded room. The volume was turned up too loud, and everyone was talking at once. A female runner was ascending a long staircase with a torch in her hand, heading to the mystery final torch bearer. The television announcer's voice was excited as he speculated about who it would be. Then a spotlight swept the crowd and focused on the top of the stairs. Dressed in white, Muhammad Ali stood waiting for the torch.

The crowd in the living room erupted in a mixed chorus of applause and cheers and a few mumbling groans. The adulation was not unanimous, but it was the majority. I could see that some of the students were having to explain who Ali was to a few of the other students. Agnes Rose was crying.

Everyone was watching the television screen except me. I was watching Dell at the back of the room. He was staring at the screen, hands in his pockets, a desperate look on his face. Not quiet desperation, almost fear. Then he saw me and morphed into a man on stage, the matinee idol. I was his audience.

Virginity and Birth

Education is a progressive discovery of our own ignorance.—Will Durant

I'm not proud of it, even though all the women's magazines tell me I'm a liberated woman and should take advantage of my sexuality as much as any man does. Jack slept around while he was married to me. I paid him back after he died. It made sense to me, especially when I did it with the husband of a woman he had bedded. As if anything made sense.

I went through phases. Revenge first, when quantity counted. Then curiosity, to test a few limits and break a few taboos. And then the stuff I probably needed to tell a therapist, except I knew what it all meant. I dated older men and slept with younger men. I wanted someone to replace Jack and make me feel like he did in the beginning. Jack, the wealthy Presbyterian from Atlanta, who heard my voice as I stood in line in front of him at a movie in South Bend, tapped me on the shoulder and asked, "You're not from around here, are you?" I'd been working to eliminate my accent ever since I got to Notre Dame, tired of having some professor tell me I sounded so *colorful*. So damn colorful, I wanted to sound like I was from Iowa. Jack was five years older than me, but he looked like he was forty. Thinning hair, but a gentleman, and tall. Jack, who would almost make me forget Russell.

The best time? I was thirty-four and the boy was twenty-eight, and he spent an hour looking at me. Like I was perfect. He made me walk around naked, walk up the stairs in his apartment, lay on the bed by myself. I wish I could have bottled the look on his face. The worst? I was drunk, so was the guy, and his wife walked in the front door as I was being hustled out a bedroom window. Out a window! How pathetic was that? Out a goddam window with my underwear in my hand.

I never told Kris those stories. Certainly not Russell. My new widow's freedom and being the cuckolded wife, I used both to explain my behavior. Still, I did too many dumb things to admit, and rationalized all of them. After all, everyone thought I was too smart to be stupid, too sure of myself to be self-destructive. I kept it all to myself, like swallowing my own blood.

It was all going to change after I moved back to my mother's house. The old Nancy Adams was back, battered by experience, wiser for it. That was the official line, and my reputation was intact. I think I was saved because I had come home from the North, which for a lot of people in Fort Jackson meant I had come to my senses. Somehow, my living in Atlanta didn't register with them. I had gone to Indiana, that's all they remembered.

I was home, I still had money in the bank and time on my hands. Men could go to hell, all of them except Russell. I was a virgin again. And then I found the Flamingo Room in Gainesville. Rather, I was taken to the Flamingo Room by a post-Jack flame who called me and asked for a date. His words...*a date*...why not? I was a virgin in Fort Jackson, that's all that counted. Gainesville might as well have been the moon.

I drove to Gainesville by myself, and he led me to the Flamingo. Two drinks down, I thought he had taken me to a New Orleans brothel. The walls were hot pink, but the room was so dark that they looked almost maroon. Dark? It was a dungeon of small tables far enough apart so that every conversation was private. Small tables to accommodate couples only. Small tables with a tiny lamp in the center that cast a circle of light to the edge of the tablecloth and not much further. I could look around and see the hands of men and women as they hovered in that light to eat or reach for a drink, but, as each lover leaned back, their faces seemed to disappear to everyone but the person across from them. The Flamingo had obviously been designed by someone who cheated on a spouse at one time.

An ocean of dimly lit islands, with dark drapes over the windows, and a profoundly surreal mural covering one entire wall. That first night, I sat across from my *date* and kept trying to focus on the scene over his shoulder in the dark distance. I asked him to turn around and explain it to me. He laughed and poured me another glass of wine. "It's this room," he said, very pleased with himself.

And so it was. An entire wall replicating the room itself, the dim tables and faceless couples, the candles like bright dots, almost starry, and tuxedo-clad waiters floating on the wall much like they seemed in reality, appearing out of nowhere to whisper to the man of the table and return with silver trays of food and drink. The only thing missing from the wall was the music of the room, a continuous thread of opera arias and slow strings, an unobtrusive soundtrack to whatever movie each couple thought they were in.

I couldn't decide if the room was incredibly tacky, or irresistibly sensual. One more glass of wine, and I reached a verdict. If the man across from me had suggested it, I would have laid on the table for him. But he was a gentleman, just like the early Jack, in so many ways.

As we left that night, bound for his hotel, we passed the bar in the next room. Sitting under the racks of upside-down glasses which hovered over the counter-top were a half dozen versions of me, women alone and waiting.

I went back to the Flamingo Room with a few men who thought they knew me, but I stopped a year ago, when I found myself sitting at the bar watching other women walk past me, women who were not alone.

The Flamingo became my secret. I began to re-virginize myself.

After Agnes's party, I went home and cleaned my already clean guns. I wanted to call Russell, but I was tired of being obvious. I was also trying to process Dell Rose, but that effort kept leading back to Russell.

Nobody knew about the first time he had touched me. Not even Kris. In fact, I had specifically lied to Kris years earlier when we were walking across the campus of Notre Dame. The subject was sex, a subject that Kris never tired of analyzing. She and her first husband Tom had been married two years, and I could already read between the lines of her description of their marriage. Kris wanted to see other men. She didn't want Tom to be the last man she ever had sex with. She kept telling me, "I'm too young to be married, to settle down. Dammit, Nance, I'm too young to get old like my mother."

Kris was always asking me about who was asking me out and what we did. I had told the truth except for one question. "What's the most exciting thing a guy has ever done to you? I mean, really turned you on," she had asked.

I told her a story about a party I had gone to the semester before, a frat party in a rented barn, with too much beer and loud music and fast dancing that turned into soft music and slow dancing. It was a good story, and mostly true, and Kris was satisfied. The truer story of my most turned-on time, however, was that I had been seventeen years old and a senior at Kennedy High, sitting in a chair in Russell's classroom, after school had let out for the day, and he was standing behind me with his hands on my neck and shoulders.

I had gone to see him about plans for the Christmas formal. He was one of three faculty sponsors. I was in charge of decorations and music, so my seeing him after school wasn't all that unusual. I had done it before for other reasons, and our conversations always went beyond school business. I would tell Kris that he always made me feel like an adult, that he would talk to me as if we were the same age, him a few years younger, me a few years older.

Music and decoration questions finally settled that afternoon, I had complained about how tired I was, about how everyone else seemed to expect me to do all the work, about how Betsy Elizondo was trying to organize an alternative *Holiday* program rather than a Christmas program. My neck felt like concrete, I had told him, rolling my shoulders as if trying to massage myself. It was all very premeditated. I knew that. It was an opening, a test. But it was also safe. We were in a classroom. Nothing could happen. The door was shut, and the classroom was at the end of a long hall. I knew that only a few people were left in the building, but I also knew that my mother was one of those people.

Russell had looked at me, smiled, that damn charming smile, and told me to sit in the chair next to his desk. I sat down and closed my eyes. It was cool outside, December in north Florida, about fifty degrees, and the late afternoon sun was flooding the west side classroom with warmth and light. He pulled my collar back and pushed my hair away from the back of my neck. I had unbuttoned the top two buttons of my blouse before I went to see him. He put his hands around my neck and started to gently rub both sides at the same time, his thumbs pushing into the tight flesh where my neck became my shoulders.

I had felt his touch all the way down my body, down to my stomach and down further. I kept my legs squeezed together, tightening the muscles in my thighs and then relaxing, surprised at how my toes curled against my will. He talked as he touched me, telling me about when he was in high school, about his being in charge of finding a band for the Christmas dance and how the band turned up drunk and sang dirty lyrics to sappy songs, about how his school's yearbook staff laid out the Social Life section with extra pictures from that dance with those lyrics euphemistically reproduced underneath the pictures. I asked him to bring me that yearbook, so I could see what he looked like when he was my age.

Perhaps it was only a few minutes, perhaps a half hour. I don't remember exactly how long he had touched me. But I do remember that when he stopped I had been very disappointed. Then, with his hands off me, he had asked me if I would like to have lunch with him sometime, on a Saturday afternoon, somewhere "comfortable," but somewhere that was my choice. Always a gentleman, he never surprised me. I should have paid more attention to the obvious.

I had known immediately where we could go. In Jacksonville, an old robber baron hotel, *The Flagler*, had converted its mammoth lobby into a gift shop and restaurant area. My father had always taken me and my mother there for my birthday. The restaurant was called the *First Coast Room*, and I had been intrigued by how, if only a few people were there, I could always hear an echo.

Thus began our secret life. Russell would meet me at a Denny's restaurant on the county line, and we would go to Jacksonville in his new Toyota. We always sat across from each other at the *First Coast*. Soon enough, we had a regular waiter who looked for us every Saturday, a red-headed man in his thirties named Sully who sometimes managed to sneak us a free piece of chocolate peanut butter pie for dessert, one giant piece with two forks.

After a month of Saturday lunches, Sully had asked us if we had a "thing" going. Russell had shocked me into silence when he laughed and told him "More than a thing, an affair. I'm married and this is one of my students." I kicked him under the table. Sully had simply taken a deep breath and seemed to think it over, as if he was not sure if Russell was kidding him, and then he said, "That's even better. That means I'm going be the best man when you two get married eventually."

I had been blushing, and I had been genuinely embarrassed. On the drive back that afternoon, I had sat as far away from him as I could, looking out the window, wondering what it would be like to be married to him, knowing that he and Stella Malone, not he and Nancy Adams, were probably headed for the altar.

We went to the *First Coast* less and less after that, as if by un-spoken mutual consent. We would eat, spar with Sully, and then window-shop at the boutiques surrounding the restaurant. We would talk about things at school, about books, about the news, and we would joke about the people around us. I had a knack for seeing strangers at the *First Coast* as older versions of Kennedy students, and he always seemed impressed with my ability to mim-ic the quirks of other Kennedy teachers. He told me that I was witty. Everyone else at school just thought I was sarcastic. Nancy Adams, the jokester. Twenty years later, I shoot at coke bottles and think the joke is on me.

Sometimes we would even go to a movie matinee, sitting in the dark, shoulder to shoulder, but he never touched me. Sometimes he would lean his face down and whisper in my ear, nothing per-sonal, just some comment about the movie. I would imagine him kissing me in the dark like that, as if he was going to whisper to me but, instead, kissing me. Eventually, I would tell myself that I was actually glad that he never tried anything personal with me, that he had drawn a clear line between us that he never crossed. That he respected me. Love and respect, surely, were synonymous, right?

The last time we went to the *First Coast* we both agreed that it was not a good idea to keep doing it. I was about to graduate. We were lucky that nobody ever saw us. Most surprising to me, he thanked me for letting him talk so much. He told me to keep in touch after I went to college, neither of us knowing that I would soon make a conscious decision to put him behind me. To put childish things, schoolgirl crushes, behind me, I told myself.

I tried to put him out of my mind, but he sent me a Christmas card. Harmless enough, I told myself. I was lonely, so I called him when I went home for the holidays. He seemed glad to hear from me. I went back to Notre Dame and wrote him a long letter, asking if it was all right to write him even though he was "going with" Stella Malone. I told myself it was possible to be friends. Cards and letters for years, but sometimes not for months at a time. He always asked what I was reading. He seldom mentioned Stella, but he told me a lot about his daughters after they were born. When Jack died, I wasn't surprised to see Russell with my mother and Kris at the funeral. After that, he called once a month, always the same, on the last Sunday of the month.

He had married Stella, and she had gone crazy. There was a medical explanation for some of her behavior, but Kris and I both agreed that Stella was disjointed even before she gave birth to her twin daughters. Two days after the thirty-hour labor and then a Caesarean-section, she had had a stroke. A massive blood clot had reached her brain as she was recovering, and she almost died. Russell took his two healthy daughters home and left his wife in the hospital for three months. I remembered that time because he never wrote or called me.

When he brought Stella home, her speech was slurred, the right side of her face twitched, she drooled, she limped, and her right arm was paralyzed. Beautiful Stella Malone was an angry woman. After a year of physical therapy, on days when Russell was teaching, she would leave her infant daughters with a black neighbor and walk four blocks into the center of old Fort Jackson. She seldom spoke to anyone, even when directly addressed, but when she wanted a response from someone, or especially when she had to repeat herself because someone didn't understand her, she would stutter and curse the person in front of her, clenching her left hand into a fist that would start shaking. Everyone agreed that Russell had to be both mother and father to his children, husband and guardian to his wife. His wife's worst behavior was usually followed by a written apology from him to the offended party, *if* he knew about the incident. Those short notes, Kris had joked at the reunion, should have been anthologized. There was some grumbling when he sent his daughters to the small Catholic school instead of the public schools. If he was always so poor, people said, how could he afford tuition for a private school when he could send them to public school free. How sorry should they feel for him? But the local priest let enough people know that Russell was given reduced tuition in exchange for his free tutoring of some St. Joseph students and for other unspecified services. The resentment faded. Stella was seen less and less in town, and he always made sure he was there to walk his daughters home. Me, I was in Atlanta, headed toward widowhood.

Going Back to School

Public school is a place of detention for children placed in the care of teachers who are afraid of the principal, principals who are afraid of the school board, school boards who are afraid of the parents, parents who are afraid of the children, and children who are afraid of nobody.—Unknown Source

A week before school opened, I went to my first faculty meeting. Most of the teachers who had been at Kennedy when I was a student had already called or come by to see me at home. In fact, most of the teachers at school had contacted me in some way. I even had lunch with Ashley Prose to discuss the upcoming year, and she had done most of the talking. I kept asking myself, *Why isn't it obvious to her how I feel?*

Jerry Sinclair called me to ask about a house he was interested in buying in Fort Jackson. I told him to call Kris, and I thought to myself that he had a voice that would sound good on the radio. Fred Stein sent me a Ralph Nader brochure. April Bourne sent me a Hallmark card wishing me *Best of luck on your new job.* I did not think she was insincere.

The faculty meeting was in the cafeteria of Kennedy High. I arrived early, and Dell was already sitting at a back table, motioning that he had saved me a seat next to him. I hesitated, remembering what Kris had said about his reputation, but then I went over and sat down, making sure there was at least a three foot space separating him and me.

"Best seat in the house," he whispered without looking at me. "And your back is covered." He then saw Jerry come in and motioned for him to come over too. As Jerry was walking toward us, Dell whispered again, "We'll put the new boy on the other side of you, and you'll be the Queen of the Nile. Two handsome studs to keep the commoners away from you." He was tacky and politically incorrect, but I was glad to be sitting next to him. Still, I reached under the table and pinched his leg as hard as I could. He wasn't expecting it, and he yelled "Ow!" loud enough to have a dozen teachers turn and look at the two of us.

"Now you've done it, sister," he laughed as he rubbed his leg. "Your payback is coming but not when you expect it. Revenge is mine." And, then, without a pause, he yelled across the cafeteria, "Jerry, get over here and protect me from this woman. She can't keep her hands off me!"

I felt like I was in high school again, not teaching there. Despite my best efforts to be cautious, I actually liked Dell. Then I saw Ashley Prose and three other teachers all staring at me. With Jerry to my right, and Dell to my left, I remembered how it felt to be popular.

When Jerry sat down, he and Dell began talking about sports, talking across me as if I wasn't there. Jerry had played basketball in high school, good enough to get a scholarship to college where he was a second-stringer, and it was obvious that he was pleased to now be sitting near Dell.

As the two men talked, I looked around the cafeteria. I didn't remember there being so many vending machines when I went to school. But the tables were still arranged the same way, ten parallel rows of ten tables jammed against each other. If the benches were full, eight hundred students could be fed at one time, but I had never seen the benches full. The polished white tile floor still had the Kennedy mascot name spelled out in oversized blue tiles: THE BLUE KNIGHTS. On the largest wall was an almost-epic painting of an armored Knight with a sword raised.

Waiting for Russell to arrive, I studied how everyone sat. With me in the back row, along with Jerry and Dell, were a dozen other male teachers. I was the only woman. Agnes and a small group of older teachers sat at a table in front of us off to the left. There were only five black teachers in the entire room. The Rose family provided two of them. Younger teachers sat closer to the front, and Ashley Prose was in the middle of them.

The meeting was supposed to start at ten o'clock. At ten fifteen, a short balding man walked in with a hand full of papers and began distributing them, saying, "Russell will be late today. Some trouble at home, so he asked me to get things going."

Dell put his face in his hands and moaned just loud enough for the back row to hear, "Oh, Jesus save me, or just shoot me now." The men around me snickered, except for Jerry, who looked at me as if I understood what was happening. I just shrugged. Dell kept his head down, but turned slightly to whisper to me and Jerry, "That's Robert Skinner, principal wannabe, and a total...dipshit."

Agnes had turned to look at her son, who nodded at her and then took a deep breath, saying to himself, "I can do this. I can do this. I can do this. I can get through this without killing somebody."

Skinner laid out the agenda. New policies from the School Board. Equipment requests approved or denied. New policies from the principal. Open discussion. He was a nervous man, and Dell constantly asking him to "speak up so we can hear you in the balcony" only made him more nervous.

After thirty minutes, Skinner had not gotten past the first new change from the Board: a minor revision to the open campus policy. Dell and the back row needed a lot of clarifications so they could explain it to their students. It was obvious they were playing dumb for Skinner. After a half hour, the other teachers and I were equally irritated between Skinner's inability to control the meeting and Dell's ability to disrupt the meeting.

Just as Skinner's voice was getting more emphatic with every "that's just the way it is," Russell walked in the room. Everyone shut up. I was impressed. I noted the absolute change in the meeting, and I looked at Russell in his dark double-breasted suit. He wasn't the same man who had sat with me with his feet dangling in the Kennedy pool after dark. It was as if I was seeing him for the first time. He had always worn a tie as a teacher, never too casual, but this suit was beyond professional. He looked like a banker, a Republican banker from the Great Depression.

"Sorry about being late," he said, taking a clipboard out of Skinner's hand, thanking him as he did it. "I'll try to get us out of here before noon."

I noticed how relaxed Dell had become. I also noticed how Agnes and the teachers around her all had a yellow notepad in front of them and were ready to take notes. Jerry also noticed the change.

"I heard he used to be your teacher," he whispered to me.

"A long time ago," I said, testing my pen on the yellow pad in front of me to make sure it had ink.

"I'm going to change the order of the agenda," Russell said. "Most of the equipment requests were personal, so I'll discuss those with you individually. No need for us all to argue about Charles Yates's request for more left-handed desks...," muffled laughter in the back row, "...or Bob's desire for more printers in the computer lab. Everybody okay with that?"

Skinner raised his hand. "I made that request to help everyone else out, Russell. I think they should be allowed to comment on it. Some input might be helpful to make my case."

Russell smiled and turned to the other teachers, "Any comments?"

Ashley Prose spoke without raising her hand. "Even though I'm new here, I think Robert's request has merit. I want to..."

Russell gently interrupted her, holding one finger up. "For the record, the printers will be here before we open the doors next Monday."

Ashley stared at him, speaking softly, "Oh, well, in that case, I suppose my input isn't needed. Excuse me."

Dell leaned over to me and whispered, "I love that man." I nodded, wondering why Ashley dyed her hair.

"Most of the new policy stuff is self-explanatory, if you read the material in your mailboxes," Russell continued, looking specifically at an older teacher near the front, a man who had not shaved in two days. "All of it went through committee last year. But you do need to know it, so take the time to read the material," looking again in the same direction. "Questions? If not, let me emphasize that you will find a complete, almost final version of the new sexual harassment policy in your mailboxes..."

Dell raised his hand. "Mr. Parsons, don't you mean our person-boxes?" Everyone in the room groaned, except for Ashley's group, which redefined silence.

Russell looked over his glasses toward the back row. "Dell, you're getting predictable, so get a new writer."

Dell didn't respond, but he did salute. As he did, Ashley raised her hand. "I'm sorry I know I'm new here. But does this mean that this school did not have a sexual harassment policy before now? How is that possible?"

Russell didn't answer immediately. Instead, he looked around the room and then up at the ceiling. Then he said with an absolutely straight face, "We never had any sexual harassment?"

Ashley stood up immediately as most everyone else burst out laughing. "That is absurd. And, as a woman, I am appalled at your lack of sensitivity on this issue. I had heard that this school was a leader and that..."

Russell motioned for everyone to be quiet, looking especially hard at Dell who was almost hurting himself trying not to laugh. I then watched him do the most impressive thing I had ever seen done by someone in a position of authority. He became instantaneously, sincerely contrite and apologetic.

"You're right, Ashley. This is a serious issue. And I apologize for being so flip about it. I'm still trying, myself, to adjust to a new world. I have two daughters. I want them protected from abusive and crass behavior. No, you're right. We need to take this seriously."

Ashley sat down, disarmed. She had appointed herself the champion of her sex, but now she was reduced to accepting Russell's apology. The room was uncomfortably quiet.

"We all want to do the right thing here," he continued. I looked over at Dell. He was looking down at his hands, which were holding on to his legs.

"If we do nothing, someone might get hurt. If we do the wrong thing, someone's career might be destroyed. I have to administer this policy. I guess I'm worried about making the wrong decision. I'll need all of your help here on this one. So, let's stop making jokes about it. All of you... *all* of you... read the policy backwards and forwards. And learn to live with a cliché...better safe than sorry. Any questions?"

Dell raised his hand and I could feel the tension in the room. I hoped that he was not about to make a joke. I liked him too much to see him make a fool of himself. But Dell was calmly serious.

"Russell, I have read the policy. I've read it more than once. Can you tell me what the *hostile environment* means?"

Ashley stood up to face Dell, but Russell pointed his finger at her and shook his head, pointing to her and then to her chair. She sat down again.

"Dell, you remember when you and I were in junior high, back in the stone ages. Different schools, different towns, but I bet we had the same experience. Sex education. All the boys in one room, girls in another."

Everyone in the cafeteria was listening in on this private conversation. "The textbook facts, the locker-room facts, the street facts. Not one guy in the room had a clue as to the truth. It occurs to me now that maybe you and I and every male on this faculty ought to sit down and re-educate ourselves. Not out hugging trees like some Iron John-howling-at-our-fathers session. But something. Dell, I couldn't define the term for you. I was hoping you could help me."

I remembered when Russell had touched me in his classroom, how I had wanted him to do it. But, as I had told Jerry a few minutes earlier, that was a long time ago. Then I did something that surprised myself. I raised my hand.

"Russell, can I make a suggestion?" Everyone in the room looked at me. "Let's have a separate meeting just on this subject. But let's do it together, boys and girls. And we can all be grownups about it. You men listen to us, and we'll listen to you. But let's set aside a lot of time, time we don't have this morning."

Heads were nodding. Nancy Adams was a natural born leader for sure. My father would have been proud. A consensus was forming to move on to the next subject. I was offering an exit for everyone to leave safely, and I had one more suggestion.

"I'll even bake some cookies," I said, smiling at Russell.

At first, nobody laughed, but then Agnes stood up and offered to help. "I'll do some cakes," she said, and then the men in the room started shouting requests. "Chocolate chip...devils food...peanut butter...spice..." Most of the women soon joined in with their own suggestions. I stood there watching almost fifty adults shouting out their favorite desserts. Agnes had her yellow pad in her hand, acting like she was a waitress taking orders. Through a sea of waving raised hands, I could see Russell looking at me, mouthing silently the words *thank you*. I mouthed back at him, *you owe me.*

Decorum restored, he said, "I assume this can be interpreted as a positive response to Nancy's suggestion. If so, I'll set it up. Any questions?"

Ashley raised her hand. "I think I should be on that committee with Nancy and Agnes."

Russell looked over at me for a sign, and I knew that he would let me decide. I shrugged, then nodded. *Why not?*

"Okay, it's a done deal," he said quickly. "Ashley and Nancy and Mrs. Rose will get us on the right track. Anything else?"

Jerry raised his hand. "Can we invite President Clinton?"

I spent the next half hour watching Russell juggle questions and egos. He was better at questions than egos, but it was not for lack of trying. Some egos were heavier and more bent out of shape than others. It was obvious that he had established individual approaches to the old faculty. He treated Dell almost like a lifelong best friend, and he treated Agnes like an older woman from another generation of manners, which she was.

With the three new faculty members, this first meeting was a chance to see how they would fit into the larger group. I had seen them all at the NHS picnic, but, except for Ashley, none of them made an impression until this meeting. Jerry quickly fit into the back row clique ruled by Dell. Ashley stood out among the all-female version of the back row: young, newer female teachers who were all under thirty years old. Also in that group was Sue Rollins, a mannish young woman who was hired at the same time and from the same college as Ashley.

I had already read the material, so my attention sometimes wandered. Seemed to happen more and more lately. I kept thinking about Russell, but not listening to him. I tried to imagine him twenty years earlier, sitting in the same spot as I was at that moment. Everything that had happened to me in the past three months was leading to a conclusion so obvious that I almost wanted to slap myself for being so oblivious to the truth.

I was absolutely alone. Ever since Jack died, I had floated through life as if time would stand still for me. As if, no matter when I might make up my mind about what I was doing with my life... even as I was getting closer to forty, I would still be waiting to turn thirty, my unofficial marker of adulthood. Even after I discovered that a part of my past was a lie, that Jack had deceived me, perhaps himself, I refused to give him up. I had surrendered my life to his a long time ago, and his death hadn't set me free. I had still lived in his house, spent his money, slept with his friends and then gone back to his house to curse his ghost. Then my mother died, and I came to live in her house. Husband and mother dead, I had attached myself to Russell Parsons, who had turned out to be a living ghost.

I wasn't seventeen any more. I was the *older woman* whom Russell had asked to help an eighteen year old girl. He had no feelings for me comparable to my feelings for him. I assumed there was a thread linking us together even after I graduated in 1977, a dormant thread for twenty years, invisible sometimes even to myself, but always there. Why else had we kept seeing each other? I was wrong. He wasn't a twenty-eight year old man who still had secret lunches with me. It was obvious. Russell had never stopped being my teacher. Anything else was my desire, not his. I was now almost forty, and he was almost fifty. We were adults. He has his own life, and it doesn't include me. I wondered if it ever did, or was our *past* merely my own memory.

I looked over at Dell. He was writing a note to Jerry, something about one of the female gym teachers. Reaching around behind me, he passed the note to Jerry, who read it and wrote a response on the bottom of the page and passed it back to him. I looked at the clock on the cafeteria wall, one of those giant white-faced clocks, with thick black minute and hour hands, and a thin red sweeping second hand, wondering, *if I was alone in the cafeteria and stood directly under it, could I hear it hum?*

I looked at my yellow pad, surprised at how much I had actually put down in the last hour. I wrote a note to Dell: "Know anybody who wants to buy a house near school?" Then one to Jerry: "You still looking for a house?"

Dell read the note and gave me a puzzled look, scribbling something and pushing it back across the table to me: "We scare you off already? You quitting?"

I leaned toward him and whispered, "Not a chance, coach. I just need to find my own place. Maybe not immediately, but eventually."

The First Day of the Rest of Your Life

An educated person is one who has learned that information almost always turns out to be at best incomplete and very often false, misleading, fictitious, mendacious - just dead wrong.—Russell Baker

As I pulled into the faculty parking lot on the first day of school I heard a drum beating, an old tradition. A senior band member would stand on the front steps the first day of school and pound a bass drum from 7:30 until 8:00. I arrived promptly at 7:30, almost alone in the lot. Students parked in the back of the building, faculty in the front, but even that early in the morning I had to fight a line of cars racing through the main entrance to get to the back.

Just like 1976, there was never enough student parking. First come, first parked. Late arrivals had to park in nearby neighborhoods and walk a mile to class. It was the classic adolescent hardship.

When I was a senior, the drummer was Larry Mohn, a slow-witted boy whose internal rhythm kept time with the pounding of his oversized bass drum. I had stood with Larry that first day in 1976 as cars sped by, my friends yelling "retard lover." The drummer in 1996 was Fred Stein, wearing a Blue Knight band uniform with a *Ralph Nader for President* sticker plastered across his plumed helmet. He saw me walking toward him and smiled like he had won the Florida lottery.

"Teacher! Teacher!" he yelled. "You gotta help me!" I was about thirty feet away from him. I waved, trying to indicate that I was in a hurry to get to class, but he was adamant. "I gotta see you. I need your help!" He yelled without missing a beat on the drum.

I gave up. "What you need?" I asked, the two of us standing together as students raced by shouting at Fred that Ralph Nader was gay.

"I HAVE to like get out of your honors seminar today. I truly HAVE to. I HAVE to be at a Green Party meeting this afternoon at the public library. I'm the county chair."

My first thought was that the local Green Party had a long way to go before anyone took them seriously, but then I had to make my first teacher decision: To excuse or not. I remembered my mother's standard policy. *Always say NO first. You can change your mind easier later.*

"Not today, Fred. I'm insecure. I need an audience," I said, patting him on the back and walking into the building as he laughed. In a perfect world, I told myself, all my students would be Fred.

"The revolution comes, Miss Adams, you're going to need a favor from me. I've got a memory like an elephant. And payback WILL be mine."

"Fred, when the revolution comes, will you be wearing that uniform?" I shouted back to him. He missed a beat.

From 8:00 to 8:55 I was free and alone in my classroom. It had been Russell's idea. "Let you get your feet on the ground," he had told me. This first day of school, I had nothing to do. I had spent July and August getting prepared. I had read and re-read the textbooks I would be using. I had outlined lectures for the first six weeks, printed syllabi for the three different courses I would be teaching, laid out daily assignment plans for the five classes, gone through the school library checking on resource materials relevant to the courses I would be teaching, and even searched websites that had been recommended by other teachers. Russell had warned me about the internet being the new source of plagiarized papers, so I needed to get familiar with it.

I had also met Donna Parton, the head counselor, and Donna had given me a personality profile of potential problem students I would be having. Donna knew everything about every student at Kennedy. When I had gotten the computer printouts of class rolls in my office mailbox, Donna had already put red X's by a dozen names.

Donna was a tall woman, her long hair always slightly frazzled. She was also the only adult at Kennedy who was in perpetual motion. Sitting in my empty classroom the first day, I heard her walk by the door and say "Hi, how's it going?," but before I could turn and answer she was gone, and I could hear another teacher in the hall, "Donna, Donna, I need to talk to you about......"

I had already replaced the old inspirational posters with my own new clichés. I had also put up new picture posters: James Dean smoking, Albert Einstein on a bicycle, Neil Diamond with long hair, John and Bobby Kennedy huddled together discussing missiles in Cuba, Theodore Roosevelt pointing directly at someone taking his picture, Rosa Parks being led to jail, Eleanor Roosevelt at the Lincoln Memorial, a kneeling young woman at Kent State.

Alone, drinking another cup of coffee, I heard music. At the end of the hall was the orchestra room, and someone had forgotten to close the two sets of doors separating it from the rest of the classrooms. Kennedy had a symphony orchestra, a marching band, and a jazz band. Even as far back as 1976, the symphony was winning state awards. I sat there the first day listening to something from Lizst or Beethoven or someone from the Romantic period. Then the music abruptly stopped as another teacher, closer to the source, closed the doors. I was disappointed. It had been a good way, an almost inspiring way, to start the day, the new school year. This wasn't going to be as bad I had thought last night.

I left my room to stand in the hall so I could hear better. Listening to the orchestra this morning, I told myself, *If I had had any real musical talent, I would have wanted to be a music teacher. How could you not look forward to coming to work if you got to do this every day, make this kind of music?* I walked closer to the band room, forgetting one of the basic instructions for all teachers: At break, we were supposed to be outside our own classroom doors, acting as adult hall monitors. As I neared the band-room door, the bell sounded and a thousand bodies of teenage energy gushed out of dozens of classroom doors and flooded the hall with me in the middle. I was in a sea of hormones.

My classroom was unguarded, and I was unprepared for the noise, the sight and smell of teenagers getting out of their first class on the first day of school. I was too slow for the bodies in motion around me. Five minutes to go to their lockers, five minutes to renew friendships, to gossip, to touch each other.

"...Go fuck yourself, butt-lick."

I felt like I was in that scene in the *Ten Commandments*, when the Red Sea parts, but in reverse. I was alone, trying to cross the dry land and then the damn water, which had been held back by some hand of God, those waters were collapsing around me.

"...So, how long you been a faggot?"

The halls of Kennedy were wider than most school hallways, an architectural innovation that was noted when it was first built. Less congestion, more civility was the theory. But, like too much air filling a vacuum, student bodies, spread from wall to wall, still pressed against each other.

"... Is it true that your mother's a dyke?"

"...There she is, Lucy Hoover, sucking up everything she dates."

"...Eat me raw."

Cologne and perfume and a thousand obscenities. I had been told to expect it, and I thought I had prepared myself for what Russell and Donna and Agnes and the other teachers had told me about. But it had all been an abstraction. Truth was, I wasn't prepared. I didn't want to hear all this. Truth was, I stood there looking for help. I could not, should not, be a teacher. I wanted an adult to rescue me from those sharks.

Russell Parsons appeared in the hall. He was in his double breasted, dark and well-worn suit, walking down the middle of the hallway, students falling away as if repelled by some sort of reverse magnetism. He seemed to know all their names.

"How's it going, Mr. Parsons?" a towering boy asked, his letter jacket too small for him.

"Good, Bobby Ray. Better if you win next Friday," Russell said, patting the boy on the shoulder as he passed.

"Mr. Parsons, you know, like, you got some cigarettes?" a frail looking girl with a nose-ring asked, shaking and smiling at the same time, knowing the question was absurd and knowing the answer ahead of time, like it was a game she and the principal played every day.

"Jackie, you keep putting those nails in your coffin, we're going to have the nurse put you on a respirator."

Jackie the Smoker mimicked smoking and then walked into my classroom.

"Mr. Parsons, Mr. Parsons, I can't take Mr. Skinner's class anymore. He's killing me. You gotta, like, get me out before I go postal," a pock-faced boy pleaded, his Florida State sweatshirt hanging down almost to his knees.

"Scott, give it a week, and give me a good reason, and we'll see Mrs. Parton," Russell said, holding on to the boy's elbow to keep him from being swept away.

"Suck me and the horse I rode to school on," blared a red-headed boy wearing a RON JEREMY FOR PRESIDENT tee-shirt, his back to Russell. The boy's audience, a pudgy girl with bleached hair, was wide-eyed as she looked over his shoulder to see the principal.

I had been told that it was a losing battle. "Pick your fights carefully," Agnes Rose told me a week earlier. "We lost the language war a long time ago. Of course, I can't convince Russell of that."

"Donnie," Parsons said as he tapped the boy on his shoulder, "Why don't you come see me at lunch. My table."

As he spoke, the throng of students flowing past him had slowed down so they could hear every word and carry it back to their classes. Agnes had also told me how most students had learned to watch their language around the principal. If nothing else, he was consistent. A lot was said behind his back, but there were consequences for anything he actually heard.

Russell turned to the girl in front of Donnie. "And you, Denise, you might get more respect if you wore something other than those kind of clothes."

Under the Nike swoosh on her shirt was JUST DO ME.

A short ring of the bell, and the halls emptied as fast as they had filled. Russell looked at me, pointed to the clock on the wall, arched his eyebrows, and laughed. "And you, Miss Adams, you better get to class before you're late. Not a good precedent for your debut."

"Yessir," I said, resisting the temptation to salute.

"And, Nancy," he said as I turned, "how about lunch in the cafeteria? You and me and Donnie Yarborough. I'll introduce you to Fort Jackson's next serial killer."

He waved, walked away, and I went to be a teacher, unable to put it off any longer.

My first class was a sophomore American history survey: *Revolution through Reconstruction*. Twenty-seven students looked at me when I came through the door. I was probably their first female history teacher, but they were not impressed.

"Hello, I'm going to hand out some material and we...," I began.

"Are you Frances Adams's daughter?" a male voice interrupted me, and I realized that, although I was speaking to them, I hadn't been looking at them. In their direction, my eyes forward and in line with their faces, but not *at* them. So, for a split second, I didn't know who spoke.

"Yes, I am. Is that important?" I answered to the whole class, wishing that whoever had spoken would speak again.

A black-haired boy in the back row said, "Not really. Just wondering. My brother had your mother, like, for a short story class a million years ago. Just wondering."

Benign or intentional, he had thrown me off the first five minutes of a carefully scripted class. After that, as every other teacher and my mother had told me, it was all improvisation. I had thought that I knew exactly what I was going to do, but he stopped me cold.

"She flunked him."

That wasn't the explanation I expected, and I wondered what sort of reaction he expected. The rest of the class was silent, waiting to see how I responded.

"Burk, everybody flunked your brother, dork-face," Jackie the Smoker finally said. "And *you* even flunked Domestic Economics, for chrissakes."

"Look, Jack-off Jackie, you better...." he began to say as the class started laughing.

"That's...*enough!*" I interrupted him and the class both. "All of you...look at the bottom of the first page of the syllabus." It dawned on me that I didn't even know the boy's last name yet. At the bottom of that first page was a short paragraph headed: CLASSROOM DECORUM. "Read it out loud, Burk."

Burk "Blackey" Barkley read, with a noticeable shrug: "All of us will treat each other with respect and courtesy. Profanity, unwanted physical contact, racial and sexual slurs, and inappropriate gestures will not be tolerated."

He looked up. "Okay, so what's the problem."

"Read it again," I said, watching Jackie the Smoker smirk.

Burk read it again, and then said slowly, with all seriousness, "Okay, I still don't see the problem."

That was odd. This kid genuinely didn't have a clue. He didn't even understand himself, much less my old-fashioned adult view of decorum. Burk Barkley needed me, or somebody, to teach him more than history. Where was *that* in my job description?

"Profanity...sexual slurs, Burk."

"I didn't slur anybody. I didn't cuss. Mrs. Adams, I didn't. You heard me. All I said was..." and he was almost crying.

"Jack-off, Jack-off Jackie. That's what you said," I said, thinking that this was not the first lesson I thought I would be giving as a teacher. Somehow, *jack-off* was not a phrase I expected to encounter two minutes into my career.

He was incredulous. "That's cussing?!"

"In this classroom, it is. You clear with that? Is everybody clear with that?"

The room was still silent, except for Jackie the Smoker.

"You sure you're not Mr. Parsons's sister?"

After my second class, I wondered why I had learned nothing when I had done my student teaching back in Indiana. More correctly, why hadn't I *remembered* anything? Why hadn't I remembered that classes, as well as individuals, have personalities? My first class was chatty and animated. The second, also American history, was a tomb. The second would turn out to have better grades, but I didn't look forward to seeing them. Both classes were sophomores, but the first had Jackie the Smoker, Mike Lankford the drummer, Harry Hellas the long-haired photographer, Ben Russell the soccer star, Gary Kirk the jock, Jenny Baker the flute player, and even Burk Barkley the troublemaker. Seven kids who provoked each other and the rest of the class. Seven kids who were consistently fun to watch grow up in front of me. The second class had an overall 3.3 GPA, but not much else going for it.

My third class, government, was clearly going to have the most interesting discussion because, as Dell explained to me, "These kids don't have to really know anything to have an opinion about government or politics. Just like their parents. History, they assume the teacher knows it all. Government? Hell, Nancy, a little bit of knowledge never gets in the way of anybody's opinion about that. Even these turnip seeds think they know it all."

Five minutes before that third class was over, Jerry Sinclair stood outside my classroom and waved at me to come out. Just as I was almost to the door, Dell Rose's head appeared, sticking out at a right angle to the door. Just his head, almost under Jerry's armpit, like he was peeking around a corner, the lookout for a gang of burglars.

"Miz Adams," Dell whispered loud enough for my entire class to hear, "you gots a date for lunch?"

Jerry shoved him back out of sight with his elbow, and the whole class could all hear Dell say, "Jeez, Jerry, take it easy on an old man."

My first impulse was embarrassment, then anger. I turned back to my class and saw two different reactions. Most of the students were grinning, as if they were pleased that adults were as silly as they were. Some of the others, mostly girls, were looking at me like those students at Agnes Rose's picnic when they saw me with Dell. As if... *interpreting?*

"Excuse me," I said to the class. "I have to go deal with Moe and Curly." Most of them didn't laugh. My first class would have howled.

Outside, I poked my finger into Jerry's chest and whispered, "Could this have waited five minutes? I'm trying to get some respect in there and you two..." looking over at Dell, "...you two show up and make it look like you want me to go play hooky. I'm trying to be...a...goddam...adult in there. Or...am I missing something? Am I supposed to be flattered?"

Jerry blushed. Dell wouldn't look at me. Both men were at least eight inches taller than me. Just then, Ashley Prose stepped out of a classroom two doors down from mine, stared at the three of us, processed, and went back inside.

"We were just trying to make the new kid on the block feel welcome," Dell whispered, "No reason to be so uptight."

Jerry put his hand over his heart and said, "We promise, no more surprises. But we did think you would need some sympathy after your first few classes. We were going to invite Ashley, too, but then we thought we would have to mind our manners around her."

"And not around me?" I said, trying to be serious.

"Oh, Nancy, you know what we mean," Dell said. "Your backside isn't welded on as tight as hers. You know that. So how about lunch with the two handsomest men in the building?"

"Dell, I'm trying very hard to be offended here."

He laughed, "Can't do it, can you?"

I shook my head. "Not really."

"Then lunch with us. We'll treat you to one of those delicious salads with the brown lettuce that the lunch room people saved from last year."

"Sorry, guys, I've already got a date with Russell. I'll be at the captain's table today."

Jerry and Dell looked at each other, as if reading each other's mind and flipping a mental coin to see who was going to respond to me. Dell won. "Come on, Jerry. Miss Scarlett here is having vittles with Master Rhett at the big house. Us field hands gotta go play with ourselves."

"That's right, boys. You two go play with yourselves," I said. "And do me a favor. Don't call me out of class unless the building is on fire. Okay?"

Jerry gave me a thumbs up sign, and Dell nodded. As they strutted off, Dell turned back and said, "Don't forget. We're your favorites." Then, seeing Donna Parton turn the corner at the end of the hall, he and Jerry began singing in unison, "Donna, Donna, the prima donna....Donna, Donna..."

Four adults in an otherwise empty hallway. Four educated, mature adults. Jerry and Dell were singing to Donna, who never slowed down as she smiled at the two men, stuck out her tongue, and raised her middle finger.

I saw Russell when I walked into the lunchroom, but as soon as I had my tray loaded Donna appeared out of nowhere, grabbed my arm, and steered me to another table so she could formally introduce me to some teachers I hadn't met at the faculty meeting. Each of them was the "best" teacher at Kennedy, Donna said, making them roll their eyes. Evidently, I joked to myself, Kennedy had no bad teachers. I looked back over my shoulder at Russell, who was still talking to Donnie Yarborough.

"Okay, enough pleasantries," Donna said. "Russell wants to see you. Go, go, go. And when you get some free time, I want to talk to you about someone in your honors class."

Donnie Yarborough's conversation with the principal was soon over, he was dismissed and Russell and I sat alone. The other adult table was packed, but nobody seemed inclined to sit with the principal and the new teacher. "You get him straightened out?" I asked, looking around to see how many students from my first three classes had this late lunch period.

"Oh... Donnie. He and I go back a long way. He and I and his father. Donnie's a bit...verbally challenged, as they say. But he's a poet compared to his old man. I've had him as a student in some of my classes in the past. Lots of charity D's. He's old town Fort Jackson. Born here, probably get some Jackson High School girl pregnant, can't get to first base with the debutantes at Kennedy, die here. Unless he ends up at the state penitentiary."

"So, you going to turn him around?"

"Nancy, that boy is lost. I'm just doing damage control. But, don't worry, Donnie isn't like the overwhelming majority of the kids here. And this school isn't like a lot of the other schools in this country. Most of the students are like you were. From good homes, educated parents, solid middle class money behind them. In fact, in the past twenty years this school has become more and more unreal to me. It's a teacher's wet dream..."

He was making a speech, a speech that I'm sure he had delivered to himself more than once. I wondered who his real audience was supposed to be. I also wondered who *he* really was. If he wasn't the man I thought he was, my former teacher, the man I designated as the man who was going to rescue me from my self-imposed emotional...for lack of a better word...*funk*, then who was he? He looked a lot older than he did at my welcome home party years ago. Not being in love with Russell Parsons, I thought, was becoming more interesting than thinking I was in love with him.

"...But don't get me wrong. I'm lucky, you're lucky, to be here. Even Donnie, whose father sent him here to keep him away from all the black students at Jackson High, even Donnie is lucky. His father might tell you that he arranged for Donnie to be here because of the academics, but I know old man Yarborough. You will too. He hates black people, and his son is too good to go to school with them. Academics are a rationalization."

"I'll know his father?"

"Nancy, you're going into your fifth period class after lunch and you're going to have Donnie. In about fifteen minutes. First thing, make him take off his cap."

"Do you know everyone in my classes?"

He shrugged. I noticed he didn't have a tray of food in front of him. Agnes told me that he always ate lunch alone in his office. But he was in the lunchroom almost every day for at least two of the three lunch periods.

"Not all, just the interesting ones. And you, courtesy of Donna and I, have a lot of interesting students. Just remember rule number one: As much as you might like them, don't cut them any slack about their grades. Donnie, Jackie Foster, April Bourne, Freddy Stein, nobody. Too many A's expected here as a right, not enough C's given. Nancy, make sure you understand your own expectations, and then don't compromise. Your A students should be as smart as you were when you were a student of mine."

What did Kris say? If I'm so smart, how come I'm not happy?

"Agnes tells me that the parents can be a problem."

He laughed so loud that the other teachers turned in our direction. "You *are* in for a treat," slapping his palm on the table. "Just remember, you can call me anytime if you've got a problem. Anyway, how's everything going so far this morning?" he asked, sitting back in his chair.

"Am I supposed to have a valid opinion right now? Most of the time I feel like I'm in a daze, then as soon as I think I'm in control, something happens, like Dell and Jerry trying to pull me out of class early, or..."

"You know," he interrupted, "when I hired Jerry I knew that he and Dell would get along. Trouble is, they get along too well. And I don't want Jerry to think he can get away with the things that Dell does."

"Things?"

"You're not blind or deaf, Nancy. Things, I mean things. You know what I mean."

"Russell, why do you let Dell unroll more rope to hang himself with? You seem so in charge of everything else."

He just looked at me.

"Don't get me wrong. I like Dell, in spite of myself," I said, trying another approach, but then the bell rang. I had five minutes to get to class.

Russell stood up. "Get to know him better. His problems aren't what people think. If those rumors were true, I'd fire him. But, see if you can get through that bogus jive and shuffle routine of his. Then, ask me again."

"Russell, you can talk to me."

"I know, Nancy. I knew that when I hired you. But you need to get to know Dell before anything I might tell you would make any difference."

"Okay, fair enough," I said. "It seems like a game, but I'll play. But, tell me this now. I've noticed that Donna tells me that everyone here is the 'best' teacher at Kennedy. Would she say that about Dell?"

"First of all, keep tabs on who Donna says that about. If she introduces you to somebody...and *doesn't* say that...pay attention. In her world, if you're good you're the best. If Donna doesn't think a teacher is good, you won't hear her use the word 'best.' She won't criticize, but the lack of a compliment always means something. If you're good, you're the best. Not good, you don't get an adjective at all. Make sense? If not, ask her what she thinks of Bob Skinner. See how she maneuvers around that. As for Dell, ask her about him too. If nothing else, Dell will tell you himself that he's the best basketball coach in the state. He's also a very good social studies teacher when he has to be. You should have been here when he failed his own starting point guard."

"To make a point, I suppose," I said. Pretty good pun, I thought, but Russell ignored me.

"A big point. The kid was off the team."

He walked around the table and escorted me out of the lunchroom, greeting students along the way. At one point, he put his hand on my arm and held it there as he talked to an under-dressed girl, as if trying to keep me from wandering off. Then, outside my classroom door, he said, "Something else, too. Dana O'Connor is in your honors seminar. Couple of weeks from now, tell me what you think of her. I'd be interested to know."

If my first class was fun, the second dull, and the third had the most discussion, my fourth class could only be described as a necessary evil, the bridge from lunch to my senior honors seminar. More than a necessary evil...a positive evil. Of the twelve students on my class rolls whom Donna Parton had red-X'd, seven were in my fourth class. Except for Donnie Yarborough, whose primary trait was a sullen grunt when spoken to, most of the other students were bright enough, even the red X's. But on that first day, when nobody, including me, expected any real work to be done, they all seemed to resist any effort to simply even be civil to each other. Most were juniors, two were seniors. Some, like Donnie, were juniors twice over.

The subject was ancient civilizations. Nothing I did for that fifty-five minutes could bring students and subject into the same universe. They spent most of their time clarifying my classroom decorum paragraph. In between, I was getting assorted lessons in how to irritate the teacher.

Donnie's contribution was to ask, "Do we have to diagram sentences in here like in Mrs. Rose's class?"

Where did that come from? The point? Did this kid have some hidden agenda? Or was I giving him too much credit for subtlety? And why the hell was I so tired so soon?

"You do realize that this is a history class, don't you?" I answered, hoping my sarcasm was not too obvious.

My mother had always told me that if a teacher is too ironic or sarcastic, students would "return the trait in bushel baskets." Donna had even warned me, "You get in a pee-fight with students, trading snippy remarks, *you* lose control. They'll always get in the last cute remark. So, you've got to watch the irony." Luckily, Donnie was a one-line warrior, weak on the follow-up. Not so with the others.

"Teacher, Teacher...." a girl in the front row raised her hand.

"Miss Adams, please," I said.

"Yeah, right, whatever. Mrs. Adams, do we have to do papers for this class?"

Pick your fights, I remembered. I held up the syllabus, "We went through the course requirements. Go back to the second page. A long research paper and a dozen one-page summaries of chapters."

A collective groan rolled toward me. "That sucks," came a muffled voice from the back, then a mumbled, "Fuck."

"Look, folks," I said, trying to speak firmly without appearing shrill, but I was getting nervous. I was losing control. "I want this to be a relaxed class, but some things are not acceptable. *Fuck* is not acceptable."

I immediately knew it was a mistake, a major fuck-up, especially with this class. A chorus of whistles and shouting erupted. "If we can't say fuck, Mrs. Adams, how about suck? Is that okay?" said the girl in the front row. "If you don't want us to fuck in this class, can we suck?"

Look somewhere else, Nancy Adams, I told myself, look anywhere but at her. Or else she'll read your mind and know that you want to slap the hell out of her, as hard as you can. But maybe there's more happening here, maybe you just wanted to hit somebody, or something, for a long time. Thankfully, you're not close to putting names on bullets. Look at the clock, for chrissakes. This class is only half over. Where are Jerry and

Dell when you really need them? If this school is such a wet dream, like Russell said, why are you in this particular nightmare? You need a diversion, anything to get time for you to think.

"And who are you?" I asked, retrieving as much neutrality in my tone of voice as I could.

A male voice answered, "She's Cunnie Lynn Porter. Kennedy High School expert on sucking."

That was enough to focus me again.

"And who are *you?*" I snapped, slamming the textbook down on my desk, my voice telling them something that I was only beginning to feel myself. I had had enough. I was pissed.

"I'm Dylan Abrams," he said calmly, looking at me with a combination of contempt and fear.

I looked at the class roll. Dylan Abrams was a senior, taking a course he should have taken the year before. There was no red X by his name. I then looked at Bonnie Lynn Porter on the roll, a red X by her name. I looked back up, first at Bonnie, who was sniffling, and then at Dylan, fascinated by how handsome he looked, like a young male model, but obviously with muscles. Dark hair and eyes, chiseled facial lines, perfect symmetry. He was going to be a very handsome adult man. I wished I knew his weak spot, his greatest fear. But I had time. This was just round one.

"Dylan," I said slowly, "you and I, and everyone else in this class, we're going to be together five days a week, almost an hour a day, for fifteen weeks. We can look forward to seeing each other, or not. Right now, I'm not looking forward to it. Trouble is, if I don't look forward to this class, neither will you. And I want to like this class because it means a lot to me. Even you, Dylan, it matters to me whether you learn anything at all. You failing this class means

I fail too. I want you to learn a lot from me. And even though this is not an English class, I want you to learn that language is important. Words count. Tone counts. The rules matter. Now, you owe Bonnie an apology."

Dylan Abrams just stared at me.

"And, Bonnie, you owe me an apology," I said to her.

Bonnie blinked, chewed her lip for a second, and muttered, "Sorry." Sincere or not, I didn't care.

I turned back at Dylan. He was silent. We looked at each other directly in the eye. I told myself that he was going to apologize, or look away, one or the other. But he was not going to win.

He looked down at his desk, and I could see his jaw clench. He mumbled something so low that nobody understood, but he could not look back up at me. Apology or not, it was enough.

I was standing behind my desk, leaning forward with my hands holding on to the edge. I looked at Dylan long enough for the rest of the class to see that he was not going to face me any more.

"Okay, now let's talk about these student information sheets I want you to fill out," I finally said, sitting down, hoping that nobody would see my leg shaking.

I sat there sat wondering if it was natural to hate an entire class. There was no other way to describe how I felt. I hated them. I had just given them a speech about how it all mattered a lot to me, but I hated them. I had lied to them, bluffed them, and now I hated them. Not one name brought back a pleasant image. How was I going to get through the entire goddam semester? If the Honors Seminar was anything like this, I would start putting names on bullets.

The bell rang and I looked up. I had been somewhere else for the entire five minutes, oblivious to the room filling up again. It was the same material classroom. Einstein and Rosa Parks and Neil Diamond were still on the walls. The map behind me still showed Europe in 1650 and the map across the room still showed America in 1776. A poster next to Einstein still said, *Never let your intelligence get in the way of your imagination.*

The eighteen faces were new. The bodies different. Fred Stein was dressed in black again, sitting under James Dean and smiling at me, pen in hand. April Bourne had wonderful posture, erect in her seat, shoulders back, pen in hand, dressed like she was going to work in a bank right after school. I recognized other students I had met at Agnes Rose's picnic. Most of them looked like young adults, college students, not really like teenagers. I took a deep breath and began again.

"Senior Honors. Are you all supposed to be here?"

An outsider would have thought that I was the funniest teacher in America. The laughter was genuine and unforced, and even April thought her teacher was funny.

Fred started, "Miss Adams, is there a chance that..."

"No, Fred, you cannot leave early for your Green Party meeting," I said, knowing where he was going.

Another round of laughter, but Fred wasn't hurt by me cutting him off. All he said was, "Okay, but just remember what happened to the Romanov family."

I waited for a response from everyone else. Enough of them groaned to let me know that they knew enough about Russian history to see the joke. I was beginning to come back to earth, back from the dark planet that had been the previous class. If the school symphony was the perfect start to a day, I was beginning to feel that this class would be the perfect finish.

A boy wearing suspenders and a tieless dress shirt spoke up, "Freddy, do you remember what happened to Rasputin?"

Fred didn't hesitate. "He became Freddie Krueger in the movies, the guy you can't kill?"

I raised my hand. "People, can I have my class back? We've got fifty-five minutes, and I still need to practice how to be a teacher." A collective nod, collective pens and pencils at attention. "I'll go through the syllabus and assignments. You'll notice that the assignment list for the entire class is fairly short. In a few weeks I'll be having conferences with each of you, and you'll be getting individual work based on your interests and how relevant it is to the overall scope of the course. This is an honors class. I expect some originality as well as academic excellence. Two major papers. One based on current events. We do have a presidential election going on, so there's lots of material out there. Then, a paper with a more historical subject..."

I talked for almost the entire period, interrupted only when something needed clarification. I actually enjoyed myself, surprised by how much adrenaline came back to me after being depleted by the previous class. Of the five classes I had stood in front of that day, this seemed like the only one that actually wanted to listen to me.

Five minutes before the end-of-school bell, I remembered that I had not taken roll. I had simply started talking and not stopped. I looked at the computer printout. April Bourne was the first name. Fred was near the bottom. In the middle was Dana O'Connor. She had a red X.

I tried to imagine what Dana might look like ever since Russell had asked me to look out for her when we had sat by the pool in the dark. Of the eighteen students in front of me that first day, ten were female. I knew April, and I knew that most of the other girls were not Dana, so I concentrated on the rest, only to be disappointed. All of them looked like each other, variations of April, of myself twenty years ago.

I looked at the roll again, nineteen names. Somehow, I knew I didn't have to call roll. Dana was absent. I wondered if April knew about Russell's plan to let Dana take some courses over, remembering what Agnes had told me about how April would take the news.

As soon as the bell rang, Jerry and Dell showed up at my door asking me to go out for a first-day-of-classes-after-school-drink, another Kennedy tradition.

"Sorry, guys, I'm beat. I'm going home," I said.

"Come on, Nance, we've got all the new people going. Even your best friend Ashley is going," Jerry said.

"Sorry, sorry," I insisted. "My old body needs rest and recuperation." I looked at Dell and read his mind. "Don't say a word. Not one smart comment about what my body needs. Save it for Ashley, or that new gym teacher. That is, if you want a real challenge."

Dell ran his finger across his lips. "My lips are zipped. But you should know, if you don't go with us we will talk about you. You better come just to defend yourself."

"I'll take my chances," I said. "Just remember, if you're going to talk about me, make me look good."

Ashley and the other new teachers were walking toward us, along with some long-timers. The Kennedy entourage was going to be bigger than Jerry and Dell expected.

"We're going to the Holiday Inn bar down the highway," Jerry said as he turned to meet the others. "You change your mind, come on down. Drinks are on me and the coach."

Dell lingered for a moment as the drinking party formed down the hall. "You okay?" he asked.

"I'm really beat," I said, thinking of how my mother felt when she came home from teaching, always tired.

"I know. You look it," he said quietly, not trying to be ironic. "Get some rest. School year's got a hundred and seventy-nine more days."

"Thanks for reminding me."

He stepped around to face me squarely, his huge body hiding me from the group down the hall. He then reached over and patted my shoulder. "Take care. And, don't forget, you promised me a dinner date."

"Dell, I never..." I started to say, but then I changed my mind, seeing him differently than when he was with Jerry or with a larger audience, "...I never forgot. Dutch, as I recall. Give me a few weeks."

He was genuinely pleased. "Dutch, hell. My treat now. You pick the place. We'll play twenty questions. Truth or Dare."

His hand trembled just a bit, but I tried not to notice.

Did my mother do this too, sit on the porch alone and read a hundred and twenty student information forms, making notes in a grade book next to certain names? It was hopeless. I was having a hard time putting names and faces together, and it was still hot outside, even at eight o'clock in the evening. The sun was just beginning to set, usually my favorite part of the day. I needed to relax, but, there I was, trying to overcompensate for a twenty-year vacation from the real world, wondering how long Jerry and Dell's drinking party had lasted, but still glad that I hadn't gone. Wondering about Burk Barkley, Jackie the Smoker, Dylan Abrams, and the few others who had separated themselves from the mass who had sat in front of me that day. And what the hell does Dana O'Connor look like?

The St. Johns looked the same. I learned to swim in that river, taught by my father as my mother sat on the dock watching us. In the summers, the three of us would take our boat and row it to the pier at Fort Jackson and then row back. Here and there, this porch and that river, my two favorite memories from when we were all together. Sitting on the porch back then, as rain pelted the tin roof, the three of us reading books, me on the wood floor, my parents in two big wicker chairs. And floating down the St. Johns ... those were my two favorites.

I was a lucky girl for sure. Russell had said something today about the difference between Kennedy and Jackson high schools, how lucky I was. That night after my first day as a teacher, I remembered how every May the *Fort Jackson Record* published pictures of all the graduating seniors. The Kennedy faces were almost all white; the Jackson faces almost all black. The *Record* had done it ever since there were two schools. Even back a million years ago, when I was still in junior high, my father had made me look at the pages, and he would tell me how lucky I was.

I drank the wine and closed my eyes. I was exhausted. I would rest, I told myself, then finish my work. Plenty of time to figure out that luck thing.

Let Me Introduce Myself

At any rate, girls are differently situated. Having no need of deep scientific knowledge, their education is confined more to the ordinary things of the world, the study of the fine arts, and of the manners and dispositions of people.—William John Wills

Dana O'Connor was absent the second and third days, but I forgot her as I worked at connecting the names and faces of my other students. The other teachers told me not to worry. It would come soon enough. So I spent the first few days trying to get all those faces to say something in class. Anything, so long as I could hear their voices. We agreed on nicknames, and seating arrangements were settled, especially in fourth period. I put Dylan Abrams and Bonnie Porter next to each other. No good reason, just because I could. In fact, fourth period was the only class in which I made any effort to arrange how the students sat.

After the first day, I walked to school most of the week. That would last until the second week, when I began bringing home assignments and tests to grade. I walked when there was almost no traffic, getting to my classroom at 7:00 and finding Agnes already at work in her room down the hall. When I began driving again I still arrived early, using that quiet time to get ready or to have some coffee with Agnes. After the first week, I also started a routine that I admitted to no one. I was home by 4:00 everyday, and I took a nap until 4:30. I wasn't about to let Dell or Jerry know about those naps because I didn't want to hear them tease me about my lack of energy. No need to share how pathetic I was.

Kennedy High School was built in 1971. The architects had combined a Spanish mission and hacienda style with Frank Lloyd Wright functionalism. From one angle, you might see a convent. From another angle, a prison. Most Fort Jackson taxpayers thought it was an ugly building, but the architects won national awards. Me, when I was a student, I thought it was a school building from Oz. I thought I was profoundly perceptive, but nobody, absolutely nobody, agreed with me. Looking at it now, as an adult, I had no idea why I ever thought it was from Oz.

The buildings and grounds couldn't be seen from the highway only a quarter mile away. An asphalt road wound its way through a thick grove of pine trees to a parking lot next to the main building. The parking lot was full of palm tree islands. Covered, arched walkways with red Spanish tile roofs connected all the other buildings. In the center of the buildings was an artificial pond, the perennial victim of rival high school pranks. Soaps, dyes, and toilet paper were seasonal additions to the pond, especially during football season, until a chain link fence discouraged all but the most rabid Kennedy haters.

Walking to school the first Thursday of the new term, I stopped at the parking lot entrance and looked at the school, thinking how I was beginning to see the Kennedy High building in a way that the architects had themselves envisioned. It wasn't really ugly. There was some hard-to-define quality that I felt, some combination of permanence and compatibility with the landscape around it.

"Need a lift?" a woman's voice said as I stood there on the curb. I turned around and saw a woman in her late twenties leaning out of the driver's side window of an ancient battered Toyota.

"No thanks," I said. "I'm almost there."

The woman nodded, turning off the Toyota's engine. "Sure?" she asked, stepping out and leaning on the door.

I was puzzled. I was less than a quarter mile from the front door, a five minute walk. Why would this woman stop and get out? Why not just wave and drive on? The woman just looked at me, and then she looked toward the school, then back at me. I first thought that she was a teacher, or one of the teacher's aides I hadn't met yet, but her clothes were too worn and they didn't really fit her body. Russell would have expected more from someone who worked for him. Her face was attractive, but she didn't look healthy. Dark lines under her eyes, pale skin, reddish-brown hair tied back but with strands hanging out. And she needed to lose weight.

"You're a new teacher, right?" the woman said.

"Yes, I'm Nancy Adams. Social Studies." I said, expecting the other woman to introduce herself, but she just nodded.

"I thought so."

"Do you work here?" I asked, assuming she would identify herself somehow.

The woman just shrugged. "Every morning, cleaning in the kitchen, but I haven't been there in a couple of days. I gotta go now."

"Well, thanks again for the offer. I guess I'll see you?" I said, beginning to lose interest in her.

"You will, yes," she said, but she didn't get back in her car. Then, "You know the story about this school?"

"The story?" I was suddenly interested again.

"They designed the buildings first," she said, pointing toward the steps leading up to the front door. "Then they laid out the grounds and trees to surround the buildings. None of this was here like this originally. The ponds, the palm trees, the way the ground slopes up over there..." pointing to the east, "...and flattens out over there near the gymnasium. It was all one package. Dirt, water, and trees on paper first, then hauled in."

"Odd, I was beginning to like how it looked. But now you make it sound like I was tricked," I said, trying to joke.

"Nope, no tricks. And I like it too," she said, opening the car door, "I just thought it was interesting how it all happened. I've seen pictures of how it looked originally. This is probably better," pausing, "...so, see you around."

"*That* was Dana O'Connor," Agnes told me as we had coffee in the faculty lounge.

"Agnes, it couldn't be. This was a woman," I insisted.

Agnes got up and went to a cabinet and returned with the previous year's annual. In the junior class section, Dana Jean O'Connor matched the woman I had just met. Much younger, much healthier, but it was Dana. "That her?" Agnes asked, her shiny fingernail tapping the picture. I nodded. "Having a baby can make you old," Agnes said, stroking the picture. "Sometimes, a lot."

"But she said she worked here," I kept insisting, refusing to believe that the young woman I had just met was only eighteen.

"Dana works two hours in the morning in the kitchen, dishwashing and scrubbing. Dana works after school for a few hours in some office in Fort Jackson near her house, typing and filing. Dana works on the weekends...." Agnes said.

"Agnes, I thought Dana had a baby. She can't...."

"Dana works at that too. Works hard at that. She even used to work for Russell, helping him with Stella a few years ago. Fact is, Dana's worked for just about everybody at this school at one time or another. Babysitting, cleaning, errands, odd jobs."

"She worked for Russell? Helping with Stella?"

"Oh, lord, yes. Back when she was in ninth grade. Helping him with his own children who were still in middle school. Miss Stella went through a bad time, sort of a relapse of her mind problems. Some pneumonia too. A rough time for him. Everybody here had already heard about this Dana girl that the junior high teachers were telling us was on the way. Dana needed some help, he needed some help, and the school insurance helped pay for most of the home care. She moved in with him for a year."

"She was just a child, Agnes, a child! Insurance wouldn't pay for a child to care for an adult," I protested, thinking all this was too absurd.

Agnes was silent for a minute, stirring her coffee and carefully wiping her hands with a napkin. She kept looking at her coffee as she spoke. "I'd appreciate it, you keeping what I just said to yourself. I slipped up. Nobody knows about the insurance part. It was my idea. My second daughter is a nurse. We used her name. She was okay with it, I promise. Check went to her, and she cashed it and gave it to Russell who gave it to Dana."

"Agnes, you're not serious! You are *not* serious!"

She kept stirring her coffee.

"Agnes?"

Silence.

"Agnes, you committed insurance fraud. You know that, don't you? You and two other adults in collusion. A felony, the last time I looked."

"Dana worked for it, Nancy."

"Dana wasn't entitled to that money. You know that. Jesus, I'm working in the midst of insurance scam artists."

Agnes flinched when I said Jesus, but then she looked me straight in the eye.

"You have to understand that Dana earned that money. Now, are you going to tell Russell that I told you?"

"Russell!? Agnes, shouldn't you be more worried that I'll tell some state insurance commissioner in Tallahassee?"

"Are you?"

I burst out laughing. "Of course not!"

"I knew you wouldn't," Agnes said, beaming.

Then, ever composed, I began stammering, "...I just ...don't know how to...take all this. My first week of my first job and I'm part of... a criminal cover-up. Do you see how I might not be ready to absorb all this right now? Dana's strange enough, and I was beginning to think Russell was a bit weirder than I remembered him. But *you*? Agnes, *you* seemed like the moral Rock of Gibraltar! And you tell me that..." I stopped myself and literally jumped up out of my chair. "Jesus God!" I almost screamed, ignoring Agnes flinch again at the sound of Jesus's name. "The car! That car! That's Russell's car. That's what I felt when I was talking to her, something familiar about something. That's the Toyota he drove to take me to Gainesville twenty years ago, when we went to lunch."

Agnes looked up at me. "Well, it's Dana's now. He gave it to her last year. It's not much to look at, and it probably has a million miles on it, but it still runs. Finally bought him a new one. That's how I knew it was her you were talking about, when you told me about her car."

I blinked, wishing that my mother was alive. Frances Adams knew all these people. She could help me understand. Forget about the school from Oz, I thought, I'm in Wonderland.

"So, you and Russell went out together when you were a student," Agnes asked innocently. "Anybody know? Did your mama?"

I stood there in front of my first class and wondered who my students thought they were looking at. I asked them a series of simple questions about the upcoming election, trying to make connections between the issues in 1996 and the issues of 1896. It was the wrong approach, as hard as I tried. These were sophomores. For them, the biggest issue in 1996 was whether Bob Dole was too old to be President. Or whether Bill Clinton inhaled back in college. Somehow, I needed to get them to see a bigger picture before I asked them about the small details. But I was also having an even bigger problem. I was trying to focus on them, but I couldn't get Agnes and Russell and Dana out of my mind. I was a

113

hypocrite. I wondered if I looked at my teachers in 1976 and saw anything other than an adult whose life was boring and routine. I thought about Russell a lot back then, imagining him in Vietnam or wrestling with some moral dilemma about the two of us. But the others? It was as if I had assumed that getting older made life simple. As if those other teachers had no life outside the classroom they were in at that moment. Were those kids now as clueless as I was then?

"Miss Adams," Jackie the Smoker asked, "is all this going to, like, be on the test? If it ain't, I don't wanna take notes. My hand is cramping."

I took a deep breath as Donna Parton's advice came back: Pick your fights, don't sweat the small stuff.

"Jackie, my whole body is cramping..." I said without thinking. Other advice came back: *Don't get in a wit fight*. I was doing everything wrong this morning.

"I hear you," Jackie said.

I then realized that Jackie was one of the few students who was listening to anything at that moment. I looked over at Ben Russell, who was reading a copy of *Sports Illustrated*. Jenny Baker was drawing. Mike Lankford was quietly drumming on his notebook. Harry Hellas was staring at me with unnaturally wide eyes, but he wasn't listening. Chickie Williams was arranging pep rally ribbons on her desk. Gary Kirk was too big for his desk and he kept fidgeting.

Am I that boring, I asked myself. "Planet earth calling Nancy Adams's history class. Planet earth calling..." I said in a loud voice.

Heads turned in my direction.

"We all back from summer vacation yet?" I asked.

114

"Oh, Miss Adams, you gotta cut us some slack. First week is, like, always a fuzzball. Besides, we've got a game tomorrow," Burk Barkley said, offering an explanation that was completely rational in his world.

"What is this 'we' business, white man?" Gary Kirk jumped in. Although only a sophomore, Gary was already a varsity starting linebacker. "I don't see you at practice."

"Can we get back to…" I started to say.

"Down, Bronco," Jackie said to Gary. "Save it for the…say, Chickie, who are we playing this week?" Chickie Williams proudly held up a blue and gold ribbon: *Bury the Buffaloes!* "So, Kirker, save all that testosterone for burying those buttaholes. Honeypot here couldn't make the tackling dummy team."

"Jackie," I stopped her before she could continue, "If it's okay with you, I'll try to have a class now."

"You're the teach," she replied, winking at me and pulling on her nose ring at the same time.

The Teacher Taught

Some people drink from the fountain of knowledge,
others just gargle.—Robert Anthony

It took all semester, but my first class taught me how to be a teacher. All the things that college education courses miss. The only lesson I learned from my fourth class was humility. Nothing I did worked. I even tried falling back on some advice that Dell had given me: *Find at least one student you care about and focus on him or her. Teach to that person, hoping some of the others were eavesdropping.*

In that class, I couldn't find one student I even liked. Not that semester, at least. Some of them would show up in classes the next semester or the one after that, and they would emerge as individuals. I would kick myself for missing their obvious desire to learn or their obvious worth. But not that first semester. They were on an island, or in a prison, feeding off each other's worst attributes. For the first few weeks I never enjoyed lunch, knowing that they were waiting for me.

"You going to the pep rally?" Dylan Abrams asked me as I walked into my fourth period class that first Thursday.

"Of course," I said, arranging a stack of handouts. "Isn't it required?"

"Only if you want to be liked," Dylan said, but without a hint of humor.

"Oh, then, I'm there for sure," I said, walking down the rows of desks handing out first-essay assignments. Standing over him, "You going to be there?" killing time until I had all the sheets distributed.

As soon as I said it, I heard Donnie mutter behind me to someone behind him, but loud enough to be heard by most of the class, "Where has *she* been?"

"Donnie?" I asked, turning to face him, my hands still full of assignment sheets. Bonnie answered for him.

"Dylan..."she said the name with as much acid as her sixteen-year-old body could produce, "...is our star. He has to be there."

I purposely didn't turn around to face Dylan as I finished passing out assignments, not wanting to see him mouth *fuck you* to Bonnie, as I knew he would do. I simply chose to ignore the entire exchange, sorry that I had been sucked into it.

As the class was reading about the rise of the Greek city-state, I studied Dylan. How could someone that physically gifted, in face and form, be so unlikeable? I told myself that Dylan had better not be one point, a half point, away from an A in this course because he wasn't going to get a break from me. How many ways could I resent him? I looked at his clothes, always a mature first step in judging somebody, or so I learned in high school. Bonnie and Donnie and a dozen other students in class—-their entire wardrobes put together probably weren't worth as much as the clothes on Dylan's body that morning.

Dana O'Connor was at the door when the bell rang at the end of Dylan's class, standing aside as the adolescents from hell left, sliding in and going to a desk near the window. Now knowing who she was, I could see that Dana was not as old as she looked that morning. Still, she looked older than eighteen. She sat down and glanced in my direction, smiled, then looked back out the window.

Everyone else filed in, and a few went over to talk to Dana as soon as they saw her. "Dana's here! Dana's here!" was a chorus. Fred started to put his books down on the desk where he had sat the first two days, but, seeing Dana, he shifted over to sit behind her. I immediately imagined a semester of notes passed back and forth between them.

April was late to class. When she saw Dana, her body language almost gave her away. A slight twitch of the jaw but then an impressively quick recovery. She was all smiles. I was even more impressed with April's self-control when I realized that Dana was sitting in the desk that April had used for the first two days of class.

Donna had assured me: Senior Honors had the best and brightest of Kennedy's students. I had been in Russell's honors class twenty years earlier, and I copied his approach. *You do not teach a class like this,* he told me. *You direct it. Let them go where they want to go. Let them show off. Let them compete with each other. But never let them get too far away from your script.*

"Okay, take out a piece of paper," I began. "Let's get this reading quiz out of the way."

If this had been the previous class I would have had to endure some collective abuse from students unprepared for a quiz they had been warned about the day before.

"You don't trust us to read the material, Miss Adams?" Fred feigned shock.

"With my life I trust you, Fred, but, believe it or not, even you Einsteins would slack off if you didn't get checked once in a while. Besides, you knew this was coming." I looked at Dana, who had a pen and paper ready. "Dana, you don't have to take this quiz. You weren't here to get a syllabus, so I..."

"I got one," she said, tapping her pen on the paper. "It's okay, really," she said. "It's okay. I'm ready."

"Dana, the offer still stands. You can skip this quiz since you didn't have the assignment."

"It's okay, really. I finished the chapter last night. I got my copy a week ago."

Russell wanted to know what I thought of Dana. At that moment I wanted her to be real. I wasn't sure she was. Nobody could be like her. But I knew that she was telling me the truth right then at that precise moment. She had read the assignment, all of it. I absolutely believed her. The quiz would prove it. But I wasn't sure about anything else, except that I had to resist the temptation to turn and see the expression on April's face.

Pagan Rites

Cauliflower is nothing but cabbage with a college education.—Mark Twain

If I had gone to enough Popular Culture conferences when I was a graduate student, I might have come across some panel that was discussing the origins of the high school pep rally. Surely, I told myself, someone had traced the roots back to some pagan frenzy of adrenalin and testosterone, complete with virgin sacrifices and sexual orgies.

In high school, the first rally was always the best. New year, new season, new seniors, new cheerleaders, new skits, new teachers, old coaches, old rivalries.

As editor of the school newspaper, I had published a column by Betsy Elizondo arguing that Kennedy should have pep rallies for the fledgling girls athletic teams as well as the boys. No one took her seriously, no more than they did when the basketball coach had also written about the lack of pep rallies for his team. Betsy wanted equal support for the girls; Coach Byrd wanted equal time for the boys who were not football players. By 1996, the girls still didn't have separate rallies, but the basketball team, with Dell Rose coaching them to an annual district championship, was guaranteed at least one sanctioned chest thumping in December as their season began.

When I was a senior, I tried to be cynical about pep rallies. I thought they were contrived and adolescent. But I always went, and I always ended up cheering as loud as anyone else. I always felt excited, stimulated, like everyone else. Pep rallies were where pent-up frustrations, out-of-control hormones, and repressed resentment of parents—all those emotions—were displaced into an outpouring of rage and pride directed against some common threat, some other equally frustrated and resentful mob of teenagers at another school. I once started a senior column comparing pep rallies to Nazi rallies in the 1930s. My mother, thankfully, deep-sixed it. Even Russell thought I had gone too far.

The first Friday at Kennedy was a lost cause as far as serious teaching went. Nobody paid attention. At 10:30 I heard a drummer coming down the hall leading a parade of students to the gym. Seniors first, sophomores last. I was in my second class when the drumming began. Then the screaming, the pounding on locker doors, the whistles, the songs. Fred Stein was leading the parade. I was beginning to like Fred more than any other student. For someone so young to be so politically aware, so committed to bucking the system, Fred was incredibly happy simply being a teenager. He was willing to act like a clown as long as he was part of that nebulous concept known as school spirit. Even the jocks liked Fred.

"Miss Adams!!" he yelled from the end of the hall, "Let my people go!" Fred was a one-man drum and bugle corps. Three snares welded together at his waist, a cow-bell hanging off either side of him, a bass drum on his back, a silver coronet rigged up with leather straps and aluminum braces to hang in front of his mouth, a halo-like wire over his head which held a floating cymbal, and a Ralph Nader bumper sticker plastered across his chest. A son that John Phillips Sousa and Eugene Debs would have been proud of. He was leading three sophomores, all from my first class. John Reardon was blaring his trombone as loud as he could; Mike Lankford had a harmonica. Both were trying to get their feet and music in sync. Harry Hellas trailed the parade, taking pictures for the school paper. But the biggest surprise was who was following directly behind Fred, pounding the bass drum on his back. The Queen of Cynicism—Jackie the Smoker.

Jackie saw me, and, as hundreds of students poured out of classrooms and fell in behind her, she started laughing hysterically in my direction. Jackie had done nothing all week except make fun of the upcoming pep rally, but she and I made eye contact at that moment and I could read her mind. *I must be, like, totally out of my head, Teach.* But she kept pounding that drum, rolling her eyes and giggling as if she had been caught with her hands in some proverbial cookie jar.

Then it hit me, the closer Jackie got to my door. The wonderful absurdity of having your whole life ahead of you. At that moment, trading places with Jackie Foster seemed like the best of all possible worlds to me.

I pointed at Jackie, and then motioned for her to come over. I knew something else about Jackie at that moment as well, something I had learned at Notre Dame. As Jackie began weaving her way through the Blue Knight horde, I dismissed my class and stood out of their way as they almost dismantled their desks racing to catch up with their friends in the hall. Jackie cursed all of them as they surged past her, swimming against the current, yelling, "I've got a damn stick and I'm not afraid to use it."

Finally next to me in the doorway, Jackie's glassy eyes and smell confirmed what I thought.

"You're stoned," I whispered to her, my arm around her shoulder. She froze as stiff as death. "Don't *ever* do this again," I said. "If you do, you're history. Understand?"

Jackie nodded like she was having a seizure.

"And just remember...you owe me. Now, go catch up with Fred. And be careful," I said, pushing her back into the hallway. She didn't look back.

Within minutes I was alone in the hall, but still able to smell the marijuana trail following Jackie. I shook my head as I looked in my purse for a hair brush. I was beginning to collect secrets about a lot of people here, and it was only the first week of class.

Agnes and Dell soon came to my room and walked me to the gymnasium. I made sure Agnes was in the middle. Dell seemed to go out of his way to tease his mother, and I wondered if he would have done the same if I were not there to be his audience.

"Mama, you ever going to watch one of these games?" he asked, bumping his hip into hers.

"You know I work the concession stand," she said.

"But, Mama, for fifteen years? Lord, Mama, you're probably the reason this school hasn't won a football championship ever.

You got the good karma. Mama-Karma, that's what I'm going to call you from now on."

On the way to the gym, he reached around his mother's back and poked his finger into my shoulder a dozen times, trying to get my attention while he was talking to his mother. I looked over and frowned at him, then motioned with my head toward his mother, who was even shorter than me.

"Mama, you're going to be a bad influence on Nancy here. She'll think it's okay to waste her time dishing up that popcorn and taffy. Like it's her main responsibility to help make money for those candy-ass football players' new uniforms."

"Delano!" Agnes snapped.

Dell winked at me and squeezed his mother even harder. "It's your life, Mama." Then he started to sing her a song about mockingbirds and diamond rings.

"For your information, have I ever missed one of your games?" she interrupted just as we were about to open the gym door.

"Which just proves my point. You're my charm, and I've got the best record at this school. You need to share some of that charma-karma stuff with old Coach Grimsby. Man's gonna die in the saddle waiting for a winning season. You watch the game tonight. Hear me? Get him started right."

Hand on the door, Agnes said, "I'll think about it."

With the double doors wide open, the three of us were swallowed in sound and color and heat. Agnes walked in and I followed, only to have my arm grabbed by Dell and pulled in another direction. He almost had to yell at me, "Wait until December. Then you'll see a real pep rally."

It was all so irresistible. Even as Dell pulled me to a bleacher I wanted to stop and clap my hands. My ears hurt and I had to read Dell's lips as he kept tugging at me. Just as we were about to sit down with some other teachers, Jerry Sinclair raced up and pulled me away from Dell, like cutting in at a dance, and I could see Dell's surprised expression as his new best friend stole his girl. Jerry had me running with him to the other side of the gym, but I could look back over my shoulder and see Dell's expression change from surprise to mock-anger and then to pleasure as he pointed his finger at Jerry as if to say, *You got me this time, little brother, but we'll meet again.*

On the other side of the gym, Jerry pointed me to a seat beside Sue Rollins, the new phys ed teacher, a young woman with almost zero body fat. I hadn't seen her since the first faculty meeting. As soon as I sat down, Sue leaned over and said, "I love this shit!" Sitting between Sue and Jerry was like being between Jerry and Dell, and I wondered if jock bonding was as strong as male bonding.

Then, with the theme from *Spartacus* amplified through the public address system, enhanced with extra bass and kettle drums from the band, the football team marched into the gym. Coach Grimsby led, followed by his five assistants, the senior captains, and then the rest of the team, fifty-five teenage boys wearing football jerseys and almost identical dark jeans. My first impression was that this team would have killed the Kennedy team I cheered for twenty years ago. These boys were huge. Big Gary Kirk from my class was far from the biggest player on this team.

Jerry leaned around in front of me and spoke to Sue, "A lot of hard boy bodies there." I flinched. Surely, I thought, Sue wouldn't think sexist jokes were funny. But I was wrong.

"All for you, Jerry. Me, I have my eye on the cheerleaders," she said, arching her eyebrows at me.

Was I the only uptight person at this school? Me and Russell?

"You better get in line behind Dell," Jerry laughed.

"Will you two stop it." I protested, afraid that they would be overheard by the students behind them.

"Relax!" Jerry and Sue said at the same time.

I looked from side to side at both of them. They had somehow reached a comfort level with each other that I envied, and from which I was excluded. The noise around us discouraged me from trying to say anything else, but I made myself a mental note to accept their next invitation to go out drinking with them after school. But only on Friday.

"Quiet! Father Grimm speaks," Jerry whispered loudly.

Another part of the script, Coach Grimsby's speech had not changed in twenty years. Mixed metaphors of war and sports. Civilian support on the home front. Sacrifice. If Fred Stein was the child of Sousa and Debs, Grimsby was the bastard union of a Woodrow Wilson, Knute Rockne, and George S. Patton *menage a'trois.*

Halfway through Grimsby's three-minute talk, Sue put her head on my shoulder, closed her eyes, and said, "Wake me when this is over."

I looked for familiar faces in the crowd. Agnes and the older teachers were grouped together as they had been at the faculty meeting. Dell was, surprisingly, now sitting by himself. Russell was standing in one of the doorways, arms folded and feet apart, like a hall monitor. I wondered what he was thinking, if he was listening to the Coach who had still not forgiven him for what he did years earlier to the football team, flunking three stars before the season was over. I looked for my students and saw most of them. Dana was nowhere to be seen, but I wasn't surprised.

An hour later, my voice hoarse and my back hurting from being too long on the bleachers, I was ready for the fun to be over. I looked over at Dell. He wasn't having fun at all. Getting close to 11:30, I saw him start to leave early. As he walked past the rows of students, watched by dozens of southern belles, one girl on the front row reached out and grabbed his pants leg as he went by, forcing him to stop and lean down to say something to her as he took her hand off his pants. The girl laughed, and he continued down the line trying to get to Russell at the door.

Russell was watching him too, and frowning. As soon as Dell got close to him, he said something that he emphasized with a chopping motion of his hand. The two men faced each other and seemed to be arguing intently, but quietly, as if through clenched teeth.

I looked around. Nobody seemed to be paying any attention to the principal and basketball coach. The cheerleaders were in the center of the gym floor, doing a surprisingly good version of the Rockettes. I looked back toward the door. Dell was gone.

A Peaceable Kingdom

Everyone who remembers his own education remembers
teachers, not methods and techniques. The teacher is the
heart of the educational system.—Sidney Hook

Getting to know more of the teachers at Kennedy, I began to wonder about their maturity level. Some, like Coach Grimsby, were
like stern grandparents. Of course, they *were* grandparents. The
new teachers seemed older than those who had been there for a
few years. But there was no safe generalization. All I knew was
that my students seemed clueless about how narrow the maturity
gap was between them and some of their teachers. Every time I
went to a faculty meeting I had to fight the temptation to become
sixteen again. I helped myself a lot by deciding not to sit with Jerry
and Dell like I did at the first meeting that summer.

By the end of September, I also figured out how the faculty was divided in their view of the principal. Most were disciples, like Agnes. Some, like Robert Skinner, were heretics. The new teachers were still wandering in the wilderness, except for Ashley Prose, who made up her mind early. Her eyes seemed to squint every time Russell spoke.

The last Friday of the month, we were back in the gym. I sat with Agnes and some of the other older teachers, my age making me their table-mate more than my experience. Jerry and Dell had convinced Sue to sit with them at the back table, and they all waved at me to sit with them, but I waved back and shouted, "I'm sitting with the adults this year." Jerry put his thumb on his nose and wiggled his fingers. Dell was leaning against the wall, his hands tucked under his arms. Sue mimicked taking a drink.

Russell laid out the agenda: dress code suggestions, amendments to the national Honor Society membership requirements, curriculum coordination with Jackson High, and a nebulous category called *Items Not On The Agenda*.

Before he could start, Ashley raised her hand. "Russell, may I make a suggestion?"

"Of course," he said, looking up from his clipboard.

"I was thinking that all these things are worthy of discussion, and I have some ideas I would like to share, but don't you think it might be premature to reach any decisions now, especially since there are three new members on the school board, a new majority, and a new board might want some input on these items."

The teachers around Ashley were all nodding. Agnes quickly sat up straight beside me. The back table was passing a note among themselves while looking at Russell.

"Ashley, I didn't assume we would reach any definitive decisions today. But, in the long run, these are items, except for the Jackson High issue, that will eventually be settled by us, not the board."

Ashley was unfazed. "Of course, for now. But it's my understanding that the board is considering a major overhaul of the district operating manual. Some of these things might come under their purview for approval. So, I thought we might want to wait and have them involved from the beginning. And, I also understand..."

From the back of the room, Jerry spoke up without raising his hand, "Ashley, how come you seem to understand so much more than the rest of us?"

I expected Dell to say that, but he would have said it with a touch of irony, as if reaching for a laugh. Jerry was absolutely serious.

"Jerry, the new board members had platforms. Some of the incumbents have expressed their feelings. I've talked to a few of them. Look, I'm not trying to be adversarial here. I was just raising what I thought was a legitimate question. If everyone else agrees with you, I will be glad to...shut up."

Bob Skinner and the table with Ashley seemingly spoke at once, "No, no, Ashley...We need to use our time effectively...No harm in raising the question..."

I had read the newspapers and knew where Prose was going. I assumed that Agnes did too, but Agnes was silent.

"People, if you want to have a debate, go rent a hall," Russell finally said. "We're going to discuss *this* agenda and then we're going home, the sooner the better." Turning to Ashley, "I appreciate your concerns, but until the rules change, this is our school and we make the decisions. That's the district operating policy I'm using now."

I wished I were a lip reader. I could have sworn that Bob Skinner whispered to Coach Grimsby, *He means this is my school and I make the decisions.*

Russell suggested a more formal dress code: clearer, enforceable standards about cleanliness and permissible styles. We all agreed that there was a problem. Some of the clothes the girls wore would have gotten me expelled twenty years earlier, but I was the first person to speak up about how times were different, even though I wished they were not. Russell suggested a policy about message content on clothes: No more Big Johnson or Coed Naked shirts allowed, period; no more pictures of semi-nude women on t-shirts; no more sexual puns.

I watched him lead the discussion, and I remembered Donna's advice: *Pick your fights carefully.* Russell was losing this argument. When Ashley objected on the grounds that students had the Constitutional right to express themselves and suggested that a student committee be formed "to get their input about the balance between individual expression and communal responsibility," and even Jerry agreed with her, I knew that Russell was going to let the issue drop.

"Okay, does this mean that you all agree with me about the need for black and white uniforms," he said, with a resigned tone in his voice but still smiling.

"Yessir, Captain Bligh," Dell said, throwing both his hands up in the air in mock surrender. "And while you're at it, can we have a rule that says you're expelled for life if you wear your baseball cap backwards, and another rule that says that any white kid that dresses like a black gang member from Los Angeles...that kid has to study ebonics."

Everyone laughed except Ashley's table. Then Agnes raised her hand. "This is not on the agenda, but it's related," she said. "It's about the school newspaper. Why do we have to..." and she seemed embarrassed. "Why do we have to keep having some of those articles, the ones like...," and she cleared her throat, "... *Crack Whore of the Month*...," and then she turned to specifically address Ashley, "If nothing else, they're in bad taste and demeaning to women, even if they are meant to be satires."

Ashley was the new journalism sponsor, and I knew that Agnes had waited for this moment to put her in a corner. Ashley Prose: self-anointed feminist monitor and First Amendment defender. I could almost hear Agnes purring.

Ashley flinched, but Russell saved her.

"Agnes, I agree with you, you know that, but we've had this discussion for the last three years. For the benefit of the new teachers, would anybody care to recite what Frances Adams always said?"

Spontaneously, and almost in unison, a chorus of older teachers all said at the same time, like a mantra, "High School *is* bad taste!" Then they all applauded.

"My mother!?" I gasped, blushing when I realized everyone had turned to look at me. "My mother wouldn't let me say *damn* at home."

Russell was laughing with everyone else, "Nancy, times change, your mother would say, and she changed with them. Sort of like what *you* said about the clothes issue. She always reminded me it was a student newspaper, not the *New York Times*. Their paper, it had to reflect them, not her. I disagreed, but she always had the best paper in the state, crack whores and all. Go figure."

"Welcome to Kennedy High School, Nancy," Agnes said, sitting down.

The next issue, changes in the National Honor Society admission guidelines, was less contentious. Russell suggested a higher GPA minimum and less emphasis on participation in school activities. Then, almost as an aside, he also raised the possibility that the valedictorian selection should be based only on grades and nothing else. Just a thought, he said, perhaps to be raised later, after some consensus was reached on the NHS standards.

The faculty discussed his proposal for fifteen minutes, with no bruised egos. My initial response was to favor keeping outside activities as a factor, but also raising the minimum GPA required. I suggested that change, and a majority agreed. I also admitted that I didn't really have a sense of whether this was a real problem or not.

"Nancy, the NHS question is just a reflection of a larger problem that we always put off because we don't want to deal with it," Russell said. Like Agnes's concern over the newspaper content, Russell was about to raise an issue that most of these teachers had discussed in previous years. "The real problem is grade inflation in general. Too many of these kids are making A's when they ought to be making B's. And I was as guilty as everyone else when I taught," he continued.

Heads were nodding.

"But, we'll fight that fight later," he said, trying to move to the next issue.

As he began to talk about his plans for coordinating services with Jackson High, I thought back to his seemingly offhand remark about the valedictorian criteria. I wrote a note to Agnes: *Valedictorian standards??... Dana O'Connor??* Agnes looked at the yellow pad and wrote under what I had written: *Congratulations. You know the code.*

When Russell brought up the subject of Jackson High, I immediately noticed a drop in the room temperature. About the dress code and NHS requirements, everyone seemed to have an opinion. Not so with Jackson High.

"Look, this is one of those subjects that we'll eventually have to have the school board's support, I know that, but before I go to them I need to have all of us on board with the program here," he said. A few heads nodded, but most everyone looked down or at the clock. "In the next week or so, I'll have a written proposal in everyone's mailbox, but the core of the program is that we have to figure out some way to bring Jackson along with us. I've talked at length with Garry Klein, the principal over there, and he'll come to talk to us in a month or so. But he agrees with me."

Jackson and Kennedy each got the same per student tax allocation. Each got the same capital project fund allocations, perhaps with Jackson even getting more some years. But the schools were not the same. I had never stepped foot inside Jackson High, but I had heard stories. Some, long ago from my mother, some from Kris, and some from Agnes recently. Kennedy got the same tax support, but for twenty-five years it had generated millions of dollars in extra revenue through private fund-raising or through special grants from the state and federal governments. Kennedy parents were generous.

"All of us are lucky here," Russell said. "The primary schools out here in the county have been feeding us good students for years, and they had all the money they needed."

Bob Skinner started to speak, but Russell refused to recognize him, "Let me finish, Bob." The room temperature was dropping in direct proportion to how anger levels were rising. "In a nutshell, we have to take some responsibility for helping Jackson do what we do. Higher SAT scores, fewer dropouts, more college-bound students, all those things and more. I want some faculty input on this from you, and we have to be united on this because when we go to the parents of our own students we can expect a lot of re-sistance. Especially when I suggest that the school board adopt a policy that gifts and donations be allocated to the district instead of the school itself, so the whole system benefits. Jackson and the city grade schools are never going to have the deep money pool we do..."

"Russell..." Bob Skinner refused to be silent, "...nobody dis-agrees with you about Jackson's problems, but..."

The two men looked at each other as Bob paused. There was a history between them that I was not privy to, a personal history, some animosity that went beyond professional rivalry.

"But, Russell, you can't elevate them at our expense. It's that simple. You put strings on those donations and those donations will dry up. Worse yet, in a few years we'll have our own white flight schools here in the county."

"Bob, what the hell do you think *this* school is?"

I looked at Dell, then over to Agnes, then around to the few other black faces in the group. I thought of my father. I thought of myself. I was free, white, pushing forty, and female. I had never had to make a decision about race that actually altered my life in any way. As much as I knew about American history, the hundreds of books, more than most of the other educated men and women in that room, as much as I knew about southern history, I knew it only as an abstraction, not experience. In that respect, I was as vir-ginal as my students. I had grown up on the fringes of Fort Jackson

County, not in the town of Fort Jackson. Nobody said anything when Russell forced us to confront the truth. We could joke with each other about clothes and grades, but not about race.

"Look," Russell spoke more quietly, as if embarrassed by his previous outburst, "I've talked to some of you privately about this." Acknowledging Skinner with a nod in his direction. "I've known your feelings for a long time. And if this approach is wrong, and your collective judgment is that we have no responsibility...no, that's not fair to you...I apologize. You may be right. It may be our responsibility, but perhaps beyond our ability. You may be right. Good intentions are only so valuable. But I want us to give these ideas some thought. More than sacrificing some of our resources, we might have to sacrifice some of our own time and personal convenience. There's a lot to talk about. About this, about that sexual harassment meeting we committed ourselves to this summer, about a lot of things. Read the report coming to you." Turning in my direction, "You and Agnes are supposed to organize that harassment meeting. Let me know when you're ready. Now, any questions?"

Nobody spoke. If I had been sitting in the back with Dell and Jerry, I knew I would have seen a flurry of notes being passed back and forth throughout the meeting, editorial comments whispered incessantly. Agnes and the other teachers around me had been quiet for most of the meeting.

"Now, anybody got anything not on the agenda, anything we can cover quickly before five o'clock?" Russell had his clipboard under his arm and was ready to leave. He had told me before the meeting that he needed to get home to take his daughters shopping.

Heads shook, and I knew that everyone was looking around to make sure that nobody had anything else to say. All of us wanted to be somewhere else.

Old Friend

I ain't got much education, but I got some sense.—Loretta Lynn

Kris called the next day. I was grading short essays, and I had plans to outline my October schedule. We hadn't seen each other for almost a month. Hearing her voice, I was suddenly tired of grading papers. I wanted to drink and talk. Kris was certainly willing to avoid the subject of teaching, but it did not take her more than two drinks to open the other subject I didn't want to talk about... myself.

"So, how are you and Russell getting along?" she asked. We were sitting on my porch, one bottle of wine almost empty. "Any prospects there?"

"Kris, I told you before. Russell and I have a professional relationship."

"Yeah, right."

"I told you. I told you. I told you. I had that moment when I realized that he was absolutely uninterested in me in any way other than as a teacher. Do you know how embarrassed I was to realize I had created a fantasy about him and me and simply assumed that he would step right in."

"You *sure* he's not interested?"

"I'm sure."

"Too bad," she said, stretching out on the porch couch, wine glass tilted in her hand. "But I suppose there are other fish in the ocean."

"Kris, why is it so important to you that I have some man in my life? Why do you think I need to be involved with someone to be happy?"

"You're happy now?" she said. "Excuse me, somehow I missed that."

"Happiness is not the point here," I insisted.

"Oh, shut up, Nancy," she said, rolling her eyes. "And listen to yourself. 'Happiness is not the point here.' What the hell is the point, then?"

"And you're happy, Kris? Married to one man, sleeping with another?"

"I'm so happy I'm pissing diamonds. And for your information, I'm sleeping with two men, which is two more than you've slept with in the past two years."

"Remind me to never discuss my sex life with you again, ever," I said. I couldn't avoid the fact that I really didn't like Kris as much as I did in the past. In fact, I was beginning to dislike my best friend. And I didn't have a backup friend.

"Your lack of a sex life, you mean," Kris snipped.

"Why does it all come back down to that? Why is it that I can't turn on the TV without being told that every tube of toothpaste I buy will get me laid, or car, or shampoo. Toothpaste equals sex equals happiness. I look at all those kids at school and see how they've bought into it, that they won't be accepted or happy unless they're having sex."

"You need to get laid, Nancy. You're starting to get cranky."

"No, Kris, what I really need is to *want* to get laid," I snapped, shaking my glass so hard I spilled some wine.

"Okay, we're out of my league here," Kris said, her voice trailing off. "I'm just trying to help. That's all."

The two of us looked anywhere except at each other.

"I'm sorry for barking at you," I finally said. "...course, you should be used to it. Me being myself."

Kris shook her head. "No, that's the problem. You're not yourself, and you haven't been for a long time. Probably not since you went to college. You changed a lot there. Hell, Nancy, you don't even talk like you used to. It's like you think too much before you say anything, like you analyze everything and how it relates to you, like you can't even relax and have fun like we used to have. Like your education ruined you. *And* your damn accent is almost gone."

"Kris..."

"Let me finish. That's another thing you do. You interrupt. You used to be fun, and I miss that."

"I was never fun," I protested.

"Shut up, for chrissakes, you were too. Bitchy fun, remember? You could put down anybody, make fun of anybody. Smart funny in a way I wished I was. But college, or that awful marriage, or something, made you different."

"So, how long have I been dull?"

"Too damn long."

"Any suggestions? Solutions?..." I said, and then added, "...That don't involve sex."

An hour later, after two bottles of wine, we were in the house washing day-old dishes and listening to a Neil Diamond CD, trying to be friends again, Kris doing her imitation of a traveling salvation man. Lucky that the house was so far from any neighbors, we could turn the volume up as loud as we wanted. I was using a fork as a drum stick, beating on a fiestaware plate until it broke, sending Kris into spasms of laughter first and then into a coughing fit that made her cry.

After she left, I was alone on the porch, looking out toward the St. Johns. The setting sun was hitting the water and giving off that orange glare I had first seen as a child. I could see the end of the dock, and I could hear crickets and mosquitoes, but all I could think about was my first reaction when I broke that plate. I had stood motionless and whispered, "Oh, God, my mother will kill me."

I started to feel sorry for myself. It was easy. I was alone, and I was tired of being alone. I wasn't looking for a man, I told myself. Not a man in the way that Kris meant a man. But somebody, or something, that could give me *something*. I laughed at myself, too drunk to be articulate, too drunk to analyze myself. I tried to stand up, but found myself getting dizzy, so I collapsed back into the cushioned lounge chair. A few minutes later, finally standing, I wondered what Dell was doing at that exact moment. I looked for my phone but then stopped myself. How many ways was it possible to be a fool?

Rumors

I have what passes for an education in this day and time,
but I am not deceived by it—Flannery O'Connor

With my five classes, I could stereotype the entire school. My first three were the great middle range. Probably above average academically when compared to other schools, but not outstanding at Kennedy. Individuals stood out, but they didn't represent the whole group. Most students at Kennedy were like my first three classes. My fourth, the class with Dylan Abrams, had those students whose behavior or grades absorbed a disproportionate amount of my time and energy. I worked harder with them with less satisfying results. Donna Parton saw students like them everyday, and red X's trailed them everywhere. Of anybody at school, she was guaranteed job security.

The *Fort Jackson Record,* however, only had one view of the Kennedy faculty and students... we were all fair game, if it would increase circulation. It also had the typical Florida attitude toward crime: capital punishment for burglary. Minors' names were seldom protected. Mug shots were published if available. Public shame as moral lesson. The year before, a Kennedy art teacher was arrested for drunk driving and a photographer was at the scene in time to get a picture of her with finger on nose, right foot in the air, trying to walk a straight line. A front page picture the next morning. Anybody on the public payroll was fair game. The paper even listed every speeding ticket issued in the previous week. I always checked for names I recognized.

Students like Fred and April were Kennedy's Cadillac poster children. With their award-winning science projects, debate championships, volunteer work, they were our official greeters when celebrity adults visited. Getting as much negative attention in their own way were students like Donnie Yarborough.

Jackie the Smoker, in the broad middle range, simplified the distinctions, "Miss Adams, unless we murder somebody or invent a cure for cancer, nobody ever notices kids like me or Mike Lankford or Harry Hellas."

Jerry Sinclair and I would often exchange names of our favorite students, and the lists never matched completely, but we both agreed about our least favorite colleague. We each wrote a name on a piece of paper and exchanged nominees. It was our secret evaluation: arbitrary, subjective, unscientific, and unforgivingly immature.

Robert Skinner was our unanimous choice, but for different reasons. For Jerry, Bob was simply the perfect bureaucrat.

"Jerry, you're missing the big picture," I said, reaching over my desk to put my hand on his to make him stop talking. "Something Agnes told me, same thing I think my mother told me years ago, it hit me after that first faculty meeting in August. Bob Skinner has no children."

"You gotta have kids to be a good teacher? Nancy, you just eliminated me, you, and half the faculty."

"No, no, listen. Agnes is right. No matter how smart you are... or, to use your categories, how big or small your ego is, you'll never be a good teacher unless you actually like kids this age. You really have to empathize with them, somehow, to understand how they feel, feel how they feel. So, being a parent helps, but it won't save a bad teacher by itself."

"Feel their pain, like Clinton?"

"Jerry!"

"Sorry, pretty lame, I know."

"But you *do* know what I mean, I know you do. And the thing that surprised me most about this last six weeks is that I think I know what I mean. As much as some of these kids irritate the fire out of me, especially some like Dylan and Donnie and my entire fourth class, I actually care what happens to most of them, even Donnie. That's not anything I expected to feel when I took this job. I didn't think I was capable of feeling anything about anybody but myself, but I do."

"Did you say Dylan Abrams?" he asked.

I took a deep breath and tried to keep a straight face. "Dylan is the exception that proves the rule. How's that for a cliché? I care that Dylan makes me hate him. He's a kid. Kids *should* be forgiven for being jerks. I know that. Thirteen to twenty-one, they should be on the moon with saints as teachers. Even my mother would laugh about that. There were times when she threatened to send me there. Dylan... I want to send to hell."

"And so Bob Skinner doesn't care?" Jerry asked.

"That pool of his, the betting pool," was all I had to say, and Jerry immediately understood.

"Oh, Jeez, of course, of course! Nancy, you ought to be a shrink!" I thought he was going to hug me.

Every fall, the first week of school, Bob Skinner tried to form a betting pool about which Kennedy student would die that year, and how. At first, I thought he was joking, but Russell told me that, as soon as he had become principal, he told Skinner to never do it again. Mr. Smith, the old principal, had ignored Skinner for years as long as he kept it quiet. Skinner would put in the first twenty dollars, and only he ever knew which of the faculty actually participated. Agnes insisted that none of the other teachers would ever do it, but she never knew for sure. Maybe Skinner had really stopped it. Who knew? All I knew for sure was that when I told Russell about being approached by Skinner he actually clenched his fist.

When Skinner asked me after the first faculty meeting, I knew he was cloaking his idea in ironic terms, so he could always say later that he was joking. But I could see how somebody might see the literal offer beneath the irony. I also sensed that he never approached younger teachers. Never a virgin teacher whose first job was at Kennedy. No idealists. I was the exception because I was pushing forty and I had been at Kennedy before.

I understood the law of averages. The actuarial tables began the first year Kennedy was open. A sophomore died in a car crash; a senior drowned in the St. Johns. The first suicide happened in

1984. There had only been one year that some Kennedy student had not died.

Skinner's pool had four options: car wreck, drowning in the St. Johns, suicide, and miscellaneous. In the beginning, you won half the pool if you matched the month, all of it if you also got the method of death. No winners, the pool grew. Only once or twice in twenty years had someone actually admitted that they won. But, sooner or later, somebody always did. Adolescent death became predictable and bankable.

Russell told me that Dell had shoved Skinner into a locker when he was asked to join a long time ago. After Skinner approached me, I asked Dell if he knew about it, even though I thought I already knew the answer. I was wrong.

"Not a thing, Nance. It's just one of those urban high school myth things that you hear about. But, of course, you watch that bastard as the year goes along. If nobody's died yet, he gets awfully grumpy," Dell had said.

I became a link in the rumor chain. Donna Parton snorting cocaine was an old rumor, only way to explain her energy. The gossips agreed, no way she could like her job *that* much. Dell Rose had slept with three senior cheerleaders. I told him that rumor, and all he said was "I wish." The football team was on steroids. A rumor made less plausible when it lost three straight games after the opening win. Jackie the Smoker was anorexic. I paid more attention to her. Some student Satan worshippers were plotting the death of Robert Skinner. I told Dell that one, and all he said was "I wish." Some sophomore girls had formed a sex club, requiring participation in an orgy for membership initiation. I didn't tell Dell that one. Russell was planning a secret locker search after school, using police dogs with drug sniffing noses, to find drugs. I asked him about that one, and all he said was, "Um, interesting idea." Dylan Abrams was gay. Dylan found the source of that rumor and knocked the kid into a wall, extracting an apology and blood. I was sleeping with Dell. I went to the gym to tell him about that rumor, and before he could say "I wish" I hit him with a basketball. Jackson High School was going to be closed and all the Jackson students transferred to Kennedy. Jerry thought it would help Coach Grimsby. Kennedy was built on a toxic dump from the Fifties. Donna Parton said *that* would explain Grimsby's glowing silver hair. The marching band was always stoned in their half-time routines at football games. Jerry said that explained their preoccupation with music from the Sixties. Agnes was going to get fired because she made her students read the Bible during class. Agnes *did* always read the Bible to *herself* in class when her students were studying. I was sleeping with the principal. Why did that rumor bother me more than the one about Dell and me? Ashley Prose was organizing a new FFA club at Kennedy—Future Feminists of America. Dell started that rumor. The school board was going to authorize hiring a full time soccer coach for Kennedy, but only on the condition that the team be coed. Sue Rollins started that rumor, thinking it was hilarious, but then Ashley heard about it and made a formal proposal to the board for such a conditional position. Dell Rose was sleeping with the head of the School Board, Betsy Elizondo. That smear died at birth as not being halfway credible. Too bad, I thought. I had started *that* rumor. Dell wasn't as amused as the rest of the faculty.

Dana O'Connor was a rumor all by herself. Before she came to Kennedy, she was a junior high myth. Russell and Agnes had told me most of it, but every other teacher had their own favorite detail. Brilliant, beautiful, infectiously happy despite a family background that confirmed every Northern cliché about the South, a family background that made her an adult as soon as she turned thirteen. A father who deserted a pregnant mother, the mother a drunk, their newborn baby partially retarded but sent home to be raised by the barely teen daughter Dana, while the mother poured more and more welfare money down her own throat instead of putting food in her children's stomachs. Dana working two jobs. Dana coming to Kennedy and stunning her teachers with a mind and energy that threatened some of them and made others even more sure that they themselves had chosen the right careers. Dana, in Agnes's words, "sanctified everyone else's sacrifice."

Dana had no academic competition. She was going to be the valedictorian, an honor tied to a $15,000 scholarship supplied by three Fort Jackson banks, an honor which would open other doors, doors that could lead her out of Fort Jackson and away from her family.

In the middle of her junior year, Dana fell to earth. For an entire semester, her grades went from A+ to B. She missed more and more school, and she was sick when she was in class. By March, she could not hide her pregnancy. She finished the semester a mother. Doors began opening for April Bourne, whose grandparents owned one of the banks supplying the scholarship money, doors which would have opened even if April had been an idiot.

In my honors class, Dana seldom spoke for the first three weeks, and I slowly began re-evaluating the entire group. That first day, I had been impressed by how much more seriously they seemed to take me as a teacher and themselves as students. They let their teacher do the talking, and I could tell that they were actually paying attention.

When Dana finally came to class, I noticed that she didn't take notes. But, days later, in class discussion or on a quiz, she could almost quote verbatim something that I had said. In class discussion especially, it could be devastating for other students, their own words turned against them, and I was never sure if it was intended to be as damaging as it seemed. Dana seemed oblivious to other people's reactions to her. Fred never seemed bothered by it. In fact, when he wasn't telling me that I was his favorite adult female and "primary dream stimulus," he was following Dana around the halls asking her for advice or a date. He was one of the few people who could make her smile.

Learning to be an Older Woman

Anyone who tries to make a distinction between education and entertainment doesn't know the first thing about either.—Marshall McLuhan

Good teaching is one-fourth preparation and three-fourths pure theatre.—Gail Godwin

I was at my desk during my first period prep time, trying to decipher an essay by Jackie the Smoker about the history of hemp farming in America, an extra credit assignment. Jackie had convinced me that she was serious about wanting to make a B instead of a C. I gave her the bibliographical information, walked her to the library, and told her to summarize three articles. Reading that work later, it was obvious to me that Jackie had not mastered the science of quotation marks and the art of paraphrasing. I knew I would have to send her to Agnes Rose for some extra help.

Dana walked in without knocking and stood in front of me. "You said to come see you."

Without looking up from Jackie's paper, I raised my hand and motioned for her to sit down.

"No thanks," she said, and for the next few minutes she walked around the room as we talked, touching posters and desks as if she had never seen them before.

"Actually, Dana, I said to come see me two weeks ago."

"I'm sorry. I've been busy. I thought Russell told you."

"That's not Mr. Parsons's responsibility."

"You're a lot like him, you know," she said, turning to look directly at me, and then slowly turning back to look at a new poster which Fred had brought to class showing migrant workers in California harvesting grapes. "Fred?" she asked.

"Fred, indeed," I said.

"I like him. He's very... *earnest*." Dana said it as if she thought that abstract virtues could be personified in people.

"Dana, we need to talk about you. Not Fred, not me...you."

"I know," almost smiling as she said it. Then she pulled an armless chair over in front of the desk, turned its back to me, sat down, put her arms across the back, and rested her chin on her hands. "I apologize. I've been practicing melodrama so long it gets to be second nature after a while. You have my permission to do what Russell does when I get too coy. Go ahead and slap me." Then, seeing my face, "I'm kidding, Nancy."

If Dana were healthier, I thought, she would be pretty. Her eyes were ringed by dark circles, her skin unfashionably pale to be living in Florida. Her hands were scraped, and the skin on her fingertips was peeling. Her wardrobe was her usual second-hand jeans and shirt, both too baggy for her. There was something about her face, however, I couldn't pin down. She never wore makeup, as if beauty didn't matter to her. But at that moment she was clearly happier than I had ever seen her.

"Seems like you're having a good day," I said.

"I finally got some more hours where I work downtown, so I can quit the kitchen job here. God, I was beginning to hate hot water, and they use some sort of chemical to sterilize the dishes or get the grease off or something. I think I can actually start growing fingernails again. I was beginning to think I'd turn into a professional dishwasher." She worked for a lawyer downtown as a receptionist, file clerk, researcher, coffeemaker, and copyreader. She had keys to his office, and used it on the weekends to study. Russell had made sure I knew all that. "So, Nancy, you ever think you would turn into a vegetable?" she asked, studying the papers on the desk, as if she was reading them upside down. "I mean, like whatever you were doing at that moment was going to turn your brain to mush?"

"I was married once," I said, and Dana laughed as if her designated older woman had intentionally told the funniest joke in the world. "No, no, that's not what I meant," I corrected myself. "I was trying to say that I was married, then not married, and I realized something about my life afterwards, not at the moment. I had been happy..." but then I stopped. "Dana, let's get back to *your* brain."

"Oh, yeah, *my* brain," she said, looking bored.

"Are you catching up in your other classes?" I asked, taking Jackie's paper out of Dana's hands, wanting her to look at me and get serious. "I can work out a schedule for the history makeup that lets you get everything else done first. No hurry. Russell said you had to be finished by April first. Will that be a problem?"

"Not a problem."

"Russell showed me your work from last year. He and I agreed that you should do something completely different, not a revision of the old stuff. He also said to not give you an extension. April first, or the deal's off. Fair enough?"

"Imminently fair, and typically Russell. Set your standards, take no prisoners, separate the wheat from the chaff. I'll have it done by the first. No fooling. I wouldn't want to disappoint him."

"It seems to me that all this is not for him. It's for you."

"Nancy, I thought you knew him better."

"I haven't got a clue what you're talking about, Dana."

She shrugged and then changed the subject again. "You know his daughters, right? I was wondering what you thought of them. They're my best friends. I like them both, but they're much more different than people think. You know, them being twins. But they're different. Theresa is a lot sweeter than Sally. You think?"

I was being sucked into something, some sort of *arrangement* between Russell and Dana that only they understood. Right then, I almost resented her. Russell had hired me to *help* this girl, but all I felt was that I was being used. Still, she was right. I knew less about him and his family than she did. What I resented most was that I was tempted to ask her about Russell, to ask a girl twenty years younger than me to help me understand a man ten years older than me and thirty years older than her.

"Russell wants me to be valedictorian," Dana said. "He thinks it's important."

"It could be important, Dana. The scholarships, the recognition. I know enough about you to know that it could make a real difference in your life."

"Nancy, I told you, you're a lot like Russell. That's a compliment, believe me."

I was frustrated. "Dana, I still don't have a clue about where you're going with this. All I know is that Russell is giving you a second chance. He asked me to help make that happen. And you know very well, just like me and every other teacher at this school know, that as soon as you finish this work you're going to be valedictorian."

"A mind is a terrible thing to waste, eh?"

"Dana! Stop this! Stop taking yourself so lightly," I said, angry at her for making me angry.

She leaned closer as I looked at the clock on my desk and then the clock on the wall. The bell would ring in five minutes. She started to chew a fingernail, then stopped herself. "Nancy, *you* stop," she said in a voice that seemed to be uncoiling. "Don't do to me what Russell and the others have done. Don't make me out to be something I'm not. I'm not brilliant or talented. I'm not even mysterious. You wanna know why I know so much. Because I force myself to know those things. I read and I read. I remember things. And some things come easier than others. Math and science? I hate them. I hope I never have to take another math course in my whole life as soon as I get out of here. Never. Stuff that you and Mrs. Rose teach, a piece of cake. Chemistry? I hate it, not because it's boring, but just because it's so hard, and it's takes up so much of my time reading and re-reading the books. But I do it. And everyone thinks it's all so easy for me. So damn easy."

"Dana, stop selling yourself so short, so...."

"*You* stop making me something I'm not. Don't become Russell Parsons. At least he's got a reason to be so wrong about me."

I looked at the clock on the wall again. I looked through the window in the door, seeing Jackie and Burk Barkley talking to each other while other students started to pile up behind them. I turned back to Dana, only a few years older than the students outside my door but living in a different world. "Can you come see me again soon?" I asked. "We need to talk, but I have to start class now. Okay?"

She shrugged, and I could see her going back into the shell that she wore to the honors class. "Whatever," she said. "Tell Russell that we got the schedule all straightened out. You and me, we'll make him happy."

"How's your baby?" I asked as she was about to leave. She paused but did not answer, and I thought about the most commonly repeated rumor about Dana and Russell. "She okay?" I persisted.

Dana slowly dissolved into an unhappy unwed teenage mother. "She'll be fine," was all she said as she left.

So I sat there as she vanished. A *presence* and then gone. There was something about her, something that pulled you in. Lucky for me, I wasn't a man. She was some sort of temptation. Not sexual, but certainly emotional. A weak man would be in trouble around her. And most men were weak. The sum of my pushing forty education: men are weak. But Dana had another appeal for me too. I wanted to see her baby. I wanted to see if Russell's face was in that child's face. I didn't believe it was possible. If he had never been interested in me, surely, he wasn't going to tumble for her? I did what Kris and I used to do when we heard that he and Stella were getting married… imagine how their children would look. So,

Russell and Dana? I put his face next to hers, anticipating the moment when I finally saw her baby. Dana and Russell, side by side, me becoming as much of a voyeur as everyone else. How would that gene pool evolve? It was useless. I would have to see the actual union, if such a thing existed. All I saw when I considered them together was that Dana looked a little like Russell.

Homecoming

Education is a method whereby one acquires a higher
grade of prejudices. —Laurence J. Peter

A week after Dana and I had talked about a make-up schedule,
April Bourne heard about Dana being allowed to take courses
over. Agnes had been right. Dealing with April was not going to
be easy.

"I need to talk to you, Miss Adams." April had called me at
home. "And I would prefer to do it face to face."

"How about after class on Monday?" I suggested, getting ready
to go to the homecoming football game with Kris and Tom, the
ex-husband she was still sleeping with.

"I would prefer to do it immediately," April said, in a tone that
made prefer synonymous with demand.

"April, I'm in a bit of a rush getting ready to meet some friends to go to the game tonight. Could we..."

"That's fine with me. I'll meet you there."

I gave up. At least, she wasn't coming to my house. "Okay, tell me where you want me to meet you."

"I'll find you."

Kris and I, along with Kris's first husband Tom Turner, were in line at the concession stand when Dell asked to cut in. "My date needs a hot dog," he said, nudging Tom with his shoulder.

"Aren't you a little old to have a *date*?" Kris kidded him.

"Never too old for a date, young lady. And, say, Krissy, aren't you tired of this old cripple yet?" he joked back, bumping his shoulder into Tom again, and then handing him some money for food. "Call me, honey, when you wanna stop doing charity work."

Seconds later, Kris nudged me with her elbow, turning me to watch Dell walk away so that I could see his date. Not much older than other students, the girl was wearing a skirt that was struggling to cover her bottom and a tissue-thin blouse that looked like a body tattoo. Her blond hair was electrified.

"Chrissakes, that's Terry McDonald! She was one of *my* students ten years ago," Kris said. "I had to explain her period to her in fifth grade sex ed."

"She was one of my students, too," Tom added. "Ninth grade. Perfect breasts even then."

Kris knocked a bag of popcorn out of his hand and steamed off. Tom and I stayed in line. We had seen Kris get angry enough times to ignore her. Tom kept looking back at Dell and his date. "I wish he wouldn't do that," he said.

"Date girls half his age?" I said.

"No, do it in public, like here tonight. He wouldn't have done it last year. Somebody like Terry would have been his private business. All of us knew he was seeing young girls, but he wouldn't rub our noses in it. He wouldn't act like a fool, like tonight."

"You going to talk to him about it? Man to...."

"I've talked to him about it. So has Russell and every other friend he's got."

"Tom, do you see anything wrong with this picture? You worried about Dell's public behavior, when you and Kris are here tonight with each other?"

"That's different. Besides, you know that we're here with our girls. It's homecoming. Everybody's here."

"But you're not sitting with your spouses...."

"Who...did... not... come!" he protested.

"Tom, would you sit with your wife if she was here?"

"Of course, Nancy, because I know the rules! That's my point about Dell."

"There are rules for adultery?" I laughed, my hands full of food for Kris and me. Tom was carrying Dell's order on a cardboard tray, and we were weaving our way toward him trying to avoid the frenetic bodies swirling around us.

"Do it sometime. You'll understand," Tom said, raising his voice to be heard above the yelling and the music amplified through the public address system.

"About time," Dell said as Tom handed over the tray.

"Hello, Terry," Tom said to his former student.

"Hi, Mr. Turner, how's it going?" she answered. "This is so much fun, seeing everybody again. Thanks for getting this stuff for us."

Food transferred, Tom leaned over and, like a lover embracing his love, whispered something in Dell's ear. All I could think about at that moment was how Dell was wasted on that child. As Tom and I walked away, I asked him what he said.

"I told him he was stupid."

The Kennedy home bleachers were built into the side of a hill. Two thousand wooden stadium seats with backs and arm rests that could be flipped up if you wanted to sit really close to the person you were with. The visitors side had room for about a thousand people on flat metal benches piled ten rows high.

Kris and Tom and I sat in the adult section of the bleachers, high up above the fifty yard line and just below the press box. Jerry Sinclair and Sue Rollins were together two rows in front of us. Most of the faculty were nearby. Dell and Terry McDonald were nowhere to be seen. Just when I thought that Russell wouldn't be there, I saw him walking up the bleacher steps with his two daughters. He saw me and the other teachers and waved. As the game progressed, Tom sat between Kris and me, happily explaining the intricacies of football to us as Kennedy dissected the Mandarin Ospreys, telling us a hundred times to "watch the line, watch the line."

Kris's oldest daughter, named after me, was home from college. I had to tell her to stop calling me *Aunt Nancy*. With Kennedy safely ahead 28-0 at halftime, Kris and I and young Nancy fought our way to the restrooms behind the concession stand. The smell had not improved in twenty years. The line was out the door, and, since I didn't have to go as badly as Kris and her daughter, I waited outside. Standing next to a graffiti-covered payphone, I felt a hand on my shoulder.

"Miss Adams, we need to talk."

I shouldn't have been surprised at April's persistence, but I was getting irritated, and my voice gave me away. "April, is this absolutely necessary right now? Right here? Wouldn't you rather..."

Words thrown against a brick wall.

"I would rather not have this conversation at all," April interrupted. "I mean, I would rather not *have to* have this conversation at all."

I was suddenly fascinated. April was about to do an un-April thing—lose control of herself. In front of strangers and friends, she was trembling and about to cry and scream simultaneously. "Okay, okay, let's go somewhere quieter and more private," I said. "Let me tell some friends that I'll meet them later."

April nodded her head furiously, but she didn't speak. Her fists were clenched. We went to the parking lot. It was not as private as I expected because Kennedy was so far ahead that the game itself was boring, so students had headed for their cars to drink or have sex. That much, at least, had not changed in twenty years.

I found my car and made April get in, asking, "What's this about?"

She disintegrated. "It's not fair, Miss Adams. It's not fair. Not fair! He can't do this to me. You have to talk to him. You have to."

"April, who are you...."

"Mr. Parsons! He's letting Dana O'Connor do her classes over from last year. So she can be valedictorian. It's not fair. I did all the work I was supposed to do, and did it on time. I followed the rules, just like he always tells us to do." She was about to hyperventilate.

I took her hand. "April, slow down, and breathe easier."

She stopped talking and started crying in earnest. Deep sobs, with her nose dripping, and her white blouse soaked with tears and sweat. I was intrigued by the contrast between Dana and April.

162

Dana was indifferent to the prospect of being valedictorian. For April, it was life and death.

She recovered and began again. "This is so unfair. He's playing favorites. Everyone knows that. She's no smarter than me. In fact, she's stupid. She got pregnant. How stupid is that? She kept her baby. How stupid is that? She had her chance. She had her chance, don't you see that? She had her chance and she blew it. Miss Adams, you have to help me."

For that moment, I felt sorry for April. Unlike Dana, April actually wanted something. Things mattered to her. In the cosmic big picture perhaps it was trivial, but, for seventeen-year-old bright and ambitious April Bourne, being valedictorian was a reward that she felt she deserved and had earned. In her world, she was being robbed.

"April, I'm not sure how I can help you."

"But you're friends with Mr. Parsons. He will listen to you. You were valedictorian. You know what I'm talking about. He likes you. That's what I heard. He will listen to you. Just talk to him, please, Miss Adams."

I listened to her and almost laughed out loud. Not at April, at myself. I had completely forgotten that I had been valedictorian twenty years ago. It had meant a scholarship, nothing else. I made a speech that nobody listened to. It was a line in the senior biography of my yearbook when I was seventeen. It meant nothing now. I wanted to tell April that, but I said the wrong thing.

"Look, I can talk to him, but he's already decided. Dana is making up his history class with me, but that doesn't mean that she'll automatically be..."

In the dark car, half of April's face was illuminated by the orange parking lot floodlights. "You knew?" she whispered, staring wide-eyed at me.

"Listen to me," I said. "It doesn't mean that..."

"*You* knew," April repeated, a statement instead of a question.

"April, why don't we sit down with Russell and..."

"Oh, Miss Adams, I am so sorry to do this to you. And I do apologize for crying like a baby in front of you. I was just so, so very wrong about you, about thinking you could help me. That you would understand. I was so wrong."

Before I could answer, April was out of the car. I expected her to slam the door, but she closed it like it was made of crystal, pushing it shut with only the exact amount of pressure required, in complete control of herself. I sat in the dark, suddenly very tired. I didn't want to go back to the game, didn't want to go home. I wanted a vacation.

I was parked in the last row of the parking lot, where the ground was higher than the first row. If I dropped a basketball out of my window, it would have rolled all the way to the concession stand. In the distance, I could see the back of the press box. The building was like an optical illusion, itself at ground level but still high above the actual playing field at the bottom of the hill. The stadium flood lights pointed down to the field, but the light seemed to bounce back straight up, and the sky above the field went from white to light blue to dark blue and then, if I looked directly overhead, it was black. I could hear the crowd, an occasional air horn piercing through the yelling, and I knew the Kennedy band was on the field. When it faced the home side, the music floated all the way to my car. Facing the visitors side, the sound would have been like a whisper.

When I was a student at Kennedy, I never missed a home football game. Since I began teaching here, I had often thought about the past, about the things I did, but tonight was the first time I had physically felt the past, as if I was there again. It was the humidity. I sat in my car, and I could smell the rain that was coming, remembering how it rained a lot at Kennedy games. Fall in Florida could still be hot and muggy, and at least twice a season the second half of a game was played in a warm rain. It was like that tonight. The clouds were flying in, and thunder rolled in the distance.

When I was a senior, I had a game date with a boy whose name I can't remember twenty years later, but I do remember that I had left him watching the game as it started to rain. He had kidded me about having no school spirit, about being a "sunshine Knight." I told him that the rain was coming, not a sprinkle, but buckets and buckets. He was a nice boy, I knew that. He had tried to hold my hand in the car as we drove to the stadium, but I had pulled away. It was the first time we had been alone. As the rains came that night, he gave me the keys to his car, and as I walked up the bleachers I tried to count the steps. I was sweating. Out of the stadium, halfway across the parking lot, I realized that he had parked in the back row even though we had arrived early and there were lots of spaces near the entrance gate, but I still thought he was a nice boy.

Having failed to console April, I smelled my past come back. The humidity tonight was the bridge from the past to the present. Always at that moment right before the skies finally opened up and rain poured down, the moisture in the air was being absorbed by every green plant until the bursting ripeness became a palpable smell. I had taken a deep breath twenty years ago and took another tonight. I knew enough about Florida history to know that, unlike any other state, my home was originally a jungle. Plants and wildlife like no other part of America. Most of it gone by the time I was born. Kennedy might have been modern, but it was still surrounded by the woods.

When the rain finally came that night twenty years ago, it was Biblical. The smell of palm trees and pine trees and tall grass was blown by sheets of almost horizontal rain. I had been safe in a nice boy's car. Safe even when a four-foot rattlesnake was blown onto the windshield a few inches from my face, rolling on to the hood, struggling to coil around anything to hold on to, and then being blown away and lost somewhere in the parking lot. I had screamed and locked the car doors. When the nice boy showed up a few minutes later, soaked and yelling to let him in, I had refused, afraid to open the door. If he were ever asked years later about the worst date he ever had, Nancy Adams was in a category all by herself.

The green smell in the air this humid night with April was the same as twenty years earlier. A big rain was coming. I sat in my car, with my eyes closed, trying to convince myself to go warn Tom and Kris to leave early, and then I remembered that snake on the windshield, and I shuddered. At that moment something hit the window beside my head. I screamed, whipping my head around and being blinded by a light directly in my face.

"Miss Adams? You okay?" Fred Stein was standing outside my car, flashlight in hand, a white policeman's cap on his head, wearing an orange reflecting safety vest that highway construction crews always wore.

"Fred Stein! I'm going to fail you, and your brother, for scaring the crap out of me!" I laughed hysterically, yelling at him as I jumped out of the car. "Exactly what are you doing?"

"Parking lot patrol," he grinned, raising his flashlight like a baton. "I'm president of the Kennedy S.A.D.D. chapter. We volunteer to walk the parking lot and try to discourage the kids from drinking and driving."

I just looked at him.

"Sorry about scaring you," he said sheepishly. "I didn't know it was you. Didn't mean to scare the...crap...out of you," he said, trying not to grin.

"Fred, don't let this go to your head," I said, knowing exactly the effect I was about to have on him, "but at this exact moment I wish you were forty years old."

Fred Stein was beaming brighter than his flashlight. I had not been insincere. He was a wonderful boy who was going to make some lucky girl a wonderful husband. Seeing him at that exact moment had made me feel very happy. Fred seemed like the most uncomplicated teenager at Kennedy High School.

"Gimme time, Miss Adams. When I'm forty I plan on being America's first Jewish socialist president."

"Fred, when you're forty, I plan on being sixty-one. But I would appreciate a dance at your inaugural ball."

He stepped back and looked at me, I knew, trying to imagine me at sixty-one. Seeing his head tilt slightly to one side, I thought I caught a glimpse of him at forty. Some grey hair, his thin body filled out, more stylish glasses, not handsome, but attractive in a mature way. Still *earnest*.

"Miss Adams..."

"Forget it, Fred, I'll always be too old for you."

I leaned back against the car door, taking in another deep breath. Looking over Fred's shoulder, I could see a few students darting in and out and around cars, some of them wearing Halloween masks, adolescent goblin impersonations of Bill Clinton or Bob Dole or Madonna.

"Yeah, I know. That's my problem," he sighed. "I always go for the girls who'll never give me the time of day. I figure the only way I'll ever have a girlfriend is if I actually do become president. I might even get to have sex. Say, Miss Adams, did presidents have sex when you were my age?"

"Only in their hearts," I said, remembering Jimmy Carter's admission. Fred laughed, and I was pleased that he knew the allusion.

"My dad says that's the difference between then and now. Lust in your heart versus lust in your loins. I'm glad I didn't live back then."

"Fred, you make it sound like so long ago."

"No, no, I didn't mean it that way," he stammered, obviously afraid that he had said something wrong. "I just mean that times have changed, you know, in politics. I just..."

"It's okay, Fred. But you can tell your dad that there was plenty of loin sex back in 1976, a lot of it in this parking lot on nights like this."

Fred smiled at me, fidgeting with his flashlight, trying to think of a response.

"And, for your information," I said, "I know all about this because I heard about it. I was pure until I got married."

"I didn't mean...Miss Adams...I never thought..."

The clouds were getting thicker and moving faster as the wind started picking up trash off the ground and blowing it around the parking lot. I sat on the hood, letting my shoes drop to the ground and tapping my bare heels against the side of my car. "Am I keeping you from your appointed rounds?" I asked him.

"Well, actually, I do need to go check on some other club members. I've been finding them hanging around the fence watching the game instead of the parking lot. It's no big deal. I mean, they're mostly sophomores and juniors, so you have to expect some slackers," he said, but he didn't move.

"So, Fred, you got a date for after the game? Surely there are lots of parties going on tonight," I said, actually pleased that he wanted to stay with me a little longer. "Always were when I was your age."

"Oh, sure, I'll be going out later," he said, but he didn't look at me when he said it.

"Fred?"

"Well, I *am* going to see somebody."

"Fred?"

"Dana O'Connor, I'm going to see Dana."

"Fred! You have a date with Dana O'Connor?!" I exclaimed, seeing him squirm.

"Miss Adams, nobody has ever *dated* Dana. She's not a date type girl. Does that make sense? I don't have a date. I'm just giving her a ride home from work tonight after the game. Her car is broken again. She asked me for a ride. It's not a date."

"Dana works on Friday nights?" I asked, imagining Dana in that law office downtown with her baby and books.

Fred nodded. "She's at Mr. Parsons' house, staying with Mrs. Parsons while he takes his girls to the game. As soon as he gets home, Dana can leave."

Neither one of us spoke for a noticeable minute. Across the parking lot, two girls were laughing as they ran toward the field.

When Fred decided that I had nothing to say, he continued, "She helps him out sometimes. Everybody knows that. He doesn't like to leave his wife alone too much. Dana helps him. That's all."

I finally managed to say, "Have you ever met his wife?"

"I've seen her."

"Met her? Been introduced? Had a conversation with?"

Fred was clearly uncomfortable. "Introduced, yes."

"And?"

"I thought you knew her. Dana said you had her as a teacher, that you were a student of hers."

"That was a long time ago, before she had her babies. She's not the same now."

Fred let out a deep breath, "Whoa! Miss Adams, I don't know how she was then, but, man, she's...she's..."

"It's okay, Fred. She's different now, I know that."

"No shi...no kidding," he said, arching his eyebrows.

Fred was having a hard time trying not to blink too much, and I could tell that he didn't want to talk about Stella. "So, tell me about Dana," I said, and his face gave him away. Fred thought about Dana a lot.

"You mean Wonder Woman?"

"You like her?"

"Nobody *dates* Dana and nobody really *likes* her. She's not interested in either thing."

"But *you* like her."

"Of course I like her. I just wish she liked me. Know what I mean? I mean, does that make sense?"

I nodded, "How does everyone else feel about her?"

Fred looked directly at me. "You know that already."

"Fred, like I said before," I smiled, resisting the urge to put my arm around his shoulder, like a parent. "I wish you were forty. You've got a lot of potential, especially in not letting people trick you."

"Well, all I know is that if I *was* forty then Dana might pay attention to me."

"Well...I know that she does like you," I said, remembering the tone of Dana's voice as she talked about him in my classroom.

"I wish," he shrugged, looking up at the sky, then back down at the ground. "I owe her a lot. She really helped me my sophomore year. Got me through chemistry. It was amazing how much she knew. Proofread some essays of mine that I did for Mrs. Rose too. Put me over the hump from A to A+. My dad paid her for tutoring me. It was my idea. I told him I was in more trouble than I actually was. But, you know, it was more that she listened to me a lot, didn't make fun of my plans. Didn't...."

"Fred, you more than like her, don't you."

"Oh, Miss Adams, it broke my heart last year when I found out she was pregnant. To see what happened to her. There was nothing I could do to help her. Broke my heart."

I got down off the hood of my car and put on my shoes just as a clap of thunder rolled across north Florida. Fred pulled a tiny plastic bag out of his back pocket.

"I've got a raincoat in here if you need it," he said.

"Fred, that's sweet, but you'll need it more than me. I've got a car here."

"No problem," he said, reaching into his pocket again. "I always carry two on nights like this, in case somebody needs one."

The parking lot was beginning to fill up with hundreds of people, mostly adults, heading for their cars.

"You get going. You'll probably be using that flashlight in a few minutes to direct traffic. Come see me Monday and we'll get you into Harvard," I said, reaching for the door handle and looking for Tom and Kris in the crowd that was coming toward us.

"One last thing, Miss Adams," he said. "You want to know how much I like Dana? I like her so much I don't even care that she's going to cost me five thousand dollars in scholarship money."

"Excuse me?" I said.

"The salutatorian scholarship. With her getting to do those courses over, she's bound to be valedictorian. April gets knocked back to second. I drop to third, and third gets a star in the graduation program, but no scholarship. A month ago everybody assumed April was a shoo-in and I was second. Now, with Mr. Parsons letting her repeat that stuff, the food chain's been re-established. But that's fair."

"Fred, how do you know all this now?"

"It's all over school today. Everybody knows. Miss Prose told April and April told me, me and just about everyone else at Kennedy. And April is not a happy camper."

"You're not bothered?" I asked him, knowing the answer.

"Nope. My dad is richer than April's dad, so the money's nothing to me. All I need is a letter from you and some other teachers that makes me look like I'd be doing Harvard a favor by going there. And, you get down to it, being salutatorian is like being vice-president. Who cares and who remembers?"

"You're being very generous about all this, Fred," I said, being absolutely sincere.

"Yeah, I'm a prince among men," he said, adjusting his cap and buttoning his orange vest. "But, I'm in the minority, especially when it comes to Dana." He flicked his flashlight on and off several times to test the beam. "Okay, I'm outta here. See you on Monday, Teach. And, remember, your job in life is to make me look good." Then, as he was about to leave, he turned back to me and asked, "You're not going to tell Dana what I said about her, are you?"

I shook my head and said, "It's just between us guys."

He waved happily and ran toward the west gate, passing hundreds of people racing back to their cars, football programs held over their heads as the rain began to come down.

The Fruit Doesn't Fall Far From the Tree

A man who has never gone to school may steal from a freight car; but if he has a university education, he may steal the whole railroad.—Theodore Roosevelt

Donna Parton came to see me an hour before the official start of Parents Night. She was making her rounds, reminding everyone that she would cover for them if they suddenly developed *parentitis colonitis*, a disease she had discovered.

"My bet with first-time teachers," she said, waving a sheet of paper. "These parents will be here. If three parents show up who aren't on this list, I owe you lunch."

I studied the names. Donna's pessimism had been expressed by Agnes and Jerry and other teachers with a few years experience, so I wasn't surprised to see that most of the parents of students who had been given one of Donna's red Xs at the beginning of the year were not on the list.

"Do I still get lunch," I asked, "if I called a parent not on this list and asked them to come see me?"

"If they show up, you get the credit," Donna said. "So, who'd you call?"

I told her about Donnie Yarborough, Jackie the Smoker, Mike Lankford, a few others. I had made a specific point of talking to the parents themselves, not just sending a message with their child. Donna wasn't impressed. "You might get Jackie's mom, Fort Jackson's last flower child, but the others? The odds are still in my favor. And, next time, if you call a parent, send me a note, okay?"

"FBI file?" I joked.

"Sort of. Truth is, I'm always getting parents who call me complaining that they're shocked at how bad their kids are doing in school and their *why wasn't I told* self-righteousness is a bit harder and harder to swallow the longer I do this job, so my knowing who you've contacted will be helpful. And, I promise you, if somebody calls me to complain about you, you'll know immediately."

"You get a lot of those complaints about teachers here?"

"Nancy, I said I'd tell you about you. My job is to know everything about everybody, not to tell everybody about anybody."

"Dolly Parton!"

We both looked toward the door as soon as we heard Dell's voice, but he had already gone down the hall. I looked back at Donna, expecting her to be irritated, but she merely laughed. "That man has too much free time on his hands. You going for a drink with us after conferences?"

"I'll see. Depends on how tired I am." Waiting for my first parent, I was already beginning to anticipate how tired I would be at the end of the night. Not as bad as the first few weeks, when I was asleep before ten every night. "Probably not," I finally said.

In front of me, my grade book was open to page one. Next to the grade book was a stack of work from all my classes, samples of each student's writing or perhaps a test. Things to show a parent who was interested. Totally prepared, I sat in my classroom alone for a half hour. My first appointment was a no-show. For that unscripted half hour, I sat there and thought about the books I hadn't read since I began teaching.

For years, I had been able to read a book a week, sometimes more. I loved reading, and it was essential to my writing good reviews. No book existed by itself, no book could be evaluated without knowledge of other work on the same subject. Teaching and reviewing were both forms of evaluation. But that was it. I seldom met a writer I reviewed. Still, I had loved the process. I was totally independent, and print deadlines were never a problem. I absorbed a book and shut out the rest of my nonexistent life. But I never had illusions about the value of my opinion. I never killed a book, even those I tried my best to expose as shallow or factually distorted, never sent an author crying to a parent. I had had writers write to thank me, write to curse me, write to contradict me, and one even asked me out to dinner. I got lots of free books, more than I could ever read. It was a great job as long as I never depended on it to support me.

I didn't absorb teaching, as I did books. Teaching absorbed me. I had no life away from Kennedy. I stayed home, and I lost weight. I went days without reading a newspaper or magazine. Every social event of my life was tied to school. A football game, a drink with other teachers, committee meetings: I had become my work.

"Nancy?"

I looked up to see a bronzed man extend his hand.

"David Abrams, Dylan's father," he smiled.

Father and son reunion. The oak to Dylan's acorn. David Abrams wasn't much older than me. He was tan and trim and not the first parent I wanted to see.

"Dylan was right. You *are* the best looking teacher here. So, why haven't we met before?"

I blinked. Dylan's father was flirting with me. Seriously, with his son's teacher? I looked around for his wife, but we were alone. "This is my first year," I managed to say, trying hard not to shake my head in astonishment or laugh out loud, secretly pleased that Dylan had sprung from this particular gene pool. If I had liked his parents, then I would have felt guilty about disliking him.

"Well, that's too bad," he said. "If you had been here the past few years, I would have looked forward to these conferences a lot more than I have."

"Mr. Abrams, thanks, but can we..."

"David."

"Okay, sure, David," I said, smiling like I was paid to do it. "We need to focus on Dylan. Was there anything in particular you were concerned about?"

He sat in the chair beside my desk, his left hand too close to my gradebook. I shifted in my seat to face him more directly, wondering how it would feel to slap him. Out of nowhere, I wanted to pop him across his smirky mouth.

"Oh, absolutely not," he said. "Dylan has been a great kid. A lot more mature than his older brother. *There* was a problem child. Dylan, he's got a bright future ahead of him. You know he wants to be a doctor, don't you?"

I nodded. "Yes, he's mentioned that a few times. And he's certainly smart enough to get into med school."

"Well, now that you mention it, there is something that I did want to ask you. I'm sure it's just a misunderstanding between you and Dylan, but he tells me that he's probably getting a B in your class. I was surprised, so I told him I would talk to you."

"Actually, he's probably headed for a B+. An A- is not impossible, depending on his final exam and a few more quizzes. But a B+ is nothing to be ashamed of," I said, wondering if David Abrams had been told that all women wanted a man to maintain constant eye contact with them.

"Dylan has always been an A student," he said firmly.

I knew that was not true. When Dylan had complained to me about an early essay grade and told me the same story, that he was a solid A student, I went to see Donna Parton. She showed me his transcript. Mostly A's, a few B's, but a couple of C+'s as well. "Yes, he's a bright boy," I said, trying to be conciliatory. "A bright underachiever."

Abrams maintained his eye contact, but he abandoned his charm, "You know he's taking college prep courses."

"Of course, most of our curriculum is geared toward college preparation," I said, trying not to seem like I was correcting him.

"That's not what I meant," he corrected me. "I meant that he's taking courses for college credit. CLEP credits through that FSU early admission program. He's already performing at the college level. I expect him to be in med school in three years."

"My class is not going to change that," I said, trying to figure out where he was going with this discussion. "His college grades will be more important."

"Okay, I'll cut to the chase. Dylan says that you don't like him personally and that's why he's getting a B," he said, a vein in his forehead starting to throb. Then, realizing that he was showing too much anger, and, I suspected, wanting the woman across from him to still find him attractive, he changed his tone of voice back to that of a young man meeting his date's father for the first time.

"Of course, I assumed he was wrong. Being his father, I was concerned, so I thought we could clear up that misconception easily in a face to face like this." He leaned back and smiled. I paused for a moment, seeing Dylan's face across from me, trying to imagine his mother's face, knowing that I was about to say the wrong thing. Honest, but still the wrong thing to say.

"David, that's crap," I said, smiling as I reached across my desk, making eye contact and patting his hand at the same time.

He flinched but immediately did a gold medal recovery. "Of course it is. I wouldn't have thought otherwise."

We looked at each other momentarily, and then he stood up, reached in his coat pocket, pulled out his wallet, and handed me his business card. "I know you have a lot of people to see tonight. If you have any problems with Dylan, or there is anything I can do for you, or you just want to talk, call me. My office number is on the card."

In the next three hours, I met nineteen sets of parents, five mothers who came by themselves, and Mike Lankford's much older brother. Jackie's mother came to see me, telling me how I was her daughter's favorite teacher. She talked more about herself than she did Jackie, how she was a college graduate who had learned more on the streets than in the classroom, how Jackie's father had been killed in a bar fight in Tampa, and how corporations were ruining America.

Donna had been right. I didn't get three parents who were not on her list. Still, I was pleased. I was intrigued by how most of the parents were older dead ringers for their children. Faces and mannerisms. Sometimes in how they smiled or frowned. Fred Stein's parents, however, were the biggest shock. His father was the epitome of a Republican banker. Despite Fred's political persona, his father being a banker was no real surprise. His mother was a librarian at UF. No surprise, either. But there was something amiss about them. They came to school separately and met in my classroom. I didn't figure out what was wrong until they were almost finished talking.

"We're worried about Freddy," his father said, sitting to my left, his mother on the opposite side. "He seems to be taking his schoolwork too seriously this semester."

"*Too* seriously?" I asked. I had never heard that parental concern before.

"Actually, Morris is not quite right," Fred's mother said, and I soon found myself turning my head from left to right and back again in order to follow their comments. "Freddy is doing too much of everything this term. Studying too hard, working too many hours at his store job, involved in too many extra-curricular activities..."

"Which is what I was starting to say," the father said.

"Excuse me," the mother said, turning her head away.

"No, I'm sorry for interrupting. Go ahead."

I was silent, aware of how nervous Morris Stein was.

"I was saying that Freddy seems to think he can do more than is humanly possible," the mother continued.

"The boy is..." the father began to say, but stopped.

"Fred is probably my favorite student," I said, trying to fill a void, and his parents looked across the desk at each other and smiled. "I mean it. I'm not sure what the word here is that I'm looking for, but it has something to do with Fred being more *alive* than most of my other students. He's energetic, he's smart, and he cares about things. I've only been teaching two months, but that's enough to know that Fred is different from the others. I look forward to seeing him in class everyday."

Morris Stein tried not to, but he started crying.

"Excuse me," he said, his hand trying to cover his face, and then he left the room.

I turned toward Fred's mother, who said, herself sniffling, "You must excuse Morris. Our divorce has been very hard on him, especially with Freddy living with me."

"Oh..." I said slowly, my stomach tying a knot with itself. My first job, my first Parents Night, I was learning more than I expected. "Oh..." I repeated, ashamed of my verbal failure, but I didn't have the words to describe how painfully sorry I was at that moment. And disappointed in myself. Fred hadn't told me about his parents divorcing, but surely I should have figured it out, his constant efforts to be...to be...what? Every encounter I had already had with him had to be reinterpreted in the context of this new knowledge.

"Just...one of those things," Fred's mother said, trying to make me feel better. "We'll get through it. And we do appreciate what you said about Freddy. Morris and I are very proud of him. And we would appreciate it if you would look out for him, perhaps call us if you see a problem."

The night should have ended with Fred's parents, but a dozen more followed. Each with their own story, some more happy than others, some bored at being there, some surprisingly hostile toward me about their child's performance, less subtle versions of Dylan's father, some just interested in seeing, as Mike Lankford's brother said, "who this Miss Adams was."

My last conference was with April's mother and father. They had gone to all of April's other teachers first, saving me for the last. Amy Bourne did most of the talking while I kept trying to remember where I had met her before.

"April says you're her favorite teacher," Amy Bourne said. Her husband nodded. I knew she was lying.

"That's flattering," I said, trying not to stare. Amy Bourne was extraordinarily attractive, as if her face and body had been coddled since birth, and her hands were younger looking than anything else about her. "April is one of the best students I have." I thought it was a safe compliment.

"We think she's the smartest student here," Amy said.

"Well, she's certainly doing well in my class, and I'm sure she's doing fine in her other classes too." Something made me resist being too lavish in my opinion. I knew that Amy Bourne was not fishing for compliments about her daughter.

Then it hit me, the connection. "Did you go to Kennedy with me twenty years ago?" I asked. Sometimes, strangers finding a common thread in their past lives will make them open up to each other, I told myself. Wrong. So totally wrong this time.

"I was a sophomore when you were a senior. Amy Gordon was my name then."

"Yes, that's it. I thought you looked familiar."

"You didn't know me. I was a sophomore," she said, with all the warmth of a corpse. "You were a senior."

"Oh, sure I do," I lied. Not really a lie, an exaggeration. All I could remember, memory prodded at this conference, was Amy Gordon the sophomore class president.

"I was saying, about April, I think she's the best in her class," Amy said. Political consultants would describe her as *on message*. Her husband was looking at the posters scattered around the room as she continued, "But I'm bothered by some information that she's brought home."

"Information?" I said, being as disingenuous as I could be, but I knew where Amy was going.

My pose was too transparent for her. "This is your first year here, Nancy, and you can be excused for not knowing all the background to this issue, but you *do* know what I'm talking about. April talked to you about it."

"Dana O'Connor?" I said, studying the other woman's face. If names were poison, I had just killed April's mother.

Her jaw tightened, and her shoulders noticeably shrank before she finally said, "Dana O'Connor, indeed. I don't know how much you know about her, nor do I care. But I think it would be in the best interests of this school if someone talked to Russell Parsons about his decision to let her take those courses over. And in his best interests, too."

"You think that someone ought to be me?" I said, fascinated by how oblivious Amy's husband seemed to everything being said around him.

"I'll start with you," Amy said.

"Why is it that you and April think that Russell will listen to me? Or anybody else, for that matter?" I asked.

"I know about Russell Parsons," the husband said, looking directly at me for the first and only time, his first and only words, and then turning away again.

"Nancy, we're both adults," Amy said slowly. "I'm almost as old as you. I haven't got time to be coy. You and Russell have known each other since you were his pet student twenty years ago. Everyone knows that, and everyone knows how you got this job. I don't care about you and him, then or now. All I care about is that my daughter is not being treated fairly by the principal of this high school. He hasn't changed in twenty years. He still plays favorites. You then, Dana now. All I'm saying is that if you care about him you might talk to him about the mistake he is making."

I stood up, shaking, feeling like I had just seen a Peeping Tom outside my window. "Amy, if you...and your husband...would like to go see Russell and talk about this, I'll be glad to go with you. But threatening him through me is a waste of my time and your time. Is that clear?"

Amy looked up. "I've never had any trouble seeing things, Nancy, then or now."

Ten minutes later, still shaking, I was standing in my classroom alone, throwing erasable ink markers against the white board, satisfying my desire to hit something. I was on my twelfth marker when Donna Parton poked her head through the door and said, "A drink, teacher?"

"Donna, I'm taking my car home," I said, making my last toss. "Follow me and give me a ride to wherever everyone is going. I want more than one drink, and I'm going to need a ride home.

And, soon, I need to talk to you about some problems with a few of my students."

"And their parents?"

"Am I that obvious, so merely typical?" I tried to laugh. "Does every first year teacher need to come see you?"

"Nancy, they all come see me, but I'm not sure they listen."

Sent to the Principal's Office

Change is the end result of all true learning.—Leo Buscaglia

Russell's office didn't have an open door policy. He was seldom in it, so *dropping in* usually meant being told he was somewhere else. The secretary outside his door, Mrs. Pullman, a leather-skinned woman who had run interference for every Kennedy principal since 1971, put visitors on a list and gave them a time to come back. If a teacher or student needed to see him in a hurry, Mrs. Pullman told them where he was last seen, but with no guarantee that he was still there. He moved around constantly, a *presence* whose most predictable appearance was in the cafeteria during the lunch periods. He was seldom alone anywhere in the building, except in his office. He was almost always in the halls at recess and wandered from classroom to classroom, stopping to wave at a teacher. Sometimes he would ask if he could sit in on a class, a habit that irritated some teachers. With others, he sometimes participated in the class discussion. I wondered if I had never met him before, would I be one of the ones who were irritated with him.

I made an appointment, but before I could meet him, April stopped me after the honors class. As she talked, I kept thinking that if April were merely vapid and simplistic she would have made a wonderful 1955 Miss America. She was pretty, talented, motivated, programmed, and a credit to her middle class culture. But April was neither vapid nor simplistic. She was opaquely deep.

"I want to apologize for my behavior at the game awhile back," she smiled at me. "I was out of line. You shouldn't have been asked to solve my problems. In fact, I took your suggestion. I went to see Mr. Parsons. I think he understands my concerns, and he was very sympathetic."

I was at my desk. "That's good," I said, looking up and remembering my first impression of April, how she reminded me of myself at that age. "Like I told you, you have every chance of being the valedictorian, as much as anyone else." I intentionally didn't say Dana's name.

"Oh, absolutely," April laughed. "I have no doubt. I just over-reacted. Sold myself too short. I'll do my best and we'll just have to wait and see what happens. I'd say my chances are as good as anybody's."

She walked toward the door as I looked up at the overhead clock.

"Oh, I almost forgot," she said, casually turning back to face me. "I want to apologize for my mother's behavior, too. She was way out of line. We talked after she came home from her meeting you. I'm very sorry," shaking her head, looking down at her feet. "It won't happen again."

Mrs. Pullman, sitting with her purse in her lap, was waiting for me when I got to the main office. "Mr. Parsons told me to tell you to go wait in his office. He had to go see Mr. Rose. Said he would be right back, that I could lock up and leave as soon as you got here."

I suddenly felt like I was in high school again, alone in the principal's office. But this was different. When Russell was my teacher, he didn't have an office, and I never saw the inside of his apartment. This was the first time I had ever seen his private space. The door to his office was always closed, regardless of whether or not he was inside. I knew his reputation. As he did with all the teachers, he and I had always had our private conferences in a classroom or in the teachers lounge.

In his office, a table lamp in the corner was always on, even when the building was empty. He never used the overhead light. Behind his desk was a large double-window overlooking the parking lot, but the blinds were always closed. The walls were paneled in cherry-wood. Facing the desk on each side of the door, the walls were covered with bookshelves, the books carefully arranged by subject. Two black leather chairs faced the desk, exactly parallel. The desk itself was immaculate. No loose papers, no discarded pen or pencil, nothing except a single pad of blank yellow paper in the corner.

The wall to the left of the desk was covered with framed pictures, all of them related to Kennedy High School: senior class group pictures, faculty group shots, athletic events, newspaper articles clipped and matted. To the right of the desk were pictures relevant only to him. Lots of pictures of his daughters at various ages. A picture of him and Stella on their wedding day. Next to it, a tenth anniversary picture, his arm around her as they sat in a front porch swing, her face contorted and her eyes almost closed.

The only non-family pictures were from Vietnam. One was of Russell standing next to a short Vietnamese man who was holding a child. Russell was wearing aviator sunglasses and holding some sort of bag in his left hand. He looked like an actor playing the role of soldier. The other was a group of young soldiers, standing and kneeling, bunched together, some with cigarettes in their hands, some pointing their middle fingers toward the camera, all of them looking like they needed a shower and shave, more white boys than black. A young Russell Parsons, looking not much older than Dylan Abrams or Fred Stein, was standing next to a much older black man. Next to that group picture was a framed American flag. Soiled and stained, the size of one of those children's flags that people waved at parades, but with only forty-eight stars. I was looking at that flag when Russell came in.

"Sorry about being late," he said, walking around to sit behind his desk.

"You get Dell straightened out?" I asked.

"Probably too late for that," he almost smiled. "Nope, I was letting him know that I had arranged that scrimmage he wanted with St. Joe's downtown."

"The Catholic school?"

"Yeah, where my girls go. I bet Dell that St. Joseph could beat Kennedy. At least, give them a real test."

"Russell, Dell keeps telling anybody who will listen that Kennedy will be the state champs this year. And, don't get me wrong, but isn't St. Joe about one-tenth the size of this place?"

"St. Joe's has been the parochial state champs twice in the past five years," he said, as animated as I had ever seen him. "Small school, for sure, and only ten players on the entire team, usually a lot of short white kids, but they are fun to watch."

"Russell, your lack of Knight loyalty is obvious," I kidded him.

"Oh, Dell knows he has my support. That's why I set up this scrimmage. He thinks his kids are getting too cocky, so we'll have an unannounced scrimmage. No crowd, just the players and coaches. No witnesses." He saw my puzzled expression. "Not even you. There are a lot of rules governing high school sports. Technically, this scrimmage is illegal. It never happened," looking from side to side with feigned suspicion, "and since I told you now I have to kill you."

"Can we talk about some *other* technicalities?" I said.

He cocked his head to one side and let out a deep breath. "Sure, sure. April and Dana?" His demeanor had changed. He was no longer happy.

"Actually, just April," I said. "Dana's not your biggest problem right now, but April has the potential to be a major headache for you. And, I'm not so sure that she isn't right."

Russell had to see that he was a contradiction. I had been telling myself that all day. A twenty-year reputation as someone who played life like a game with unbreakable rules, he had decided that he could change the rules at his leisure and expect all the other players to agree. All I wanted at that moment in his office was for him to be honest with me, with himself.

"I talked to April," he said, "and although she doesn't agree, I think she understands."

"You're wrong, you have to see that, don't you." I wasn't going to let him get off so easy. "April thinks she is being cheated by you. What she *understands* is that you are playing favorites..."

"Nancy, all I'm doing is trying to make the valedictorian award a true reflection of scholarship, not all that other stuff that has been piled on over the years to make it a test of *citizenship,* so smart students who know how to work the system can pad their credentials by having their picture all over the school annual..."

"You told her that?"

"I was more diplomatic."

"How did you explain letting Dana take those courses over again?" I asked, surprised by the confused reaction on his face.

"We didn't talk about that," he said.

"You mean to tell me that she didn't ask you about Dana's second chance?"

"Not a word. She came to see me about my plan to select the valedictorian solely on GPA. That's all."

"And you think that's all she was concerned about?"

"That's all we discussed."

I was getting exasperated. "Russell, you're setting up an absolutely inevitable confrontation with April and her parents. A fight I don't think you can win."

He got up from behind his desk and came around to sit in the chair next to mine, turning it to face me. "Nancy, two separate issues. Changing the valedictorian criteria is merely a suggestion of mine. If a majority of the faculty doesn't want to go along with it, it's not going to happen. But letting Dana take those courses over is a done deal. My decision, my prerogative, by the book, non-negotiable."

I took a deep breath and said nothing.

"Look, there are actually bigger issues to worry about at this school, and I do want you to help me on those," he said, getting back up and going to a file cabinet to get a set of drawings and some other papers. "Take a look at this," he said, laying out the sketches on his desk.

In front of me were pages of plans for a new high school in Fort Jackson County. It was huge, a mall for the twenty-first century. A central library bigger than any Barnes and Noble superstore, a gym that was more like a health club, complete with a sauna and an indoor rock climbing wall, a food court to replace the cafeteria, complete with Taco Bell and Arby's counters, each classroom fitted with its own computer lab, a parking ramp instead of a parking lot, a school that was its own community.

Russell, however, wasn't impressed. "This is floating around the school board. And I'll be the first to admit that we're overcrowded here, and with each new addition to this building we keep getting more and more fragmented," he said. "And some of Betsy Elizondo's curriculum proposals, like going to a three semester school year, are overdue."

"But?" I offered him a transition to what he really wanted to say.

"But this is the wrong solution."

"Too expensive?"

"Nancy, Betsy has been working on this for two years. She's wanted a mega-charter school forever. She's lining up state money, federal money, corporate sponsorships, soft-drink franchise tie-ins, and then there's that damned Kennedy endowment drive that keeps belching money in its sleep. She's even been lining up a campaign committee to get the bond referendum passed. All this will become public late this spring, assuming she gets the other votes she needs on the board. I need people to help me come up with a counter-proposal. That's where you come in."

"Russell, I'm not sure this..." I said, pointing to the plans, "...is a bad idea. You have to show..."

"Do we need some new facilities? Of course. But the foundation, the basic premise is flawed."

"I'm missing something here," I said.

"Her main selling point will be cost savings. She'll propose closing down Jackson High School completely, bussing those kids to Kennedy and filling the new school with Kennedy kids. But with a twist. Her plan will pull out the best Jackson students, get them to the new school, and provide them with opportunities they never had before. Jackson *is* a rat-hole school. And facilities *do* count. But ... "

I remembered my father's story, the history of Fort Jackson. No money for buses when integration came to Fort Jackson, but money now. New schools but old ideas.

"I've got a plan, Nancy, and I need you to help me sell it to the others. You and Agnes and Jerry and Dell and Sue and a few others who can bring over the rest of the faculty, at least a clear majority, and then the school board and the Jackson faculty." He handed me a two-page memo. "Read this. It's bare bones now, but tell me what you think."

I read the proposal quickly and then stared at Russell as if he had escaped from a mental institution. But I also realized something about why I had thought I had been in love with him before.

My parents had given me two goals in life. My father, who had marched with Andrew Young in St. Augustine and been beaten by a white mob, insisted that I should *do good*. My mother, who had gone to the hospital to bring him home, told me to *be happy*. It was my father's admonition and Russell's character: The purpose of life was to *do good*. In twenty years, Russell hadn't changed. Doing good was more important than being happy.

"Russell, you know, of course, that you are certifiably crazy and this plan hasn't got a chance of being adopted."

"Not if it's just my plan, Nancy. It has to come from more than me."

Russell had a vision. There was no denying that Kennedy was over-crowded. No denying that Jackson was a decrepit, budget-draining sink hole, a school half the size of Kennedy with three times the air conditioning bill. Other glaring facts. Even though the proposal in front of me was brief, I knew that Russell had probably dissected and absorbed the entire Fort Jackson school system budget. He understood it down to the last dime and paper towel. More than money, however, Russell was proposing a shift in educational philosophy.

A new school building, somewhere, was unavoidable. The demographics could not be denied. But he wanted to keep Jackson open and completely renovate it. The new county school would be scaled back, with almost as much money going back into Jackson High renovations. Most dramatic, he wanted to restructure how students were to be assigned, to redefine the use of those buildings that already existed. He wanted to divide the county into three zones, each its own neighborhood. More than just a new high school was needed. Russell wanted educational complexes.

He wanted to integrate every grade into the same facility. Instead of separate elementary, middle-school, and high school facilities, he wanted every complex to be a K-12 school. Parents would have all their children in the same building. Instead of a thousand high schoolers, there would be a thousand students from age five through eighteen. Teenagers would go to school with their younger siblings. Older students would help with the younger students activities. High school teachers would eat lunch with elementary school teachers.

School *choice* would be eliminated in his plan. Where you lived in the county determined where you went to school. Teachers themselves would be initially assigned to the schools closest to where *they* lived, unless there was a need for a particular specialty at any particular school. No satellite, magnet, or charter schools, there would be no better or best school. If more blacks lived nearer to the Jackson complex, Jackson would be mostly black. But Jackson would be as good as Kennedy or the new school, offer as much, have the same quality teachers, the same standards.

"Russell, does the name Don Quixote ring a bell with you?" I asked him, handing the papers back. "You might win all your pedagogical battles, but that last paragraph is an impossible dream."

"It's the lynchpin, Nancy. I have to have..."

"Wrong, Russell, it's the poison pill."

Kennedy High School had pulled away from Jackson in the past twenty years because of an endowment fund that had provided computers, pool enhancements, landscaping, teacher bonuses, athletic equipment, musical instruments and a performing auditorium, televisions, VCRs, private vans for club road trips, scholarships, excursions to foreign countries for the foreign language clubs...money compounding money compounding status and comfort for Kennedy High School.

Russell's proposal was simple. The school board had to adopt a policy that all contributions were to be made to the district, not to a particular school. The board could then allocate according to need. Or, as a counter-proposal, a contribution could be designated for a particular school but only as long as an equal amount was pledged to the district.

"You know the response, don't you?" I asked him.

He nodded. "A firestorm first, and, if it miraculously happens to pass, the donations will dry up for a few years. But, eventually, a lot of the money will come back. Most of these parents will support their kids, wherever they are. Not all, I know, but I'm assuming the best, that most will."

"Russell, is there a pill I can take to be as optimistic as you are?" I smiled at him, trying to make him smile.

"Nancy, the worst thing that will ever happen to me...it's already happened. I think I told you that before. Everything in the future is gravy."

He was sitting on the edge of his desk, his feet tapping each other. I thought of Humpty-Dumpty, then of Dylan's father and April's mother. Then I thought of myself in pieces along with Russell. The two of us hitting the ground at the same time. I was mixing metaphors—Sancho Panza as an egg.

"You talk to anyone else about this yet?"

"Dell and Agnes."

"Russell, you're going to need a lot more white friends than black ones for this to succeed. Sorry to be so blunt. Another thing," I said, standing up and pausing inches away from him. "You can't have any baggage. No enemies over small things. Dana is baggage, and you have to stop carrying it. You have to look at yourself in the mirror and ask yourself what's more important."

He looked at me and tried to smile. I felt like I was looking at a dead man.

That Damn Henry Adams

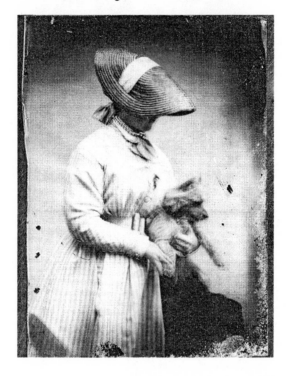

An education isn't how much you have committed to memory, or even how much you know. It's being able to differentiate between what you know and what you don't.—Anatole France

I left his office convinced that if Russell wouldn't un-graft himself from Dana O'Connor, then Dana would have to do it for him. For Dana to understand why she had to do it, then I had to confront her. I called Donna Parton and got Dana's address, but I failed to get directions. After an hour of driving up and down gravel roads seeing nothing but turnoffs without markers, I began to invent metaphors about the triangle I was in with Russell and Dana, metaphors about being lost in the woods, metaphors about lost causes, metaphors about messengers being killed because of their message. An hour of metaphors and historical parallels later, exhausted, I gave up and went back to Fort Jackson to call Donna again, who told me to go by the lawyer's office downtown where Dana worked.

I called from a payphone outside a *Lil' Champ* convenience store, across the street from St. Mary's, where me and mama and daddy worshipped until he died.

The most useless book I ever read? One of my father's favorites, so I had heard about it even before I went to Notre Dame. My favorite history professor at Notre Dame, you would have thought that book was his Bible. Useless, and a pain to read. Henry Adams and his *Education.*

Adams spanned the nineteenth century. I was a woman living at the end of the twentieth. He had written his *Education* for himself and a hundred friends. He had never imagined me. Never imagined himself as part of *my* education. But there he was in my junior year, the first required book on the syllabus of a twentieth-century American culture course. The professor had laughed about separating the real versus amateur students early in the semester. "The twentieth century begins with Adams," he had said, "be sure to read the end-notes." It was 1980. I was one of only three women in the class.

I read it, and all the endnotes. I was clueless. I was a smart young woman and I was still hiding the fact that the first vote I had ever cast in my life was probably going to go to Ronald Reagan. I was sure that all my professors, even at Notre Dame, were flaming liberals. But I also read it because I remembered my father telling me the same thing, almost verbatim, "The twentieth century begins…"

I read it when I was twenty, and then I read it again when I was thirty because some editor at the *Atlanta Journal* wanted me to do a book review of a new Adams biography. I had an MA in history. I was the logical choice. I protested. I told the editor that Adams bored the hell out of me. His voice over the phone was not subtle, "I thought you were an educated woman." I called Russell and asked him if he wanted to write the review. He was more considerate than my editor, "Give it a second chance. You can't really write an intelligent review unless the *Education* is fresh in your mind."

I gave Adams a second chance. I had nothing else to do with my life. I understood more. And then I forgot about him, until I went looking for Dana.

How many times had I sat in that church and asked Jesus to come down off that cross? How many times did I ask him why my father died? How many times did I get an answer? Not one damn time, not one time. My father had tricked me all those years. I knew my mother was going through the motions whenever we went to Mass, but I believed because my father believed. His name is still on a brass plate on the armrest at the end of a pew. My mother's last contribution had preserved his name, and that was the only reason I ever went back the few times I did.

Three in the afternoon, I had the space to myself. St. Mary's wasn't one of those ornately beautiful Catholic churches that I had seen in books and movies, or that I had seen in person when Jack had taken me to Europe. It was a simple church. I had never seen it full. Not much artwork, but a gold cross supported Jesus as he wept and bled. At certain times of the morning, depending on the season, the sunlight would come through a clear glass window and hit the cross and make it burn, and the crucified Jesus would be pale within the gold light surrounding him. I had asked my father about it, asked why the cross was gold and not wood, but he had no answer. Nobody did. The cross had been there since the church was built in 1896. It was merely gold plate over wood, and it had to be re-laminated every few decades, but nobody had ever suggested they replace it with something more traditional.

Waiting to go visit Dana, I heard someone walking around behind the wall on which the cross was hung, but whoever it was never appeared.

Another danger of being too educated was that someone else's profound insight or wisdom, learned by you as a student from a book, *that* insight would crowd out any chance that you could have your own wisdom. Someone else's insight, at first acting as a revelation to you, could eventually become a veil that kept you from having your own vision. In church that afternoon, I was looking at a painting of Mary, remembering Henry Adams's chapter about the Virgin and the Dynamo. I was beginning to understand my own education. And I was sure that Adams would be laughing at me right then.

I wanted to understand all this myself, this moment and this place and the trip I was about to make to see Dana, but Adams kept getting in the way. He wrote too gracefully, too perceptively, as if there was nothing else to say. He had anticipated me at that moment. How could I break away from him, feeling about him as I was sure he must have felt about his own father and his father's father and then, compounding that debt, his great-grandfather. Two presidents and an ambassador, and then Henry the history teacher. Charles Adams, my college teacher father; Frances Adams, my high school teacher mother. Nancy Adams, me. Henry Adams had known Lincoln and Grant and Roosevelt. I had grown up on Nixon, Carter, Reagan, Bush, and Clinton. It took me a long time, but I started to understand his comment about Darwin and evolution and American politicians. Churches did that to me, made me remember Henry Adams. I had become an educated woman, in spite of myself. But there was a big difference between Adams and me, between him and almost everyone who ever read him. He could mock himself as being irrelevant, but he knew he wasn't, not really. He could belittle his role, but he was still on stage with the greatest players of his time. I was sitting in my dying church in Fort Jackson, Florida, taking shots at a dead man. And how utterly pretentious all this was.

Faith as power, the Virgin. The Machine as power, the Dynamo. Absolutely profound, and absolutely irrelevant to me at that moment. I wasn't a historian. I was a high school history teacher in northeast Florida searching for an unwed mother in an attempt to help a man I thought I had loved but who was as much a mystery to me now as the death and resurrection of Christ and the automobile must have been to Henry Adams.

Russell was certainly no Jesus Christ. But, at that moment, if I had possessed the faith I had had before my father died, I knew I would have been guilty of blasphemy for even comparing the mysteries. But I was safe. The church was empty except for my father's name in brass, and Henry Adams was more real to me than God. And I finally had the question I wanted to ask Adams after all these years.

Tell me why you left her out of your book. All those pages and in-sights, but you kept her to yourself. Tell me about her. Tell me about your wife who killed herself. Tell me about that pain. Tell me about the woman you loved, who inflicted a horrible death on herself. Tell me what you learned about life...then. Forget about Chaos and Sequences. Tell me about Love. Tell me about her.

"Nancy, child."

I was up and turned around in one motion, childishly fright-ened by a voice in an empty church. Agnes Rose was standing in the aisle.

"I thought that was you, sitting here by yourself," Agnes said, as pleasantly as if we had crossed paths in a Kennedy hallway. She was holding a plastic bag full of groceries in one hand, her Bible in the other. My biggest shock was that this was the only time I had ever seen Agnes in mismatched clothes. She was wearing faded jeans and a Kennedy blue and gold t-shirt.

"Agnes...Agnes..." I stammered.

"That's my name, don't wear it out," she laughed, setting the groceries down in the pew.

I could only say, "I didn't think you were Catholic."

Another happy laugh from Agnes, "Lord no, I'm an old fat African Methodist, just doing my Saturday chores."

"But, you're...here," I said, waving meekly at the walls around us.

Agnes's eyes opened wide in mock disbelief and she looked from side to side, as if wondering how she got there. Then she exhaled, pushing out her lips and letting her breath escape with a wet flapping sound. "Nancy, you've got to promise me that you won't tell the Reverend Jefferson down at the AME. That man isn't as enlightened as you and me. He still thinks the Pope has some explaining to do in front of St. Peter."

"Agnes, why I am so totally confused about you?"

"Because I'm much too simple for you," she said, sitting down next to her groceries. "No deep thing why I'm here. I live a few blocks away. You've been there. Every Saturday I walk to the Winn-Dixie and do my shopping. I always stop here on the way back. The AME is two miles away. I'll drive there on Sundays and Wednesdays, but I ain't walking anymore, not since my arthritis got me. Been doing this for almost as many years as you've been alive."

"You just...you just stop in?"

"Nancy, I stop, I rest, and I pray. Then I take my butter beans and corn meal," shaking the bag next to her, "and I go home, grade some papers, listen to some music, and visit my neighbors when the sun cools down. Not a big deal, and I don't think this old church is gonna boot out an old Protestant like me."

I expected Agnes to ask me what I was doing there, but she didn't. So, I asked her what she thought of Russell's school reorganization plan, as nonchalantly as if we were having lunch in the cafeteria.

"I think...," she began to say but then paused, leaning forward with her elbows resting on the pew in front of her, "...I think it is the positively right thing to do. But, if he tries to win on every point, he'll lose everything. He's got to compromise. That's what I think, and that's what I told him. He has to compromise."

She turned to face me. I had been staring at the gold cross on the wall. With her right hand, she touched my cheek to force me to make eye contact again, "And he has to stop being so obvious in trying to help the girl."

Turning the corner, I could see Dana's battered Toyota parked in front of the lawyer's office. Shopping on Saturdays in downtown Fort Jackson was almost nonexistent since a new discount mall had opened, so I easily found a parking space right behind the Toyota. As soon as I opened my car door, Dana was standing in the office doorway, waving and putting a finger to her lips as if I was making too much noise. "Tess is asleep," she said.

She held the door open and ushered me in quietly. The office was dark except for one corner where she had been working at a computer. In the opposite corner, on a black leather couch, her baby was asleep in a child car seat.

"So, this is your other life," I said, self-consciously lowering my voice.

"One of many," she said, shutting down the computer, leaving the room even quieter than before. "But this pays better than most."

"Getting some schoolwork done?" I asked.

"Later. I was just posting some bills and transcribing some depositions. Pretty dry stuff. I don't think Dave's going to be arguing any Supreme Court cases anytime soon."

"Dave, your boss?"

"Yep, David Darrow, the people's champion."

"David Darrow! You're..."

"Yes, Nancy, I'm kidding. Didn't you see his name on the door? Small-town David O'Leary...personal injury, divorce, and criminal defense lawyer...everyone's favorite villain."

"He treats you okay?"

Dana shrugged. "Fine. Pays good, leaves me alone, usually, lets me use the office for myself. I keep him from forgetting his briefcase and make sure he can find anything in here anytime he needs it."

For the next half hour she talked about her job, some of the cases her boss was handling, how she did the paperwork, and a lot about David O'Leary's personal life. "I thought Dave was just another amoral spineless lawyer," she finally said, "but I got him to agree with me that some scum didn't deserve a good defense, that some criminals are not defensible. That's when I thought there was hope for him."

"For example?" I asked, imagining Dana debating the issue at some public forum, being the center of attention in a courtroom.

"That guy that was just sentenced to death in California for killing that Polly Klass girl."

"Richard Allen Davis?" I said.

"Oh, Nancy," she beamed, "I am so glad you knew immediately who I was talking about. It's one of my tests. And you passed."

"So, a knowledge of serial rapists is an important criterion in your choice of friends?" I tried to joke, while wondering at the same time why we had taken this direction in the conversation.

"Not all serial rapists deserve to die. Sick bastards or not. But, Richard Allen Davis does. As painfully as possible. Nancy, in my world, knowing who deserves to die, that's a list everyone ought to have."

"You're awfully young to..."

"Nancy! Don't lecture me," she whispered slowly, looking back at her baby as if she was afraid of being overheard and understood by an infant. "Young? I'm too damn young to be *me*."

We looked at each other in the dark office. The only sound was a baby breathing fitfully, a weak cough and some short gasps and then another cough.

"She's about to wake up," Dana said, less agitated than she was just a few seconds earlier. "Time for dinner."

"Dana, I want to talk to you about Russell," I said. "Is now okay, or should we get together some other time?"

"If she wakes up, I can talk and nurse at the same time. What's on your mind?"

I gave her my five-minute prepared speech. I told her about April and April's mother, about the growing perception that there was something *unprofessional* between her and Russell. That, Russell was headed for trouble by letting her take those courses over and by his suggesting that the rules for valedictorian be changed. That people were beginning to talk about the other favors he was doing for her. Dana listened without responding, but she nodded enough to let me know that she knew all this and agreed with some of it.

"There's something else, isn't there?" Dana finally said. "You've described and summarized. Where's the ad-vo-ca-cy? The other shoe, what you want me to do about it?"

"Dana, to be honest with you, I haven't got a clue about what to do. I was hoping you did."

"You were hoping that I would tell him not to change the rules for me, to not let me take those courses over, or maybe to just tell him that I'm not taking those courses over even if I could? Is that what I should do?"

"Look, all I'm telling you is that Russell is jeopardizing his ability to do a lot of good for this entire school district. And, right now, he's running the risk of losing that chance and the chance to help you too."

"You left out something else. He's also jeopardizing his marriage. Isn't that something you also wanted to say?"

I stiffened and leaned back in my chair. I had never thought about that possibility. But Dana said it, and it suddenly became obvious, or so I thought. "No, I had not intended to say that," I said honestly.

"But now?"

"But now it's probably a valid point."

"Wrong, wrong. Absolutely invalid."

"Dana, you're hardly capable of being objective."

"And *you* are?"

"Dana..."

"Nancy," she said, putting both her palms up.

We both stopped talking. Dana, Stella, and Russell. Nancy, Stella, and Russell. Nancy, Dana, and Russell. Triangles bumping into each other.

"I'm no threat to his marriage," I said. "I never was."

"But you thought about it," Dana said, turning her palms over, as if offering me her hands.

Basic rule of courtroom interrogation: Never ask a question unless you already know the answer. Dana knew what I would say, if I were honest.

"I thought about it. For awhile, not recently. I thought I loved him," I said, my hands folded in my lap.

Dana was obviously pleased. "It's okay," she said. "I understand. I understand completely."

"But he never loved me. He cared for me, I know that now, but he never loved me."

Dana nodded, sliding her hands toward me, but I kept my hands folded. Seeing me hesitate, she said, "You have to trust me. I do understand."

"I don't understand it, Dana. How can you?"

"I do."

"This is not the conversation I had planned, Dana, you know that, don't you. I had wanted to help Russell, not confess to one of my students about...other things."

"Russell will be fine," she said. "I told him a long time ago I didn't care that much about being valedictorian. Told him that changing the rules was dumb and unfair to everyone else. And I know enough about the system to know that he won't get it done, not this year to help me. But, Nancy, taking those courses over *is* important to me. I'm going to do that, for me. April will probably be valedictorian, probably. But, I'll be truthful. I'd love to end up with a higher GPA than her. Who knows, I might even beat her fair and square under the old rules. Doesn't matter in the long run, but it would be nice."

She was about to take my hands in hers, but the baby started crying. She jerked her head around to that corner of the room, looked back at me, and then got up and walked over to the couch, singing softly, "Tessy Tessy Tessy, mama's little messy. Tessy Tessy Tessy."

She sat on the couch and began nursing, her eyes closed as she hummed songs I had never heard. I found myself staring at the baby. Tess was small and pale. I could see that from where I was sitting. But I wanted to look for something else, so I went over and sat beside Dana on the couch.

Without opening her eyes, Dana said, "Do me a favor. Get a cloth out of that bag over there."

Putting the cloth in her hands, I looked at Dana's face. She lifted Tess off her breast and wiped her own blouse and then Tess's face. Nursing her child, she looked very different than when she had made me confess earlier. She now seemed utterly defenseless to me. This Dana was herself a child.

"You know," she said, opening her eyes and seeing me stare, "this is the only time that I think I'm a good mother. Most of the other times, I feel like I'm cheating her. Sometimes, I think I'll lose her when we stop doing this. That's the main reason I hate school now, having to be away from her. Does that make sense?"

I studied the child's face, especially the eyes with dark circles underneath; the nose, the ears, the cheeks, the eyebrows. All I could see in that face was Dana.

"Go ahead and ask," she said, smiling at me and gently patting Tess's back. "Everybody else already has."

"About the father?"

"Who killed Kennedy and who's the father of Dana's baby...the only important questions in American history. Go ahead, Nancy, I don't mind."

"You won't tell me anyway, will you?" I said.

"Of course not. But I'll do something for you that I wouldn't do for anybody else. I'll tell you who's *not* the father."

"Russell?"

She took a deep breath, and Tess seemed to float upward as her mother's lungs filled with air, "Russell Stewart Parsons is not the father of Theresa Mary O'Connor. Never was, never will be."

"You okay?" was all I could say at that moment.

Dana was crying. "Oh, Nancy, I wish he was her father. Hell, sometimes I wish he was *my* father," was the last thing either one of us said for a long time.

210

As I sat there in the darkening room, I came to a conclusion about the father of Dana's child. Something about Dana was becoming clear, not any word she said, but something. Whomever it was, he had not been gentle, and he had not been her choice.

Back home, I was in one of those moods I had tried for years to deny. I was outside of myself again, me flaying me. Before I became a teacher, my life seemed simple. I had been alone. I took care of myself. I was responsible for no one else. I wrote reviews, but the process was simple. I read a book, and I wrote about it. I never read more than one book at a time. Sometimes I could read a two pound book over the weekend. The review writing took a day, and then I revised for a few more days. In between writing a review, I read lots of other books, but that process was linear. One book had my attention, it was finished, and then I read another. I liked the sequential neatness of my life: choose a book, read the book, go to another book. A sense that I was in control.

Teaching wasn't like that. Teaching was Chaos. If Dana and Russell were a book, so was Dell. So were April and her mother, Dylan and his father. Before, a book waited for me to pick it up. Not with teaching. The stories kept imposing themselves on me. Some stories were simpler and shorter, like Fred or Jackie the Smoker. I tried to explain it to Kris but she didn't understand. Not until the right book analogy came along. These stories were not in print, I told Kris. They were more modern. They were audio-books. Like dozens of cassettes playing all at once, the volume on some louder than others, and the volumes shifting so that one story drowned out the others at one moment but then fading as another swelled, but they were all there regardless, being told as if each thought itself the only story. Each student was like a story, but I couldn't listen to them all, so some were never heard. But, unlike books that could be picked up at my leisure when I made time for them, these stories were being told whether or not I was listening, and the tapes could not be stopped or rewound. Some were just a hum, white noise, in the background. If I could shut out Dana, I might hear Dell more clearly, or some of the other stories, but it would be like walking into a movie an hour after it started.

So my life before teaching was simpler. The only real book I had been reading was me, the only story I was hearing had been mine. Henry Adams had a hundred readers. I had one.

Body Art

Education is an admirable thing, but it is well to remember from time to time that nothing that is worth knowing can be taught.—Oscar Wilde

When Dell asked me where I wanted him to take me to dinner, I pointed out that it was not a date and that I would pay for my own meal.

"Nancy, you don't have to find me irresistible just because I spring for a steak...you do eat meat, don't you, or are you one of those carrot fanatics...but I'd feel better if you let it be my treat. You know, guy thing, like holding the door open for you," he said outside my classroom.

"Okay, you can pay," I said, "if you let me pick out the restaurant."

"You are so easy. See you tonight at seven, after practice."

"Dell, I'll pick you up. I'll drive. You mind going to a place I know in Gainesville?"

"You are such a tight-ass," he laughed, rolling his eyes. "I'll be sitting on my porch. Don't be late."

We went to *Flamingo Room*.

Dell was mystified. Two drinks down, he told me why. "This just doesn't look like a place you would ever go to. It's too...something."

"I thought you would like it," I said.

"Nancy, don't be a tease. Leave that to the kids. You say something like that, you know I have to ask you why you said it. You keep deflecting things away from yourself. Why?"

The restaurant was still cheaply decadent. Still the red curtains, the dim lights, the discreetly scurrying waiters. The only difference was the music. Still quietly in the background, but some sort of elevator music jazz ballads instead of opera arias. Still the same shadowy couples, but Dell and I were the only black and white lovers, as surely we must have seemed to the others around us, and all of us, Dell and I included, were leaning toward our partners across small tables, the white tablecloths the brightest things in the room, a room that could have held many more tables, tables now far enough apart so that none of us had to whisper for fear of being overheard.

"Dell, I brought you here mainly because I didn't think we would see anyone we knew. You *do* have a reputation."

"That's it? That's the reason we're here?"

"Mainly," I insisted.

"You're embarrassed being seen with me?" he asked, tilting his head to one side.

"Doesn't it bother you, what people say about you?"

"That I sleep around with students? Is that what I do, so you're afraid to be seen with me?"

"I'm not afraid."

"Embarrassed?"

"I'm not embarrassed."

"Uncomfortable?"

"Why are you trying to deflect things off you, and back on me? Isn't that what you accused me of?"

"Nancy, you know why I was surprised you brought me here?" Dell started softly tapping the table with his fork, waving off a waiter who was approaching.

"*Do* you sleep with your students?" I interrupted.

He ignored me. "You know why you don't fit in here?"

"You didn't answer my question," I said.

"Your question can wait. You want the truth about me, you can have it. Right now, I'm going to tell you the difference between you and me. Between you and most of the people around you. How unlike you are to this room."

"Dell, can you be any more cryptic! Now I'm unlike a room. How am I supposed to interpret *that?*"

The fingers of his left hand were trembling, so he pushed them flat on the table, and I could see the tips almost turn white with the pressure he was applying. "Wait a minute," he said, his voice tightening.

"You were taking the lead on this dance and now you want me to wait on you," I snapped at him. "How am I..." I stopped. Dell's jaw was clinched, his fingers still pushing into the tablecloth, but then he slowly relaxed and let out a deep breath. "You okay?" I asked.

"Fine, now," he said, picking up his wine glass and looking around for a waiter. "The problem with this place is they don't have any waitresses. Too many gay men."

"Dell, what's wrong with you?"

"Sorry, didn't mean to insult my diverse brothers."

"Quit it. Quit being so glib. Tell me what's wrong with you, physically."

"Nancy, I'm physically turning to shit. That's what's wrong with me. And I want to kill somebody because of it. Right now, Bob Skinner is heading my list. You keep asking me and I might bump you up on the same list. That's part of the truth, but you don't know me well enough for me to tell you the whole truth."

"Does anybody?"

"Nancy, forget me for a second. You know your problem?" he said, putting one hand over the other to make a time-out sign. "You haven't got a body."

How was I supposed to respond to *that*?

"It all goes back to this room. This room is not where you belong because this room is full of people who have bodies. Hell, this room is a body itself. With a touch and a taste and a smell, on a good night you can probably hear this room moan. And you're right, even if you didn't know why. This is a room I like. I like it because I like my body. I don't think you like yours. And, Nancy sweet Golden Adams, lots of women would trade their bodies for yours in a split second. Fact is, your body's wasted on you."

Sometimes I wished I were like Kris. She would have had a response for Dell at that moment. Something to stop him cold, and then to tease him back to life. Me, I could have told Dell about a lot of times my body wasn't wasted on anybody. But I was drinking, something I hadn't done in weeks, and I had a nagging suspicion that Dell might be right. Would I admit it to him? Not a chance.

"Dell, you want to know what I was thinking about as I drove you here? I was wondering if you were going to find some excuse to casually touch me. And you don't think I know I have a body!"

"How'd you feel about that, Nancy? You want me to guess. I'm guessing you didn't want me to, did you?"

"Dell, you know what I'm sick of? I'm sick of seeing every television ad or stupid tv sitcom tell me that the only way I'll be happy is if I'm having sex twenty-four hours a day. I'm tired of people vomiting up their every dirty little secret on some talk show. I'm tired of people prying into my private life or assuming they can make me happy by fixing me up with some desperately love-starved friend of theirs. I'm just about..."

"The biggest hypocrite in the world," he said, calling time-out again. "You want people to leave you alone but you're always trying to figure other people out, to get inside their heads, analyze *their* problems. You want to know about me, but you want to sit back and keep yourself to yourself. But you can't do it, not here in this job in this world, with your students and the rest of us..."

"Dell, do you want to sleep with me?"

"Go to bed with you?"

"Yeah, all the euphemisms, all of them, do you want that?"

"Of course," he said, smiling. "I did the first time I saw you, at my mother's house. I would have done the deed upstairs while the kids were watching tv in the living room. But then I got to know you. All your distance and thinking and self-doubt. Even your over-educated irony. And I also figured out that you didn't want to go to bed with me, that was clear, me or anybody else. Well, except maybe for Russell, but that's not going to happen. Nancy, I like you. I hope you get happy. But I don't have enough time to put my body next to a woman who lost her body a long time ago. I don't have the time to help you find yourself."

"Dell, you talk like you've got some terminal disease, like you're going to die."

"No, I'm not dying. I'll be breathing a long time," he said, but he wasn't smiling, and he wasn't looking at me.

"Why did you say that about me and Russell?" I asked.

He gave me one of those chin-down, eye-rolling ask-a-dumb-question looks that students always gave their teachers. "Russell is my best friend, I know how you feel about him."

"How I felt, past tense, that's all Russell knows. I never told him, but he knew. But not now. I don't think he's got a clue."

"So, you don't want to hear any more about yourself from me? You just want to hear about Russell?" he said.

"You want to know what I really like about this exact moment?" I asked, changing the subject and wanting him to agree with me.

He nodded.

"I feel like I'm having an adult conversation. Does that make sense? As if this matters, even if you are full of crap about me. I lived by myself for so long, and now I'm surrounded by children, and my soon to be former best friend Kris seems more and more unrelated to me the past few months. I talk to Russell, but he still keeps this wall around him. Your mother, as much as I like her, she talks to me like a daughter," provoking a laugh and a nod from him, "and everyone else seems so busy. Russell keeps telling me to give you a chance, that there's more to you than your sex life. And I think I know what he means, here and now."

Dell cleared his throat and raised his hand like he was in one of my classes. "Teacher," he said. "You asked about me sleeping with my students. The answer's...yes, but..."

"You're a fool, Dell Rose," I said quickly. "A lucky fool, but a fool still the same. All I can tell you is that next month Ashley Prose and I are laying out the new policy to the faculty...and you... you're headed for big trouble. And the way the court cases are going, Russell being your friend won't save you. He'll protect the school because he has to, but you won't make it possible for him to protect you."

"Won't happen, Nancy. I've never propositioned anybody, never touched anybody in school, never done most of that stuff you hear about. My biggest problem is that I just can't say no when somebody makes me an offer. I just can't say no."

"Oh, Dell, you can't be that naive. Facts don't matter in things like this. Perceptions matter. As soon as the policy is adopted, all it will take is some little girl who just doesn't like your smile and she'll start screaming hostile environment to her parents, and Betsy Elizondo will jump on you like you were the embodiment of every male sex organ in America. You've gotten away with it for..."

"Because, Nancy dear, and here, to use your lovely phrase, is the dirty little secret about all that harassment pudding, I am an attractive *single* man. And that statement has nothing to do with ego. You think I haven't thought about this before? I know for a fact that sexual harassment complaints are overwhelmingly against married men. Usually older married men. Me, I know my audience. I never make the first move. Girls, women, *they* seek me out."

"Jesus, Dell, that sounds so calculating, and delusional. You can't seriously believe you're safe, can you? Handsome or single, you're still a black man in a southern high school full of white southern belles. Forget what I said about this being an adult conversation. You're incredibly dumb. Forget about the harassment policy. Just be an adult. Stop screwing girls. Are you afraid of women?"

"No, Nancy, I'm not afraid of them. My real problem is that they're like a drug."

"Women, Dell, not girls."

"For the record, I haven't slept with a woman under twenty-one in five years. Not one Kennedy female student. Lots of former students, a few mothers here and there."

"I don't believe you."

"You not believing doesn't change the truth."

"And that's the problem. Dell, I like you. I want you to be safe. I want to believe you, but I don't. And if your friends don't believe you, what do you expect others to believe? That you're just misunderstood or misperceived?"

"Nancy, do you like sex?"

"Dell, this conversation is not about me!"

"Funny, I thought it was," he said. "You're an attractive, single, intelligent, articulate woman. When's the last time you had sex? The last time you had sex just for the sake of having sex? The pleasure of it."

"I am not like you."

"Never? Too bad."

"No, no, no, it's not too bad. You're wrong about me. I could tell you stories about me after my husband died, about me and men and nights, and days, about stupid mindless fu... stupid mindless sex. But that's my past, and that's my private life. And I'm not the one with the problem here. You are."

"Forget sex, Nancy. You ever do anything physical in your life? Did you ever feel like you were your body and nothing else, not a mind or a soul, just your body? That you were your *body*?"

"Is that a jock question, Dell?"

"You don't have to be a jock, you just got to be alive."

"Dell, you know the flaw here, don't you? What's wrong with loving your own body. It goes away eventually. You get older and gravity wins. Exercise all you want to, the only thing that happens when you get older, if you work at it, is that you get smarter. From what people have been telling me about you, from what I've seen, that's not happening in your case."

We had already eaten dinner and had two drinks. I wanted a third at that moment, breaking my self-imposed limit. For almost two hours we had enjoyed each other as long as we did not talk about each other. We gossiped, we talked about basketball, complained about our students. We talked about why we had both decided to study history in college, our favorite history books, our favorite historians, how we both liked Barbara Tuchman and Richard Hofstader, and we disagreed about Howard Zinn. I told him all about how Russell had encouraged me to submit my first review. How Russell and I had kept in touch over the years. I even told him about how I met Jack Vandergriff and how Jack died. Dell told me about his mother, his brothers and sisters. He even told me stories about my own mother. I listened to him, thinking that I would eventually know more about my mother than my father. I told him that, and he told me to ask his mother about Charles Adams, how they had worked together years ago to integrate the Fort Jackson school system and to get the bond issues passed to build the new schools. It had been a thoroughly pleasant dinner for the two of us until the only topic was us.

"Nancy, I don't think you'll understand me," he said, after a noticeable silence. "I used to be really good at sports. I was good enough at football to be all-state..."

"Oh, Dell, I certainly remember that. I saw you play against us. You were a...marvel."

"Yes, I *were* that...I were a marvel."

"Stop it! You're too smart to be one of those pathetic over the hill jocks who sits around in his letter jacket moaning about his glory days. Don't act like a cliché."

The music had changed. Dell noticed as soon as I did. "Charlie Haden," he said. "I've got this at home. Love that sound. You like?"

"Sure, I like," I said. "You want another drink before we head back, one for the road?"

"You going to be able to drive?"

"I'll be fine. Your mother will be proud of both of us. And, Dell, I didn't mean to jump all over you just now."

We had two more drinks instead of one. The second was our substitution for dessert. I was beginning to feel like I did the first time I had been there, a cloudy buzz in my head, to feel that this place was a wonderful escape, and Dell's eyes were getting a little glazed themselves.

"Basketball was my game," he began again, waving his hand to stop me from interrupting. "I was more than marvelous. I was magic. I didn't understand it myself. Sometimes, in a tight game, I knew I would make the winning shot. It was my secret. Like my feet weren't on the ground. I could float past the mortal fool who thought he was guarding me and I would push that damn ball into space and I could see the line it was traveling to the basket. See it, like some sort of red laser beam from my hand to the net and the ball never strayed. It just stayed on that red line. Every moment has its moment. I knew the game was over before anybody else did. Nancy, there was no better feeling. There was no drug that could do that for me. And I know, I know, I accept the fact that those days are gone. I really do. Part of the pleasure of coaching now, I know, is that sometimes I see that feeling in the boys I teach, and I can live vicariously through them."

"So, why aren't you at peace with it, Dell. You tell me you accept it, but there's something wrong here."

"I know you won't understand this, but listen anyway. You worry about me sleeping around. You're probably right. I know that I've been a lot more careless the past year. But the only thing that ever came close to that moment on the court when I was completely my body, the only thing comparable was touching a woman."

"Dell, I can't..."

"You *can* be quiet," he almost pleaded. "Just listen to me. Touching a woman, touching and seeing and tasting and smelling a woman...there's nothing like it. If I'm pathetic, your word, it's because I'm like a junkie looking for a fix. But the high, the high of the fix. Not just the finish, the whole long extended moment. The delirious happy pleasure of feeling the woman I'm with share the same eternal moment. Oh, Nancy, I never rush that moment because I'm always afraid I'll never be able to do it again. See, that's what I don't think you'll understand. If I didn't have that to look forward to, I don't think living is worth the effort. Can you understand that?"

I looked at him, wondering if he had always had those words in his mind and had just been waiting for the right audience, wondering if he had ever said it all before. "No, Dell, I don't understand. You deserve an honest answer. I don't understand. I think...I think you're wrong. There's more to life than sex."

He looked down at his wine glass, watching the dark liquid swirl as he slowly tilted the glass back and forth. He was still looking at the wine when he said, "You weren't listening. I wasn't talking about sex."

"I wasn't listening?" I said, resisting my first urge to laugh. "You could have fooled me."

He shook his head, "I was talking about being alive."

I was drunk. So was Dell. It was like we were both twenty again, on our third date, comfortable enough to tell the other person all our young profound thoughts about life, trying to explain ourselves to each other and perhaps to ourselves. I was the virgin girl. Dell was the experienced boy. I was fascinated and frightened by him. I had grown up avoiding boys like him. But I was away from home now, on my own.

"Can you drive?" I finally said.

"No problem," he smiled across the table at me.

I handed him my keys, "Good, you be the boy. You drive."

We walked to the cloak room, my arm through his and me leaning against him for support. As he was helping me put on my coat, I looked back into the dimly lit room.

Dana O'Connor, I was sure, was sitting at a corner table with an older man. Her hair was tied high on her head, and she was wearing too much makeup. She had on a dark dress that plunged low in the front, and the man was lighting a cigarette in her mouth. She was looking directly at me.

I fell back against Dell. He put his hands on my arms to hold me up, laughing kindly, "Nancy, you got to get in a twelve-step program."

"Dell, look over there, in that corner. Who do you see?"

He held me steady and stared into the room. Standing behind me, he seemed to take a long time before he replied, "People, just people. Am I supposed to see somebody we know? We been outed?"

"You don't see Dana O'Connor in the corner, that woman with the older man?" I was adamant.

He looked again, pausing before he spoke, "Nope, that's not Dana, and the guy's not much older than her. I better get you home. Next thing, you'll tell me you see Russell, too."

Dell was right, I knew that. I needed to go home. I took one more look at the woman in the corner. She looked back at me and then turned her attention back to the man she was with, nodding at something he was saying. Sure, I was wrong. It couldn't be Dana.

Outside, Dell opened the car door for me, putting something in my hand as I eased past him. "Put this in your souvenir collection. Something to remember me by."

Sitting by myself in the front seat as he walked around to get in the driver's side, I looked at the matchbook in my hand. On the pink cover in teal lettering was printed: *THE FLAMINGO ROOM—Discreet Dining for Discerning People.*

"One last question," he said as he slid behind the wheel. "You do *not* have a thing for Russell? Am I right?"

"Absolutely right," I said softly.

He looked straight ahead and smiled. "Good. Just needed to make sure. And now I'll drive Miss Daisy home."

I was alone on the boat dock near my house. The moon was hidden by clouds, so it was too dark to see the St. Johns, but I could hear the river flow past me. I sat on a bench, wondering if the water was warm enough to go swimming. Wondering why I was working so hard to keep myself safe from Dell. I was actually be-ginning to want to see him away from school. But he had so much baggage, and he didn't want what I wanted. I wanted to trust him, and I wanted to touch him. But I couldn't trust him, not now, now soon, not with those demons that controlled his life. And I couldn't change him.

I had told him the truth. I was tired of everyone assuming that all I needed was a man. Dell wasn't like any other man I had known since Jack died, but Jack had destroyed something about me that I was only now missing. If I had told Dell the complete truth, I would have said that as soon as I believed I was the only woman he was interested in, then everything would be different. But that would have been to let my guard down. The real truth was, I was tired of being alone. I was tired of not being in love, and I was tired of thinking too much. I had grown up a long time ago, and I was tired of feeling old.

Hostile Environment

In the first place, God made idiots. That was for practice.
Then he made school boards.—Mark Twain

Even though Agnes had volunteered to help present the new sexual harassment policy, she quietly refused to work with me after Ashley also volunteered. She had "schedule conflicts" every time I called her. Actually, I discovered, Agnes's help wasn't needed. Most of the policy language was boilerplate lifted from other schools, and I let Ashley tinker with some nouns and verbs, but we seldom disagreed.

Ashley was very pleased when I agreed to let her take the lead in the actual presentation to the faculty. I didn't tell her that I had a perverse pleasure in anticipating how she would handle Jerry and Dell, especially when she tried to explain *hostile environment.*

The only area where we had a substantial disagreement was in the actual grievance process, the steps a person had to go through to make a complaint. Ashley wanted the complaint to go directly to the district Office of Equal Opportunity, to be reviewed by the OEO and a school board subcommittee. The OEO, I protested, should only be involved in those cases that couldn't be resolved at a lower level. A fact-finding inquiry might not always be necessary, I said, when a third party, usually the principal, could mediate. Any second complaint against the same person, I agreed, should go directly to the OEO. I was obviously behind the curve.

Ashley had an unbeatable rebuttal, "This is the way Liz wants it. She wants a record of everything. Of course, confidentiality will be guaranteed."

"Of course," I said. "And, let me guess, Betsy Elizondo is on the subcommittee."

"Liz *is* the subcommittee," Ashley replied, with a look that told me that she and I had been working four hours on a policy that Betsy Elizondo had already written by herself.

"So, Ashley, why are we doing this?" I asked. "Why are we going through the motions, wasting our time?"

"I'm not wasting my time. If you feel like you've been wasting yours, I'm sorry. But, Liz feels strongly that the process of adopting this policy is just as important as the policy itself. In fact, I'm sure you'll agree, with your appreciation of history, that sometimes process *is* policy. She wants public and faculty input so that the policy has legitimacy. She's a great believer in quality circle team management. She's merely facilitating that process."

"I can't wait to hear what Dell says when you tell him that he has been facilitated by Betsy Elizondo," I said, shaking my head, looking down and trying not to laugh.

"Dell has as much right to contribute to this debate as anyone else," Ashley said without a trace of irony.

A week later, in the Kennedy cafeteria after school, Ashley and I sat at a table in front of the faculty and support staff. Russell had personally gone to every adult employee of Kennedy and made it clear that their attendance was required, even the teacher aides and Darrell the janitor.

Agnes delivered on her promise to provide refreshments. As everyone filed in they passed a table weighted down with donuts, cakes, candy, rolls, buns, pies, soft drinks, coffee, tea, lemonade, and four milk options: whole white, low-fat white and chocolate, and skim milk. She stood next to the table and insisted that everyone take a napkin and fill the paper plate she handed them. Even I had to sit at the front table with my plate full.

The first half hour of Ashley's presentation passed without a word from her audience. I had told Russell to tell Dell to be quiet. He agreed that everything that was said in this meeting would probably go directly back to Betsy, and Dell's ice was already thin enough.

The problem was, I realized later, that after thirty minutes of snacking, enough sugar was racing through a hundred healthy adults to kill an army of diabetics. Everybody had come to the meeting with an empty stomach, and nobody turned down Agnes's heaping plates. Only Russell had abstained.

I had eaten two donuts and finished a Coke, and I found myself trying to tap out Harry Nilsson's "Me and My Arrow" on the table in front of me. I hadn't been listening to Ashley, and, looking at the crowd in front of me, I suspected I wasn't alone.

Agnes raised her hand.

"Ashley, I understand how all this relates to conduct between the adults, and conduct of teachers around students, but are you seriously proposing that we have a sexual harassment policy for student-student relationships?"

I snapped to attention. Ashley had agreed to save that discussion for a later meeting because it was all too vague right now. It wasn't on the rough draft we all had in front of us, but Ashley had now introduced it anyway. "The courts will be expecting us to have a policy and guidelines. And, please remember, Agnes, this is not *my* proposal. It's from the board."

Agnes turned to me. "Is that right?"

I tried to be diplomatic. "Yes, the board is trying to catch up with the rest of the districts."

"That's not what I asked," she shot back. I was puzzled. I had never seen Agnes hostile. "I asked specifically about the part about the children having the ability to file charges against each other."

"You mean the girls against the boys," somebody muttered behind me.

"The courts will..." Ashley began to say, and at that moment I saw the meeting start to implode.

Dell stood up. I tried to make eye contact with him, to tell him to sit down, but he said, "Ash... ," his new pet name for her, which she had already told him not to use, "...can I file a complaint against some of these girls who are harassing me?"

Howls of laughter, as Dell expected. I looked for Russell to stop this before it got out of hand, but he was standing in the corner, arms folded across his chest, letting Dell hang himself.

"Franklin," Ashley said dryly, provoking more moans than laughs, "anybody can file any complaint as long as they follow the rules. If *your* work environment becomes hostile because a student behaves inappropriately toward you, then you should absolutely file a complaint and pursue a remedy."

"Suppose, just for the sake of supposing," he said, "suppose that girl I complain about, she counter-files, says I harassed her first. Who are you gonna believe?"

"That wouldn't be my decision. I'm not involved in the process."

"Of course not, Ash. That wasn't my point. The *you* I'm talking about is the process. Who does the process favor?"

"This process does not play favorites."

A collective groan, and I saw small groups of teachers whispering back and forth, arguing among themselves. Russell was still silent. Agnes kept looking at me. Jerry stood up, but Dell didn't sit down.

"I want to go back to that definition of hostile environment," Jerry said. "I mean, that's the core issue here, isn't it?"

Unlike Dell, Jerry's tone was not adversarial, and I was glad he was trying to bring us back to the most troubling part of the policy, the part that had the potential for the most misunderstanding.

"With or without a policy, we're adults here and we should be able to agree that some things are clearly taboo," he said. "Teachers don't date their students. Teachers don't offer better grades for sex.

Teachers don't even socialize, however pristinely, with individual students away from school. Teachers don't touch their students."

He paused there and turned back to Agnes. "I know, Agnes, you and I have talked about this. You disagree because you're a toucher. I've even seen you take a comb to one of your students. But I don't think *that* freedom is going to last here or anywhere else."

Agnes was quiet, but she shook her head. Not in disagreement, I thought, but in disappointment. Her son, however, disagreed.

"Jerry, if this process was fair, you'd be right. But you know as well as I do that my mother can put her arm around any male student she wants to, but as soon as *you* put your arm around a female student your reasonable backside will be toast. My mother can tell one of her boys he's 'looking mighty fine this morning' and get a smile. You say the same thing to some girl who's got a grudge on you and your reasonable backside will be burnt toast."

"Franklin, you seem to be overly sensitive to this issue," Ashley started to say, with a not so subtle sneer in her voice. "You don't seem to understand that this policy is designed to protect everyone."

I stood up. If for nothing else, to save Ashley from being murdered. "You're right, Ashley, of course," I began, waiting for Dell and Jerry to sit down, and then waiting a few seconds more to let Ashley know that I expected her to sit down as well. "This is designed to protect us all. But, we can be honest with each other here in this room," knowing what I was saying would be relayed to Betsy Elizondo within an hour. "Up until a few years ago, most women teachers and female students put up with a lot of...a lot of crap from the men and boys around them."

Sue Rollins was nodding vigorously and punching the woman next to her. Other women in front of me were also nodding. I couldn't see Ashley behind me, but I knew that she was nodding as well, nodding with more attitude than most of the others.

"You guys," I continued, panning the room, "have been insufferable. This is 1996. None of this ought to be news to you. Am I right?" Before anybody could respond, I said, "This is not a dialogue right now. And I don't want to hear any jokes about our recently re-elected President."

Jerry mimicked Clinton's bent thumbs-up salute, but I was the only person to see him do it. I looked at him for a split second, I then focused on Russell, now standing behind everyone else. Only Ashley and I could see him.

"But, as I said, let's be honest. Jerry's also right. We're adults. We should be able to control our own actions and do the right thing. Times have changed, and common sense has to change with them. Did I say we ought to be honest with ourselves? But, if we do now...admit the truth...then Dell's right. This policy is objectively neutral and subjectively biased."

I looked at Russell, but he was looking at Ashley behind me. I knew he would tell me later how Ashley was reacting. As I stood there, I began to make mental notes about the faces in front of me. In the months since school had started, I was beginning to know the people in that room well enough to predict who would support Russell's educational proposals, who would support his other proposals, who was agreeing with me at that moment. I could feel Ashley stiffen behind me, and Russell was trying to hide a smile at the back of the room. Dell was nodding but looking down at the floor. Even Bob Skinner, no friend of Dell or Russell, was nodding grimly.

"This policy is payback for a few centuries of abuse," I said, "but that doesn't make it wrong. It's biased against men because men have been the problem. I know, I know, not any of you... the mature guys in this room," trying to slip a split second glance at Dell without being obvious. "The other guys. You're paying for their sins. But if you've got a lick of sense you'll see that Jerry is right. Some things are absolutely unacceptable. Propositioning, touching, openly admiring the young breasts of your female students..." I paused to let that word sink in, knowing it would make a few people in front of me uncomfortable. "...*and* the mature breasts of your fellow teachers."

I knew I would get a laugh with that last line. I also wondered if Dell would try to respond, but he was silent. Instead, Jerry raised his hand.

"Nancy, am I missing a page of the handout? The one that defines mature?"

I knew I had given *somebody* a straight line, and I was glad it was Jerry because he could say it in a way that Dell couldn't. Jerry was on my side. I knew that.

"Thanks for setting up my next point, Jerry," I said. "About humor. Teacher school 101 should have taught us that most students have no sense of irony. All those harmless cute lines you guys think are so obviously funny are going right over most of these kids' heads. Or, worse, being misinterpreted. So, stop being so cute. All of you."

Jerry rubbed a finger across his lips.

"On the other hand," I said, "all of us who are adults...mature... ought to have a sense of humor and cut ourselves some slack. If you're genuinely offended by somebody, tell them face to face. If they don't change, then you can make a federal case out of it. Work it out among yourselves before you go hire David O'Leary...," instantly realizing that almost nobody knew who I was talking about, "...I mean, before you start filing a lawsuit."

Agnes raised her hand. "But, Nancy, about the students complaining about themselves?"

"That's not part of this proposal," I said, hoping that Ashley behind me was embarrassed. Hoping, not really expecting. "That's not to say that something like it might not be coming. My suggestion is that we act like parents and not let the students...male or female...harass each other when we're around. Let's face facts, sexual teasing is a requirement for adolescence. But I think we can draw a clear line between raging teenage hormones and genuine abuse."

I knew that Ashley had reached the end of her proverbial rope. She *had* to respond to that last statement. In front of me, I could see Dell and Jerry and a dozen other men in the room start grinding their teeth as Ashley stood up.

"With all due respect," she began without coming around to stand beside me or to face me, "my experience as an educator...,"

I could hear Agnes almost snort at the idea that Ashley had any experience.

"...has led me to understand that our role requires more than just filling our students with information. We have to have behavioral as well as intellectual expectations for them. Every adolescent psychologist will tell you that the younger we get to these students the better chance we have at shaping their adult behavior."

"I agree," I said, still facing the group in front of me, not looking at Ashley. I could see eyes shifting back and forth, from me to Ashley behind me, back and forth waiting for the next volley. I made eye contact with Russell in the back, and then Jerry in the front. They had been watching me throughout the entire exchange.

"That was not my impression," Ashley finally said.

"No, I really do," I said. "But we need to do it even before high school, and we need to do it without turning girls into victims and boys into villains. That's my point. I'm not sure a sexual harassment policy doesn't do that when it comes to the hostile environment section. Even between adults, but especially with students. *That's* my point."

I stood there waiting for Ashley to respond, listening for her to take a deep breath. Just when I thought she was about to open her mouth, Russell spoke from the back of the room.

"This is not going as well as I had hoped. I appreciate the work that Nancy and Ashley have done, but I'm not sure we can resolve anything today. I'll arrange another meeting, perhaps in smaller groups, and then another group meeting. Then..."

"Russell." Ashley almost shouted, "I have two more pages to cover."

"And you'll get to cover it at the next meeting, I promise," he said.

"I would like a vote on your motion," she said firmly.

"I don't recall making a motion," he said, less kindly.

Bob Skinner spoke, "I'll second Ashley's motion."

"I'll second Russell's motion," Dell immediately said.

"Whose motion was first?" Sue Rollins asked.

"Who's on first?" Jerry said.

I frowned at him, then smiled, and the shrug of his shoulders told me that he thought we were all past comedy and approaching farce, again.

"There are no motions on the table," Russell said dryly. "But, if...if a majority of us want to continue this, I will be glad to step back. Is that what you want?" he said as everyone turned around to face him.

"I'm outta here," Dell said, but I knew that he wasn't the support that Russell needed at that moment.

I was fascinated by the inability of the people in front of me to make a decision. It had only been a few seconds since he gave them a choice, but everyone seemed to be waiting for someone else to make the first move.

"Russell's right," I said, folding the papers in my hand. Then, before anyone else spoke, I walked out of the cafeteria by myself.

The Games Boys Play

I read Shakespeare and the Bible, and I can shoot dice. That's
what I call a liberal education.—Tallulah Bankhead

When I was a senior at Kennedy, basketball was a short season,
described by me in the school paper as "the shorter of two evils."
I thought it was a wonderful pun, but Coach Grimsby and the
basketball coach both went to my mother demanding an apology.
Frances Adams told them to go see her daughter, but the two men
never confronted me. Russell, I heard later, told them in a faculty
meeting that they should worry more about seventeen-point losses

than seventeen year old girls.

Dell Rose changed all that. It took him two years to get a winning record, but since then his teams had never lost more than five games in a season. The reasons for his success were simple, his famous three C's: Coaching, Concentration, and Conditioning. Those were his public explanations, but there was another simple reason for Dell's success, a reason he admitted but did not turn into scripture.

He recruited the best players in the county. He even lured potential stars in from other counties whose parents might work somewhere else but who just coincidentally moved into Fort Jackson County. After Dell started coaching at Kennedy, the downtown Jackson basketball team, which had always humiliated Kennedy, never came close to winning. Dell would scout seventh and eighth grade games, spotting future talent and then start talking to their parents. Even though most black kids in Fort Jackson County could seldom make the fifteen-mile drive from downtown to Kennedy High School, transportation was somehow always available if you could shoot baskets.

But that was only raw material. Everyone agreed that Dell was the best high school coach in Florida. His teams were in better condition than their opponents, and they played defense better than they played offense. Every year, at least one of his starters was all-state. Dell's favorite statistic, however, was less publicized. Every year, his teams were called for fewer fouls than the year before, setting a state record that other coaches thought impossible. That, as he told his audiences, was what concentration meant.

The reward for Kennedy was a district championship every year and state championships in 1987, 88, 92, 93, and 96. Two year cycles, with 1997 a foregone conclusion for most fans. The rewards for his players, in addition to the usual female adulation, were scholarships. The big stars always went to big schools. Even his lesser players were scouted by small schools, so their college education at some level was almost a guarantee if they could play for him.

The standard joke at Kennedy was that Grimsby coached high school football, but Dell Rose coached professional basketball. Until I went to the first game, I never understood the distinction.

The pep rally was prologue. Unlike the morning football rally three months earlier, Dell had shifted the season-opening basketball rally to the hour immediately before the first game. You had to have game tickets to this rally because there were never enough seats for those who wanted in. Since it was held in the same gym as the game itself, the 300-ticket allotment for the visiting school was sometimes bought by the Kennedy booster club which offered them triple the printed price. Most schools declined, concerned about leaving their players like orphan Christians in the Kennedy lions den.

"Come early, come often," Dell had yelled at me as I left school that afternoon. "See what I mean about concentration, how much it's worth."

Jerry warned me about the change in Dell once basketball season began. "Nancy, watch out for the next few weeks. Dell isn't a gracious loser. Hell, he's not much of a gracious winner, either. Fact is, he wants more than just winning. You'll see tonight. It's personal with him. A test between him and the other coach. I remember watching him play years ago. He was so focused then, it was scary. And he's even more intense now. Me, I wouldn't want to coach against him. I even had some second thoughts about being his assistant coach. The game starts, he takes no prisoners."

Jerry was walking me to my car after school.

"Oh, Jerry, please don't tell me that easygoing Dell is one of those screaming coaches who runs up and down the sideline throwing towels, foaming at the mouth," I laughed.

"No, no, that's my job," Jerry smiled, opening my door for me. "I get to yell, but if I get too many technicals called against me I'm out of a job. Dell, he's not a screamer. And *that* is the scary thing. Dell whispers, that's all. He whispers and he points. But, I swear, I've seen it in practice. He'll point at a player and whisper, and that player hears him...or else. You watch it tonight, even with all the noise, our kids will hear every word he says. And you'll swear, that pointing finger of his is a loaded gun."

The game began at seven o'clock. The noise began at five-thirty. I sat with Agnes, who worked the concession stands at every other Kennedy athletic event, but not when her son was coaching. She was wearing solid Kennedy blue with a Kennedy gold scarf. She also had blue and gold mini-pompoms.

For the next hour I thought I was in one of those Soma drug orgies from *Brave New World*. All the standard music and dancing of any pep rally, but notched four octaves higher. And drums that never stopped beating, like the first morning of school. A smaller version of the symphony orchestra was at one end of the gym, the jazz band at the other, alternating with each other and then joining together on the same song. The smaller jazz band was behind the visitor's goal, and every so often they had to dodge a wayward shot from the visitors warm-up. The symphony orchestra would play abridged Aaron Copland or George Gershwin; the jazz band would counter with Duke Ellington or Glenn Miller, heavy on the trombones.

Kennedy basketball, especially this first game, had developed other traditions since Dell had arrived. All long hair, male or female, was in a ponytail. Hundreds of girls were in blue micro miniskirts; the boys were in gold t-shirts. Blue Knight plumed helmets were worn by the sophomores, foam rubber swords waved by the juniors, but it was the smell that was overpowering. In Dell's first year, a small group of senior girls all wore the same perfume to a game against the defending state champions. Kennedy was an obvious underdog, but they won. Dell bought those girls an ounce of the same perfume and asked them to wear it every game.

I had noticed the same smell in the halls a few times during the year, but at the game this night it seemed as if five hundred female bodies were pulsating with some fragrance that only Dell could have brewed. Russell had warned me, had told me to make sure I ate before I went to the game, had told me that he had had extra fans installed in the gym just to increase the ventilation, that he kept the air conditioning turned lower than usual for this first game, but I was still almost overwhelmed.

When I was in high school, a core group of malcontents had always refused to take sports seriously. Betsy Elizondo was their leader. She hated jocks and she always sat with her followers in one corner of the gym and refused to stand up and cheer even in those rare moments when Kennedy actually played well. She also refused to stand up for the National Anthem. Now, as school board chair, she tried to come to as many games as possible.

Getting ready for tonight's game, I scanned the crowd looking for apathy or insincerity. I knew some of my students were cultivating their own version of *I refuse to worship at the altar of maleness* identities. None of them were at the game tonight. The gym was full of true believers.

The closer to seven o'clock, the more intense the emotion. I tried to step back and watch everybody else, but I was soon rising with Agnes to my right and some glazed Kennedy parent to my left, swaying as we all leaned with the wave that would sweep the crowd.

I looked for Dell. His team was doing warmup drills, but Jerry was the only coach on the floor. Why did Kennedy only have eight players when the other team had fifteen, I wondered. Why did the other team look older than Kennedy's? Why were the Kennedy cheerleader uniforms tonight different from the uniforms they wore at the football pep rally? Shorter, tighter, more revealing. Why was the gym slowly getting darker? Why was Jerry wearing a suit instead of casual clothes? I wondered all this as I clapped along with the others, laughing at myself as I started yelling across the gym to Fred Stein, seeing him sitting next to Jackie the Smoker, wishing they were together, laughing to myself as I saw Dylan's father staring up at me from his seat two rows below, laughing to myself as I intentionally smiled at him and waved, knowing that he would misinterpret and then "process" all the way home that night, smiling to myself as I saw Sue Rollins with her arm around another pretty woman, happy to see most of my favorite students there, like huge Bobby Ray Dearing and even sad Bonnie Lynn Porter; others, all of them with springs in their bottoms. Russell was there too, flanked by his daughters, visiting from their parochial world, taking turns making their father smile.

Perhaps it was the smell, genuinely seductive perfume tinted with sweat. Perhaps the noise, the sound waves pounding into me and a thousand other bodies. All of us wanting to see the young men below, extensions of ourselves, to simply see them win a game. With my last rational brain wave before I gave myself over to that desire, I wanted to step outside of my body and say to Nancy Adams, *A few weeks ago you were in an empty church contemplating God and Henry Adams and now you're about to lose your voice yelling at teenage boys. Nancy, Nancy, how did you get here?* It was a good question, but I never got that far. The gym went completely black. In the dark, I could feel myself rising along with everyone else. Most of the others knew what was coming; I was about to be initiated.

"Ladies and Gentlemen," a booming bass voice jumped out of the public address system, "Kennedy High School is pleased to present the 1996-97 Knight basketball team!" Then the dark gym was flooded with red laser beams and white blinking strobe lights. On the wall across from me, a giant laser image of a Blue Knight helmet appeared, a single shaft of red light then went from one corner of the gym to the floor, forming an empty red circle. Then, as we all silently held our collective breath, the orchestra began "Thus Spake Zarathustra" and I felt like I was swelling up and about to explode unless I got some relief. I was giddy, like everyone else, suspended in anticipation because we all knew how that music ended, knew where we were being led. I thought to myself: *How utterly silly, how utterly contrived, how utterly perfect, and how dare Dell tell me that I had no body.* Then, with a final symphonic crescendo of horns and drums, Dell Rose stepped slowly into the red circle.

I screamed along with everyone else.

Dell raised both hands over his head, held them up for a few seconds, and then slowly lowered his right arm as he stepped out of the circle, leaving only that arm in the light, his hand palm up, and the announcer began: "Six-four senior guard Steve Beaumont..." and, with Dell's hand like a magician pointing to his assistants, two seniors and three juniors were introduced, in and out of the circle with thunderous applause.

With the last introduction, the gym was flooded with light again. It was more than showmanship, it was psychological warfare. From darkness to stark light again, all of us were disoriented. From visual deprivation to sensory overload, we went from focusing on single players in that circle to dozens of moving bodies all in sync throughout the gym. Motion in every direction, choreographed to begin as soon as the lights came back on. Pompom girls and cheerleaders, their tan legs in the air, others cartwheeling in front of the benches. The jazz band and orchestra playing Queen's "We Are The Champions" while marching up into the stands where seats had been reserved for them. The visitors were already beaten, and they knew it. Losing, however, was only the beginning. They thought they were there to only play a game. Everyone else was there for a party.

The Kennedy bench now had thirteen players. Dell had kept the starters out of sight during the pregame warmups. He had perfected his opening game over the years. First, he always scheduled a non-conference opponent who had never been to the Kennedy gym before. Whoever it was, they knew about Kennedy, knew the record, knew they were themselves chosen as a sacrifice, knew about the first-game circus. But Dell never failed to find a coach who thought he wanted to test himself and his team against the best team in Florida. They signed the scheduling contract and told their team that Kennedy was beatable. It was a necessary fiction.

Dell's opponents also knew that he did not play his starters for the first quarter, not a minute. "Take your best shot," he seemed to tell the other coaches, "Get ahead if you can. It won't matter. I'll catch up."

I was skeptical of other women who generalize about men. I was old enough, smart enough, I was so sure, to avoid pigeon-holing men by types or to lump them all into one big stereotype. Age, education, and experience: I could dissect the individual. I had read enough books. I was so damn smart, despite my marriage to Jack Vandergriff, right? But as I looked at Dell and Jerry, their boys, the other coach and his boys, I kept thinking that there must be something in the blood of most men that makes them the same, but different from me and other women. Something more than hormones, something older and deeper, more primeval. Sometimes, it wasn't very attractive; indeed, often ugly. Sometimes, like this night, it was magnetic and irresistible.

At the end of the first quarter, the visitors were ahead by nine points, but none of the Kennedy fans were worried. Dell stood up for the entire quarter, but as soon as he put his starters in for the second quarter he sat down and seemed to lose interest in the game. Jerry took over, and Kennedy went from a nine-point deficit to a twenty-three point lead. For the fourth quarter, the starters were pulled and sat out the rest of the game. Most of the crowd began leaving then, and Kennedy eventually won by twenty-five. The rest of the season would not be this easy, they all knew, but that was the future. This was the moment.

Dell never raised his voice, but he never took his eyes off the court. Nothing distracted him. When it was obvious that one of his players could not guard someone on the other team, Dell raised both his hands, one forefinger pointing to his struggling player and the other to a teammate. Then, with fingers still pointing, he crossed his hands and the players switched assignments. Even though nobody ever saw them look in Dell's direction, we knew that the players had been aware of him. They were concentrating on the floor, but still wired into their coach.

After the game, as everyone was congratulating the players, Dell motioned Jerry off to one side, then the two men called over one of the sophomore first-quarter players, a scrawny black kid who had lost his temper after a foul was called against him. The two tall men made him sit on the bench in front of them, and then they each got down on one knee so they were all at the same eye level. The boy kept his head down at first, but Dell reached over and put a hand under his chin and nudged him back up. The boy was angry, almost to tears, but he kept nodding as Dell and Jerry talked to him. Conference over, Jerry patted the boy on his knee and sent him to the locker room.

I was sitting in the bleachers alone, and exhausted. Jerry looked up, saw me, and waved. Dell looked up, saw me, looked over at Jerry, and then back at me. Then Jerry leaned over and whispered something in Dell's ear. Dell looked down, and then he looked back up at me and we made eye contact. Jerry was still talking to him, and he began nodding, never taking his eyes off of me.

Will Tymeson

I think it is totally wrong and terribly harmful if education
is defined as acquiring knowledge.—William Glasser

The beginning of basketball season also meant that the first semester was about to end. My students thought their lives were a living hell because of the work that was being compressed together. Projects, essays, oral reports, final exams competed for their attention. I pointed out to my first class that, while they had to do their own work, I had to read and grade everyone's work; that, while they had to write one essay and do one exam, I had to read and grade hundreds of them.

Jackie the Smoker put her hand on her chest and said, "Teacher, you're like ... breaking my heart." Then Harry Hellas, of the sun-bleached hair and constant camera, opened his eyes and said, "Miss Adams, you get paid the big bucks to do that, don't you? Somebody paid me, I'd study. Pay me enough, I'd even study for somebody else." Jackie looked at Harry and then shifted her entire body so that he couldn't see any part of her face, looking at me instead with a smile that said, *Isn't he so cute.*

Chickie Williams, the student council rep, raised her hand frantically, "Miss Adams, I need an extension..." I immediately wished that Chickie hadn't used that word in this class. "...I am, like, really tied up..." Another wrong choice of words for this class. "... being in charge of decorations for the Christmas dance. So I was wondering if I could turn in my essay after the dance."

"Certainly," I said with a straight face, knowing that half the class would see where I was going while the other half began raising their hands to ask for the same slack. "You can turn it in next year..." I said, seeing Chickie's eyes widen, "...but there will still be a letter grade drop for every day it's late."

Chickie blinked, and the other hands dropped like stones. "Miss Adams, you are so unfair," she said, her face red.

"And so predictable," added Jackie.

After class, I asked Jackie about her request to do more extra-credit work to raise her grade from C to B. I had told her that she could do what the honors class was doing: interview an adult who was a teenager in the Sixties. I had suggested that she interview her own mother. "You going to take my offer, Jackie? Interview your mother?" I asked.

"Absolutely, as soon as she gets back to planet earth," Jackie said. "I expect that'll be about the time you retire."

"Give her a chance," I said. "The trick on these interviews is to ask the right questions and *pay attention* to the answers so you can do a follow-up. You might be surprised, might learn something about her you didn't know."

"Whatever," was Jackie's only response.

"Jackie, give your mother a break."

"Whatever," she repeated.

"Okay, it's your decision. But interviewing your mother is the only option I'm giving you for extra credit," I said. "Take it or leave it."

Jackie rolled her eyes up almost to the back of her head, and then mimicked Chickie Williams, "Miss Adams, you are so unfair."

"And predictable," I smiled.

"Okay, I'll interview Mama Cass..."

"Jackie!"

"Okay, okay, I'll get the dirt on my mum," she shrugged.

I was pleased. I knew Jackie's mother would appreciate that her daughter wanted to know about her past. Before Jackie could leave, I also asked her about the first basketball game. "I saw you at the game sitting with Fred Stein. You and him got something going?"

Jackie acted as if I had asked her if she was going to join the *Young Life* club. "Miss Adams!!! That was the worst coincidence of my life. Freddy Stein is like the mega-King of the Nerds!! I could be ruined if you even joke about me and him seeing each other. I... will...fuc...frigging...die!"

"Your loss, Jackie," I said. "Fred's a great guy."

Jackie's mouth was open wide enough to see her molars. "Miss Adams, can you see the children we would have? Can you imagine that? Freddy Stein and Jackie Foster? Mr. Brainy do-gooder and Miss ... Miss ... Miss ... Freddy and ME!"

I nodded, "Don't rule it out."

Jackie picked up her backpack off the desk, shaking her head as she left muttering, "So unfair, so predictable, and, like, so very very weird."

Final assignments for most students would not change their eventual final grades. Most would be easy to figure, but not in my honors class. Dana was ruining the implicit curve. It wasn't a matter of who would get an A grade. That was easy. Almost everyone in the class was an obviously bright student, and most would get an A. But I had decided that A- and A+ should be rare grades. Unless I was teaching math like Jerry, with clearly objective scores and a precise point value for each letter grade, I had come to the conclusion that an A- was simply an excuse for me to avoid hurting a student's feelings with a B+. In my emerging world of standards, an A- diminished the value of an A. But the real problem in my honors class was how to differentiate between better and best. Should students be measured solely against my expectations, or should they also be measured in relation to the other students?

Put in its starkest terms, the problem was Dana. If she weren't in the class, April would be the best. Perhaps even Fred would be the best after all the final reports and tests, either of them an A+ student when compared to their competition. But Dana *was* there, a clear level above everyone else. If an A+ had any real meaning as an indicator of atypical excellence, Dana and April could not get the same grade. April Bourne was an A+ only in a world without Dana O'Connor.

At certain times of the month, I looked at the stack of papers in front of me, then at my grade book, and I thought about the final grade columns inside that green leather book. I wanted to walk out to my boat dock and throw everything in the St. Johns and then jump in after it.

When it came time to give the oral reports in class, Dana was absent the first two days. If I thought hard about it, I could have come to the conclusion that Dana did it on purpose to let everyone else establish some sort of norm that she could then demolish. Then again, she had been absent enough in the past so that these particular absences probably meant nothing. Dana still inspired interpretation; sometimes, misinterpretation.

Most of the students chose their parents or some other relative to interview. I expected a lot of Vietnam stories, but most of my students' fathers hadn't been in the service. Fred's father and mother had both been in college, as had April's parents. Fred's father had been the only Jewish Republican at Dartmouth. As Fred talked about his parents' college romance—their both being engaged to other people when they met and how they had a lot of explaining to do to their own parents—I thought of the man who had broken down in front of me a few months earlier. Fred had many of his features.

April's mother and father had gone to Florida State together, and her report was well organized, surprising in its honesty about her father. She even managed to work in a description of conservative student activities on the 1980 FSU campus when her parents were there, putting them in an environment that was more interesting than they were themselves. April's thesis was that her parents' college life was symbolic of the Reagan Revolution backlash against the Sixties. It was an impressive report.

The real surprise for me was big Bobby Ray Dearing talking about his father's aircraft carrier duty aboard the *U.S.S. Forrestal* off the coast of Vietnam. Bobby Ray wasn't a good public speaker, he mumbled too much, but the impression he created was of a young man who had actually *learned* something that had changed how he related to his father. Concluding his report, he announced that he was seriously considering not going to college next year and was instead looking to first enlist in the Air Force and then go to college when he was older. Everyone was shocked, including me. Bobby Ray was sure-fire football scholarship material, especially with his good grades. In that first few seconds after he looked up from his paper in front of him, we all sat silent, and then Fred softly applauded. It was spontaneous and sincere, but Fred quickly stopped when he realized that he was alone. Bobby Ray looked at him and nodded a *thank you*. Trying to shift attention from himself, Fred asked, "So, why the Air Force? Why not the Navy, like your dad?"

A logical and innocent question, but I could see Bobby Ray turn tomato red. Still, he straightened his shoulders and answered with a grin, "Because I swim like a damn rock, Freddy. But, thanks for asking."

The entire class, Bobby Ray included, laughed hysterically, and I was a happy teacher. It was more than the humor. It was a moment I had had with other students, but usually by ourselves or in small groups. We would forget that we were supposed to be students and teachers. Instead, we were all sharing the same experience, surprised at turning the same corner hand-in-hand and Life yelling *Gotcha* at us, lost in the funhouse.

Big, intimidating Bobby Ray Dearing was blushing but not embarrassed. Fred was tilting his head and slapping his ear, as if shaking out river water. Even April was giggling. I liked everyone in front of me at that moment. My only regret was that Dana wasn't there to be part of it.

"Bobby Ray, why not do both," I asked when everyone quieted down. "Why not apply to the Air Force Academy? You're smart enough, and they probably need every good football player they can get. The application deadline might have passed, but your all-state credentials and grades will get some serious retroactive consideration, but we need to get some recommendations immediately."

I wish I had a picture of his face at that moment to put in a scrapbook. It was as if he had been reserving judgment about me for the entire semester. But, with that suggestion, I had suddenly been accepted by Bobby Ray Dearing. I had finally said something that was actually relevant to *his* life, something more than facts about other people's lives. His face told me that a burden had been lifted off him, as if his own repressed ambivalence had been resolved, and he was grateful to Nancy Adams. He was still standing by my desk. "I never thought of that," he said. "Will you write me a recommendation?"

"I'll be glad to," I said. "After class, let's go see Donna Parton and start the paperwork. No guarantees, and you still have to get some political support from somebody in Congress, but it's not too late."

Bobby Ray sat down, and I knew he would not hear anybody else's report that afternoon. He was planning his future.

Dana's report the next day was the last one. I wasn't surprised by it's substance, even though I soon realized that Dana was lying about whom she had interviewed.

"I want to talk about my uncle, my mother's brother. His name is Will Tymeson. He was a combat medic in Vietnam thirty years ago, right after the troop buildup under LBJ."

Dana was standing at the podium next to the desk, so all I could see was her right profile. After that opening, she turned and handed me a large manila envelope. "Everything's in there," she said, turning back to face the class and speaking without notes for fifteen minutes. "You ready, Freddy?" she asked. He waved and pointed to a tape recorder on his desk. "Okay, let me tell you about Will."

Will Tymeson was Russell Parsons.

"Will volunteered right out of high school. He told me that he believed in what he was doing, that he had been inspired by John Kennedy, but that he specifically asked to be a medic because he had plans to be a doctor anyway after he got out of the army. When he told me this, I thought of that play we read in class..."

I had had everyone read Ron Kovic's *Born on the Fourth of July*. Dana was connecting classwork to the outside assignment. I suspected that she threw in the reference to Kovic because it would satisfy an expectation of the teacher, not that she actually thought of it at the time of the interview. That was okay. It was more than most of my students did.

"... but his experience was not what he expected. He had grown up with two parents, my grandparents..."

A lie, I knew, but consistent with the bigger lie, and I noticed Dana's subtle, perhaps unconscious, emphasis on the word *two*. I knew enough about Russell's parents to know that Dana was describing them. "... who tried to talk him out of volunteering.

They were educated anti-war activists long before it was fashionable. Will assured them that he was going to help people. But he told me that he had never imagined in his wildest dreams that he would be holding a pint of plasma in one hand trying to put a needle in the arm of a wounded soldier while he was firing a rifle with his other hand, trying to kill somebody who was trying to kill him while he was trying to save someone else. Will often used the word *surreal* to describe his tour in Vietnam. He told me that combat medics were often the first target of the Viet Cong, so he stopped wearing the red cross insignia on his sleeve."

Russell had told me that same story once, but he had also told me that he never killed anybody while he was there.

"I asked Will if he had read any of the books about the war in Vietnam or seen any of the movies, if any of those were accurate. He told me to watch *Hamburger Hill*, not *Platoon* or *Apocalypse Now*. He also told me to read Tim O'Brien novels, especially *The Things They Carried*. I asked him, if I read those would I understand him any better..."

Dana had two audiences, and she knew it. The class was hearing one story. I was hearing another. I had seen all those movies myself, read all those books and more. I had asked Russell question after question, but he had stopped answering when I asked why, if his first tour was so bad, why he had volunteered for a second, why he had put himself at risk again when he could have gone home.

"Will wrote his parents every week, and he had a girlfriend back home who he wrote to almost everyday, but she eventually stopped writing back..."

Parsons had never told me about his high school sweetheart. I wondered if Dana knew because he had simply told her or whether she had just asked him a direct question.

"I asked Will if there was a major misperception about being a soldier in Vietnam that people might have had. He didn't answer that question the first time I asked it, but I asked again another day. He finally told me that he had always been bothered by some people's image of him and his friends as being either some sort of insensitive killer rapists or them being too dumb to see that Vietnam was an immoral war and they should not have gone, that they should have stayed home and protested."

Dana stopped, and it dawned on me that she didn't know what she was going to say next. The manila envelope was sitting on the desk in front of me. Without taking my eyes off her, I slowly pulled it off the desk and on to my lap. Not looking down, I opened the envelope and pulled out the papers. Then, in a quick glance down, I saw that the pages were blank. Dana was improvising, and then I made a stunning leap. The blank pages made me think of something Dana had said about the unknown father of her child. No logical connection, but I remembered that moment back in the lawyer's office, when I had realized that something bad had happened to Dana O'Connor, something very bad. Like a silent slow-motion scene in a movie, my stomach constricting, I forced myself to look up from the blank pages and back toward Dana.

"No, I'm not being accurate," Dana was saying. "I was trying to paraphrase Will. His exact words were, 'They thought they were better than us because they hadn't gone. They thought they were smarter.' I thought about what he said, and what we had read in class, and I asked him if he thought Vietnam was a noble cause like Reagan said. He told me there was no such thing as a noble war, not even against somebody like Hitler."

I found myself looking at Bobby Ray Dearing. His father had never set foot in Vietnam, but he had seen the fighter-bombers come back to his ship. Bobby Ray had described his father's anguish at counting planes, those that left versus those that returned. The sinking feeling when the numbers didn't match. He had also described his father's courage when the *Forrestal* lost hundreds of men during an explosion on deck. Bobby Ray was looking out the window, but I knew he was listening.

"I asked Uncle Will how he was changed by his experience, and he told me that he wasn't. I told him that he was not telling the truth ..." another hesitation, "...but he explained that Vietnam only reinforced certain core values he had. It did not change him. It only made him grow up faster into the person he was going to be anyway. Of course, he admitted that he was speaking from hindsight, that at the time he was actually there he thought he was going to go crazy. He was eighteen, then nineteen, just a little older than Freddy or Bobby Ray or you other guys," looking around the room and making eye contact with whomever would look back. Fred looked down, but Bobby Ray looked right at her. "Putting his hands inside the wounds of men without legs or arms or sometimes even faces, looking for bullets or shrapnel, and scared to death that he was next."

When Russell was in Vietnam, I was nine years old. He was an adult. I was a child. Dana was making it easy for me to see that the gap between Russell and me wasn't just our age.

"Will told me that he went to Vietnam thinking he was fighting for America, but he ended up fighting for the men around him. That's why he volunteered for a second tour. In addition to being a company medic, he was also the company historian, he told me. His company captain would ask him to write letters back to the families of the men who had died there. Will respected the captain, he told me, because the captain was a cautious man, unlike some of the other officers he knew. So Will would write to the parents and wives of dead men, telling them the truth, and lies if necessary. Every man in his company was given a story in which he was brave and in which he always thought of home at some point before he died. Will had a secret, he told me, a secret that he shared only with his best friend, the company sergeant, an older black man who was career army. Near the end of his first tour, after a dozen eulogies... his word, *eulogies*... back to America, he began to go out of his way to get to know the men in his company. He would ask them questions about home, about their lives back in the States, their families, and he would remember everything. He told me that he began keeping files on them all, assuming that any one of them could be dead soon and that he would have to *re*-create them in a letter back home. He wanted every letter to be as individual as the person he was writing about. Of all the letters he wrote, the hardest was about his best friend, the sergeant."

A picture on a wall. Russell's office, how often had Dana been there? How much more had she seen? And why did she know more than me?

"The sergeant had come to Vietnam the same time as Will, but he had served one tour in Korea before. Not in that war, but still across the line from an enemy who was very real. And he had been a drill instructor back in the States. He could have avoided actual combat, but he insisted on going to Vietnam. He told Will he felt like a hypocrite staying back in Texas and training kids to do the real fighting. But the more my uncle knew this sergeant, the more he realized that the sergeant was intimidated by his own father, a black man who had served in a segregated unit in World War II but who had seen combat and been wounded. The sergeant's father, segregated or not, had been proud to fight in the war. When his son, the future sergeant, enlisted, he gave him a good luck charm, a small American flag that he carried with him throughout Europe. The sergeant would pull out that flag and show it to Will every time they went back into the jungle on a mission. And tell Will that it was going to be *his* flag when he left, his good luck. The sergeant had sons of his own, but he told Will that he was 'gonna be goddamed if those boys ever put on a uniform.' My uncle didn't tell me how the sergeant died, only that it was a month before they were scheduled to be rotated back to America, a month before their tour was over. My uncle was wounded in the same fight, but he wouldn't tell me the details, and I didn't ask. It was a serious wound, and my uncle could have certainly gone home early, but he volunteered for a second tour."

Dana talked for a few more minutes, getting her "uncle" home from Vietnam and into college, where he used the GI Bill but not his parents help. She finally carried Will Tymeson into marriage.

"He got a job as a college teacher and fell in love with another teacher. She was a beautiful woman, he told me, and he felt like he was the luckiest man in the world..."

I had assumed that I was important to Russell. Had assumed I understood him and knew all about his life, but Dana was about to explain something to me, to explain what should have been obvious about Russell and Stella, but which I, and everyone else, refused to believe.

As Dana's voice lowered, she spoke slower. "A few years ago his wife died. She was killed in a car wreck. He tells me that he sees her every day, but everyone knows she's dead. I know for a fact that my uncle has had other women interested in him, women who might have loved him as much as his wife did, women that he might have loved if he would just cut himself off from his first wife's memory. But my uncle tells me that I'm too young to understand what love means. He tells me that he took a vow to her, that loyalty and commitment were not abstractions to him. I told him that wedding vows had an escape clause, a *till death do you part* line. He told me that marriage might be a contract, but love was not."

Dana stopped talking, stood there a second, and I thought she might be preparing some sort of summation, something to tie everything together, but she simply paused, looked over to me as if wanting to see if her teacher had any questions, and then she walked back to her seat.

"Thank you, Dana," I said, as I had thanked every student. April was smiling to herself, and I knew why. As an assignment, April's speech, even though merely read from the complete paper in front of her, had been more organized, more focused on the specific topic, more relevant to the work we had done in class. It had a clear beginning, a substantial middle with supporting illustrations, and a conclusion that came back to the beginning. As a written exercise, April's report was flawless. Dana had written nothing, but only I knew that. April assumed that Dana's written work paralleled her speech, and Dana's speech, if judged objectively, was not as good as April's had been. In April's mind, *she* had the A+.

Dana stayed to see me after class. "Can I get that envelope back?" she asked. "I need to do a few revisions. I'll get it back to you in three hours. I can bring it back here or drop it off at your house."

"Dana, I've already looked in the envelope."

"Caught, eh?" she sighed.

"Red-handed," I said, keeping my voice neutral. "You know, technically, I don't have to accept late work."

"No, you don't," she said calmly. "You owe me nothing."

"Oh, Dana, don't be so indifferent. And don't be a..." I was about to tell her not to be a martyr, but I instinctively knew that she would snap back at that word. "... don't jerk me around. Do me a favor, tell me ahead of time that you need a cushion. We know each other well enough for you to do that."

"Fine. This is what I need. Two hours. I had Freddy tape what I said. I'll go back to David's office and listen to the tape and write the report. I'm sorry, and you're right. I should have talked to you sooner. But I've been swamped with a lot of things lately and I got behind."

"Are you simply going to transcribe the tape?"

"Hell no!" she laughed. "I was improvising like crazy for this speech. When I get through with the written report, it'll be publishable."

"I want the tape too," I told her. "I want it along with your report. You got a problem with that?"

Dana looked down at me, thought a second, and said, "Not at all. I'll take it to your house. If you're not there, I'll leave it on the porch. All I need is a couple of hours."

"Dana, for the record..."

"This is just between us," she said, turning to leave. "Our secret."

"No, not that, but that's okay too. For the record, I want us to talk more about some other things. About you."

She stared at me like I was a complete stranger, and then left without a word.

The next day I met Russell in his office and gave him the tape and a copy of Dana's paper. The written report didn't mention Will Tymeson's marriage. When I told Russell how Dana had turned him into her uncle, he shook his head, "Nancy, she never talked to me."

"Never talked to you?" I asked. "But, she had to ..."

"Well, she never actually interviewed me," he said. "She never sat down and asked me about my experience in Vietnam."

"But I knew some of the things in her report were true," I said, beginning to be afraid that Dana had simply invented a life for Will Tymeson. "I just assumed that..."

Russell was leaning back in his chair, his feet uncharacteristically propped on the edge of his desk. "Dana's not going to lie to you, Nancy. Let me listen to the tape. You come see me tomorrow. I'll know what to think then."

I didn't have to wait until the next day. He called me that night as I was watching the late news on television. "Relax, Nancy," he said. "Dana got it right."

"Everything?" I asked, reaching for a copy of Dana's report, remembering the tape. I could hear him take a deep breath at the other end of the line before he spoke.

"Enough," he finally said. "Some things I didn't tell her, but they're not wrong."

"You want to explain that distinction to me?"

"Nancy, I'm not sure I can explain it to myself. For now, I'm really tired. I'm going to bed. So should you."

I didn't want to go to bed. Instead, I went out to my boat dock and sat on the edge, my feet barely skimming the surface. I thought that I might go swimming, but I surprised myself when I realized that I hadn't shot my guns in over a month. Had I been that busy? That distracted? I got up and went back to the house intending to get my twenty-two pistol, but as soon as I walked into the kitchen I saw what I had been avoiding. Two stacks of assignments on the table: essays and tests. I wondered if Henry Adams ever got tired of his paperwork. I wondered if he and his wife would sit together as he graded papers. He taught at Harvard, but the house in which I always imagined him was in Washington, just around from the White House. Was his parlor lit by candles or kerosene lamps? When did he get electricity? Did he sit in the same room after she killed herself? Did he forget that she was dead? Immersed in some book, would he instinctively start to read out loud some passage that he wanted to share with her, lifting his eyes as he spoke, seeing her ghost? Or, sadder, *not* seeing her ghost. I needed to read his book again. I felt like I was catching up. My century was ending in a few years. He finally found his symbols. All I had were two stacks of papers. I sat down.

Fred is Dead, Christ is Born

I only had a high school education and believe me, I

had to cheat to get that.—Sparky Anderson

A week before the Christmas dance, Fred Stein was dead for ten minutes. I was alone in my classroom during my morning prep period when I heard a scream in the hall. I rushed out to check and found little Jenny Baker and Chickie Williams both wide-eyed and white-faced.

"Miss Adams! Miss Adams! Did you hear! Freddy Stein was killed in a car wreck this morning on his way to school," Chickie said breathlessly, tears in her eyes.

I was dizzy and nauseous at the same time, and I put my hand on Chickie's shoulder for support. As soon as I touched Chickie, she and Jenny both put their arms around me and we stood there holding each other up. "How do you know..." I asked Chickie, my throat suddenly very dry.

"I heard it from Ginger. She saw the wreck!" Chickie was gasping for breath as she tried to talk.

I saw Donna Parton running down the hall, but, before she could speak, she raced by me toward Russell's office, saying, "I know, I know. I have to make some calls."

More students were filling the halls, but they seemed oblivious to the news. I told Jenny and Chickie to go sit in my classroom while I went to the office. As I went to find Donna, I felt like I was stoned again at Notre Dame, in slow motion and light-headed. At that moment, Fred turned the corner and waved.

"Miss Adams, you gotta help me," he said sheepishly as he approached. "I am like under a mile high pile of manure. And my father is going to kill me."

"Fred!" was all I could say.

"I think I totaled his car this morning. Rolled it over in a ditch and ..."

"Fred! Forget about your father. I'm going to kill you," I began laughing. Behind him, Donna and Russell were turning the same corner in a hurry until they saw me with Fred. They slowed down and almost grinned.

"Freddy Stein!" Donna shouted, "Don't you ever do this again!"

Fred glanced at them, and then back at me, a confused look on his face. "Excuse me?" he said.

"We thought you were dead," I said. "That was the rumor."

He shuddered, but began smiling, then laughing. "I died for your sins, Miss Adams, you and the other gentiles around here. Fred Stein, another Jew for Jesus."

I held up my hand and said, "Shut up, Fred, and let me hug you." As I put my arms around him, Donna and Russell came up and did the same, three relieved adults wrapped around their prior grief.

Standing back, I told him, "Now, I want you to go in my classroom. Two girls are waiting for you."

A few seconds after he walked into my classroom, we three adults outside heard the shriek, "FREDDY!!!!!" We went to the room to see Fred being pulled back and forth between Jenny and Chickie like they were fighting over the last man on earth. If the expression *shit-eating grin* needed personification, Fred Stein was it.

My relief lasted until I remembered Bob Skinner's betting pool. I wondered if anyone had picked Fred.

I had been in charge of the Christmas dance arrangements when I was a senior in 1976. This year was Fred's responsibility, and he always managed to point out the obvious irony of him, the self-proclaimed designated Jew at Kennedy, being in charge of a Christian fete. Ashley Prose reminded him that it was now called a Holiday dance and no longer a Christmas dance, but Fred ignored her.

"You people are too insecure about your own heritage. I said that to Miss Prose in honors English," he told me. "My people, I told her, we know we're the brand name and ya'll are just a knock-off."

"Fred, you did *not* say that to her," I said, backing him down.

"Well, no, I didn't. But I thought about it. I would have said it to you, *could* have said it to you," he said.

"Is this a compliment? That you can make flip remarks about religion around me but not Miss Prose?"

"Well, duh, Miss Adams. Of course it is."

"So, Fred, tell me this. Would you say the same thing around Mrs. Rose?" she asked.

"No way," he said, stepping back from me.

"So Agnes and Miss Prose are the same?" I pressed.

"Not hardly. I like Mrs. Rose. I thought she was a great teacher. Miss Prose..."

"Fred, think about what you're about to say," I said like a parent.

"I'm digging myself into a hole?"

"Knee deep right now," I said.

"Well, for the record, I love everybody here at Kennedy," he said, pushing his glasses back over his nose.

"Good, now go ask Miss Prose if she'll be one of the chaperones for the dance."

"Miss Adams!" he whined. "You are so..."

"I know, Fred," I interrupted him. "I am so unfair."

After I graduated, the Christmas dance was held at the Fort Jackson Country Club. But as soon as Russell became principal, he insisted that the dance come back to the school gymnasium. It was held the last Friday night of the semester, and it was supposed to be a formal dance, but even Russell couldn't enforce that. In years past, a local rock and roll band was hired, but Fred scrapped that tradition in favor of an elaborate sound system and a local radio disc jockey serving as master-of-ceremonies. By the time the dance was over, I was convinced that my students had no idea what real music was, even real rock and roll.

I had joked with Mike Lankford, my drummer student, about his generation's taste in music. Mike, out of my class and therefore free of the no-hat rule, had tipped his baseball cap and told me, "Don't you worry, Miss Adams, that Big Band sound is coming back. You and the other teachers can show us how to jitterbug."

Mike was right, I admitted, but not to him. I was out of step with the adolescents swirling around me, irrevocably now an adult. In a letter long ago from Russell, after I had written to him about my feeling that I was just drifting in life, that I couldn't imagine myself in the future, he had asked me if I was *trapped* in my past, asked if I was still re-living my life with Jack, trapped in a routine of what-if questions. I told him that I wasn't living in my past. In fact, I had erased my past with Jack, all the knowledge of his infidelities had erased the memory of the good times we had. Like a game of paper-rock-scissors. Paper covers rock, rock breaks scissors, scissors cut paper, knowledge trumps memory. I wasn't living in the past, I told him, I was living in a vacuum. No children, no pets, alone in Atlanta. I had no past, and there was nothing in my present to fill up the emptiness. But even that *present* had become the past.

For the first hour of the dance, I realized that tonight was both work and play for me. I was fascinated how all the kids were more alive here than they were in the classroom. I wasn't surprised, just fascinated. I was having fun watching all those hormones unrestricted by the daytime rules.

Most of the students came with a date, but there were still small groups of boys and girls clinging to each other, each group distinguished by how informally they were dressed. From my first class, kids like Ben Russell were wearing the same clothes they wore to school. Jenny Baker and Chickie Williams were dressed like magazine ads. Fred was wearing a tuxedo, and Mike Lankford was wearing a powder-blue seersucker suit along with his ever-present baseball cap. Fred didn't have a date. His excuse was that he was too busy to pay attention to a girl. Mike's date was a black girl from Jackson High, two inches taller and twenty pounds heavier, but the two of them were always on the floor dancing. By the end of the night, she was wearing his cap.

Sue Rollins, Ashley, Bob Skinner, Agnes, Jerry, and Dell were the other faculty chaperones. I suggested that one of them be patrolling the parking lot at all times, taking turns. Ashley thought I was being "too paternalistic." Bob then informed me that Russell had arranged for the daytime security guard to be in the parking lot all night, constantly checking cars. *In loco parentis* was his policy.

Dell heard that and pulled me off to one side, whispering, "That wind-up cop is worthless. He'll sniff around for drugs, but if he finds some kids making out in a car he'll stand there and stare, and you could be selling or smoking crack behind him and he wouldn't turn around." We were standing by ourselves near the buffet table and Dell started to whisper something to me again, but the music volume suddenly went up with a new fast dance. "You want some fresh air and peace and quiet?" he said, raising his voice.

"Parking lot patrol?" I asked.

He nodded, and then said, "I'm going to do restroom patrol first. You might check the girls' room. Be sure to check the ledge along the top of the stalls. Meet you at the door in a couple of minutes."

In the restroom, I immediately smelled cigarette smoke. Floating over one stall was a cloud. Without really thinking, I said in my sternest voice, "Jackie!"

I heard, "Oh, shit," and a toilet flushing at the same time. Then a meek voice, "Miss Adams?"

"Get out here, Jackie. Right now," I said, but there was no response, no movement inside the stall. "Jackie," I repeated.

"Leave me alone, please," a trembling voice said.

I softened my tone, "Jackie, it's okay. Come on out."

The stall door swung open, but Jackie didn't come out. I walked over and stood in the open space looking down at her, resting on the toilet looking like a punk rock version of Olivia Newton-John in *Grease*: Poodle skirt, purple streaked hair, nose-ring, bloody lip and swelling cheek.

"Jackie! Are you okay?" I gasped, reaching in to pull her off the toilet and over to the sink where I started rinsing off her face. Jackie was absolutely passive, sniffling and trembling.

"How did this happen?" I asked, holding on to Jackie's shoulders as she started shaking.

"Just an asshole, that's all! Just an asshole who thinks I'm a whore, that's how this happened," Jackie blurted out, her nose dripping blood now. "I'm sorry, Miss Adams, I'm sorry, I'm sorry. I'm just shit, I know that. I'm a joke at this school, I know that. I don't deserve to..."

She started collapsing in my arms.

"Tell me who did this," I said as firmly as I could while also trying to hold her up.

"Oh yeah, *right*. *That* will make a big fucking difference at *this* fucking school," she almost screamed.

I put my hands around the wilting girl, and with a strength that surprised me, I picked Jackie up and sat her on the counter top. "Take a slow deep breath and calm down. You hear me?" I said, but just as Jackie was about to speak again there was a knock on the restroom door.

"Nancy, you in there? You fall in?" Dell said as he opened the door about six inches. "Nancy?"

Jackie's eyes opened wide and I could see an immediate change in her as she said, "That's Coach Rose! Oh, Miss Adams, you can't tell him anything, *especially* him. Promise me that. Please, don't tell anybody, especially him."

"Dell, hold on a minute," I yelled to him, and then turned back to Jackie, "Are you sure you're okay now?"

She nodded, dabbing her eyes dry with a Kleenex I had given her.

"Okay, we'll wait here another minute, just to make sure you're okay," I said, stepping away. "And I'll keep this a secret on one condition. You come see me on Monday..."

Jackie almost laughed, "There's, like, no school Monday, Miss Adams. Christmas vacation, remember?"

"Okay, do this. Call me this weekend. We'll go out for lunch. Just us. But you better be honest with me when I see you. Or else I call your mother. Okay?"

I already knew that I was going to talk to Donna about this when I saw her, perhaps even Russell.

Jackie kept her head down, "Okay. Just don't tell anybody, okay? Never ever, please."

"I promise," I lied to her.

A minute later, with her face more presentable, Jackie and I made our exit. Dell looked at us and joked, "Women in restrooms... when do we guys ever find out what you're talking about?"

"Never," I said, nudging Jackie past him. "That's the source of our power." Jackie giggled. "Now, Jackie, there's a young man wearing a tuxedo running around this gym like he's a hall monitor. Go find him and tell him that Miss Adams said he is supposed to dance one dance with you. And, if you really want to make an impression on him, tell him how disappointed you are that Bill Clinton got re-elected last month." Then, I realized that I had forgotten the obvious question. "Jackie, do you already have a date for tonight?"

"Not anymore, Miss Adams," she said happily.

Dell held the door open for Jackie, and I watched how she kept her head down as she eased around him, as if afraid to make eye contact. He noticed too.

"I do something wrong?" he asked as we walked to the parking lot.

"No, no, it's just a girl thing. Some boy was hassling her tonight. You just happened to be the only male around at the moment, so you're the villain."

Outside, the air was warm and humid, despite being mid-December. When I asked him how good his basketball team was this year, Dell's mood shifted from glib to serious.

"Something weird is going on this year," he said, scanning the parking lot as he talked, watching the couples dart in and out of cars. "The younger players aren't responding the way they used to. I mean, don't get me wrong, this is probably the best team in the state, especially the juniors, but the young guys, especially a couple of those juniors, seem...for lack of a better word, they seem spoiled.

A ton of talent, but almost impossible to make them really put out a real effort."

"But you're undefeated," I said, pulling his tie back off his shoulder after the wind had blown it there.

"First third of the season is always easy. Non-conference, patsy teams. No, the first clue we had was that scrimmage with St. Joe's downtown. Those little Catholic boys almost beat us. Jerry was yelling his head off, but I was calm as death. On the outside. Nine guys on their team, none of them over six-four. And they ran us ragged. Snap snap snap, they could really pass the ball around. I tried that gimmick of not using the starters right away, and those little Catholic boys were ten points ahead in the first five minutes. They had this one tiny kid, the only black one on their team, who must have stolen the ball every time we tried to come up court."

"But you won," I said, thinking that was the key point.

"Oh, we won, okay. Wore them down, got them in foul trouble with our subs, finally got some scoring from our seniors. Yeah, we won, but they beat us."

"Did you and Jerry explain that distinction to your players?" she asked.

"The seniors understood. But you see, we only have two seniors as starters. And those guys aren't even our best athletes. Every coach in Florida knows that it's next year's team that's going to be the powerhouse. Supposed to be. But the younger kids learned nothing from that scrimmage, and that's what bothers me."

Over Dell's shoulder, I could see Chickie Williams and David Pillow, the smartest boy in my first class, holding hands and walking toward a top-down convertible. As David opened the car door, he touched his mouth with two fingers and then reached out to put those fingers on Chickie's lips. She reached up and held his hand against her face.

Dell had stopped talking as I focused on Chickie and David. When I looked back at him, he was staring at me.

"You look great tonight," he said slowly. "And that's a compliment, not a proposition."

"I need a drink," I smiled at him, trying not to show him how pleased I was. "And thanks. Really, thanks," I said as I reached for his tie again.

"You don't need a drink," he smiled back. "You need a dance."

I almost stopped breathing. Was he serious?

"Here in the parking lot?"

"No, Nancy Adams, you need a proper dance with the proper music with the proper audience."

"Dell, I don't think..."

"Exactly, Nancy, don't think."

He took my hand, pulled me away from the car I was resting against, and set me in motion. We walked back into the gymnasium without touching. Inside, I looked for familiar faces. The music was too loud and too fast. Mike Lankford and his black date were dancing. Chickie and David were dancing, back from the parking lot. Fred was talking to Jackie the Smoker. Bobby Ray Dearing was dancing with two girls half his size. I then saw Dylan Abrams's father and April Bourne...dancing. I turned to point them out to Dell, but he was gone. I turned back to look at April. Dylan had cut in on his father.

"Have a drink," Dell said, appearing out of nowhere with a plastic cup full of red punch. I was parched.

"You missed it," I said. "April Bourne was dancing with Dylan Abrams father."

"Practicing for the wedding, I suppose," he laughed, taking a sip of punch and then handing the cup to her.

"Wedding?"

"Oh, Nancy, you are wonderful. So smart, so always thinking the big thoughts, so wonderfully out of touch with the obvious." Dell was beginning to keep time with the music by snapping his fingers. Then, with a clap, he did a complete 360 spin, coming around to face me again, almost having to shout over the music, "Dylan and April have been a couple for a long time. I would have thought you would have known, but, by the look on your face, you didn't have a clue. Dylan Abrams and April Bourne...Nancy, how could they *not* be made for each other."

I started to laugh, catching up with Dell's laughter. I was almost giddy. Why the pattern, I asked myself. Glum, then giddy. Overwhelmed, and then free as a jaybird. Dylan and April! How very, very logical. All my ambivalence about April disappeared. I was totally relieved, even happy. I was now completely on Dana's side. And not looking back. The music ended, and for a moment all the bodies on the floor seemed frozen in mid-step, then they dissolved into each other.

"This is the last dance," Dell said. "I paid the piper and the song is mine. And you, Miss Adams, owe me a dance."

We were at the edge of the dance floor as the music began. A slow song, as I expected, an old slow song. I heard some of the teenage boys around me groan, but the girls pulled them out on the hardwood floor. Dell looked at me. "I'm not a good dancer," I said, holding out my hands for him to take.

How many years? Dell was three feet away. In the time it took him to make contact with me, I counted back to my first dance in the eighth grade. I was more poised *then*.

I took his right hand with my left, his left with my right. We were less than a foot apart. The top of my head would barely reach his chin, if we had been that close. I felt the pressure of his hands as he began to guide me in the dance, turning us both in a circle. His palms were sweaty, or were mine? We were soon too close for me to see his face, but I could feel his breath on my hair. Strange, I found myself staring at the knot in his tie. The song had words, but I couldn't understand them. There were muted trumpets, and trombones, a sound like muffled clarinets, but it might have been saxophones. I wasn't sure. I was still facing him squarely, my nose pointed straight at his chest. Then the smell hit me, some blur of cologne and sweat. My head wasn't clear. I was dizzy. I hadn't been this close to a man in a long time. My right hand still held by his left, Dell released my other hand and put his free hand on my waist. For a brief moment I was helpless, unable to move my newly free hand anywhere, and it hung there in the air until, of its own volition, it moved around Dell and drew him close enough to me that our bodies finally touched. My head turned and I settled my face into the soft-hard spot between his shoulder and chest. I kept track of every motion, forgetting about April and Russell and Dana and all the rest. Dell was a good dancer. I remembered him lecturing me at the *Flamingo Room*, about me not having a body. Now, at this moment, surrounded by children, I wanted to tell him that he was wrong. Instead, with my lips feeling the texture of his jacket lapel and my eyes closed, I said again, "I'm not a good dancer."

I felt his hand squeeze my waist as he said, "First times are always awkward. You have to do it more than once, over and over, until you get it right."

The New Year

Education: the inculcation of the incomprehensible into the indifferent by the incompetent.—John Maynard Keynes

With no school for almost three weeks, I slept late every morning. December was sometimes cold in Atlanta. Not so in Florida, not this year. I could sit on my porch in the morning, drink tea, and finally catch up on the reading I had put off for the previous three months. I even found myself re-reading books I had read a decade earlier, but I kept Henry Adams on the shelf.

The last day of 1996, Kris came to see me. With the two of us sitting on my dock, she asked me when I was going to sell my parents' house and find a place of my own. "You keep putting it off," she said, rubbing suntan lotion on her legs.

I had already told her about Dell, about our dancing with hundreds of teenagers around us, about seeing him for lunch a few times, about him coming to see me at home. She asked, "You done the deed yet?" but I ignored her. I shifted the topic to teaching, how much I was beginning to like it, how happy I was that I had accepted Russell's offer, but Kris tried to bring it back to sex. I ignored her again, so she gave up, "You used to at least like *talking* about it."

The sun was putting me to sleep, but there was just enough of a breeze to keep me from getting hot. Tuning out Kris, I thought, *this would be a pleasant way to die.*

It was at that moment, in between being awake and being fully asleep, it was then that I found myself dancing again. It had been Dell's body next to mine but in my dream that body belonged to Russell. We were in that dark hallway again, back to last summer when we had met late at night at school. Somebody was watching us, I felt that. In my dream, I thought that other person was an unseen Dana O'Connor, but then I saw that it was my own mother. My mother when I was seventeen. I heard a bell ring and then a whispery voice.

"Oh, no, it's no bother. I'm here by myself."

I opened her eyes to see Kris talking to Tom on a cell phone. Seeing me, she put her hand over the phone and said, "This might take a long time. Go back to sleep."

I shook my head, stood up, waving at her to stay there, and then I walked back to the house. I called Dell and accepted his invitation to go out with him and a dozen other teachers to a New

Year's Eve party at his mother's house. He pointed out that there was no better chaperone than his mother.

Four hours later, wearing my best dress, waiting for Dell, drinking a glass of water, feeling good about life, I read the *Fort Jackson Press* list of "Notable Names Gone in 1996": Dorothy Lamour, Gene Kelly, Carl Sagan, Marcello Mastroiani, Timothy Leary, Audrey Meadows, Barbara Jordan, Francois Mitterand, Spiro Agnew, Erma Bombeck, George Burns, Ron Brown, Ed Muskie, Claudette Colbert.

I wondered if any newspaper ever had a list of "Notable Births of the Year." A special category for adults who were starting over.

I was too old to act like a teenager. Too old to sit by the phone. Too old to worry about how I looked to some boy. After the dance, however, I thought I'd see Dell a lot, was looking forward to it, surprised at how easy it seemed, and I actually stopped worrying about Russell and Dana and all the others. Kris kept asking about sex, and I kept being evasive because she wouldn't have believed that Dell had not touched me, the Nancy Adams whom she had known in high school.

Between the fall and spring terms, we had three weeks without students. But Dell wasn't as free as I was because Kennedy still played basketball over the Christmas break. Three games, three wins, and I went to each one, even if it meant driving to Tampa. I called Agnes and told her what I was doing, but she already knew. I called Donna to talk about Jackie Foster's trauma at the dance, and Donna asked me if I was seeing Dell. I even talked to Jackie and *she* asked me if I was "seeing the Coach."

The truth? I was seeing Dell several times a week, talking on the phone with him almost every day. Sometimes only a minute, an exchange of information and then goodbye. He called me more than I called him. We went to a movie, went to dinner, went to Gainesville for lunch. Our only really awkward moment was when he asked me to have dinner with him at the *Flamingo Room* again. I turned him down, pleading a schedule conflict. He then offered another night. I was typically evasive and non-committal, and too obvious about it. But he was a gentleman, asking for a raincheck.

Since the Christmas dance, in all that time, we had never been as physically close as we were that night. Left to the imagination of someone like Jackie the Smoker, we were sweating over each other's body all the time. Jackie lived in a time-zone where everything moved too fast. The twenty-two year age gap between her and me was more than a generation. It was a different country.

I was in no hurry. I just assumed there would be time. I was wrong, again. All it took was a call from Russell.

"We need to talk."

I was home, reading a book as if I had nothing else to do. "Dana?" I asked. "I have an idea about her I want to ask you about too, about what happened to her last year."

"No, you and Dell," he said quietly. "Come see me at school. We can get some scheduling things settled as well."

I wanted him to get to the point as soon as we sat down in his office to sort out the Spring schedule, but he insisted that we do "first things first." He was letting me pick students I wanted, blackball those I wanted to avoid, a reward for my first semester initiation. I would never have to deal with Dylan Abrams again. I laughed about that, but he told me that there was a Dylan every semester for every teacher. The names changed, not the types.

"Russell, are you always so slow to get to the real reason for a conversation?" I finally asked. "Last summer about Dana, about Dell now. We could have done this schedule stuff anytime."

"You like Dell?" he asked, not looking at me.

"Of course," I said. "Next question."

"Why?"

"Excuse me?" I stammered.

"Where are you going with him?"

"Russell…"

"I knew you'd like him…eventually…but not this. And I knew he would like you, but not like he does."

"Matchmaking wasn't your goal?" I tried to joke.

"Oh, Nancy, I feel so damn foolish, I just wanted to help people like you and Dana and Dell, people I care about. But it's all getting away from me."

As I waited for Russell to stop talking, the same old cloud started to come back over me. I was about to cry, but couldn't explain why. I had thought Russell was going to make me happy last year but I had been wrong, like I had been wrong about Jack, wrong about Russell when he was my teacher. For the past three weeks I thought I was happy again, for the absurd reason that I cared about a man who had disappointed me *before* I cared about him, not after. I had assumed I knew the worst about Dell Rose, so I couldn't be disappointed again.

"Russell, there's nothing you can tell me about Dell that I don't know."

"You haven't been to bed with him, have you, haven't even kissed him, have you?"

"Russell, you and everyone else can go to hell! And don't think you're being noble by trying to protect me from Dell, or from myself! Our private life is none of your or anybody else's business!"

I stood up to leave.

"He told me, Nancy, he told me everything."

I sat back down, beyond anger. Neither of us spoke, not until he could finally look me in the eye. "Not what you think," he said. "Not any sort of locker room talk, that sort of thing."

"You know, I never thought *that*," I sighed. "I was just wondering why he would tell you anything personal about us, since he seldom talks to me directly about his feelings, even though I know he likes me."

"Dell thinks he loves you, Nancy. Or something close. All he knows is that he has never felt this way before."

It was my turn to look down. A philandering black basketball coach thought he was in love with me. A fact that made me profoundly happy, and I wanted that feeling to last more than three weeks. I kept looking down, assuming that Russell wanted me to tell him how I felt about Dell, but he never gave me the chance.

"But he doesn't want to be," he said. "He's a fool, and he's prideful, and in his world it all makes sense, him stopping himself, but he's also a coward. I told him that. He was a coward, who should have been truthful with you. Thing is, he's never cared so much for someone before, like he does for you. I can't wait for him to put this off anymore, so I'm going to tell you…"

"Russell, please," I stopped him. "Don't do whatever you're going to do. Let me…let me…" and I stopped. He probably thought I was going to say something like *let me confront him* or *let him tell me himself*, but I whispered, "Let me be happy. For a little bit longer, just let me be happy."

He was silent, waiting for me to continue, but I just stared at the pictures on his office wall. "Dell is leaving Kennedy," he finally said, very quietly.

I jumped at a small thread of irrational hope, thinking I knew the reason immediately. Dell's conduct had finally become unacceptable. The school district was trying to avoid a lawsuit. He was politically incorrect and legally indefensible. "His conduct?" I asked, swelling with the idea that this was actually a good thing, for him to get away from real trouble later, and his reluctance about me was simply his not knowing where he was going to be next year.

"You really don't know, do you?" Russell said. "Well, he'll be glad to know that he's managed to fool even you. He thought he would never have to tell you, but then all this, this relationship, happened between you two and then he didn't know how to backtrack. Then he wakes up liking you."

"Russell, has this got anything to do with..., " I started to ask, remembering all those times I had seen Dell seem to lose control of himself.

"Dell has Parkinson's," Russell said. "He's known, I've known, for over a year."

All I could say, as I leaned back in my chair, trying not to cry, looking around again at pictures on Russell's office wall, was, "He's too young."

"He's the exception, and he's tried everything, even some brain surgery two summers ago, and every kind of pill, but it's getting worse. Accelerating in weird ways that even his doctors can't explain. Me, I'm amazed he can force himself to stop shaking sometimes."

"He's too young," I repeated.

"He's forty. Old enough," Russell said, getting up to come around and stand beside me.

"But he'll be okay eventually, won't he? I mean, he's not going to die," I said, shaking my head, trying to organize Dell's future in my mind. His own words came back to me, from when we had dinner. Something about men such as him and Jerry, as he tried to explain what he had that I lacked. Dell loved his body because it had been gifted. His body had separated him from lesser men and drawn women to him. Perhaps beautiful women felt the same about themselves. I never had. But women athletes, as gifted as their bodies might have been, couldn't have felt about themselves the way that Dell and men like him felt about their bodies. I knew that I could see Dell and tell him that as men got older they also got wiser, that his mind and heart were more important. I could say that to him, but I knew he would simply look back and tell me that I didn't understand. Nancy Adams didn't have a body, wasn't that what he had told me?

"I'm not sure you understand, Nancy, why Dell can't tell you how he feels."

"Oh, I think I do, I think I can try," I protested meekly. "I really do. I saw Dell when I was seventeen. I knew how different he was then. But ... but, Russell, Dell's more than his body, he has to know that. *You* have to know that. He can still coach. He can still be a teacher. He can still... "

"Nancy, Dell doesn't want to be a role model for how to be a graceful cripple. He's not ready for that yet. Not here, at least, at this school. And he's not ready to ask you to share all this with him."

After another long silence, I said, "You know, it should have been obvious."

"He did his best to divert attention away from all the signs. Told me that he would feign anger sometimes, anything, anytime he felt his hands begin to twitch. Keep his whole body in motion, or hide his hands. You see, he knew, people like him know, that their bodies will desert them eventually. But he's not ready. Not now, not this way. And he's angry."

"Who else knows?" I wondered aloud.

"You, me, and I'll tell Jerry soon. Dell handpicked him to be his successor and Jerry never knew. Dell wanted to make sure he had the right stuff, and part of that stuff was being willing and able to go from head coach at one school to assistant here and learn from him without any other assumptions. To see how big his ego was. Jerry hasn't disappointed us."

"And Agnes?" I asked.

"She was the first to know. Dell said his mama knew even before the doctors did. He's still her first-born."

"Oh, God, poor Agnes," I whispered as I began to cry. "Oh, crap crap crap, I hate all this. This is so. . ."

"So very. . . unfair?" Russell said, offering me a hand. "Sorry, I beat you to that line a long time ago." He helped me up and held my hand as I started to shake. "You probably need to talk to him, about you and him," he said. "He's afraid of losing more than his body. But you need to give him some space, too."

Walking back into the main office, he then asked me about my own future, "You need to decide if you're going to be back here next year, even if Dell isn't."

I leaned into his shoulder, first making sure we were alone. "First day of class the answer was no, a month later, maybe, then for the last few weeks I was definitely sure. But let me think about Dell for awhile, okay?"

"I want you to be happy," he said, "with your life and your work. I know how unhappy you've been for the last few years. I could hear it in the tone of your voice, the way you used to drink too much. But, whether you want to admit it or not, I think you like being a teacher. And from what your students say, I know you're a good teacher."

"You obviously haven't been talking to April Bourne," I almost laughed.

"Oh...*her*," he rolled his eyes. "She and I have talked a lot, even some about you. And you, my dear Nancy Adams, will be glad to know that I've given up on my idea to change the selection criteria for valedictorian. April's happy now. Any statistical tie between top students will be settled by looking at their extra-curricular activities."

"Finally, a smart move, Russell. You were being a little too upfront about trying to help certain other people," I said, pausing before I asked the obvious question. "Do you think Dana still has a chance?"

"Does it matter to you?" he asked.

"Actually, yes. And you knew I'd feel this way eventually, didn't you?"

"I was hoping you would get to this point. Not everybody does. I would've been disappointed if you didn't."

"So, for the record, how I feel about Dana determines how you feel about me? You want to think about *that?*"

It wasn't the response he expected. I could tell by how he wouldn't look me in the eye when he spoke. "Yes, it does matter," was all he said. "But how you feel about Dell and Agnes, and others, that matters too."

"Russell?"

He finally looked at me. "Dana matters to me. Do I have to explain that? You matter to me. Do I have to explain that? Jerry and Agnes and Donna and Sue, and Dell more than most, other teachers, and almost every kid at this school, they all matter to me. Some people here don't matter at all. But, do me a favor, don't make me explain why Dana matters so much."

Back in my classroom, I decided to wait for the right moment to talk to Dell. I had never been an impulsive person, so I set a deadline: a month. Let him tell me on his own terms. Russell's description of Dell kept coming back. More than proud, Dell Rose was a *prideful* man. And all of my proverbial audio-books kept playing at the same time. I listened to Dell's story, and Dana was in the background, Russell in the corner. Kennedy kept winning basketball games and a new semester started with new student names and faces. Life goes on, and on. Surely, there was a better cliché.

Crunching Numbers

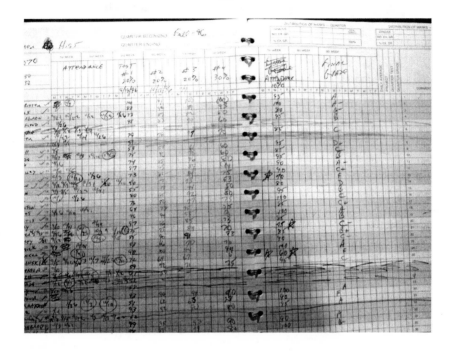

The world is run by C students. —Unknown Source

Jackie the Smoker was in my world civ class and hated it from the first day. "I went to the bookstore downtown, Miss Adams, looking for some Cliffs Notes to this class, and the guy laughs at me," she said. "The butthead. So, like are you gonna cut me some slack in here. I mean, this stuff is so very boring."

Dylan Abrams was gone, but his clone, Billy Hunter, a junior basketball player nine inches taller than me, was in the same class as Jackie. This time, however, I didn't let it bother me. But when Jackie saw Billy, she moved as far away from him as possible.

Fred and Dana were back for my spring honors class, but not April. Fred had a list of spring projects—get a Kennedy chapter of the Green Party organized, get a lackluster Kennedy debate team re-organized, get Dana to go out with him, get his parents back together. He also discovered coffee. The second week of class, Dana brought a stick to class and threatened to hit him if he didn't stop tapping his foot on the leg of her desk. Fred just beamed.

Every Kennedy faculty member got a letter from the school board asking for an *Equity Statement*. How did each teacher propose to "incorporate the values of gender equity in your classroom? How can your subject matter be used to ensure that students understand and recognize the fundamental sameness of men and women?" *The fundamental sameness?* Who wrote crap like that? I read the letter and waited for Dell to stand up in the faculty lounge waving the sheet of paper and declaring war, but he never said a word. Ashley Prose and Bob Skinner requested the issue be put on the agenda for the next faculty meeting, but Russell told them his "plate was full."

Dana kept turning in assignments for her make-up work. A+ in Honors, A+ work in her regular classes. Without April in my spring honors class, Dana talked less. She missed at least one class a week, usually because her baby was sick, but she never missed an assignment. She would bring me articles about the topics we were discussing in class that she had clipped out of magazines.

Russell told the faculty he was dropping the proposal to choose the valedictorian based only on grades. In the case of a statistical tie between students, he had said, extra-curricular activities could determine who was landed on top. When I went to see Donna to talk about Dana, and Russell's seeming capitulation, Donna pulled out Dana's transcript and showed it to me.

"Read 'em and weep, Nancy," she laughed.

In three years, except for the semester she was having a baby, Dana had five A's. The rest were A+'s.

"Check out how many of those A+'s have stars by them," Donna said, running her finger down the margins of the transcript as she stood over me. "Those are weighted courses, supposedly harder than the average class. An A+ in one of those carries a little bonus for your GPA. That's the rule, and Russell knows it."

"Is Dana really that smart? I mean, really?"

"Nancy, you know her. Do you really need to ask me?"

"I suppose not," I said. "I guess I'm too much of a cynic. I just don't believe in perfection."

Donna sat down across from me. "Dana O'Connor is brilliant, for sure, and even her standardized test scores back that up. But brilliant is not the same as perfect. Trust me, if she keeps at the pace and level she's doing now, Dana will be the 1997 Kennedy valedictorian, outside activities or not. Russell came to see me. I could do for you what I did for him. I could show you April's transcript, but *that* would be unprofessional of me, right? Just take my word for it. Absolutely sterling. But if Dana does all that make-up work as well as she seems to be doing it... there will *not* be a statistical tie, not even close, in her GPA and April's. April could join the few remaining clubs she doesn't belong to and it wouldn't make a difference. Russell knows the math. He's known for weeks."

"Has April figured that out too?" I asked. "That it's almost a foregone conclusion about Dana?"

"April's a very smart girl. Not brilliant, but certainly smarter than the average smart person. She'll figure it out soon enough, and I'd love to be there when she tells her mother."

"So, tell me," I started to tease her, "Are you in that Kennedy crowd that seems to love Dana O'Connor?"

Donna wasn't bothered. In fact, she laughed and clapped her hands. "Oh God, yes, Nancy. I love Dana Jean O'Connor. Have ever since I met her. A charter member of the fan club."

We looked at each other but didn't speak. I closed Dana's folder and shoved it across the table. Then, in a transition so smooth that I didn't see it coming, Donna asked, "So, when are you going to talk to me about you and Dell?"

"After I talk to Dell about Dell," I answered.

Bits and Pieces Add Up

I didn't go to high school, and I didn't go to grade school either. Education, I think, is for refinement and is probably a liability.—H. L. Hunt

Dell and I had already begun our conversation, in bits and pieces, as I waited for him to tell me the complete truth first. A month into the spring semester, right on schedule, I finally forced the issue with him. I had watched him for those few weeks, noticing how he seemed less angry, less prone to look for an argument with Bob Skinner or Ashley Prose. More often than not, in a faculty meeting or in the hall, he would smile at me, kick my leg under the table, joke about Jerry and me getting together, but he never laughed and he never raised his voice.

The change was noticeable to everyone. Ashley even tried to spar with him, to provoke him with a comment about gender equity or gender-neutral language in school board reports. So, just as she was beginning to become more comfortable being Betsy Elizondo's surrogate at Kennedy, and after she had lined up her allies among the other teachers, she was ready to go after Dell and Russell. But Russell ignored her, and Dell refused to play anymore.

Dell cared only about one thing. If this was his last year at Kennedy, he wanted a state championship. As the season headed for the playoffs, that championship seemed an inevitability. We had only lost one game, an away game with bad officiating and miracle baskets by the opponent, or so the Kennedy school paper had written, but that was enough to put a dark cloud over both Jerry and Dell for a week afterwards.

Jerry had told me that he wanted me to come watch the team practice. Watching a game was exciting, I admitted, but watching practice? He insisted, "Humor me."

He stayed on the floor with the team, and Dell sat in the bleachers, which I thought was odd because I knew that Dell was surely not interested in having any company as he watched his team. But Jerry was insistent. "Coach, you tell her how the game works and how smart I am," he had said, nudging me toward Dell.

As I sat on the bleacher next to Dell, I realized that I had been set up. Russell had already talked to Jerry, and I wondered if Jerry had set up Dell too. "I *know* how the game works. I was on the girls' team when I was a student here. All-state," I said.

Jerry blew his whistle as loud as he could and walked onto the court. "Foul for lying, Nancy. Kennedy didn't have a girls team in 1912 or whenever you went here. I already researched your career."

Even Dell laughed.

"For your information, smart guy," I said, "we did so have a team and..."

"*You* never tried out, Nancy, and I know that's the truth. You were too busy being a pain in the butt for all the coaches with your newspaper stories."

I started to respond, but then I was speechless. I had never told Jerry about my newspaper work when I was a student.

"Jerry's a good man, Nancy." Dell sat beside me, not looking in my direction.

Without thinking, I put my hand on Dell's arm, near his wrist as it rested on his leg. As soon as I did, he flinched, but he said nothing. I took my hand off and looked at Jerry at the far end of the gym. He was leading the team in a warmup drill. With them in some sort of rhythm, he looked back across the gym at Dell and I, and it was then that I realized why he had invited me to practice. Now was the time to talk to Dell. There was no subtle opening.

"What are you going to do next year?" I asked, neither of us looking at the other, both of us watching Jerry lead the team. Dell didn't answer. "You *can* talk to me, you know. I would have thought you would know that."

"Coach!" Dell suddenly shouted across the gym to Jerry, ignoring me. "Coach, remind them about posting up!"

"Dell..."

"Nancy, what do you want me to tell you? That I've come to terms with all this, all this that you seem to already know about, that I will be stoic and brave and a role model for everyone else?" he said without looking at me. "That this is not the end of the world? That I can still be a good coach and I can still do the same things I've always done? Is that what you want to hear?"

"Actually, yes, I was hoping to hear that," I said, trying to get him to look at me. "I was hoping..."

"I was hoping to do this on my own terms," he interrupted. "How many other people has Russell told?"

"Just me," she said. "And probably Jerry."

He nodded, and then he slid a few feet away on the bleacher, enough to turn so he could face me.

"You're okay, I guess. And I shouldn't be upset that Russell would tell you. I told him things about us," he said.

"So did I," she said.

Dell watched the court. Jerry had his hand on Billy Hunter's shoulder. Barely seventeen, Hunter was already taller than both his coaches.

"Student of yours?" Dell asked me.

"World Civ, and, no offense Dell, but I wish he were somebody else's problem."

"I'll talk to him."

"Jerry's already talked to him," I said.

Dell took a deep breath, flaring his nostrils and letting it out slowly. "The boy's all talent, but not a bone of charm anywhere. Jerry will have his hands full next year."

That was my opening. "Full circle, Dell. What are you doing next year? Are you going to be okay?"

"Coach!" he shouted again, pointing to Jerry and then to one of his seniors who had missed an easy layup. Then he turned back to me. "I suppose I'll be okay. I'm not going to die, am I? But I'm not gonna go to hell in front of these people here. You can call me immature, but I refuse to let anybody here see me turn cripple in the next few years. I'll win my last championship here this year. Then I'm gone..."

"Gone to where and what?"

"I've got options. My name is still worth something, and I'll be upfront with all of them. They'll know the truth. Even got one offer with Nike sales that will pay me triple what I make as a coach. Traveling, making endorsement deals with coaches around the country. Lots of virgin territory at the high school level."

"Nike..." I started to say.

"Don't lecture me about Nike and all those third-world kids in sweatshops. I know the devil I'm dancing with. *You* fight that fight. Me, I've got maybe three years before I can't even walk by myself. Five, tops. And I know that this don't mean squat to you, but I got maybe a year left that any pretty woman will give me the time of day. And, excuse my French, but I'm not interested in a charity fuck from some woman who'll ignore my spastic hands just so she can say she bagged the once-famous Dell Rose. You'll never understand, but I'll miss *that* as much as I miss coaching. Doing it, and knowing that a world of pretty women want to do it with me. I'll miss the hell out of that. But, like I said, you wouldn't understand."

The gym was beginning to smell like sweat. Thirteen young men were running back and forth across a hardwood floor, their hundred-dollar shoes squeaking when they pivoted to reverse direction. From north to south, and then back again. Dell was watching them, looking for signs of fatigue.

"You know, I still have that article you wrote about me a long time ago, the one they wouldn't let you publish," he said after awhile, standing up to go out on the floor. "The one about me being first in line if they ever started a new human race and needed a physical model."

I was mystified, "How's that possible?"

"You showed it to Russell when he was your teacher. He kept it, showed it to me when I told him about the Parkinson's. I was angry and down at the same time. Thing was, he was taking a chance. Something like that, about how I was *perfect* back then, something like that could have made me even more down. But it didn't. He gave me a copy, and I showed it to my mama. She appreciated it too."

"Thank you," I mumbled, sure that I was blushing.

"No, Nancy, I'm the one to thank you. I appreciate what you said back then. There never was a way to thank you before now. So, thanks."

I was on the fourth bleacher row looking down at him on the floor. He was still a stunning human form. "You're welcome, Dell. I just wish there was something I could say or do to help you now," I said, almost choking.

"I'll be okay eventually. I'll deal with this better *eventually*. You don't worry about me. You just take care of my mama and Jerry and your students. Most of all, you help Russell. He's gonna need you more than I do. And one more thing, Nancy, about us."

"You don't need to say anything right now. . ."

He put his finger on his lips. "Shush, I do need to say something, and we can sort it out later."

I waited as he looked at the court and then back at me. "I'm sorry. That's all I can say now. I'm sorry if I misled you, maybe misled myself. I guess I'm one of those guys who gets smart too late. And for that I'm sorry."

He turned and ran out on the floor, yelling for a ball. Jerry grinned at him, faked a pass, and then lofted the ball effortlessly into the basket from the corner of the court. Dell didn't stop moving. He raced to the basket, retrieved the ball, dribbled to an invisible mark forty feet away and, in one fluid motion, turned and lifted himself off the ground, suspended himself in mid-air, and released the ball. As his feet touched the floor, the ball went through the net with a swish that was almost a whisper.

Jerry raised his hands in surrender.

Ten months earlier, I had felt sorry for myself. I was alone. I thought other people were happier than me. I was desperate for something, even though I wouldn't have admitted it then. I had accepted Russell's job offer for the wrong reasons. I wasn't a teacher, I knew then. I was an educated book reviewer.

After talking to Dell about his future, I took a look at myself in the metaphorical mirror. I actually liked teaching. Most of my students liked me. I knew more about history than I would ever use in a classroom, but that was okay. It wasn't wasted. This spring term I knew more about teaching than I did when I began that first day, things no education course could ever teach me. In a few years, I told myself, I would be as good as any other experienced teacher. I might not be at Kennedy, but I would be teaching somewhere.

Control? I was learning to let go of things that I couldn't control. Wisdom, eh? Especially other people. I finally had my own life to lead, and I didn't have to live vicariously through others. I was beginning to make myself happy. My mother would be proud of me. I wouldn't change places with anyone I knew. Compared to most adults around me, my life was incredibly simple. I was healthy. I probably had job security. No other person was a threat to me. My parents were dead, I had no children, but for the first time in my adult life I felt like I had friends who cared about me and who would help me if I needed them. For every reason to be unhappy, I had another to justify happiness. This couldn't last, I was sure.

I went to visit Agnes to see how she was feeling about Dell, to tell her that I understood a lot of what she had been trying to tell me last summer. But as I sat in her kitchen, with that giant picture of Jesus looking down at me, I never mentioned Dell. Sitting at the table, I watched Agnes make pies, smelled apples and cinnamon baking, and remembered my mother's cooking.

We had been talking about Betsy Elizondo's plans for the district and what chance Russell had with his counter-proposals. Agnes was rolling dough into pie crusts, sprinkling flour all over the kitchen, hitting me and the dog who wandered in and out. As I watched her smooth out the dough with too much force, as if Betsy was under the roller, I suddenly changed the subject. "Tell me about Dell's father. Is Dell like him?"

Almost in mid-sentence, with both hands holding the roller, Agnes sat down, her dark face spotted with flour. "That's why Dell is different, because of his daddy," she smiled as she talked. "I was lucky to find him. I see Dell, I see his daddy. Nancy, you know how it is when you find someone who fills up your heart? You know that feeling?"

I wanted to tell her the truth, that I didn't know that feeling. At least, not for a long time. Instead, I merely nodded. Agnes accepted my insincere agreement as permission to speak in a language she assumed that I understood, but I felt like I was in a foreign land.

She told me how she had met her first husband, that first look and touch, the flowers of their first date, how her parents let him sleep on their couch, their going to Atlanta to hear Martin Luther King, Jr. preach, their marching together in downtown Fort Jackson in 1961 with a dozen other blacks as well as my own father, who had thought they would be part of a much larger crowd. "There we were, waiting at the AME for all those other folks who had promised to march with us," Agnes spoke as if it had happened yesterday. "We knew there'd be trouble down at the courthouse, but if there'd been enough of us then we thought we'd be safe. Dell was barely able to walk, and I was chilled, Nancy, but Thomas stood up and told us he'd go by himself if he had to. Lord God, how could I not love that man, I said to myself at that moment."

I was spellbound. "What happened?"

She laughed and slammed her palm down on the table, raising a white cloud of flour. "Went down there, through the town, past a lot of angry white folks, most of 'em grandparents of the kids I teach now, went to the registrar's office, Thomas in the lead. Of course, the office was closed. They knew we were coming. But we told them we'd be back. When it finally happened, us finally voting, Thomas wasn't there to see it."

We sat there smelling pies in the oven as I asked one more question, "How did you deal with...with him dying?"

If Agnes had burst out crying, I would have understood and probably cried with her. But she took a deep breath and smiled the sweetest smile I had ever seen.

"My children, and everybody, I guess, think I've been a Christian all my life. But I took the faith only after Thomas died. If Jesus hadn't filled up my heart, the sacred place that Thomas created, then I'm sure I would have died. Truth is, Jesus was the only one I could have loved as much as I loved Dell's father."

I left Agnes's kitchen and walked to downtown Fort Jackson. Another postcard spring day in Florida. Outdoor sales were going on all over town, and sometimes I had to step around a rack of clothes or table full of bags that were blocking the narrow sidewalks. There were almost as many black people as white in town this afternoon. I saw the girl who had danced so much with Mike Lankford at the Christmas dance, still wearing Mike's baseball cap, but she was walking hand in hand with a tall black boy who was wearing a Jackson High School athletic t-shirt. Some of my new students were there too. If they were with their parents, they would point at me and I would be introduced.

Sitting alone at an outdoor table in front of the Walgreen's, drinking a Coke, thinking about possible test questions, I looked across the street and saw Dana and Russell. I shouldn't have been surprised, but I was. In my mind they were always together, but I had never saw them physically together at Kennedy or anywhere else. They were both wearing sunglasses, but not as a disguise. It was a bright sunny day. Dana was in her usual baggy clothes, Russell in jeans and a white dress shirt with the sleeves rolled up to his elbows.

With shoppers walking in front of me, I lost sight of them for a moment. When I found Russell again, Dana was gone, replaced by an old woman standing next to him. He was showing her a dress on the rack behind them. Then his daughters walked up to him and the old woman, one of them pushing a baby stroller. The two girls stood on either side of the woman, pushing their father aside as they started pulling dresses off the hangers and holding them up against the woman and themselves. Russell pushed the baby stroller into the store and disappeared. Then Dana emerged, pushing the same stroller, but with the baby in her arms.

Russell walked out of the store with a package and put it in the stroller, and then he held out his arms to Dana for the baby. Dana shook her head and laughed. Russell walked over to his daughters and started putting dresses on hangers, but the woman wouldn't give one of the dresses back. She kept holding it against her body, rubbing the sleeve on her face. He didn't seem to mind. One of his daughters whispered to him and he turned to look across the street, his eyes searching until he found me. He stared for a second, motionless, and then he waved at me to come over. I waved back, holding up my glass to show him that I hadn't finished, but then also holding up two fingers to let him know that I would be there in a few minutes. I took my time finishing the Coke. Dana saw me and waved too, then walked over to the woman and talked to her as she pointed back to me.

Halfway across the street a few minutes later, I stopped cold. The old woman was Stella Malone Parsons.

"You directing traffic?" Russell yelled to me as I stood in the middle of the street.

When I got across, one daughter was holding Dana's baby, the other seemed to be hiding behind her father's back. Stella was still holding the dress. Russell re-introduced his daughters to me, after reminding them that they had met me at the first football game. As he turned to his wife, I was keenly aware that Dana was watching me.

"Stel, you remember Nancy Adams, don't you," he said, nodding in my direction. "Class of 77, the valedictorian, and just starting at Kennedy this year as a teacher."

She didn't respond. And all of us—father, daughters, Dana, and me—were suspended in time and motion.

"Stel..." Russell started to say again, but she spoke abruptly.

"Russ, my memory is fine," she said in a voice that made each word sound like it had been pounded by a stone crusher. "I remember her fine," her head slowly tilting over as if she was trying to rest it on her own shoulder. "But I doubt that she remembers me."

"Of course I do, Miss ... Stella," I said, instinctively extending my hand. Stella remained motionless, so I stopped my hand halfway across. "How have you been?" I asked, a formality. Unlike my hand, however, I immediately realized that I couldn't pull the question back. Stella stared at me, and I tried to not look directly at her contorted face, the white crust at the corner of her lips, the droop of one eyelid, the remains of a once beautiful woman.

Dana stood next to Stella, her hand moving from Russell's arm to Stella's, taking the dress out of Stella's hands and giving it to him. "Thank you, Stella," she said.

Stella finally spoke, but I didn't understand her at first. The words were clear enough, but not the meaning. "How do you think she will look?" Stella said, her left arm limp at her side, her right trying to point at Dana.

I looked at Dana, then Russell.

"It's my graduation dress," Dana said. "A present from the Parsons."

The daughter behind Russell, who had not spoken even when we met in the fall, suddenly chimed in, "I think it's gorgeous, and daddy picked it out himself."

"He did not!" Dana almost squealed, laughing and reaching around Russell to slap at his daughter.

"I did too. I have impeccable taste," Russell said, winking at me while keeping his body between Dana and his daughter as they made faces at each other.

Dana was acting like a teenager, something I had seldom ever seen before. She was acting her age. She took a deep breath and turned to face me as if to say something profound and I thought she might morph back into the Dana I knew, the myth and rumor. Seeming to ignore Russell's daughter, she looked straight at me, but at the same time she reached back and poked the daughter in her ribs, setting off another round of laughter from everyone except Stella and me.

Dana was having fun. Russell and she and the two younger girls were a family. Stella and I were outsiders, or so I thought at first. Until Stella spoke.

"Dana, I picked it out," she said, in the same gravelly voice but without the benefit of a face that could express emotion. Hurt or happy, the tone was always the same.

Dana changed from playful daughter to grateful daughter in a blink. "I knew that. That's why I thanked you first."

I suppose that if I had known Stella since her stroke, had been around her more, I might have learned to interpret that face better. Perhaps I was over-interpreting at that moment, but I thought I saw something in an otherwise blank look, something that told me that Stella Malone loved Dana O'Connor. *They* were a family, and I finally understood. I was the outsider.

Five minutes later we parted. After idle conversation about clothes and the weather, with the twins pulling at their father's sleeves as if to get him to leave me, the boring adult, and pay attention to them, five minutes of pleasant quips about Dana's refusal to dress better and Russell's refusal to dress in anything other than those double-breasted suits for school, five minutes in which Stella never spoke again, we said good-by and I watched them walk away. The twins in front taking turns pushing the baby stroller, Dana and Russell flanking Stella as they walked behind the twins. At first, Dana had her arm entwined with Stella's, but she soon surrendered possession to Russell, who put his arm across Stella's shoulders and then, in a motion that was as natural as breathing, he leaned down and kissed his wife lightly on the top of her head.

Dana moved ahead of Russell to line up with the twins. I thought she was going to take back the baby stroller, but then the universe shifted right before my eyes. How else to explain the sudden and irrevocable truth about Dana that had always been hidden out in the open and which explained everything about her and Russell. I had sometimes wondered, suspected, that Russell could have even been Dana's real father. Anything was possible, right? And there were subtle signs. Dana's mother had been one of his students a long time ago. Russell wasn't a saint... except around me, right? Some secrets *could* be kept, right?

I was wrong. I was so goddam wrong I almost cried there that sunny day in Florida in the middle of my hometown. Dana and one of the twins dropped behind Russell and Stella... and why at that moment couldn't I remember the twin's name... I owed her that much, the simple courtesy of knowing her name, the simple respect. Which one was it? Sally or Theresa? And it came to me as I watched her and Dana put their arms around each other's waist, walking hip to hip behind Russell and Stella, shoulder to shoulder, each face leaning toward the other, taking turns whispering to each other, each whisper lasting long enough so that their lips seemed to caress the other's earlobe. That caress was seamless as I saw their faces turn toward each other, and they kissed like two people in love.

The twin was Theresa, as was Dana's daughter.

Without turning around or breaking stride, Russell motioned over his shoulder for the two girls behind him to move back ahead of him. Two adults, three teenage girls, and a baby... six moving bodies all synchronized in a family procession. Dana and Theresa had gotten out of place, but Russell directed them back to the middle. Dana went to the right, Theresa to the left, and they met again in front of Russell and Stella. Met and rejoined. Arm and arm again, with Russell and Stella watching over them. I was merely a spectator, but I knew that I had become complicit in their lives, in Dana's future, just like Agnes and the others, but I knew more than they did.

Water and Death

It is the mark of an educated mind to be able to entertain
a thought without accepting it.—Aristotle

A week after seeing Russell and his family downtown, I asked him
to let me have the keys to the Kennedy swimming pool. I then
called Dana and asked if she wanted to go swimming. Just the two
of us, late in the evening, lights out.

"How do we sneak past Darrell the janitor?" Dana had laughed.
"Doesn't he live in some closet at school?"

"Dana, a friend of mine and I used to sneak in there all the time. Darrell never caught us. Unless you plan on bringing some jazz band with you, we'll be fine."

"Can I bring Tess?" she asked. "She's still sick, and I don't want to leave her."

"No problem," I said. It occurred to me that Dana's child was the quietest baby I had ever been around. "But, aren't you even going to ask me why I'm inviting you to go swimming like this?"

"Okay, Nancy, I'll bite. Why are you inviting me to go swimming like this? You planning on seducing me?"

"You never seemed to be the seducible type, Dana. If anything, you seem…" and I stopped myself. I waited, but there was silence on the other end of the phone. I listened for breathing, but there was nothing. "Dana?" I finally said. "You still there?"

"I suppose you're right," Dana said. "I'm not the seducible type. Too suspicious of motives, too cautious, just like you. But, you know, I'm a helluva swimmer. Would you believe me if I told you about swimming with some dolphins over in the ocean near St. Augustine? An inlet near that fort they have, on a dare. You ever swim in the ocean at night?"

"Dana, how well do you think you know me? Is that something you would expect me to do?"

"Odd thing is, even if you don't believe it, I think you know me better than I know you. So, is this swimming party your idea, or Russell's?"

"Mine."

"Good," she said. "We can play *Truth or Dare*. Me first. About your question, how well do I know you, the answer is that I don't think I know you at all. But I'd be surprised if you told me that you liked swimming in the ocean."

"I used to like swimming in the St. Johns, day and night."

"That's a start," Dana said. "See you tonight."

I picked her up at the lawyer's office and we drove to Kennedy in my car. Dana's Toyota was crumbling, and it could have been heard coming a mile off. Darrell wasn't *that* deaf.

Tess was already asleep in a portable car seat when I arrived at the office, and Dana kept the seat in her lap as we drove. She had a trait that most mothers have, she constantly touched her child. A pat or a soft stroke across the forehead, and her eyes were always alert to see if the baby was awake.

The trick to sneaking into the Kennedy pool, I explained to Dana, was not to park around back where the sliding glass doors to the pool were located. Cars back there were always a tip-off. Park in front, then go through the whole building, always knowing where Darrell was sleeping, and enter through the locker rooms. Having Russell's keys made it easy. When I was a student, however, I had had to leave door locks taped or windows unlocked during the day, assuming that Darrell wouldn't check.

No indoor lights, just the parking lot orange lights shining through all that glass. The pool had an underwater floodlight, but that could have been seen from the outside. As we opened the sliding doors to get a breeze, Dana offered her first test of my courage.

"You know how to open that roof?" she asked, laying Tess on a blanket safely away from the edge of the pool.

"Too loud!" I reflexively answered. "If it needs any oil at all, you can hear it all the way to town."

"It would be nice. You know, floating, looking up at the sky," she said, unbuttoning her blouse.

I watched her undress completely, assuming she had her suit in the bag she had brought. But I was wrong. As Dana walked naked to the edge of the pool, I studied her body. Even in the dim orange light, I could see that pregnancy and birth had not been kind to her.

Turning around, she noticed me staring. "Jesus Christ!" she hissed, covering her breasts with one arm, spreading her fingers on the other hand and trying to cover her stomach. "This is not a goddam freak show."

I stammered, "Sorry...I wasn't staring...I was just surprised you were going to swim nude, that's all. I just assumed, I mean, that you had a suit."

It was a lame excuse, but enough to satisfy her.

"Dana O'Connor swims naked, isn't that what you really expected?" she said. "I mean, it is Dana O'Connor, after all, the rule-breaker. Isn't this so typical of her?"

"I'll open the roof," I said, the irritation in my voice obvious. As I walked away, I yelled back, "And, Dana, you don't always have to be a legend in your own mind, you know." All I heard was a splash.

Standing in front of the control panel, I took a deep breath and pulled the roof switch. Except for a brief pop and surge of electrical current, the roof slid open with a low hum. When I got back to the edge of the pool, Dana was waiting in the water.

"Race you!" she laughed, splashing water on my feet. She then pushed away and floated on her back. I had been wearing my own bathing suit under my clothes, and it only took a few seconds before I was in the water. Dana had been right. Floating, looking at the night sky, it was not unpleasant. It was even more than pleasant. It was good.

We ignored each other for the first few minutes, swimming by ourselves, doing slow laps across the width of the pool. Dana would swim to the edge every few minutes, raise herself up out of the water and look to where Tess was sleeping. Satisfied, she would swim back. She and I met at the floating rope-divider in the center of the pool. Both of us were breathing hard, our arms draped over the rope.

"What's your excuse?" Dana asked me. "Me, I just had a baby. I've got a right to be out of shape. Why are you huffing and puffing?"

"I'm thirty-eight, Dana. Pushing forty. And I've been sitting on my backside grading papers for too long."

She cupped her hands together, squirting water out like a fountain. "Thirty-eight, that's not old. You're just out of shape. Exercising your brain and not your butt...no disrespect intended. And you haven't been teaching *that* long."

"None taken," I said. "I'll admit to a complete disregard for my body."

Dana suddenly shivered, turning her head toward her baby. Neither she nor I spoke for minutes, listening to the wind blowing over the open roof and the pool waves lapping the edge. Then she relaxed. "She'll be okay, don't you think," she said.

"Sure," I agreed.

We swam some more and then ended up back at the rope.

"Why are we here?" Dana asked. We were on opposite sides of the rope, about six feet apart. "Exercise ain't the reason."

"Did Russell tell you about the night last summer that he and I sat on the edge of this pool?"

I could see Dana's eyes get bigger, the orange light bouncing off the water and reflecting off her face.

"No! Did you go swimming together? Did you get in the water with him?" she whispered, floating closer to me.

"No, we spent most of the time talking about you." As soon as I said it, she backed away from me. "He wanted me to help you, to be, in his words, an *older woman* for you."

Dana shook her wet hair, splattering my face with water, and said with disgust, "Yeah, I forgot, you're thirty-eight. My surrogate mother."

"Your *older woman*," I corrected.

"Nancy Adams, my older surrogate mother, to go along with my older surrogate father, Russell Parsons," she said, seemingly bored, no longer disgusted, as if hearing the same song too many times.

"You know, you *are* a textbook case of a young woman seeking a lost father through some sort of older male authority figure..." and I stopped, hearing myself sound like a textbook, sensing the opening about to close. "Am I starting to sound like..."

Dana interrupted, "You're starting to sound like that idiot Ashley Prose. And if you really think that Electra stuff explains anything about me, then you're not as smart as I think you are."

"You want to explain yourself? Cut out the middle-man?"

"Nancy, all I want to do is be happy. Is that so hard to understand? Is that so different from you?"

I told Dana about my father telling me that the goal of life was to do good, but that my mother told me to be happy, and for a long time I felt like I had been doing neither. I told her that I was beginning to think that teaching would let me do both. I was about to tell her my whole life story, but I remembered that I had asked Dana to go swimming with me so that she would talk about herself, not listen to her teacher.

"Dana, if I ask you a direct question, will you answer it without all your usual cryptic evasions…"

Her hands slapped the water. "Whoa! Cryptic evasions! How perfect! Oh God, Nancy, you are so articulate, so wonderfully precise, so much fun to listen to. Oh sure, I'll answer anything you want. As honestly as I can, but I'm not sure you'll get what you want. Fire away."

"Are you in love with Russell Parsons?"

"Absolutely and positively," she said instantly, looking directly at me, daring me to look away.

"And?" I said, offering her a chance to say more. Wasn't this a chance for her to tell me about her and Russell's daughter?

"Nancy, you asked me if I was in love with him. I answered truthfully. But I love him in a way that even I don't understand. I've never felt this way about any other man in my life, ever. If I was different, and he was younger and single, it would all make sense. But it is what it is. We are who we are. Next question."

"Have you slept with him?" I knew the answer, but I wanted Dana to think she could shock me with some other truth.

"Had sex with him, you mean? That's what you mean, right? No, he's never touched me. He could, and I've wondered what it would be like, but he hasn't."

"A lot of people think you have."

"A lot of people are full of shit."

"You want me to stop?" I asked. "You don't have to do this, you know."

"Sticks and stones can break my bones, Nancy, but questions aren't going to hurt me. You just remember the rules."

"The rules?"

"*Truth or Dare* is a two player game. You get your questions. I get mine. You think you can poke at me without getting poked back... the game is over."

"Who's the father of your baby?" I asked before she could catch her breath.

"None of your damn business, none of your goddam business," she gasped back, pushing herself away from the rope, swimming over to the edge of the pool and getting out to see how Tess was doing. She stood over the baby and looked down, dripping water, but she didn't pick her up. Then she walked to the far end of the pool, her naked body going into streams of orange light and then into darkness, in and out like a ghost. I started to swim toward her, but she waved me back, "Stay there, we're still playing."

"Sticks and stones, Dana," I called to her.

She dived into the pool with hardly a ripple and swam underwater as far as she could, coming up for air only once. Back at the rope, her first words were, "Truth or Dare, Nancy, not sticks and stones. And it's my turn."

"Ask away."

"Not a question. First, I have a dare for you."

I wasn't prepared for that. "I thought I was supposed to be given a choice. You offer, I choose, that's how it works."

"How it works now is that if you accept this dare, and do it, I answer your last question truthfully."

"What's the dare?" I asked.

"No, no. You want the truth, I get the dare."

"Well, it seems to me that you're betting that you can dare me to do something, here and now, that I won't do, so you won't have to answer. Am I right?"

"Do you accept the dare? Or not?"

"I accept," I said, wondering how I had gotten to this point.

She smiled at me, pushing wet hair away from her eyes, and said, "I dare you to take off your swimsuit. I dare you to be naked in this pool with me and to walk around the pool naked, just me and you and Tess here, and Tess is the only one with clothes."

"You don't think I'll do it, do you?"

"You're free, white, and thirty-eight, Nancy. It's your decision. Nobody here but us chickens, and nobody's got a camera. Not any way to blackmail you."

"I do it, you answer truthfully?"

She simply nodded. I looked around the pool, as if confirming the obvious. We were alone. Why this particular dare? Dana wasn't interested in my body, I was sure of that. But then I wasn't so sure. If she was in love with Russell *and* Russell's daughter, what else was possible in her world? What would this prove?

I looked around one more time and then pulled down my shoulder straps. Getting it off wasn't as easy as I expected. It was a one-piece suit that zipped up the side, but peeling out still required me to let go of the rope and slip underwater. Coming back up, suit in hand, I gasped for breath, "Satisfied?"

Dana moved closer and took the suit out of my hand. Then she threw it out of the pool. "The walk?" she said.

"I...I can't do that," I admitted.

"Nancy, you ever think that Russell wanted me to help *you*, not the other way around? You're wound so tight I'd be surprised if you pee with your eyes open."

"So, I guess you win," I said, starting to swim to the edge of the pool and get out to retrieve my suit.

"Jesus, Nancy, come back here and talk to me, please! I'll give you full credit for getting naked. Forget the walk. You earned your answer," Dana said.

Face to face once more, a few feet apart, both of us naked in the water, I asked again. "The father?"

"The absolutely honest answer is…I don't know who her father is."

"Dana, is this another…"

"Nancy, you think I'm proud of this? That I like listening to everyone whisper behind my back. Dammit to hell, if I knew I still wouldn't tell anyone. But I'd tell you at this exact moment because you earned the truth. You know what Mrs. Rose said when I told her I was pregnant? She asked the same father question, but I wouldn't tell her. She called me Hester Prynne, and I knew why. She thought Russell was the father and I was just protecting him. I like Mrs. Rose, respect her, but I wouldn't tell her what I just told you."

She was telling the truth, I knew that. But the truth had a way of creating even more questions. Sometimes the truth explained nothing. Knowing that Dana didn't know who the baby's father was, I knew I had been right about how Dana had gotten pregnant. I now had a more important question than simply the father's identity. "Why did you keep the baby? You didn't have to, you know that, don't you."

"Oh, sure, I could've done a lot of things. Gone to Gainesville and gotten an abortion, like my mother told me to do. Just not tell anybody and act like it never happened. I could have put her up for adoption, like Russell wanted me to do. After he told Stella, she even said they should adopt the baby themselves. I would keep the baby, and they would keep me and my baby together. All of us together. Me and Theresa, all of us. But that would be crazy I told them."

"Russell knew you were pregnant as soon as it happened? Does he know that you don't know who the father is?"

Dana shook her head, and for awhile I thought she wasn't going to say anything else. Overhead, the sky was getting cloudy and the stars were disappearing. "You're the only one that knows that I *don't* know. Only you, not even Russell. Everybody else has an opinion, but they don't know dick."

"You want me to change the subject?" I asked.

"I'm not sorry I did it, Nancy. Kept my baby. I just wish she had a better mother than me."

"I'm going to change the subject," I said.

"So why didn't you and your husband ever have any children?" Dana asked, changing the subject for me.

"Okay," I said, looking left and right and then back at her, "The new subject is Nancy Adams."

I talked for a long time. About how Jack and I had decided early that we would wait to have children until after he was firmly established in his practice, and then we had another reason to wait, and then another, and then he was dead. I admitted that the delay was mostly my idea. "Any regrets now?" Dana asked.

"I'm not good mother material," I said. "And now I am too old."

I talked about Jack, about falling in love and falling out, about his *other* life. I talked about a time after he died when I hated him, and to prove how much I hated him I would sleep with his friends or colleagues. If I had told Dell or Russell those things, they would have been surprised that I was capable of having sex with any man, much less a lot of them. Dana just listened. She asked if I *cared* for Dell, careful not to say love. I told her that I cared but I wasn't sure that was enough. Slapping water at me, she said, "It's a start."

She asked about my parents, if they loved each other. Of course they did, I said without reflection. But then I thought about how easily my mother seemed to get over my father's death. Where could it have gone, that love?

"Did you love Russell when you were his student?" she asked casually.

"Absolutely...positively," I tried to joke, but Dana repeated the question. I looked at her and tried to make a point about students loving their teachers, how it was understandable, how it was a phase, how I had simply gone through that phase. I was my own example, but I knew that Dana was hearing the implicit sermon about all students and teachers.

I had been hired by Russell, I thought at that moment, so I could be a living lesson for Dana. Nancy Golden Adams had become a parable, and the lesson was *life goes on.* I remembered what Jerry had told me about why he liked math. And why he liked teaching it. Math was never a matter of answers. It was process. Learn the rules, the laws of math, and you could always find the right answer. Swimming naked with Dana at that moment, I saw myself as merely a process. I was young once. I grew up. The iron law of maturity. Childish things had to be put away. If Dana understood the rules, she would come to the right answer. If A equaled B, and B equaled C, then A equaled C. I could have been more subtle, I suppose, and let Dana figure it out herself. She might be mature for her age, but she was still only eighteen. Eighteen, pushing a hundred, but still eighteen, carrying a ton of baggage, hiding the fact that she loved another girl *and* that girl's father. A lover's love and a child's love. Nobody at eighteen should have a life so complicated.

Dana swam in a circle around me, the center of a ripple.

"When you knew Russell back a million years ago, Nancy, he was older and engaged. Did that stop you from loving him?" she asked.

"Yes," I said quickly.

She swam away, but not before saying, "Yeah, right."

"You loving him doesn't mean he loves you," I shouted as Dana neared the far end of the pool, my voice echoing off the water and walls. It was a spiteful and petty line that came from the same recess of my heart that wanted to really tell her, *You can have his daughter, but you can't have him.*

I wanted her to understand another rule of life. There were no guarantees. Love, especially, guaranteed nothing.

She kept swimming, and I finally swam after her. Something made me want to confront her. To tell her to grow up for real, to accept whom she was. After all, she ought to listen to me. I was so much wiser. I was the goddam older woman. She was at the deep end of the pool, treading water, waiting for me.

As soon as I caught up with her, I realized that I was exhausted from being in the water so long. So was she. We no longer had the rope to support us, so we swam slowly in circles. Dana did all the talking, but she had to stop in mid-sentence time after time to catch her breath.

"Nancy, you're right. He's too old and he loves his wife. He's not *just* married to her. He loves her... and even if nobody else in this town likes her, I know Russell loves her. He'll never leave her. That's what nobody else understands...thinking he's unhappy because of her, but I do...I understand...he's unhappy *for* Stella...

not because of her. He loves Stella...I can live with that. Hell, I can even live with the worst thing he ever said to me and he didn't know how cruel it was."

I was about to learn something about myself.

"One time we were out for lunch together, not in this town for sure, I was only sixteen. It was obvious to me that he liked me a lot, so I asked a stupid question. I asked him *why* he liked me. And he told me the goddam truth, and for that afternoon I hated him. He told me that I reminded him of Stella, how he imagined what Stella must have been like when she was my age, before she met him, before she had that stroke and disappeared. He said I was a lot like her. I had to get up and go to the john so I could cry without him seeing me. And yet, a day later, I realized that I was in love with him. He had lost the Stella he fell in love with, and then I go and get pregnant and I knew he felt like he had lost me too. But, the pissy thing? I understood that it also meant that he lost Stella again. He had been helpless to protect her, so he was protecting me. Truth was, I didn't protect myself, but Russell blamed himself. Does that make any sense? Me, I wanted him and me to exist in a different universe. I wanted me to be the center of that universe at least one time. I wanted him to whisper something to me about a universe without Stella and a universe in which I was not who I am."

Sense? She wanted to know if it made any sense? It made too much sense. How many times was I told in high school that I was just like Stella? Kris's laughter came back, *If you're so smart, how come you aren't happy?* Right, if I was so smart why did I need an eighteen-year-old girl to explain me to myself?

"But you seem to be making the same mistake everyone else makes," she continued, getting no response from me. "About me and Russell. I love him for sure, but he's not..."

My shoulders and thighs were beginning to ache. I knew that if I stayed in the water, I would soon get muscle cramps. "Dana, I have to get out and rest," I gulped, stopping her but assuming she would finish what she was saying as soon as we were out of the pool.

"God, I was hoping you would say that," she said, obviously relieved that I surrendered first. "This truth game is wearing me out."

My clothes were at the other end of the pool, but I didn't have the strength to swim back that far. Reaching the nearest ladder, I climbed out of the water and sat on the edge of the pool. Dana was right behind me. She sat a few feet away from me and then, her feet still in the water, she laid all the way down on the concrete, her hands clasped over her eyes. I did the same, and we lay there for a few minutes listening to ourselves take deep breaths. "Time to get back to the real world," I finally said.

"Yes ma'am," was all she said.

We walked back to where Tess was sleeping, both of us naked and wet. I stopped and picked up my suit but didn't bother putting it back on. My dry clothes were near enough. Dana, still naked, got down on her hands and knees to look at her baby as I dried off and began dressing.

"Nancy?"

It was Dana, but a voice I had never heard before.

"Nancy…"

"Dana, are you okay?"

"She's cold…Tess is too cold."

In the orange light, I watched Dana O'Connor vanish.

Devolution and God

You can educate yourself right out of a relationship
with God.—Tammy Faye Bakker

After Russell told me the real reason Theresa O'Connor had died,
I went to church. I wasn't looking for comfort, or an explanation. I
was looking for that smug bastard Henry Adams. I wanted to tell
him that I finally understood how he felt when he went to see his
dying sister in Italy. Of everything in his *Education*, I had re-read
that scene more than once. It was the only time I thought he was
a real person.

I couldn't tell anyone that I went looking for Adams in a small
Catholic church in Fort Jackson, Florida. They would see it as

the pretentious gesture of an emotionally repressed woman. I was ready to plead guilty. "I could intellectualize intellect," I had admitted to Dell one night, "and I could even trivialize it." I could make it one of those simplistic homilies like I used to hear in Mass every Sunday. With a straight face, I could spin an analogy, could say that intellect was like a parasitic Georgia kudzu plant, greenery that killed the natural vegetation and spread along the telephone poles and power lines of the highway. Green, the color of life, but poison.

My students, probably not even Dana, had never heard of Henry Adams, would surely not understand him. The other teachers at Kennedy? Most had heard of him, a few had actually read him. But why should they care? And they were right. He was a luxury of the idle mind. I was a high school teacher, a life of incessant and active endeavor. I *thought* those words—incessant and active endeavor—and knew I would never say them out loud. Dana had laughed at the way I spoke, my precise and articulate words. To be a good teacher, I knew, I didn't need Henry Adams. He was a dead white male, and he had now become exactly what he perceived himself to be even then—irrelevant. I went to church after school. I went alone. I hadn't seen Dana since her baby's funeral. I took a stack of essays with me, along with a letter from Betsy Elizondo asking me to come see her. An official letter from *the* Elizabeth Elizondo, School Board Chair, with her signature written by a secretary who had printed her own initials next to Betsy's name. I was being asked to "discuss the recent unfortunate event on school property."

Adams wasn't waiting for me. I made a feeble effort to conjure up some sort of philosophical puzzle: Even with me sitting there, was the church still empty? I looked at the stained glass, the ornately painted ceiling, the gold cross. There was nothing there. I remembered how Agnes had surprised me the last time I was in that church, before I went to find Dana. If Agnes had showed up this afternoon, I could have turned her into a sign of something. But Agnes never came.

Henry Adams had been in Italy to watch his sister die. A gorgeous season of warmth and color, and a horrible death. His sister had bruised her foot, a mere bruise. The wound had become infected with tetanus ending in rot and lockjaw ending in convulsions. A beautiful woman dead. That's how I remembered Adams's description. And the conclusion: God might, indeed, be a *Substance*, but he certainly could not be a *Person*.

Adams had summer in Italy. I had spring in Florida. Was it like comparing John Adams to Ulysses Grant? Henry Adams to Nancy Adams? Adams was surely right about Darwin being wrong, I understood now. Why wasn't I so smart when I was younger, when I first had to read him? My professor at Notre Dame had insisted that the twentieth century began with Henry Adams. The twentieth was now ending, the twenty-first a few years away. Of all the books I read back in college, in a curriculum of male writers, taught by male teachers—all of whom were surprised that I was a history major and not an English major, who thought my accent was quaint and my ambitions uncharacteristic—only *The Education* was beyond my reach. But I never admitted that to them.

I could have been more self-indulgent there in church, waiting for Adams so I could tell him that my experience had finally caught up to my education, but I had to get home to grade papers.

"She's not breathing."

I kept telling Dana to put her clothes on and find a phone to call 911. I knew CPR, a legacy of hours of volunteer hospital work when I was a doctor's wife, and I worked on little Tess O'Connor as best I could, careful to not apply too much pressure, but Tess must have been dead long before her mother came back to her. For those few minutes before the EMTs arrived, I wasn't thinking. I was breathing into a baby's mouth and yelling at her mother between gasps.

Dana found a phone and called Russell first. He told her to hang up and call 911. He was at the school almost as soon as the ambulance got there. I was still working on Tess when an EMT kneeled down beside me and took over. It was then that I noticed the red lights flashing outside. The first words out of my mouth were, "I think it's SIDS." The EMT nodded grimly and put his fingers on the child's throat while listening for a heartbeat with a stethoscope.

I looked for Dana and saw her wrapped in a blanket, with Russell's arm around her. He looked at me and shook his head. With Russell and Dana to my left and the EMTs to my right, the pool room was suddenly flooded with bright overhead lights. Darrell the janitor had finally found us.

The story was dutifully reported in the *Fort Jackson Press*, but Russell and I agreed that we had been lucky. There was no reporter on the scene. No pictures. The EMTs were discreet, discretion helped by one of them being a Kennedy graduate and former student of Russell's, a student who liked him. Their report repeated my guess that the baby had died of Sudden Infant Death Syndrome. Russell had also suggested the same cause. The EMTs agreed.

A reporter called me in the morning, but he was only an intern from the journalism school at FSU. The usual newsbeat reporter was on vacation. My version and Russell's were the same, even without a conspiracy, so it was reported in three paragraphs under a small print headline on page 8A. A baby girl had died of SIDS as her unnamed mother and her mother's teacher *Nancy Grant* were discussing school activities. The reporter had never heard of Dana O'Connor, and I had suggested that Dana and the baby's name not be used, out of respect for Dana's grief. I had taken a chance that the reporter would still possess some human empathy. If the *Press* had actually been paying him, that empathy would have been put in a blind trust. As soon as the story ran, Russell called me with an obvious question, "Since when are you Nancy Grant?"

Theresa Mary O'Connor had not died of SIDS. After the funeral, Russell told me about the autopsy results. Her death was the culmination of a lingering respiratory infection. Tess was suffering from borderline pneumonia. With the proper care, she would have lived.

"I told her I would help her," Russell had said as we sat alone in his car at the cemetery. We could see Dana standing over Tess's new grave, with Fred on one side of her, Theresa Parsons on the other. The few other people who had come to the service had already gone. "I thought, she thought, we both thought, it would go away. I told her to go to the doctor, that I would pay and she could pay me back later. But she kept insisting that she knew some sort of home remedies and she would go if those didn't work. I told her I would help, Nancy, I really did."

Russell wasn't talking to me, I knew that. He was talking to himself.

"Who else knows?" I asked, waiting for him to look at me instead of Dana and Fred and his daughter.

"You, me, and Dana. The report is a public record, so the *Press* can check, but I don't think that'll happen."

I wanted to ask him why he thought Dana ignored his offer to help, but I knew the answer. Dana had expected too much of herself. She worked two jobs, was raising her child and her siblings, was going to school and doing make-up work at the same time. She was poor. She was brilliant, but she was distracted. She had juggled a dozen obligations. She was only eighteen. She was surrounded by adults who admired her, some who loved her, but she was alone. I could total up an explanation for why all those factors converged into the death of her daughter. I could explain it all, rationalize it, and even excuse her, but I knew that she couldn't excuse herself.

A few hours earlier I had listened to the priest put baby Theresa O'Connor to rest in the arms of a God who moved in ways beyond our human comprehension. *Sudden...Infant...Death* were words slowly spoken by him as some sort of parallel Holy Trinity, an incantation of the *Mystery of Faith*, and he believed himself.

Dana and Theresa Parsons had sat between Russell and Stella at the church, Sally Parsons on the mother's side, Dana's younger brothers on Russell's side. Dana wasn't Catholic, but the priest had allowed, in his sincere words to me afterwards, a "spontaneous conversion" so that Dana and her child could find "grace and comfort in the Church." He had joined the admiring sect of Dana O'Connor.

I sat behind Dana as she stared at the small white wooden coffin. I looked up, staring at the gold cross on the wall behind the coffin.

The priest offered comfort in the acceptance of his God's grace. A package deal, I smiled to myself. Tess's "sudden and inexplicable death" was part of a plan much larger than the human mind could understand. It could not be explained, only accepted. There was an implicit bargain in his words, I knew that. In between the lines was the simple message: *God did it for reasons only God understands.* When the priest finished speaking, Dana looked away from the coffin and directly at him for the first and only time.

"Bobby Ray's Very Big, You Know."

It should be possible to explain the laws of physics
to a barmaid. —Albert Einstein

Fred Stein was my new hero. As soon as he heard about Dana's baby, he took it upon himself to help raise money for the funeral expenses. He knew all about Dana's borderline existence, knew that her small income was consumed by buying food for her brothers and child, paying bills that her own mother's AFDC check could not cover.

As spare as it was, the funeral would still cost over two thousand dollars. Russell told me that he would have paid it, but Fred came to see him and asked if it was okay to solicit funds at school. It was a responsibility he wanted to assume. Russell had stepped back and let Fred lead.

I had offered a hundred dollars, but Fred insisted that nobody give more than twenty. He wanted, he expected, a hundred donations. He actually got money from almost two hundred students, but he had overestimated the charity of some and the resources of others. It was still less than he needed. April had written a check for her twenty and given it to Fred in front of me and a dozen other students in the Kennedy hallway. I had watched without comment, but I was glad to hear Fred mutter as April walked away, "Awfully damn Christian of you." He had seen through her gesture.

Fred and a hundred other Kennedy students had gone to the funeral service. A few dozen had actually gone to the cemetery. It was a school day, and attendance at the funeral was an excused absence. Russell told me that there were over three hundred "excused" absences that morning. "They must have gotten lost on the way to church," he had said grimly.

Fred was short of his goal, but not for lack of trying. Dell was at the funeral with me, along with Jerry and Donna and Agnes and a dozen other teachers, Dana's fan club. Ashley Prose and Bob Skinner were not there. I told Dell about the money shortfall as he sat beside me. He whispered back, "I've already collected from the faculty. We've got it covered."

Fred cried at the funeral service. He tried not to, but he broke down as soon as Dana stood by the coffin, leaned down, and kissed the closed cover. Fred wasn't the only one to cry, but Dana was dry-eyed. She had stood back up, a blank and cold look on her face, while I had felt my own tears dripping down to fall in my lap, where Dell's hand was holding mine, his trembling barely perceptible.

"Miss Adams, I know who the baby's father is."

Fred Stein was exhausted. He had called me at home Sunday afternoon and asked to come see me there instead of school. It was private, he said.

"Miss Adams, she told me all about it," Fred sniffled as we sat on my porch. "And I think I've done something I shouldn't have." He was convinced that he had broken the law, done something that was legally wrong, and he was trying to understand his own actions.

"Talk to me, Fred," I said. "Tell me the truth."

"I don't know who else to turn to," he said.

He talked for an hour, circling around what he really wanted to say, straying off the subject of Dana at times to express his personal disappointment about most of the other students at Kennedy, but eventually it all came out.

As soon as he had heard about the baby, Fred had gone to see Dana at her trailer. He had taken her out to eat, insisted she go, paid for a meal she only picked at, and, when she hadn't talked then, he did all the talking. He told her all about his parents, his little brother, about his plans for the future. He told her that he cared about her. She had said nothing, except that she wasn't coming back to school. Russell was going to make her come stay at his house, where Stella would become the nurse instead of the nursed.

"And then it was after the funeral itself," Fred said, his hands shaking, "that she suddenly told me everything."

"The father?" I said, pushing the conversation forward.

"More than that," he said, taking a giant breath. "Dana was raped."

"I knew that," I said quietly, my reluctant intuition confirmed by Fred's story, and then I reached out and held his hand. "And I know how hard it was for her to tell you."

"It was two guys, two guys in school here," he continued. "Oh, Miss Adams, she said it like it was nothing. She said it like it was nothing at all. She told me everything like it had happened to somebody else. And her voice was so flat, like she wasn't there."

At first, Fred didn't tell me who the boys were. He just told the story as Dana had told him.

They were clients of David O'Leary. They had gone to him with their parents to have him negotiate with the County Attorney to keep their names out of the paper. Petty theft at a store with state-of-the-art surveillance cameras. Dana had been in the office when they arrived. Later, they had called her and wanted to talk. At this part of the story, I could visualize better than Fred what had happened. He knew the details, but I knew Dana.

She and the boys met, and they had asked her to keep their secret. Dana teased them, not trying to conceal her contempt for them. They suggested a six pack of beer to seal an agreement. Dana assumed she could control them, out-drink them, but they had drugged her.

And they had taken pictures.

When Fred told me about the pictures, I stopped him. "Fred, who were the boys?"

"She made me promise not to tell."

"Fred Stein, you tell me right now."

He cracked without hesitation. "Billy Hunter and…"

The second name was a blur to me because I had never had him as a student, but Hunter's name was enough to make me dizzy. I would see him the next day in class.

"Miss Adams, I hate them. I really hate them."

I was speechless, sick at my stomach. "Fred…" I started to say, not really knowing where I was going.

"You know what she told me about why she never told anybody," he interrupted. "She said it made her feel so…so very common. I don't understand that…so very common."

I understood perfectly. Dana didn't want to be another date-rape statistic, another helpless girl who had gotten herself into a situation that had gotten out of her control. Dana didn't want to be like anyone else, to be…common. She would never have told anyone the truth anyway, but the pictures had ensured her silence.

"Fred, do you think Dana is special?" I asked.

He nodded and said, "Of course I do. I've never known anybody like her in my life."

"Did you tell her that? When she told you that she felt so very common, did you tell her that you thought she was special and would never be common, no matter what. Did you tell her that?"

He shook his head. I noticed that he hadn't drunk any of the Coke I had given him an hour earlier.

"Okay, then, Fred, this is what you do. You go back to her and you tell her how special she is to you. And, another thing. I want you to go and tell your parents everything you've told me. Tell them you want to talk to both of them at the same time, together, the three of you. Even if you don't think it makes sense now, I want you to ask them for their advice. I want you to do that for me. Okay? For me."

"I can't tell them everything," he said, eyes down. "I mean, Dana told me something else too, and I can't tell anyone, not even..."

"You mean about her and Theresa, right?"

Fred almost shuddered, but he didn't look at me as he whispered, "Yes, ma'am."

"That too, Fred. Yes, you can tell your parents. You can trust them. I wouldn't say that to all my students, but I can say it to you. You can trust your parents."

"But we hurt them. My parents won't like that."

I blinked. "*We* hurt them? You hurt who? Who is *we*? What are you talking about?"

"Oh, Miss Adams, I wanted to help her. And I had a plan, but I needed help. So I told Bobby Ray Dearing everything. Bobby Ray likes Dana a lot too."

"Bobby Ray Dearing?" I said, remembering that I had been surprised that Bobby Ray had actually gone to the cemetery with those few other students.

I was intrigued. Fred was trying not to smile, "Bobby Ray's very big, you know," he said, his head tilted down but his eyes looking up at me. The story got better.

The night before Fred came to see me, he and Bobby Ray Dearing had gone to see Billy Hunter and Tad Bishop, the other boy. Bobby Ray led interference. They went to Tad's house first, and Bobby Ray talked him into going for a ride. Once they had Tad in Fred's car, Bobby Ray told him that they knew about Billy Hunter and him. Tad denied it. Bobby Ray put his hand around Tad's throat and told him to tell the truth. Tad denied it again. Bobby Ray squeezed harder. Tad Bishop confessed. Bobby Ray asked for the pictures. Tad said he did not know what he was talking about, so Bobby Ray slapped him. Not hit, slapped.

Fred imitated Bobby Ray's hand motion as he told me about it. "You should have seen Tad's eyes when Bobby Ray slapped him," he said. It was obvious that Fred was enjoying the memory.

"Fred, I can. Don't worry, I can see this very clearly," I said, wondering if I should feel guilty about smiling, but also wishing I had been Bobby Ray at that moment.

Tad said that Billy had the pictures. With Tad tied and gagged in the back seat, Fred and Bobby Ray then drove to Billy's house. His parents were home, but they knew Bobby Ray so they let him and Fred inside and sent them to Billy's room. "You should have seen his eyes too, right when he opened the door, Miss Adams. I think he knew, he knew exactly, why we were there."

"Don't over-interpret," I said, wishing it were true.

Bobby Ray did not say a word to Billy. He simply slapped him, put his hand over his mouth, and pushed him back in the room, with Fred closing the door quietly behind them. Bobby Ray whispered to Billy that he better be quiet when he took his hand off his mouth, but Billy was not as passive as Tad had been. As soon as his mouth was free he started to raise his voice. Bobby Ray slapped him again and held him down on his bed.

"He called him a..." Fred started to tell me, lowering his voice, blushing. "...called him a motherfucker, told him to shut the fuck up...those were *his* words."

Bobby Ray had sat on Billy Hunter, but Billy wouldn't confess. Spitting though Bobby Ray's fingers over his mouth, he told Bobby Ray that he would have him thrown in jail. But, while Bobby

Ray sat on his chest, Fred ransacked his room. Drawer by drawer, closet shelf by shelf, under the bed, and he finally found a large manila envelope in a suitcase in the closet.

"I knew it was them, Miss Adams, but I didn't want to see them. Really, I didn't, but I had to be sure. Didn't I?"

"Yes, you had to see them," I said, offering absolution.

He broke down and wept convulsively, still trying to talk until I said, "Fred, it can wait. Don't talk now."

We were silent on my porch for a few minutes. I had moved over to stand behind him, taking the Coke out of his hand, putting my hands on his shoulders. His trembling came up through my hands and straight into my heart. That's how I would describe it to Russell later.

Fred looked up at me, his eyes red and his nose dripping. "You got a tissue?" Drier and calmer, he continued, "But, you see, Miss Adams, it wasn't her. I looked at the first picture and it was some other girl, some sophomore girl I met at the Christmas dance last year. I don't remember her name. But they had done it to her too. I couldn't look at anymore, so I handed the envelope to Bobby Ray. He went through all of them, and I could see his face change picture by picture. But he found it eventually, found them, the pictures of Dana. He told me, but I wouldn't look. He told me there were three girls. Dana was the last one in the stack. Bobby Ray just put the pictures back in the manila envelope and then slapped Billy with the envelope as hard as he could, but Billy kept quiet. Bobby Ray asked for the negatives, but Billy refused to talk. Bobby Ray told me to get the camera off the dresser. It must have been a three-hundred-dollar camera, and Billy got even more bug-eyed as Bobby Ray smashed that camera to smithereens. All that metal and hard plastic in a heap. And Billy wanted to scream but Bobby

Ray had that envelope in one hand. And he asked for the negatives again. Lord, Miss Adams, you should've been there."

Fred kept talking faster and faster. "Bobby Ray picked up a baseball bat and told Billy that he would smash the computer in his room if he didn't turn over those negatives in ten seconds. Billy hesitated, and Bobby Ray raised the bat. Billy found the negatives. You should've seen Bobby Ray. I was even scared. I had asked him to help me get the pictures back, but I didn't expect all the other stuff. I just thought he would intimidate them, know what I mean? But Bobby Ray was on a serious crusade. He's a big guy, you know."

"Where are the pictures now?" I asked.

"Bobby Ray took all the ones of Dana and put them in a separate envelope, and we took them to her. He told me that they were the worst of the bunch. She was tied up, and hit. Even when she was tied up, Bobby Ray told me, they must have hit her. Except for Dana, and Billy and Tad, Bobby Ray is the only one who's seen them. It was his idea, to give them back to her. Not just to destroy them and tell her we did it. To let her do it. So we gave her the pictures and the negatives late last night. We were in my car outside Mr. Parsons' house. Told her that she should destroy them herself, so she would be sure they were gone. I thought she would feel better, maybe feel free, or something like that."

"She didn't, did she, feel free," I said.

Fred shook his head. "Not really. I mean, she thanked us. She even hugged us. And she took the pictures. But she wasn't really there with us. Does that make sense?"

"Perfect sense. It was a start," I said, remembering Dana's words about me and Dell. "You helped her do that."

Fred shrugged. "I don't know what else to do. I want to help her, but I don't know what to do."

"Where are the other pictures?"

"Bobby Ray has them. He told Billy and Tad that if they ever said a word about any of the girls, or bothered them again, that he would personally make sure they went to jail for rape and got...eh, got raped themselves in prison. Tad is still petrified, but that Billy is something else."

"I'll call Bobby Ray. I want those pictures in my hands. And I want you to do what I told you. Go talk to your parents. Tell them everything. Yes, everything. Even the parts about you and Bobby Ray. The whole truth. Understand?"

"Dana didn't want anyone to know," he protested meekly.

"Tell your parents, Fred. Trust them. Dana will never know you told them. But, you talk to them, for yourself."

An hour after Fred left, I had the pictures. Bobby Ray Dearing didn't argue. All he said was, "I'll be gone next year. Those guys will still be here, but they'll know that...somebody...has the pictures. I was going to make sure of that."

"Anything else I should know about last night?"

"No ma'am," he said, towering over me but refusing to look me in the eye.

"Bobby Ray?"

"You won't tell anyone?"

I nodded.

"Fred dropped me off at home after we took those pictures back to Dana. He was satisfied, but I wasn't. I went back to see Billy and Tad. That's all I want to say now."

Tests of Character

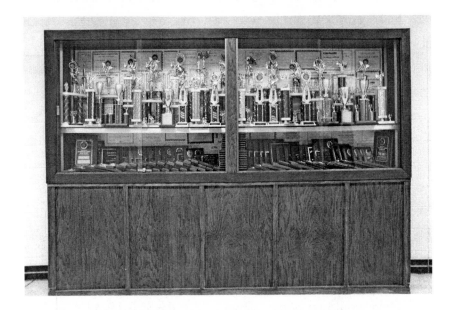

A teacher who is not dogmatic is simply a teacher who
is not teaching. —Gilbert Keith Chesterton

I had been shooting guns for thirty years. I finally had someone I
wanted to kill, to utterly destroy. In all that time I had never imagined my first victim being a seventeen year old kid who was a foot
taller than me. But all it took was for me to see those pictures. I
wondered if Fred and Bobby Ray had seen what I saw in the faces
of the other girls. There weren't any bruises or blood, and a well
paid lawyer could make a case for indifferent sex as much as forced
sex, based on the pictures. And certainly drugs were involved, that
lawyer could say. Or *she* could say, because I was seeing more and
more women attorneys defending men accused of rape. But how
could another woman not see what I saw? Absolute fear in the eyes

of one girl, absolute hate in the other. And I hadn't seen the pictures of Dana, the pictures of a girl who had fought back. Bobby Ray had seen them, but he wouldn't, couldn't, describe them, even if I had asked him.

Billy Hunter was the star, that was certain. He had had each girl stand naked next to him while he was fully clothed. His arm over her shoulder, and each girl seemed so tiny next to him. Different girls, different occasions, but the same pose for each. Like a big game hunter with his kill, Billy Hunter was the biggest man on the Kennedy campus, that was the message. Billy Hunter, long live the king. Until somebody shot his sorry self straight to hell.

I was stone cold sober and I plotted murder. And all I really wanted to do was have him look at the barrel of a gun pointed at him while I told him what a rotten sack of shit he was, and how the world would be better off with him dead. I thought all that, and I unlocked a cabinet and pulled out my shotgun. Then I went to the end of my dock and shot a box of small-spread buckshot into the St. Johns. A couple of dozen shells later, my speech delivered, Billy Hunter was safe from me, and the St. Johns just kept flowing downstream.

Late that Sunday night, I called Russell and told him about Dana and the pictures. After a long silence he asked me to meet him at school, and to bring the pictures. When I got there, Dell and Jerry were with him. When I first saw them I wondered why he had invited them, but then I remembered that Billy and Tad were basketball players. Kennedy was four wins away from a state championship, Dell's swan song and legacy.

Basketball wasn't mentioned when we first sat around Russell's desk. I watched the three men pass the envelope around and look at the pictures. Seeing the first picture, Dell's eyes narrowed, and he didn't look at all of them. "I've seen enough," he said, closing the envelope and pushing it across the desk to Russell.

"Dell, Jerry, we've got two girls raped. We know who did it. So what are you going to do about it?" Russell asked.

I felt a rage swelling in me that almost brought me up and out of my chair. Those three men seemed at that moment to be the embodiment of every male presumption I had ever known in my life. The arrogance and casual appropriation of power. The exclusion of me, the one who had made it necessary, possible, for them to be there. "Russell... ," I interrupted, my anger apparent. "What *we* do about it is obvious! And you said two girls were..."

I stopped myself as the three men turned to stare at me. Russell hadn't told Jerry and Dell about Dana. Two victims were enough. Dana was still uncommon.

"Nancy, you're right," he said, rubbing the middle finger of each hand slowly in circles across the envelope. "Obvious, but not simple. As for me, I was wondering if these girls really want anyone else to know."

"Don't you think that's *their* decision?" I almost hissed.

"I'm calling them into my office tomorrow. Donna and I will talk to them. But, Nancy, so far they haven't wanted anyone else to know. You're right, going public is their decision, their choice."

"So, why are *we* here tonight?" I asked.

"Because, regardless of what those girls want, *some* things have to be decided by us. Right, Dell?"

All of us turned to look at Dell. I was coming to understand something about Russell. Life was a puzzle to him. In my own world, no sensible person could make sense out of life. But Russell had transformed that common dilemma into a series of tests that he offered to other people. Tests of character. Dell was being test-ed. Understanding Dell, Russell could understand life. I wondered if I had passed the test that Russell gave me.

"Dell?" Russell asked again.

"Two weeks from now," Dell began to speak slowly, almost as if to himself. "Two weeks from now this school is going to be state champ. Can be, I mean. Should be. As sure as I know anything, I know that. Jerry here knows it too."

Jerry nodded, keeping his head down.

"Billy and Tad are juniors, but they're better than any senior I've got. Cosmic potential for the future. And getting better every game this year," Dell continued. "And this is my last chance. All I need is two weeks."

Russell and I were both looking directly at him, and I was also looking at his hands to see if they would start shaking. Jerry just kept looking down. Dell paused and then looked square at Russell, shaking his head and almost laughing. "Shee-it, Russell, you are the biggest turd at the table tonight. Did you honestly think this was going to be a tough call for me? Did you honestly think I was going to ask for some playoff time before we start rattling all these cages. Win one for the Negro gipper, some shit like that?"

"I had to ask," Russell said.

"Your ass, you had to ask! You know those little pricks *will* be turning in their jock straps tomorrow afternoon. Tell me you didn't know that."

"I thought you might feel this way."

"You *thought*! Screw you, Mr. Big Turd Principal, and screw the smug pony you rode in on. But you know, turd, that our young replacement here…" he ranted, turning to Jerry as Russell leaned back in his chair and smiled more than I had seen him smile all year, "...has a decision to make too. Assuming those girls keep quiet, Jerr-bear, Billy and Tad will be seniors next year, and you aren't going to win shit without them."

I was in a locker room, dodging testosterone ethics right and left. I might as well have been invisible at that moment. Macho-phony-anger was flying back and forth between three men who obviously liked each other and who were having a good time pricking each other.

"Screw you, Coach. You think they're not good enough to play for you, but good enough for me?" Jerry popped back.

"Good ain't the question," Dell humphed.

"Dell was trying to say..." Russell spoke up.

"I know whatthefuck the Coach is saying," Jerry said, holding up a hand. "And I'm telling you that next year I'll win more games with less talent than Mr. Hot Shit here could have won with a team of Michael Jordan clones."

"I'm assuming that means, regardless of anything else, that Billy and Tad are..." Russell began.

"Are fuckin' history!" Jerry and Dell said almost at the same time.

The only thing missing was a high-five slap-fest around the desk. I wish I had a picture of me at that moment. I wonder if I was too obvious when I started rolling my eyes. I was beginning to imagine what my life would have been like as a child with three older jock brothers. I should have been pissed at these three men, ignoring me like they did, but it was just as easy to be in love with all of them.

"Guys..." I said, materializing in their world as if from another planet. Despite the soft lighting, I could almost see them blush. "How do you plan on explaining all this to them?"

Dell spoke first, his tone noticeably more subdued. "Jerry and I," looking to see Jerry agreeing with him with a nod, "Jerry and I will sit them down tomorrow afternoon. While Russell and Donna talk to the girls, we'll tell them that their basketball careers are over at Kennedy, that their services are no longer needed. And if, *when,* they ask why, we'll just hold up *that* envelope and tell them that's why."

"It won't be that simple. You know that, don't you?" I said.

The three men didn't respond for a moment, Russell then spoke for all of them. "No, it won't. But we'll have to take this one step at a time."

"You'll have to deal with the parents," I said. "I've been here long enough to see that coming. Especially with a kid like Billy Hunter."

The three men all nodded silently.

"And possibly with some lawyers. After all, you're pre-judging their guilt. Even if it goes to trial, a good lawyer, and they'll have the best, will make it all look consensual. I've seen the pictures. They're proof of sex, not necessarily rape. And the girls themselves will be put on trial, every small indiscretion of their lives on public display. A lawyer will make that case. And there might even be a little issue about the admissibility of the photos, seeing as how Bobby Ray Dearing failed to get a search warrant. Somehow, beating evidence out of a suspect might not be legal, you think? So, you guys can be seen as jumping the gun, going on a witch-hunt without good cause or due process. And," I said, looking at Dell, "they're both white. White with college futures ahead of them."

They nodded again. I had told Russell earlier about how Bobby Ray had described the pictures of Dana to Fred. Dana had clearly been raped. The pictures of her would have proved it beyond a reasonable doubt, but not the other two, and Dana was out of the equation. Russell had made that decision.

"You know," Jerry finally said, "sometimes I think this school should be closed down and reshuffled. Start over from scratch. Does that make sense?"

Dell and Russell were silent, but they didn't seem to disagree.

"I think there's hope," I said. I knew he was still debating himself about his own future. "I'm willing to keep trying."

Jerry looked at me and said, "I guess that answers one question. You're going to be here next year. Right?"

"I guess I am. Didn't think I would decide tonight, but it seems like the right thing to do," I said. "You having second thoughts?"

"Not at all," he said, with Dell and Russell nodding.

"You want to know why I'm staying?" I said, looking at the other two men. "You guys want to know, too?"

They all looked at me, waiting for me to continue.

"One of these two girls is a student of mine. She's a sophomore. I want to see her graduate in a couple of years, and I'm not going to leave her behind."

Dominoes Begin to Fall

True, a little learning is a dangerous thing, but it still
beats total ignorance.—Pauline Phillips

In my world civ class the next morning, I looked at Billy Hunter
and smiled. He looked like he had bumped into a lot of doors. He
was also oblivious to what was about to happen to him. As I stared,
I wished I could be there when Jerry and Dell talked to him. To
see him get angry and deny everything, and then watch his face as
Dell held up that envelope.

After Dell and Jerry left the meeting last night, I had asked Russell to transfer Billy into another class soon, to get him out of my sight. Russell had agreed, but this morning I realized that I could deal with the Billy Hunters of this world. But I also knew that even though Billy's presence in that class wasn't a problem for me, it was unfair to someone else.

As class ended, I asked Jackie Foster to stay and talk to me. I had told Russell that I wanted to talk to her before he did.

"Miss Adams, you want see me? Am I already, like, down the toilet, or has my mother been calling you again?" Jackie said, unwrapping a piece of gum and tossing it in her mouth.

"Let's take a walk, Jackie," I said.

"Miss Adams, I got PE class, body sculpting 101, you know," she said, already popping the gum.

"I've taken care of that," I said, just as Dell came through the door to cover my next class. He looked at Jackie, and I knew he was remembering the pictures.

"Hey, Jacko," he smiled at her, his tone soft. "You okay?"

In any other context, an innocent opening. But Jackie stared at him and then back at me, putting things together. Not book-smart, Jackie was still far from dumb.

"This ain't about my grades, is it?"

"Let's take a walk," I repeated.

"Shit," Jackie muttered to herself.

We walked outside. In a few hours it would be an unpleasantly muggy Florida afternoon, but the morning was still mild and softly breezy. At the foot of the front steps was a shaded bench.

"Jackie, after we talk, Mr. Parsons wants to see you, but he let me talk to you first," I began.

Jackie was obviously nervous, obviously about to cry. "Is this about the drugs? Oh, geez, I've really cut down. You gotta believe me. I'm not like I was last semester. You gotta believe me. Please, Miss Adams, you gotta give me a chance."

"Jackie, this is about what Billy Hunter did to you. Russell… Mr. Parsons and I have seen the pictures."

Jackie shuddered, her eyes widening and flooding with tears. "Oh no, no, no, Miss Adams," she moaned. "I'm sorry, I'm sorry you saw those. He said nobody would see them as long as I was quiet and let him do me again. He promised…"

"Jackie! *You* are not in trouble. Billy and Tad are the ones in trouble. Believe me, they didn't show us those pictures of their own free will. And they're about to have a ton of bricks come down on top of them."

Trying to console her, I had only made Jackie more hysterical. "No, Miss Adams, no, please. Everyone will know. I'll be an even bigger joke around here. Please…"

"You're not the bad person here. Don't you understand that? Listen to me, you have to talk to Mr. Parsons. I'll go with you if you want…"

Jackie grabbed my arm before I could finish, pleading, "Yes, please, you have to go with me, and you have to promise not to tell my mother."

"We'll go together," I said, holding her hand. "And where we go from there is your decision. Mr. Parsons will explain that to you. And he'll support you whatever you decide. And, Jackie, you've got to understand that you're not the only girl they did this to. We have all the pictures now, and the negatives, so if you want to put this all behind you, you can. They'll have no power over you ever again."

"Nobody will ever see the pictures?"

"Jackie, you're safe. But if you want to testify against them in court, help us press charges, those pictures will be public knowledge. That's what Mr. Parsons wants to talk to you about."

"But I don't have to, right?' she said, tears streaking her makeup.

"Jackie, let me tell you what I believe. Okay?"

She nodded vigorously.

"You can be safe from Billy and Tad. And I'll support you if you don't want to go public. But *you* being safe doesn't make other girls safe. Understand? I suspect that if you go public then other girls in the same spot might have the courage to do it too, girls we don't even know about now. It's a tough spot, I know that. You go public, accuse those boys, you'll become a villain at this school…"

"Is that worse than being a joke?" she half-heartedly laughed.

"At this school…yes," I said as seriously as I could. "It's a tough choice, and only you can make it."

"Oh, Miss Adams, sometimes I wish I could just die, just kill myself or something," she started to cry again.

"If you kill yourself, I'll make you regret it," I said. Jackie kept pulling on a strand of her hair. "Let's go talk to Mr. Parsons. He's actually a pretty good guy."

Life goes on. Isn't that the simplest and most irritating of clichés? I was beginning to appreciate clichés a lot more. You can drop out, but life goes on. You can stand in the stream and put up your hand, tell life to stop and accommodate you, but the waters will split and flow around you, leaving you behind. It was an inexhaustible cliché, and flexible too. I was tempted to start drinking again, but I was too busy. Life was going on. Papers had to be graded. Jackie and Dana and Fred and Billy were four of a hundred and thirty students I had this term. Conferences had to be held, parents met, faculty meetings attended, and then there were those papers and tests, an assembly line of papers, one stack finished, another to replace it.

I played my favorite make-believe game. Putting famous people in the same room. Have them go at each other from different times and places. How about Kennedy and Clinton and Thomas Jefferson around a table, two men from the twentieth century in awe of their hero from the eighteenth. How about Eleanor Roosevelt and Hillary? Better yet, how about me and my own mother?

Why not put Neil Diamond on stage, Henry Adams in the audience. Diamond could sing *I Am, I Said* and Adams could shout from the third row, "So what! Nobody cares! Listen up, Neil, life goes on with or without you. You hear me? Life goes on."

I told Russell about my game and he suggested another singer for the show with Diamond and Adams, "Put Bob Dylan just off-stage, that awful raspy voice of his singing the most profound line in music ever."

"Which is?" I had asked. We were sitting in the cafeteria a week after we had both talked to Jackie.

"No contest, Nancy, no contest. *Time is a jet plane, it moves too fast.*"

We had both looked at the children around us. Kids were careening around full of hormones and Mountain Dew, bouncing off walls, colliding with each other and ricocheting out the double-doors.

"They would never understand that line, Russell," I said, looking for students who had been absent from my earlier classes. "They all think they're trapped here for the rest of their lives."

"Oh, they'll understand, eventually," Russell said, his shoulders drooping.

Why at that moment, I'm not sure, but I finally asked him the question I had avoided ever since I saw Stella and him downtown. "Were you ever going to tell me about Dana and your daughter?"

He kept looking around the cafeteria, and I thought he was simply going to ignore me, but then he shifted his body on the bench to face me more directly. "You know the thing about being a parent? About how I'm sure your mother and father were, and most parents. You want your kids to be safe and to be happy, to be in love with the right person and never get hurt, even though you know it never works out that way. Ever since my girls were born, and after what happened to Stella when they were born, I've never thought my girls were safe." He stopped and looked up at the clock. "Stella and I have known about Theresa for a long time, and I'll be truthful...the first time Stella and I talked about it, we admitted to each other that we were disappointed. Not because of who Theresa was...hell, she was perfect in our eyes...but because we knew how rough her life might be in the future, especially here in Fort Jackson...in Florida...in this country. A lot of hate out there for no good reason, but still there. Theresa was twelve the first time she talked to us about her feelings, so afraid we would not love her anymore. She had heard all sorts of stories about other kids coming out to their parents, the horror stories."

The noise in the cafeteria was getting louder and Russell was speaking softer and softer. I had to lean closer to him as he spoke.

"But it was okay, we told her. She was who she was, and we adored her. And it was nobody else's goddam business."

"Did you know about Dana before she moved in with you?"

Russell almost laughed. "Oh, I knew about *the* Dana, the Dana that dazzled every adult in her world, except her mother. That Dana was who I knew. And I wanted to protect her too."

"But..."

"But, no, I didn't know. But I don't think that Dana knew either. Thing is, Stella figured it out before any of us. I thought I could be Dana's father, you know, but it was Stella who became her mother, and it was Stella who helped Dana let out that long breath she had been holding in, that was choking her, and Theresa helped. But then it all went haywire when those boys walked into that office. I know that now. I wish I had known it then, but Dana closed back up."

"So, tell me, Russell, was Dana in love with you before she moved in with you, or did that happen later?"

"Nancy, Dana has never loved me like you loved me."

How close was I, at that moment, to saying out loud, *Nobody has ever loved you like I loved you.* I could have been wrong, I suppose, and it would be irrelevant. At least I had heard him acknowledge something about the two of us after all these years. He *knew* how much I had loved him. I was in a crowd all by myself. That comfort lasted only a few seconds until I remembered what Dana had taught me. She wasn't Stella, and neither was I.

Life Goes On?

The school system, custodian of print culture, has no place for the rugged individual. It is, indeed, the homogenizing hopper into which we toss our integral tots for processing. —Marshall McLuhan

Neither Jackie nor the other girl were willing to go public with the truth about Billy and Tad. Russell didn't pressure them. Life went on. Billy and Tad were off the basketball team a day before the championship playoffs began. Kennedy lost and the season was over. Dell announced his retirement. The parents of Billy and Tad threatened a lawsuit, until they saw the pictures. Rumors flared and died. Billy and Tad would see Bobby Ray Dearing in the halls and head for the nearest door. Fred would meet Dana after each of her classes, *when* she came to school, and walk her to the next one. Jackie the Smoker quit smoking. Life went on and on.

Dana didn't come back to class for two weeks. When she did it was still like she wasn't there. It was obvious that all of Russell's plans for her had been rendered irrelevant. She never spoke in class. There was no expectation that she could now do all the make-up work needed. Russell had gone to several teachers, asking them for extensions to deadlines to let her catch up. Everyone agreed, even Ashley Prose, but they all knew that it was useless. Dana was falling behind in her regular classes. Make-up work was impossible. April Bourne had won. Life went on and on and on.

Six weeks from graduation, my world was in complete equilibrium, my time and energy and concentration all balanced. I was able to listen to all the audio-book stories at the same time. I was able to sleep six hours a night and still be alert the next day. Another analogy was born. Like balls in the air, I could hold Russell in my right hand while Dell was going up and Jerry was coming down. In my left hand, Jackie and Fred were taking turns in and out. Dana, she had been set aside, no longer in motion. And, somehow, I found time to grade and grade and grade.

I told Donna about the juggling analogy, and she told me to learn how to use my feet, elbows, and knees all at once. She was old enough to remember the Ed Sullivan Show. Her favorite act, after some singing mouse, was the juggler who kept a dozen plates spinning on sticks at the same time. "Juggling six balls," she assured me, "is nothing to brag about. Just watch out that somebody doesn't toss you a new ball about the size of Texas when you're not looking."

Betsy Elizondo's *Vision 2000* plan was unveiled earlier than Russell had expected. With a luncheon/press conference combination, she lined up the editorial board of the *Fort Jackson Press* and stuffed them with charts, colored graphs, architectural site elevations, and chicken kiev. The Kennedy jazz band provided music, and the Kennedy Endowment Fund provided chartered buses for state legislators to come in from Gainesville. She didn't need their approval, but she did want their attention. Looking at Betsy's picture in the *Press*, I noticed that she was dressed like a Republican banker. Gone was her usual sartorial homage to multiculturalism.

Everyone agreed, Betsy had bigger plans than merely a mega-charter school in Fort Jackson. Even back in high school she had talked about being Florida's first woman Senator. My friends and I had all rolled our eyes and laughed, but we had all under-estimated her. She had gone to FSU and come back to Fort Jackson and worked on the political campaigns of second-rate men who would go to Tallahassee or Washington, but she had made contacts and forged bonds with a network of political professionals. Favors were owed. She had a timetable. Local politics first, a progressive record on the non-partisan school board. Opinions about environmental and gender issues, but she avoided the partisan party races for city council or the county supervisors board. Being controversial too soon was to be avoided. Secure her base, the first rule of politics. Then, let her image slowly evolve for a wider audience. After the school board, a run for the state legislature. Invite her future colleagues to be part of her *Vision-2000* launch party. Then the House of Representatives, then the Senate. She was a patient woman, and I even felt some grudging admiration for her methodical march. So there I was, with Betsy as the new ball tossed my way, something else to juggle.

I could do it. I was getting good at juggling, and then Russell tossed me a bowling ball.

"Nancy, I need to talk to you about a problem I'm having," he said in a flat voice.

I assumed that Dana was back in motion. Off the shelf, in the air, a heavier ball than before, but still falling to earth.

Sitting in his office, Russell let me do all the talking at first. I asked him about his problem, but he waved his hand and said, "No hurry. Tell me about Betsy. You said you had her figured out."

"She's not what she seems…" I began, only to have him burst out laughing.

"Oh, Jesus, Nancy, I've always known that. I was hoping you could tell me what she *is*."

"Shut up, Russell, and listen. See if this makes sense," I said, noticing him fidget with an envelope in his hand. "And don't call me a conspiracy nut."

He shrugged, and I could sense that he wasn't really paying attention to me.

"You know…I think that Betsy actually believes her own spin, her own self-invention."

"Self-invention?"

"That she is doing the right thing, that she's making life better for everyone else. I know, I know, I'm not being clear even to my-self here," I admitted, "but, when I finally saw the contradiction in her reform plan, I finally understood something about this whole town, this whole blessed country. Because the contradiction is not, like I had thought, a mistake. It's a design. She wants everyone to read between the lines, to see it, but not to talk about it."

"Nancy, I think you might be making Betsy more important than she actually is," he said, looking at me from over the top of his glasses. "I think you might be looking for some sort of pattern that doesn't really exist and…"

"It's…race. Don't you understand? Black and white," I stopped him. "Someone like Fred sees the feminism, the environmental concerns, and he projects his own version of progressive politics on to her. But, Russell, down deep, you *must* see what I see about this plan. In the name of educational reform, talking about quality of life issues, Betsy is leading us back to the 1950s in race relations, only worse, because she's willing to peel off the brightest black students and let them slip through the front door."

I was leaning forward, both my hands on the front edge of his desk. He was smiling at me. At what, I wondered. "Am I getting excited? Having too much fun?" I said, leaning back.

"I was just remembering how you used to be excited all the time when you were a student here," he said. "You used to come see me with some idea or some information or some gossip, and your face would turn red if I interrupted. All that pleasure of the proverbial light bulbs going off in your head. A new crusade every week, and when you told me about your career plans, I knew you'd make a good teacher."

I let out a deep breath, "I guess I should relax, eh? I'm all grown up now?"

"That's not what I meant to say, if that's what you heard. I was just looking at you now, thinking about how long we've known each other, in how many different lives."

We looked at each other, then looked away.

"Russell Parsons, my first love," I finally said.

"You were younger then. So was I," he said, after another long silence.

"You make it sound like we're old fossils now," I said.

"I feel old, Nancy."

"Funny thing, I don't. Not now. I feel younger now than I did when I took this job. Exhausted all the time, sure, but I don't feel old. As soon as I got off the fence about my future, after seeing Jackie's pictures in that envelope, something got lifted off my shoulders."

"I've been doing this almost twenty-five years," he said. "Fighting the fight for a quarter century. You, you're like a twenty-two year old new college graduate. Me, I think I'm burned out. I hope it doesn't happen to you."

"Russell, it probably will, eventually, like it does to most people who do the same thing for so long, but I'm enjoying it now. Twenty-five years from now? I might be cinders, but that's perfect timing. I'll be ready to retire, like my mother."

As soon as I said it, I realized the irony. My mother had worked all her life but never retired. She just died. "God, I forgot about my rotten gene pool," I laughed at myself, seeing Russell smile.

"Don't worry," he sighed. "You seldom drink anymore, you don't smoke, you walk to school twice a week, you floss twice a day, you'll live forever."

I thought it was time to change the subject.

"You want to tell me about that problem of yours?"

"In a minute," he said. "You still haven't finished with your expose' of Betsy."

"Okay, in its simplest, crassest terms, Betsy understands that affirmative action is dead. This town, this state, this country doesn't want to hear about racial remedies. Most everybody has bought into women's issues and environmental protection, even here in the Sunshine State, and I'm sure she's not the only politician who's figured out that it's okay to cut the strings to black people as long as you seem to care about the other issues. Her plan will do just that, all the while skimming off the cream of black students at the top."

He was nodding. "You're right, she's not the only politician doing it, but she *is* ours, isn't she."

"This is a Republican state, Russell, but the Republican party is a nest of religious zealots. Betsy's gamble is brilliant. A so-called moderate Republican woman named Elizondo who speaks Spanish fluently and English intelligently, with a mildly progressive record on women's issues and the Everglades but silence about race, that woman will pull voters from all directions here in Florida. Unless the Republicans in this state go bat-shit crazy, full-bore Christian full-mooners, she has a future..." Russell grimaced. Another moment to slap myself? Russell was a believer, and Agnes too. Not crazy, I was sure, but genuine, and there I was ranting about full-mooners?

Russell relaxed. "It's obvious that you've thought a lot about Betsy's future, probably as much as she has."

"Actually, working to get ready to present your plan, and thinking about Betsy, it's all been good for me," I said. "It gave me something new to think about, something other than Dana and Jackie and the other kids. And Dell. Fact is, Betsy seems like a solvable problem, a lot easier than the others around here. Betsy isn't just thinking about this school district plan. She's thinking about fifteen years from now."

He nodded, and I could see him almost smile when he said, "So how long have you really disliked her? Even back as kids?"

"Truth is, I resented her back then, all her sanctimony, all her political correctness before it was even a cliché, but I figured that we needed people like her to fight the bad guys, but I assumed she would grow up and be a flaming left-winger. *That* Betsy is gone for good. What the hell happened, Russell, what the hell happened to all of us?"

"And *that* is the perfect opening for this," he said, reaching for the envelope on his desk and holding it up for me. "A letter from Elizabeth Elizondo, informing me about the first sexual harassment charge filed at Kennedy under our new guidelines."

I immediately visualized Dell and knew that his luck had run out. "This is all so predictable," I said, reaching for the envelope. "And so sad. He only had another month until he was gone. But he wouldn't listen to any…"

"Read the letter," Russell interrupted.

Dear Mr. Parsons,

In compliance with the grievance procedures of the Fort Jackson County School District, this letter will serve as your official notification that April Bourne, a student under your supervision, has filed a complaint of sexual harassment against you in your capacity as principal of Kennedy High School. Specifically, you are alleged to have created a hostile environment which has affected Ms. Bourne's academic performance and psychological well-being. Details of the allegation will be provided in a private meeting with my office.

You have fourteen days to respond to this charge. However, you and the complainant are both advised that the district takes this charge very seriously. Confidentiality is assumed on the part of all parties involved. If a finding of merit is established, appropriate action will be forthcoming in accordance with policy guidelines. If the charge is not upheld, the file will be sealed. Either party may appeal the decision of the Board, but the assurance of confidentiality cannot be guaranteed at that point.

As this process occurs, you are reminded that there are serious consequences if you attempt to contact or in any way influence the complainant. If the charge is not upheld, you are still under notice that any action on your part that can be perceived as retribution or intimidation will result in your immediate dismissal.

This office has an obligation to impartially evaluate the evidence. It is a difficult and serious process, but that process will be greatly facilitated if all parties cooperate and understand their rights and responsibilities as outlined in the district sexual harassment policy dated March 1, 1997.

Please make arrangements to meet with this office as soon as possible.

I read the letter twice. Then I looked at him. "April and you? I don't understand."

"Nancy, you were on the review committee with Ashley. The third category, remember? About a hostile environment being created for one student by the perceived relationship of a faculty member and another student. Favoritism granted one student for sexual favors, and that favoritism affecting the environment of another."

"Oh, Christ, Russell, it all comes back to Dana."

"Yes, it all comes back to Dana."

"Does she know?" I asked.

"Of course not! You think she needs to know this now, all this... all this shit!"

"Who else knows?" I asked, handing the letter back.

"You and Donna," he said in a whisper. "I told her first, gave her the pleasure of telling me *I told you so* in so many words. It's your turn now. Go ahead and tell me what a fool I've been."

"As long as you can say it to yourself, you don't need me. I just wish I could help you somehow."

He was sagging back in his chair, almost dissolving in front of me. "I'll figure this out later," he said, putting the envelope in the desk drawer in front of him. "But, you know, the most galling part about this mess is that it's so unnecessary. We didn't change the rules about valedictorian, and Dana probably can't do that make-up work anyway. April knows that. She's probably going to get what she wants regardless of me. She's not going to be hurt. All that was obvious when Tess died."

"Russell..." I started to speak.

"Why did she do it? She filed the complaint two weeks *after* Tess died. It was all...so...unnecessary. So very very unnecessary," he said, oblivious to me.

If Russell's office was a model of order, Donna Parton's was its evil twin. Posters were curling at their corners, the tape dried yellow and no longer sticking to the walls. Somewhere under a dozen stacks of paper was her desk. Her file cabinets had papers sticking out from closed drawers. A potted plant in the corner had leaves turning brown at the edges. I could have written her name in the dust on the slats of the window blinds. Donna, obviously, did not have allergies.

"How do you keep track of everything?" I had asked the first time I had gone to her office. "You seem to know everything about everybody, but how do you retrieve it?"

"Nancy, all I can say is that this school better hope I don't drop dead or find the right man. Either way, I'm outta here. Regardless, I can't be fired. I know where too many bodies are buried," she had told me that first week of school.

"Yeah, probably right here in this office," I had laughed, and she laughed with me.

That first time was back in September. Eight months later, neither of us was in a good mood, and the office was messier.

"How does Russell get out of this?" I asked as we sat facing each other on a leather couch. Before I sat down, I found a cloth and wiped the couch clean. Eight months earlier, she would have made fun of me. Not today.

"I don't think he does," she said.

"You don't think he can disprove the charge?"

"Nancy, he's guilty," she said calmly.

"He's not the father of Dana's child. You know that. A simple blood test will rule him out."

"Irrelevant."

"The facts are irrelevant?"

"Nancy, don't play dumb with me. You know that perceptions are more important than facts, and Russell has let perceptions get out of his control long before this year. He did it with you twenty years ago, with a few others since, but at least he tried to be discreet. But this is *now* and the rules have changed. And the stakes are a lot higher."

Her saying something about the "stakes" told me that she might also be thinking about why all this had happened now.

"Donna, do you believe in conspiracies?"

"Lord, yes," she almost laughed. "I've still got money down that says JFK was killed by the CIA and the mafia. And I know where you're going with this, but that doesn't make any difference in this case. According to the policy as written, and if reasonably interpreted, Russell's still guilty."

"Do you really think he should lose his job?" I asked incredulously.

"No, of course not. That's not what I said."

"Then where are we going with this, where are we going from here?"

"Look, if I were totally objective, and if it were any other smart student except April, I would say that Russell is about to get what he deserves," she said. "He did something stupid and he was immune to anybody's feelings except Dana's. And he *was* warned, Nancy! Damn it, he took that road with full knowledge of all the dangers. I know for a fact that he knew that April's mother had gone to see Betsy, that April was telling everyone how upset she was about him and Dana. Poor baby April."

"But you're not objective, and we are talking about April here," I said, wanting her to admit what we were both thinking. "And she did file the complaint after Dana's baby died. When it was obvious that even if a hostile environment might have been present in the past, there were no consequences now and she would suffer nothing from it."

"Back to my favorite word—irrelevant."

"So, you want to tell me what you think is relevant?"

"Russell Parsons is history."

"Can you be more specific and less poetic?" I asked.

"Regardless of the resolution, it's the charge itself that counts. You know that. He will be found guilty in the beginning. He can appeal, and he might eventually win. But the appeal has to be public...eventually. Russell has a wife he loves and children he adores, and in their own way those three women worship him, just like Dana does. I've seen it. Russell knows that this charge, in these times, is like being charged with rape. Acquitted, the suspicion lingers. Your life is never the same, and the life of the people you care about. And in this profession, you're a walking target for the next time you tick off some prima donna who doesn't know crap from crayons but who can always remember the word harassment connected to your name. His career is over. And he knows it. Russell is history. Didn't I say that before?"

Every time Donna or I shifted on the couch, dust materialized from unseen crevices and floated hazily toward an air conditioning intake duct. "So, she wins?" I said, wishing I had a glass of water.

"April?"

I looked directly at her and said, "No, and you know who I mean. Betsy wins."

She stood up and held her hand out to help me up as well. "Time to go to work."

As we walked into the clean hallway, I asked again, "So, Betsy wins?"

"Nancy, you know the great thing about conspiracy theories? They're more fun if you can't prove them right or wrong. As for me, I think that the book on Russell and Betsy would go like this..." We had to dodge students late for class. "...He's known her since she was a student. Maybe it all began back then, some moment between them, some line crossed by one or the other, something you and I will never know." She talked and motioned to passing students at the same time. "Maybe not. But we, especially you and I, do know that she has big plans for herself, big plans that require that school re-organization plan to pass. And we do know that Russell is, was, the biggest obstacle to getting that plan accepted by this county."

"And, now the sweet meat of any theory, the coincidences. April's mother, as uptight and conservative as anybody in Florida, has been friends with Betsy since high school. You might go check her campaign...she's run three times...contribution records, down at the auditor's office. Look at the names. A lot of odd bedfellows. But, money is money, right? Even in a small town school board race in which less than ten percent of the registered voters bother to go to the polls. Then April, with some justification, feels wronged by Russell. Charges, irrelevant or not, are filed. Charges known only to April and her clan, and filed with none other than the woman who is now Russell's professional judge and political enemy. Call me crazy, but it seems like a lot of dots are being connected."

I wanted to stop walking, but Donna was in a hurry to get to the cafeteria. "You're worse than I am," I said, catching my breath as we opened the double-doors to the cafeteria and were hit with a flood of noise from four hundred teenagers.

"I'm older than you and I've been in this town a lot longer," she said, raising her voice.

"So, Betsy does win," I said for the last time.

"Well, all I know is that Russell loses. And Betsy knows she has his private parts in her purse. Only way to say it. He fights that charge too hard, even in private, and that confidentiality boiler-plate language means nothing. Russell knows it, knows how leaks happen when they're convenient. Knows how the press would make this a front-page story. He shames his family, he loses his public credibility on education issues. Facts, how the charge is finally resolved, they mean nothing. Nancy, he cannot win this fight. In fact, right now, I'm betting that he'll never step in the ring."

She handed me a tray and silverware, and we stood in line with a dozen giggling sophomores who had abruptly tried to get serious as soon as they fell in behind the adults. I looked for Russell, but he wasn't there.

Sitting at the end of the faculty table, we kept our voices down so low that I was sure that Bob and Ashley at the other end of the table must have thought we were talking about them. But Donna had a skill that I wanted to learn from her later. She could talk out one side of her mouth without moving her lips, all the while making eye contact with and smiling at someone across the table.

"Don't get me wrong," she whispered as I tried to look across the table like she was, neither of us making eye contact with each other. "Russell losing is not the same thing as Betsy winning."

"Explain," I muttered, trying not to move my lips, like Donna, but not being anywhere near as subtle.

She winked at Ashley, who had been staring at us, and then turned to face me, "You're going to be here this summer, next year? Right?"

I nodded, a forkful of salad headed for my mouth.

"Me too, and Agnes, and a lot of other good people," Donna said. "Russell isn't the only person around here who can throw sand in Betsy's machine. He could have been the best, but he isn't the only enemy Betsy has."

"Well, all I can say is that you never fail to amaze me. Is there anything about anybody you don't know? As for me, I thought I knew a lot too. But I'd trade a few pounds of information for a little bit of understanding. I know all about Russell and Dana, but there's still something about them I don't really understand." I paused. "Why was such a smart man so willing to potentially ruin his life over a girl young enough to be his daughter? And he wasn't even sleeping with her. You got an answer for that? When you do, come see me. If anybody can figure it out, it's probably you."

"You want me to explain that to *you*? And this is just between me and you, right?" she said, reaching across the table to hold my hand. Ashley had finished her lunch and was leaving. Donna smiled at her while leaning closer to me at the same time, "There's a category of men that Russell fits in," she said, "A category in psychology called the *Platonic Seducer*. It's one of the basics of male teachers. Older man gets his kicks from having young vulnerable girls fall in love with him. He *could* get in their pants, but he chooses not to. He wants, he manipulates, their hearts and minds, not their bodies. He wants them to totally surrender to him, to have that power over them, but it's always non-sexual, so he never gets into trouble. Russell is the poster boy for that. I've actually seen him do it with other girls in various degrees in the past ten years. Certain girls absolutely love him, serve up their virgin hearts, and he's an absolute gentleman about it. Just like he was with…"

Donna stopped abruptly and turned her head away. I finished the sentence for her, "Just like he was with me?"

"I wasn't here twenty years ago," Donna said, blushing.

"But you know enough, right?"

"Oh, Nancy, I think I know enough to make smirky innuendoes about you and Russell." She was looking at me again. "But I don't mean any harm. As for Russell, he's not even aware of what he does. As long as he never touches the girl, he sees himself as a moral person. Maybe even more moral because he could touch them but he doesn't. And he was always in control, because he was an adult and he dealt with girls, with children."

"Until he met Dana?" I said. "I was a girl when I fell in love with him. I understand that now. I wasn't the only girl who fell in love with him, either, and as long as he played with girls like me, he was safe."

"Dana wasn't a girl, was she?" Donna said, getting ready to leave the table. "No, she wasn't like you or the others. Dana was older, *is* older, than me or you at this moment. She was an adult when Russell met her, and he was utterly defenseless."

I looked at Donna and knew it was time for me to stop asking questions. I was fascinated by the realization that she might have been right about Russell and me, and maybe Russell and other girls, but she was absolutely wrong about Russell and Dana. I had assumed that Donna must have known about Russell's daughter, and how could she not have known about Dana's relationship with that daughter? Donna knew everything about everyone at this school, right? But she didn't know about Dana and Theresa. And if she didn't, neither did anyone else. It was Dana's secret first, then Russell's, and now it was mine. I could tell Donna the truth and absolve Russell of the guilt she had attached to him regarding Dana. But I knew that the truth would also be a betrayal of Dana and Theresa. Russell and Stella understood that from the very beginning. They wrapped those two girls in their arms and let them fall in love in private and without judgment. How many other kids at Kennedy, I wondered, had to hide themselves in plain view, like Dana had always done. Didn't I tell Jackie that she had a responsibility to other girls? To other past and possibly future victims. Stand up for the truth, right? And it shall set you free. I could Donna tell the truth about Dana, but that would betray

Dana. Do good, be happy, where were my parents when I really needed them? But not really, I knew, I didn't really need them to help me. I just wanted them to see me at this precise moment, and to be proud of me.

"See you later, Donna."

My Life Had Stood a Loaded Gun

His lack of education is more than compensated for by his
keenly developed moral bankruptcy.—Woody Allen

I called Betsy's office that afternoon and was told that *Ms. Elizon-do* would get back to me. I called Betsy at home and left a message on her voicemail. I went to her office unannounced and was told that the Board Chair was in Tallahassee indefinitely. I wanted to confront her, to demand that she recognize me, but Betsy seemed to feel no obligation to acknowledge my existence. I had seen her picture in the *Press*, but Elizabeth "Betsy," "Abeth," "Liz" Elizondo had become a wizard behind some curtain in the Oz of Fort Jackson. Always in the background, Betsy was finally, I understood, imposing herself on all our lives without having to reveal herself.

I gave up trying to see her. With graduation and summer vacation approaching, all the stories at Kennedy High School demanded their own conclusions. Jackie the Former Smoker struggled to pass my class. Fred finally remembered Jackie's name and her pictures in that envelope. When not escorting Dana to class, he was carrying Jackie's books and offering to help with her homework. April was all smiles and made a point of saying hello to me every time we passed each other in the halls. Bobby Ray Dearing was accepted into the Air Force Academy and given a football scholarship, but he was also told he would still have to learn to swim. Dell and I went out to dinner a few times, but we avoided any conversation more personal than exchanging gossip about the other teachers. Other than with me, Dell seemed to disappear. After announcing his retirement, he seldom came to faculty meetings and he never went out drinking with the other teachers on Friday afternoons. Dana moved back in with Russell and Stella, and Betsy Elizondo continued to ignore me.

Somewhere in Kentucky, a seventeen-year-old boy walked into his high school and shot four students and a teacher. He was unhappy, a social outcast, and he had two guns. Two days after it happened, while the MSNBC and CNBC and NBC and CBS and ABC and FOX and CNN television networks were still interviewing grieving parents and politicians were still venting, and before *Time* and *Newsweek* could do cover stories, Russell called an emergency faculty meeting.

He asked a simple question. Was it possible at Kennedy? Most of the faculty protested that he was over-reacting. Even Agnes was skeptical. But Donna stood up and read off a list of names, starting with Donnie Yarborough. "Anybody walks out of here, repeats what I just said, those names, I will make sure all those kids are in *your* class. Understand? But I don't want anybody here to think they're working in Candyland," she said, sitting down.

Bob Skinner called for more security and metal detectors, prompting Dell to nudge me and whisper, "The man knows he's on too many lists." I was happy that Dell was still capable of focused malice toward the deserving.

Ashley Prose insisted that students' Constitutional rights had to be protected, that random locker searches were "proto-fascist." That was too much for Jerry, who was about to raise his hand and respond when I touched his arm to stop him. He put his hand down and rolled his eyes at me.

Back and forth for half an hour, we settled nothing. Enough teachers were convinced that Kennedy was different from other schools, that, as Ashley said, "our students have too many collective advantages to feel individually deprived." As the words were oozing out of her mouth, I tried to make eye contact with Russell. Just as his eyes met mine, Donna stood up again and went ballistic. "We can talk this thing to death or we can face facts. Ten years ago, students like that kid in Kentucky would've taken those guns and killed themselves. That was then. From now on, they're not going alone. I gave you names, but I'd bet you that *if* something like that ever did happen here the kid might not even be on my radar screen. And I know there's no one solution to all this, but we damn sure better start thinking about it. The specific problems, not all this petty cosmic shit we seem to waste our energy on all the time."

The cafeteria was tomb silent when she finished. She stood there, one hand clenched in a fist, as if daring anyone to disagree, but the fist was also trembling as she sat down.

Russell walked back to the front of the tables to face all of us. I looked at him, knowing things about him that nobody else in that room knew, knowing how much weight he was carrying right then. He cleared his throat and spoke quietly. "Look, all I want us to do is think about it for now. There's a lot of written material about the subject. You'll hear all sorts of opinions about it in the media. But I want us to think about our situation—us, here—not some hypothetical school. Donna has been worrying about this for a long time. I know...I know what some of you are thinking, and I agree. That it's one more problem that people expect us to solve. That if we could all just go back to when we had to teach reading and writing and not worry about values and religion and sex education and race and gender and television violence and all those other issues which get dumped on us because parents and politicians have..." He stopped and scanned the room, looking at as many faces as would look back at him. "Sorry, I was about to make a speech there, as usual. I'll save it. But I do want to tell you something."

I looked down at Dell's hand. It was shaking despite his best efforts to hold on to his own leg.

"I want to tell you that working here at Kennedy has been very satisfying to me," he continued. "Some of you, I know, have disagreed with me on some things. But I want you to know that I respect all of you, and I know you'll want to do the best thing by these kids. All I'm saying now is to think about it over the summer and to get back together next year and talk again. That's all I'm saying."

The meeting was over. So was his career at Kennedy. I knew it as he spoke, as he must have known when he began the meeting. I walked with him back to his office, surprised by how relaxed he seemed to be, as if all that metaphorical weight on his shoulders had been lifted. "You're not going to be here next year, are you?" I asked, wanting to put my arm around his and lean on him.

"I've reached an agreement with Betsy's office," he said calmly. "Those charges go away if I do."

"Russell, you could fight this... ," I began to say.

"I fight, maybe I win, but I still lose. You know that. Betsy knows it too," he said. "We settled it over the phone. A lot of unspoken assumptions and agreements. I resign for whatever reason I'm comfortable with, and nobody knows about the charges. They are, however, and I love this phrase, they are part of my *confidential permanent record*. Just like my teachers used to threaten me with when I was in high school."

"And April?"

"And Betsy says she will take care of April."

"You trust her?" I asked as we both saw Donna running toward us from the far end of the hall. Russell burst out laughing.

"I trust her to anonymously send my complete file to the *Press* if I even hint that I'll criticize her re-organization plan publicly. And, fact of the matter is, she knows I'll be quiet. She knows I'll protect Dana and my family. But this is all probably for the best anyway. I have an old offer from St. Joe's I'm finally going to take, and then..."

"Russell! Stella just called," Donna said breathlessly as she got closer. "You have to get home. Dana's locked herself in the bathroom and Stella thinks..."

If I had been asked a direct question as Russell and I drove to his house, a question about Dana's future, my honest answer at that moment would have been that Dana had no future.

Russell didn't ask me if I wanted to go with him. I simply followed him to his car and got in when he did. If I had been five seconds behind him, I would have been left in the parking lot. Neither of us spoke during the fifteen-minute trip, and all I could think about was that the interior of his Volvo still had that new car smell, especially the leather. Then I kept trying to remember all the lyrics to a Neil Diamond song that began, *Stones would play, inside her head*. Dana's song.

By the time we got to his house, his daughters had just gotten back from school and were still wearing their uniforms. They were trying to calm their mother down, and all I could understand Stella saying as we went past was, "I have no strength, I have no strength."

Russell went straight to the bathroom, tried to open the door, called out Dana's name once, waited a few seconds, stepped back, and then, in a motion so swift that I didn't have time to brace myself, he raised his foot and kicked down the door.

It all happened in a few seconds, but I would remember it in slow motion. Somewhere behind us, Theresa screamed. If there had been anything left of the door, perhaps Russell or I could have closed it and kept anyone else from looking in, but it was off its hinges. Theresa screamed again as she looked inside. I yelled at her to call 911.

Slow motion. Russell took one step on to the bloody bathroom floor and almost fell down. Grabbing a towel holder for support, he told me to get some clean washcloths off the shelf. He had to tell me twice because I was fascinated by all the blood. Slow motion, what was the point? Dana had to be dead, so predictably dead. I kept staring as I handed Russell the washcloths.

Dana was sitting on the floor, her shoulders against the edge of the tub, her head down, her whole body motionless, her bloody left palm limp on the floor, the fingers of her bloody right hand still clutching a razor. Russell kneeled on the bloody floor, and I stepped back to watch them embrace.

He took the razor gently out of her hand and then held her wrists in his own hands, a clean washcloth pressed against the bleeding veins. The white cloth turned dark red, and then the blood seemed to be coming from Russell himself as it oozed out between his fingers. "Dana," he whispered, as if they were alone in the dark.

I stood over them, looking down as Russell pulled her two hands up toward his face, whispering her name over and over. She raised her head first, and then opened her eyes, blinking as she focused on the face above her. Her vision didn't go past Russell. I wished that I could have seen his face at that moment, seen what Dana was seeing, but all I could see was her reaction, her lips trying to speak but lacking power, her eyes at first glazed and then clear and then filled with tears, and her clasped hands reaching for his face, her red palms finally touching his hair and stroking her blood across his temple.

I couldn't see Russell's face, but I knew that Dana was looking into the face of a man who was deeply, truly in love with her, a man who did not want her to ever die. He was not her lover, just a man who loved her.

Everything was in slow motion, even the sound of the sirens coming from far away and the flashing red and yellow waves that flowed up toward Russell's home as if they were water instead of light. I ignored everything and concentrated on Dana's face, seeing her smile at Russell, shake her head, and then close her eyes.

"Dana!" I said, my voice intentionally loud.

Eyes still closed, her head shook again, and then Russell put his face next to hers and began whispering to her again, but so low that I couldn't understand the words. Her face buried in his shoulder, Dana began moaning. They were alone again, and I somehow knew that he was telling her what she had always wanted to hear.

Somewhere in the house a deep male voice was saying, "Where they at?" I turned toward the voice and saw Theresa kneeling, framed in the shattered doorway. I looked back at Dana. She was looking over Russell's shoulder, making eye contact with Theresa, and I could see her lips mouth the words, *I'm sorry.*

When Dana's baby had died, she had been lucky with the *Fort Jackson Press.* Not this time. Her attempted suicide was front page news, complete with pictures of her being wheeled out of Russell's house. The small figures in the background were his daughters and me.

The reporter this time was not an intern, but a professional. He went back to the story about Tess O'Connor dying, looked up the coroner's report, and made it clear that Russell and I had both been at the scene of that tragedy as well. He got the hospital to confirm that, in addition to cutting her wrists, Dana had swallowed a potentially fatal amount of tranquilizers prescribed to Russell's wife. Dana was not seeking attention, like some teenage suicides. The drugs and the angle of the razor cuts proved that she was seriously, irrevocably, trying to kill herself.

The reporter interviewed Betsy Elizondo, who expressed her condolences and concern. He interviewed Kennedy students, selecting the right quotes to make Dana look like an eccentric and despondent outsider. He resurrected a story from the previous year about another Kennedy girl who had successfully committed suicide. The second day's story had that girl's class picture posted next to Dana's.

Then, another front page scoop landed in the reporter's lap. Somehow, he found out that Russell had already resigned from Kennedy and had accepted a position as teacher/principal at St. Joseph's Academy. The headline was written by a page editor: *KENNEDY PRINCIPAL RESIGNS IN WAKE OF STUDENT TRAGEDY*. A new round of interviews with Betsy and students. Except for Betsy, who "graciously" expressed her best wishes for his success in the new position and praised him for his service at Kennedy, most others were shocked. A few teachers were outraged that Russell had not told them himself. According to the third day's story, "Questions remained about the sequence of events." The Gainesville papers got interested, but then the local paper mill closed without notice. It took sixty people losing their jobs to erase Russell and Dana and me from public view.

I was in school the day after being on the front page of the newspaper, fielding questions from students and teachers alike. Some students would bring me the latest rumor, and I would convince them that reality was a lot less dramatic. Old rumors about the paternity of Tess O'Connor came back. The fault line between Russell's supporters and his enemies, between what Agnes had described as the line between those who were teachers and those who were educators, that line was totally uncovered. In the faculty lounge, conversations would stop when I entered the room. Outside, lockers were being slammed and teenagers were bouncing off each other like pinballs. Life went on.

For no good reason, except perhaps for the relief that comes with letting go of a problem that can't be solved, I was relieved. I was free of a self-imposed burden. Things might be crashing around me, out of my control, but I was somehow different, different than the Nancy Adams of the previous day, much different than the Nancy Adams who accepted Russell's offer the previous summer.

Unfortunately for Bob Skinner, he happened to meet the new Nancy Adams at the wrong time for him but the right time for her.

I had left Agnes after our morning coffee and was going back to my own classroom when I heard Bob's voice.

"I was *so* close," Bob said, grinning as he walked toward me. "Four hundred dollars, *that* close," he cackled, holding his thumb and forefinger a half-inch apart. "*That* close!"

I was absolutely clueless, and my expression told him that I had no idea what he was talking about. He then made his mistake. He told the truth.

"The betting pool *you* weren't interested in," he smirked. "I put all my money on Dana O'Connor to be the Kennedy suicide this year. I just knew it. Just knew that she was headed that way. And then she blew it, couldn't do it right."

I was stunned numb and didn't hear anything else Bob said. He kept talking as I stared at him. The next day, I would try to explain it to Russell and Donna how inarticulate I felt at that moment, but also how I immediately knew what I was going to do. *Do*...not say. But the thing I didn't explain to them was more personal, more visceral. I wasn't staring at Skinner himself as he spoke. I intuitively knew who was *really* in front of me. It was Betsy and April and Ashley and Dylan and Billy Hunter and a Universe of Forces all beyond my control, all there in front of me at that moment, and even though Bob thought I was talking to him, I was really talking to them. I raised my hand to shut him up, speaking as slowly as I could.

"Bob...you...are...a...damned...dead man."

Blinking, he laughed weakly, "Excuse me?"

I walked away before he could finish. Students cleared out of my way as I ignored their space. I walked a straight line to my classroom. If students were in that line they either got out of the way or were pushed out of the way.

I was looking for one of those hard cardboard cylinders in which hanging wall-maps were shipped. A quarter-inch thick and four feet long. So big it had to be held with two hands. The closest thing to a baseball bat that I had. A poor substitute for a gun.

Bob's back was turned toward me as I walked into his classroom. I swung the tube with all my might, aiming for his shoulders, but he turned around. My words and weapon hit the side of his face at the same time. "You are a fucking asshole bastard, Bob Skinner!!!"

His head snapped back and his body followed, and he staggered away from me.

"A GODDAM PIECE OF SHIT BASTARD," I screamed as my second swing cleared his desk, sending books and papers and pens and pencils and pictures flying across the room. His face was crimson, and his nose had a new shape. He tried to walk toward me, his voice an octave higher and his lips bleeding as he said, "Nancy, have you lost your mind! Have you gone crazy! I'll have you fired in..."

I raised the tube again and took a step toward him, "YOU SHUT THE HELL UP...YOU FUCKING MORON!"

He put his hands in front of his face, stepping back, just as I started to swing at him again. And then I was saved from myself.

The tube froze in midair, but not because I had changed my mind. Someone behind me had grabbed it, and then two massive hands took hold of my arms and forced them down. Those two hands then lifted me completely off the ground and swung me around and away from a blubbering Bob Skinner.

"Nancy, honey, you can't do this," Dell said as he let my feet touch the floor again.

"You're damn right she can't do this!" Bob exploded, his confidence restored when he saw me held tight.

"Uh, Bob, I'd back off if I were you," Dell said, one hand on me, the other pointed at Skinner.

"You just get her out of my sight!" Bob said, puffing toward me and Dell, who let go of me and turned to face him directly, the tone of his voice a little deeper. "I don't think you ought to come any closer."

"Did you see what she did to me?!"

"Nope, I didn't see a thing," Dell said, an obvious lie. "If anything, I think maybe I saw Miss Nancy here defending herself."

Skinner was bleeding, his nose and eyelids were swelling, and he was beyond angry. "You haven't…neither one of you have heard the last of this," he stammered, edging around us and heading for the door. "I was assaulted in my own classroom. That is totally unacceptable!"

Students were stacked outside, waiting to get in as he raced by them. Some of the girls gasped, others were giggling. Dell turned to look at me. "You okay?"

"Truth is, I'm exhausted," I said with a sigh. "And thanks for coming along when you did. You probably saved me from going to jail for murder."

"Oh, a few kids saw you carrying that tube-thing and how you looked, alerted me, so I thought I'd follow you, see what was up."

"Well, thank you, you and whoever told you," I said, wanting to go wash my face.

"Actually, it was just Freddy Stein and Bobby Ray Dearing, and they went to get Russell. So, how much trouble do you think you're in?" he smiled, almost laughing.

"I'll worry about that later," I said. "Right now, I'd be honored if you walked me back to the restroom so I can powder my nose."

He offered his arm. I took it, and we left the scene of the crime. A minute later, at the restroom door, I let go of his arm and said, "You know, back there, I'm glad it was you."

He smiled again and shrugged his shoulders. "Does this mean I'm your hero?"

I reached over and squeezed his muscular arm. "My..."

He shook his head, stopping me. "I was kidding. I will kick your skinny butt all the way to the principal's office if you call me a damn white knight, and I will tell Russell that you totally flipped out back there and Bob was a poor undeserving victim. I will not tell him the truth...that I'm jealous. I've wanted to do that to Bob for a long time."

The only thing I could say at that moment, the truest feeling I had ever had, was, "I wish I could kiss you right now, right here in front of all these kids, in front of God and Russell and your mother."

He didn't respond. I understood. I knew it was too little, too late. He walked me to Russell's office.

Bob made the mistake of going to see Russell before he went anywhere else. If he had gone straight to Betsy Elizondo, I would have lost my job, but Russell let me confront Skinner one more time when he had us both in his office, "to hear both sides of the story."

Holding a handkerchief over his nose, Bob presented his case. He had "been joking about Dana O'Connor" and I obviously took it the wrong way. I was also obviously dangerous, he insisted, and my behavior was "actionable." He had even gone back and gotten the tube as evidence. I laughed when he held up the bloody and dented cardboard, which sent him into another spasm of finger-pointing.

"Nancy, you want to give me your version," Russell said, frowning at me when I rolled my eyes at Bob.

"This piece of shit here..." I began, and both men flinched. "This piece of shit..." I repeated intentionally, "admits he had bet on Dana killing herself."

"A joke, obviously, Nancy," Skinner interrupted.

"The joke is you, and you know exactly what we're talking about, and so does Russell," I shot back. "And if you think you're going to have my job then you better be prepared to talk about your betting pool with the *Press*, because I'm sure they'd love that story."

"That pool is a myth. You have no proof it exists!" Bob said, but he was less sure of himself than he was a few minutes earlier. "Your word against mine. You have no proof!"

"The *Press* doesn't need proof, Bob. They just need a story," Russell said firmly. "And I did tell you to stop that mythical pool a long time ago."

Bob looked at Russell and me, his eyes shifting back and forth, then narrowing. "Students saw me looking like this," he said. "How do *we* explain that?"

"Teachers horsing around, having fun, Nancy showing off her swing, both of you misjudging the distance, accidents happen," Russell offered. "Dumb shit happens, even between teachers."

"And how about Dell Rose?" Bob sneered.

Russell looked at me. "Dell saw me defending myself," I said. "He thought I was being attacked. Bobby Ray Dearing and Fred Stein were there too. I'm sure they saw the same thing."

Bob was whipped, and he knew it. "Just stay away from me from now on. You better do that," he said as he stood up to leave. "Just stay away from me."

As soon as Skinner was gone, Russell said to me, "And his real message was *watch your back*. Christ, he is *not* one of the things I'm going to miss about this school."

"You got a list of the things you are going to miss?"

"A mile long," he answered. "Mile wide, mile deep."

"You know, this is not the way I thought this year was going to end when I took this job last summer," I said.

"You sorry you accepted my offer?"

"Not a bit," I smiled at him. He looked a lot older than he did when he had sat in my kitchen last summer.

"If you're interested, there's an opening at St. Joe's you could fill. A big whack in pay, but a much different environment. And I've got some pull with the new principal."

I shook my head.

"You realize that Bob is probably going to be acting principal here until they get my replacement. And he'll be applying for the permanent position."

I nodded silently.

"Cat got your tongue?" he asked.

"I'm late for class. The kids will be plotting a revolution unless I get back soon."

"Aren't you worried even a little about your future?"

"Actually, Russell, I am. But I'll deal with it as it comes. Right now, I'm just really glad, happy, you offered me this job last June."

He tried to smile, but his face never made it. "Well, a few more weeks and we push some of these kids out of the nest. You, you've got a lot to do, including this," he said, handing me a manila envelope.

"And this is?" I asked.

"Dana's last make-up assignment for me. You need to grade it soon so she can get credit."

"Russell, we both know this is irrelevant now."

"Not to her," he said. "And not to me."

I took the envelope, not knowing then that it was Russell's last test for me.

"One more thing, Nancy," he said as I was about to go back to class. "Dell and I had our own bet about you."

I glared at him, "And this is funny how?"

"We both thought you were overdue about...well, we wondered when you were going to hit somebody or something."

"You and Dell can go. . ."

"Nancy, you've been uptight for too long. Sooner or later, you were due to pop a gasket, or do *something* physical. Let's just say that he and I are proud of you. And we both know that Bob is damn lucky that you didn't have time to go home and get one of your guns."

The Final Test

I know a lot of people think I'm dumb. Well, at least
I ain't no educated fool.—Leon Spinks

The envelope sat on my desk at home until the weekend. There
was no hurry because the deadline for the second grade option
had come and gone. Dana would graduate with honors, but not as
valedictorian.

After I finished grading a stack of research papers Sunday
morning, I took the envelope out to the boat dock with me and

sat in a deck chair, soaking up the morning sun. The St. Johns was almost still.

I was expecting a critical book report on a long chapter from Barbara Tuchman's *March of Folly*, about American involvement in Vietnam. About a hundred pages, but very readable. Instead, I found myself reading a report on Stanley Elkins's *Slavery*, an intellectual history of the "peculiar institution." Not an easy read at all, even for a bright college student, much less a bright high school senior. So, technically, Dana hadn't done the assignment given her, and I had no obligation to accept it. But it was also typical of Dana, to change the rules even when she was making it harder on herself.

I had read *Slavery* too long ago to remember much more than the basic premises, but that didn't matter. As I read, I was astonished by how plain the writing was, how simplistic the sentence structure, how superficial the analysis. Compared to most of my students, of course, this was "A" work, but I had read enough of Dana's work in the past to be disappointed in this report. It could be an "A" but not an "A" by Dana. I wasn't bothered by the fact that she only wrote about the first half of the Elkins book, a comparison of slavery in North and South American in the nineteenth century, but still very dense and challenging material. Her report was a dozen pages, and I read it twice. Something was wrong, but I couldn't pinpoint the problem. The writing was acceptable, but from Dana it was disappointing. I put it down and stared at the St. Johns, drifting away for a few minutes as I thought about the scene in Russell's bathroom, with him saving Dana's life while Theresa and I stood as witnesses.

It was a warm morning, a drowsy morning, and I kept slipping from conscious to semi-conscious, from daydream to dream. I thought I heard my mother's voice calling me from the house. Perhaps Kris whispering, then a voice I didn't recognize, a vague male voice calling my name, coughing quietly. My eyes were closed, but I was sure I was awake. After all, I could feel the sun and the wind.

I opened my eyes, Dana's paper still in my hands. I read it a third time, and I felt my head turn lighter and my stomach turn over. She hadn't written this paper. There was no doubt about that in my mind. It wasn't her work, which explained why it wasn't as good as I would have expected from her. But, if not her work, by definition, it was plagiarized. Dana had cheated. But *that* made no sense. Dana would not cheat.

I was very methodical, detective-like, ruling out suspects and motives and evidence, all leading to an obvious conclusion. Dana had nothing to do with this paper. Russell had intentionally, consciously, supplied me with plagiarized work, asking me to give Dana credit for work that she didn't do. But, both he and I knew that the work was irrelevant. There was no objective purpose to be served by his action. Even if accepted by me, the final outcome wouldn't change. It was simply a test of character.

I knew what Russell was trying to do, to see if I would become totally complicit in the conspiracy that had wrapped itself around Dana and had been willing to bend all the rules to protect and support her. To do that because Dana had some undefinable future to which all of them had attached themselves. Russell and Agnes and Donna, even Stella, and others. All of them believed in rules and ethics and morality, all of them were willing to cheat for Dana. I understood the seductive lure. In a world seemingly ruled by people like Betsy, who used all the rules to their advantage, who made all those rules, why not? Dana O'Connor was a higher law. The problem with Russell's plan, however, was that I had already joined that conspiracy. I joined it that day when I saw him and Dana and

391

his family downtown. This new test for *me* was completely unnecessary, but Russell had made my test more subtle. A plagiarized paper, but known only to him and me. I could give the paper an "A" and neither of us would have to mention what we both knew, our collusion. Because, surely, he knew that I would know it wasn't Dana's work. The grade wouldn't change her life, not help her in any way. Did he not think I had already completely crossed over to his side?

I sat there and read the paper again, and it finally hit me, the enormous ingenuity of the test. I laughed as loud as I could, alone there on my dock. I stood up and twirled around, holding the paper in my hand. I almost danced. I almost jumped in the St. Johns. I was *that* happy. I talked out loud, like a lunatic, talked to Henry Adams, my favorite Harvard history teacher, the deadest whitest male icon of my life, self-deprecating and ironic Henry Adams, telling him that the sum of *my* education was *this* moment of absolute clarity.

I wanted to confront Henry Adams, but I settled for Russell Parsons. Face to face would have been better, but that would have taken the edge off this exact moment. I had to give Russell my answer immediately. I wondered if Henry Adams had ever made a phone call. Who knows, I might have to read him again to see all the things I missed.

"Russell, I graded Dana's paper," I told him on the phone a few breathless minutes after I ran back to my house.

"So, is she going to get the credit?" he asked.

"No, Russell, she's not. The paper's unacceptable."

Silence.

"Certainly, I understand," he finally said.

That was exactly what I wanted him to say.

"Russell, you're the most wonderful man I've ever known," I began, knowing where I was going and hoping he could keep up. "But you don't understand."

Silence again.

"Dana wouldn't have been a part of what you did for her. You're so blinded by your...affection...for her that you're willing to cheat for her. It's one thing to bend and stretch the rules, but you can't break them. Dana understands that. She knows what she's capable of. Can you imagine how she would feel if she knew what you did? Think about it."

More silence.

"Russell, if you were in my place, I know, you would have accepted the paper. But if Dana were in my place she would have thrown it out. *That's* what I understand about her that you don't. As much as you love her, you still don't understand her. You don't, really, *know* her."

I could hear him clear his voice on the other end of the line, finally saying, "I wanted to help, just help."

"She needs your help now, and mine, and a lot of other people's, but not this kind of help. What you did here was for you, not her. She didn't need this, *you* did."

An hour later, I was listening to a Neil Diamond CD, the volume pumped up, cleaning house, moving furniture around and dusting the tops of ceiling fan blades. I was incredibly happy, and I had done a good thing. Both my parents would have been proud of me.

The law of unintended consequences. Russell had overreached in his effort to wrap me in his web. I had been tempted, but when I had finally figured out what was really bothering me about that paper, what had jolted me up out of her chair and made me laugh hysterically, it was then that I had irrevocably gotten away from Russell-My-First-Love Parsons.

It was *my* paper, written by poor, pathetic Nancy Adams over twenty years ago. Written for Mr. Parsons, her schoolgirl crush, written well enough for an "A" in 1977 but not good enough to be Dana's in 1997. Kept by him, with so many other things he had kept, for reasons only he could comprehend. Like my unpublished article about Dell Rose for the school paper, in a file probably filled with other artifacts of other students. I couldn't imagine. All I knew was that it was a test to see how much I remembered, how far I would go, a test that I had passed, a test that he failed. Not for lack of trying. He had obviously had to retype my old paper himself on a word processor and print it out so it looked like a 1997 product. It was clean, margins justified, and a failure.

Pomp and Circumstance

A good education is usually harmful to a dancer. A good calf is better than a good head.—Agnes de Mille

Russell Parsons was leaving. Dell Rose was leaving. In their own ways, their exits were predictable, but I wasn't prepared for Agnes Rose.

"You're doing what!" I gasped when Agnes told me in the cafeteria. We were sitting at a long table piled with blue and gold pamphlets, organizing the after-graduation party.

"Doing what I should've done years ago, going back to Jackson High. Taking my gifts where they're needed the most. Doing the right thing.

"Agnes, how can you do this to me?" I protested.

"Ain't about you," she said, smiling as she folded blue pamphlets. "Fact is, this isn't even about *me*."

"I know, I think I know what you mean," I sighed. "So I want to tell you something, but you have to promise that it won't go to your head."

Agnes put one folded pamphlet in an electric stapler while she reached for another. "Praise away, just so long as it doesn't go to my bottom. My head's got room."

"You're the best teacher here," I said simply.

She stopped and put her hands in her lap. Neither of us spoke for a moment. Her eyes widened and blinked, as if trying not to cry. I was almost crying myself, "You know, we could get seriously sentimental here."

She had the antidote for sentimentality, "There might be some debate about best teacher, but nobody around here is disputing that you've got the best punch."

"So I hear," I said, glad to go in a new direction. "But you know this school. More rumors than facts flying around."

"Well, honey, I'm sure not gonna cross you," Agnes said. "I'm just glad you're on my side."

"You'll keep in touch, won't you. Invite me over to cook with you sometimes? Or, watch you cook."

"Nancy, I'm going downtown," she laughed. "Not to Georgia. And you and I got a lot of work to do about that Elizondo woman. She might be a shape-shifter, but you and I know she's a skunk. Me, I plan on putting a new stink on her and I expect some help from all you pasty white folks. You, you stay and fight the good fight here. You'll have your hands full, but you won't be alone. Jerry and Sue and some others will be back, but they'll need a leader."

"I'll miss our morning coffee," I said, pushing some more folded pamphlets over to her side of the table.

"Me too. But you'll be okay. Now, I want to say something that you have to promise me not to let go to *your* head."

"I promise."

"I knew your daddy a long time ago. I know he'd be proud of you now. Your mama, too. They'd both be proud of their girl."

I stammered, "Am I as red as your blouse?"

"A nice shade of pink. But we've got to stop all this mutual admiration society stuff and get back to the important business of informing these children how to get to a party."

We folded and stapled for another fifteen minutes as I thought about my parents. My father proud of me? My mother? I was on the verge of feeling proud of myself when Donna Parton yelled from the door at the far end of the cafeteria, "Agnes, Nancy, get down to Russell's office! All's right with the world again. I want you there when I tell him!"

"You're all probably wondering why I called this meeting," Donna beamed as we sat watching her pace back and forth.

"Donna! Get to the point," Russell said.

"Oh, for chrissakes, Russell...'cuse me, Agnes...but will you let me enjoy this moment!" she laughed back.

"Let us all enjoy it, Donna," I added, wishing I had a rubber band to shoot at her.

"Well, I wanted you all here to congratulate the new valedictorian of Kennedy High School...who will be here in about three minutes."

"Donna..." Russell began.

"The prima-donna, Donna Donna...I *love* my damn job," she interrupted with a flourish. "Oops, sorry, Agnes."

"I thought..." I began.

"Freddy Stein!" Donna burst out.

Russell, Agnes, and I looked at each other like we suspected each of the others to be in on the joke. Then Agnes and I both looked at Russell, who slowly said, "Freddy Stein?"

"The one and only green people's choice, the same," Donna said, a grin from ear to ear.

Russell spoke slowly again, as if making sure we were all using the same language, "But, April always had a higher GPA."

"And our darling April insisted that you not change the rules in midstream, or horses, or something like that. And you didn't, and...," turning specifically to Agnes, "...and, Agnes, I may have to take back all those judgmental things I said behind your back about God, because somewhere, somebody, *has* to be pulling these strings!"

We all began to get as excited as Donna.

"I crunched the numbers a dozen times," she continued. "April's daddy can hire his own CPA to fight this, but the numbers are there. The weighted courses, everything Freddy took this semester was a weighted course. Maybe if she had taken your honors course this term, Nancy, maybe it might have made a difference. But the big thing, the clincher thing, and you'll all love this, was the extra-curricular activities credit, all that bogus citizenship fluff. April's holy grail! Freddy's been a madman all year long. April joined clubs, Freddy started clubs. April was president of a few, Freddy was an officer in all of them. Don't you see the beauty of all this, folks! We played by the rules and...the...good...guy...won."

Donna was right, I thought to myself. There must be, had to be, some order in the universe. How else to explain the knock on the door at that moment, and Fred Stein poking his head through, asking innocently, "You wanted to see me, Mr. Parsons?"

My class in 1977 had a hundred and forty-three graduating seniors. In 1997, Kennedy had four hundred and eighty. When I graduated, the auditorium could hold all the parents and students and relatives. In 1997, they filled one side of the football stadium.

Russell had arranged for the Kennedy symphony orchestra to play an extended version of *Pomp and Circumstance* as the seniors filed down the stadium steps, past their proud parents and other relatives, on to the field to sit on folding chairs that faced the stadium bleachers. The orchestra of juniors and sophomores was on an elevated platform behind the folding seats on the ground.

By five o'clock the day of the ceremony, Donna and I were looking for each other, to celebrate more evidence that God was smiling down on this class. The temperature was in the low seventies and the humidity had been imported from Arizona.

I arrived an hour early, wondering if I should have brought a sweater. If the wind picked up, it might actually get cold. The forecast did call for warm humid air from the Gulf to move in around midnight, the clash of hot and cold creating thunderstorms. But, for the ceremony itself, meteorological luck or divine intervention were with us. It stayed a perfect night to cut the apron strings.

Close to eight o'clock, the orchestra was in place, the bleachers were almost full, Russell and assorted dignitaries were on stage, and I was sitting by myself in the bleachers. I had seen Jerry Sinclair sit down below me earlier. He had seen me and motioned to come sit with him. I waved back, shaking my head. I would see a lot of him next year, I told myself. At that moment, on this night, I just wanted to be alone.

I had originally asked Dell to sit with me, but he told me that he had "a hot date." I was disappointed, assuming that the last image of him in many people's minds would be more embarrassing proof of his worst behavior. I had lectured him about it, and he kept his head down, meekly saying, "Just check her out." When I saw his *date* I wanted to tell him how proud I was. He and his mother were sitting together on the other side of the bleachers. Even from that distance, I could tell that he was kidding with Agnes, making her laugh, both of them happy to be with each other.

The music began.

I took a deep breath and closed my eyes, lightheaded and twenty years younger, beginning that slow walk down the auditorium aisle, up the steps of the stage to give my valedictory speech and get my diploma and go to Notre Dame and meet Jack Vandergriff and fall in love and go to his funeral and then drift until I became a teacher and swam naked as a baby died and then attacked Bob Skinner with a cardboard bat and sat on my dock reading my own work with Dana's name on it and then coming to this stadium this night and taking that deep breath at the same moment every other adult around me was remembering their own graduation, and I let the air out of my lungs and opened my eyes to see cameras flashing and parents crying.

There were two lines of seniors, one coming down the steps on the west side of the stadium, the other coming down the east. April led the west procession. Fred led the east. Salutatorian to the west, valedictorian to the east. Tradition. I had known that. I purposely sat on the outside seat of a row on the east, and I had brought my own camera.

Fred was all business, until he saw me. Then he grinned like an idiot, raising his hand and giving me a peace sign. Click, I had his picture. So did his mother and father, sitting together, two rows below me.

Alphabetical order, tradition, behind Fred was Dylan Abrams. I was unfazed. Dylan saw me and smiled, and I was fascinated by how young he looked, younger than I had ever seen him in a class-room or hall. He was just a kid. A voice called out, "Dylan, over here!" and I turned to see Dylan's father waving at him. There was nothing insincere about their happiness.

They all marched past me, half the class of 1997, down to the field and up on the stage. All the rehearsals had paid off. The pro-cession took less than thirty minutes. Russell made a welcoming speech, asking for a moment of silence in which everyone was en-couraged to be grateful for this occasion, the politically correct substitute for prayer, and then he introduced the dignitaries. In ascending order of importance, Elizabeth Elizondo was the last to be acknowledged.

I heard her name and watched a smartly dressed woman walk to the podium. I shook my head. I had looked at the stage dozens of times since I arrived. Betsy had been right there in front of me all the time and I hadn't seen her. I just stared at the woman who was supposedly Betsy Elizondo. Words came out of the woman's mouth about "pride" and "community support" and then I was watching Russell looking straight ahead of himself, scanning the crowd. I followed his eyes until I saw Stella and his daughters.

The woman who was introduced as Elizabeth Elizondo began announcing the scholarship awards, shaking hands with April and Fred and a dozen other deserving seniors. The last award went to Bobby Ray Dearing.

The woman named Elizabeth Elizondo sat down, and I remembered all I had to do in the next few weeks to organize an effective response to that woman's re-organization plans. I looked around, counting the heads of people who I thought would help me. A couple dozen, and Agnes probably had more who I didn't know. It would be enough.

When Fred was introduced, I was shocked, and pleased, by how hundreds of his classmates seemed to spontaneously rise and clap for him, some of them whistling and hooting, but all of them happy for Fred. I quickly zeroed in on April, who was still sitting. After a quick glance around, the salutatorian stood and applauded with the rest. More proof to me that April would go far in life. After April, the ovation became unanimous.

Fred had already asked me to proofread his speech, but I wasn't prepared for his new opening remarks. "Before I begin, I want to say..." he began, but his voice was too high and about to crack, so he paused and took a deep breath and let it out slowly, his face turned away from the microphone, and then he continued. "I want to tell my mother and father that I love them both, and I want to thank them for..."

I didn't hear, would not remember, a word he said after that. All I would remember is crying and looking briefly down to where Fred's parents were sitting, holding hands.

Life Goes On

To the uneducated, an A is just three sticks.—A. A. Milne

I dutifully went to the school-sanctioned after-graduation party, but an hour of chaperoning non-alcoholic fun was too much for me. I was tired, so I said my goodbyes to Fred and Bobby Ray and my other favorite seniors, wished them well, thanked them for their telling me that I was their favorite teacher, signed their yearbooks, and sincerely told them to keep in touch with me, and then I went home at midnight.

Dana O'Connor was waiting for me.

I saw the battered Toyota in my driveway, but the house was dark. Seeing Russell's old car, I wasn't surprised that Dana was there. She hadn't gone through the ceremony itself, but she still graduated with honors. I had assumed that, even after not seeing her for weeks, we would talk again, perhaps not so soon after the ceremony or so late at night, but eventually.

"Dana?" I called as soon as I got out of my car, feeling how warm the air was, much warmer than it was during graduation. The rain was coming. "Dana?" I called again.

"Up here." Dana's voice came out of the dark. She was sitting on the porch.

I opened the screen door and, my eyes adjusting in the dark, saw an outline in the swing. I walked over and sat in the chair next to a table lamp. "Can I turn this on?" I asked.

"I wish you wouldn't," Dana answered.

"Fair enough," I said, pausing. "We missed you tonight."

"Oh, I was there. Wouldn't miss my own graduation, would I?" she said. Suddenly, there was a metallic click and then a small flame in front of her. She had lit a cigarette. In that few seconds, I strained to focus on her partially obscured face, but the light was out too quickly. "My new worst habit," she said. "You want one?"

"You were there?"

"At the top of the bleachers, after everyone had marched down to the field. I hadn't planned on going, but Freddy made me promise to come listen to his speech," she said, exhaling smoke.

"You mind if I turn on the ceiling fan?" I said, already getting up to do it without her permission.

"You ever smoke?" she asked as I sat back down across from her. She had started to slowly swing in her seat.

"Sure, seems like a long time ago, but I gave it up."

"Me, too. I'll quit eventually," she said, taking a long drag, the red tip glowing brighter in the dark.

"Dana, how are you feeling? Are you okay?" I asked.

"Like a million dollars," she said, exhaling again. "You got an ashtray?"

I handed her a saucer that had been sitting on the lamp table. Cigarette stubbed, she said, "So, how'd you like the speech? I thought he was really good. Not all those cliches about *first steps of life* or *overcoming adversity* or shit like that. I thought it was very good."

"Did you help him write it?"

"Not a bit," she said. "Freddy's a smart boy, a good writer. Did you know that he went back and read every Kennedy graduation speech since..."

"Please don't say since mine," I protested mildly.

Dana laughed softly, "No, that wasn't your best work, Nancy. Heartfelt, to be sure, but not original."

"You know, I would have liked to have heard *your* valedictory speech."

"Well, that train left the station without me, didn't it."

"Still, it would have been interesting," I said.

"Thanking my mother and father, like Freddy did?"

"Dana, don't do that to yourself. Don't start to wallow..."

"In my self-pity, you were going to say?"

"Yes, in self-pity. You're better than that."

Silence.

"Sure, you're right, Nancy. But you're going to have to cut me some slack for awhile. If anybody's entitled to wallow in self-pity, it's me. I'm knee deep right now, but I'll climb out soon enough. So, cut me some slack," she finally said, slowing down the swing.

The wind was picking up outside, and the pine trees around the house were swaying into each other, their branches groaning.

"I came here to thank you," Dana said.

"Thank me?"

"For not going along with Russell's..." she began to say, but a drumroll of thunder miles away reached us and rattled my house. We both turned in the direction of the thunder, and she said, "Rain's coming."

"Russell told you?" I asked, wishing that Dana would get off that swing and come sit in the chair on the other side of the lamp table, closer to me.

"Oh, Nancy, haven't you figured out that Russell is a pathological confessor, the perfect guilt-ridden Catholic. Always seeking some sort of forgiveness," she said. "And if you listen to him long enough, he'll tell you his whole life story. You've just got to listen."

"That's not the Russell Parsons I know," I said.

"Whatever," she said, as if dismissing me. "Anyway, thanks for not going along with him."

"Is that all? Why you're here?"

"Of course not," she almost laughed, but only almost. "I owe you a favor, but I wanted to ask you if I should do this particular thing I'm thinking about. I want your opinion."

"Dana, it's not like you to ask permission first. Usually, you do what you want and announce it later."

"I'm not asking permission. I'm asking for your opinion. I could've done this, I suppose, without asking you, but, Nancy, the really pissy thing about...about things now...is that I'm not as sure of myself as I used to be. And I hate that."

"What's on your mind?"

"That sophomore girl, Jackie Foster, and the other girl."

"Russell told you?"

"No, I've always known."

"How?" I asked, smelling the rain about to come, sheets of it.

"Doesn't matter how I knew. I just did. And others too." she said. "Russell *did* tell me that you and he tried to get them to press charges, go public, and they wouldn't."

"True," I said, letting her unwind.

"Do you think I should talk to them?"

"You're asking for my advice?"

"I'm asking for your opinion. There's a big difference, especially in my world. Opinion is what you think. Advice is what you think I ought to do."

"My opinion. You should talk to them," I said quickly.

"But, I can't tell them about me. I can't do that."

"You can still talk to them, but I think they would feel better knowing that they weren't alone, that it happened to other, stronger girls."

A streak of lightning flashed across the top of the trees, followed almost instantly by thunder that rattled every window in the house. The rain was close enough to hear.

"Nancy, I can't do that. I won't let anybody ever know that's where Tess came from."

"But you *will* talk to them, right?"

The rain was hitting the tin roof of the house, like pebbles.

"Sometime this summer, I'll do it this summer," she said.

I could see her head turn toward the sound of the rain on the roof. Neither of us spoke for a minute. The damp wind was coming though the porch screens. The swing was closer to the screens than where I was, and she was getting wet. "I should go," she said. "That damn Toyota sunroof leaks. The front seat will be soaked."

"Dana, do me another favor. Stay the night. We can sleep on the porch like I used to do a long time ago. Just like my mother and I did. The rain will stop in a while, and I can set up some dry cots. It'll be nice, and we can talk some more. Do that for me. Don't leave so soon. We'll dry your car out tomorrow."

"I should call Russell and tell him I'm spending the night with you and having some sort of pajama party. I told him I'd be back in an hour. He'll worry and go looking for me."

"I'll call Russell," I said.

"Okay, deal," she said, standing up. "You want to call some boys and hang up on them? All sorts of games we could play."

As Dana stepped toward me, I reached over and turned on the table lamp next to me.

"JESUS!" we both gasped at the same time, but for different reasons.

"Jesus, Nancy, you want to warn somebody before you blind them!" she scolded.

"Jesus, Dana," I whispered to myself. "You're beautiful."

She stood above me in a thin white dress, almost a nightgown, a younger thinner version of the woman I had seen that night I went to the *Flamingo Room* with Dell. Her hair was down to her shoulders, not pinned up like she had always done it before, handled in the past as if it was a bother. She was wearing makeup, something she never did before, her eyebrows dark and her full lips tinted pale red. I was awe-struck. "Your face..." I stumbled, "... you're so much..."

She stood there, looking down at me, a different person than the one to whom I thought I had been talking. The girl I had met that first day of school, who had driven up as I walked, the girl who told me all about the history of the school's design, that girl who looked like a woman, *that* girl was gone.

"You never thought I had cheekbones? Or hipbones?" she said with a shrug, not moving, letting me stare, her bandaged wrists held behind her back out of sight. "Funny, how those things make a difference."

"You are so...how did you..."

"My own special patented diet...starvation. Eat nothing for a month and you, too, can be a supermodel."

"Well, for what's it's worth, coming from me," I said, motioning for her to sit in the chair across from me, "You look stunning."

"No warnings about beauty being skin deep?" she said, finally sitting down.

"No, but I do have to offer you something to eat. My refrigerator's full."

"Maybe breakfast," she said. "Maybe then."

There was one last obvious question to ask.

"Dana, what are you going to do now? After this summer?"

She closed her eyes and laid her head back on the padded chair. The lamp between us had a dark blue shade and only a 40-watt bulb, so the light faded beyond the small circle that she and I occupied. The rain was less intense, and we could hear the thunder moving further off.

"As soon as I think Russell will be okay," she finally said, opening her eyes but looking out toward the St. Johns. "I'm going away."

"College?"

"Oh, God no," she sighed. "I want to learn a lot more before I go back to school. I want to travel, get away from this place. Meet some new people. Maybe go to New York City, maybe Europe. Just get away."

"Have you talked to Russell about this?" I asked, shifting in my seat to face her more directly.

"Yes."

"He's going to miss you."

She didn't respond at first, but I could see that she was thinking about what I had said.

"And Theresa?" I added, the first acknowledgement to her that I knew.

Her eyes began to moisten, so she looked down and away. "I need to do it. She knows that," she finally said. "I know it too. And maybe she'll catch up with me later. I'd like that. You know, I guess, it was the first time for both of us. And you never forget your first love. Right, Nancy? But home is where she needs to be now. Me, I need to hit the road."

"You'll keep in touch?"

"Oh sure, postcards from the edge."

"Da-naaaaa," I said.

"Sorry. Sometimes I can't help being a smartass."

It had rained hard for about fifteen minutes but had now dwindled to a slow drizzle.

"Nancy, one last thing," she said. "I can only tell *you* this. And I'm not looking for advice or an opinion or permission or anything. I just need to say it out loud in front of someone else and to hear myself say it. You don't need to say anything back, or try to make me feel better, or even have an opinion. All you have to do is listen. Deal?"

"A deal."

She reached over and turned off the lamp. "I had this feeling come back as I was sitting here waiting for you tonight. Something that makes me hate myself."

"Dana, you don't have to..."

"Shush, a deal," she quieted me. "Just listen. It hit me first as I sat in that church listening to that priest talk, and then again tonight." Pausing, "I'm glad that Tess is dead."

A thousand birds were singing in the trees around my house, telling us that the rain was over.

"It just came up out of some part of me, how my life had changed as soon as she was born. How the world had gotten smaller. And I resented her. Then I sat here tonight, maybe it was because I had gone to see that graduation ceremony, and I felt something come over me like I had never felt before, not even before Tess was created. I felt truly free. Truly truly free, and I was so truly happy. And I hate myself for it. More than even at her funeral, I hate myself."

Neither of us spoke for a long time.

"I want us to do something," I finally said, standing up, offering Dana a hand in the dark. "I want us to go for a swim."

"The river?" she said quietly.

"Just for a little while, and we'll have to be careful. The current might be strong tonight after all this rain. But the water's warm, and we'll be okay if we stay close together. Will you do that for me? With me?"

"You sure about this?" she asked hesitantly.

"Positive."

She didn't resist as I pulled her up.

"Thanks," she said, still holding my hand.

"Am I allowed one last cliché before we get in the water?"

"Sure."

I pulled her toward me. I put my arms around her in a hug, my hand patting her trembling shoulders. "You've got your whole life ahead of you."

I felt her shake as she held on to me tightly, speaking softly into my shoulder, "You too, Nancy, you too."

Henry Adams

I had become an educated woman, in spite of myself.—Nancy Adams

Mike Lankford inherited Fred Stein's job as front step drummer for the first day of class for the new year. Mike was a much better drummer than Fred, but less colorful. Still wearing the ever-present baseball cap, but covering less hair, Mike was glad to see me.

"New year, Miss Adams," he called to me as I walked up the steps.

"You still going to make us take our hats off in class?"

"You bet, Mike. Rules are rules," I said, and he hit his cymbal in mock disgust.

I walked into the building and looked for Donna. I wanted to confirm a name on my sophomore American history survey course printout. Seeing her run down the hall with an armful of text-books, I yelled, "Donna, slow down. I want to. . ."

"I'm late, I'm late, for a very important date, can't wait," she yelled back, not slowing down. "First day of class, Nancy, a couple of the new teachers are already having a crisis."

I ran after her, catching up and walking beside her as fast as I could as we went to the faculty lounge.

"This one here," I said, holding the printout in front of her, one name circled in red. "Is he for real? Or are you just trying to be cute?"

"Henry Adams?" Donna huffed, shifting books from one arm to the other. "Of course he's real. A bright kid. Some self-esteem issues, but nothing to worry about."

"Thank you, Miss Parton, thank you from the bottom of my heart," I laughed.

"You are so easy to please," she said, and then she disappeared through the lounge door.

Coming down the hall from the other direction was Jackie Foster, holding hands with Harry Hellas. From what I could see, no part of Jackie's body was pierced or tattooed. Harry had gotten much taller over the summer, and more tan. Jackie saw me and waved, dragging Harry as she ran toward me.

"How was your summer?" I asked both of them.

"Like the best of my life," Jackie said. Harry just grinned and shrugged.

"You're both in my government class, I see," I said. "Looks like a lot of the same people from your class last year."

414

Jackie nodded, and then she whispered something to Harry, who promptly un-grafted his hand from hers and went away. "Miss Adams, can we talk after class about something? Something I've been thinking about," she asked, looking around to make sure nobody was listening. "About that thing last year."

"Sure, Jackie, but let's do it after school when we have more time. Okay?"

"Okay. So I guess I'll see ya second period," she said, her permed hair bouncing with each word. "And my mom says to say hello to you from her. She's back on planet earth for a while. So, hello."

I walked into my first class, the sophomore American history survey. All new faces to me. They were instantly quiet as soon as I entered. Without saying a word, I handed a stack of course handouts to a girl in the first seat of the first row, and she began the process of passing them around. For these kids, it was the first day of the first class of high school. A new world for them. Most of them would graduate in three years, the Class of 2000, and then they would start a new century.

I stood at the podium watching the papers circulate, looking at each boy in the class, wondering which one was Henry Adams, and then I began.

"My name is Nancy Adams, and I'll be your teacher."

Marion Public Library
1095 6th Avenue
Marion, Iowa 52302-3428
(319) 377-3412

CPSIA information can be obtained at www.ICGtesting.com
Printed in the USA
LVOW08s0556220414

382568LV00002B/2/P

9 781888 160789